ALSO BY COLLEEN HOUCK

Reawakened

The Tiger's Curse Series

COLLEEN HOUCK

RECREATED

DELACORTE PRESS

Visit us on the Web! randomhouseteens.com

Educators and librarians, for a variety of teaching tools, visit us at RHTeachersLibrarians.com

Library of Congress Cataloging-in-Publication Data
Houck, Colleen.
Recreated / Colleen Houck. — First edition.
pages cm. — (Reawakened ; 2)
Summary: "Lily must go into the Afterlife to save Amon and protect the world from being overthrown by the deadly Devouror of the Underworld"—Provided by publisher.
ISBN 978-0-385-37660-0 (hc) — ISBN 978-0-385-37661-7 (glb) —
ISBN 978-0-385-37662-4 (ebook)
1. Amon (Egyptian deity)—Juvenile fiction. [1. Amon (Egyptian deity)—Fiction. 2. Gods, Egyptian—Fiction. 3. Supernatural—Fiction. 4. Love—Fiction.] I. Title.
PZ7.H81143Ref 2016
[Fic]—dc23
2015015060

The text of this book is set in 10.75-point Dante.
Interior design by Heather Kelly

Printed in the United States of America
10 9 8 7 6 5 4 3 2 1
First Edition

For Matthew, Alan,
Sarah, Katie, and Chris,
who love being in my books
even if they're not mermaids or dragons

A WOMAN'S LOST LOVE

An Ancient Egyptian Love Poem

Lost! Lost! Lost! O lost my love to me!
He passes by my house, nor turns his head,
I deck myself with care; he does not see.
He loves me not.
Would God that I were dead!
God! God! God! O Amun, great of might!
My sacrifice and prayers, are they in vain?
I offer to thee all that can delight,
Hear thou my cry and bring my love again.
Sweet, sweet, sweet as honey in my mouth,
His kisses on my lips, my breast, my hair;
But now my heart is as the sun-scorched South,
Where lie the fields deserted, grey and bare.
Come! Come! Come! And kiss me when I die,
For life, compelling life, is in thy breath;
And at that kiss, though in the tomb I lie,
I will arise and break the bands of Death.

PROLOGUE
Lost

How could I have done something so foolish? Amon thought. Leaving the safety of the afterlife for the uncertainty of the netherworld had been a bad decision, a dangerous one. But Amon had felt as if there were no other option. Besides, death was what he sought, though admittedly he would have preferred a gentler one.

As he wandered the stone path leading to, he hoped, a temporary refuge, Amon wondered what form death would take. Would he be swallowed up by a monster that would slowly digest him over centuries? Would he be flayed alive by a creature whose expertise was in making a man suffer? The best case he could think of would be death by venom. The netherworld was full of venomous creatures bent on the destruction of those who wandered into their nests.

Even though Amon courted death, he didn't wish to succumb to it just yet. Lily had only recently returned to her mortal life, and it would be years before there was even a remote chance that he could be with her again. Amon had promised to meet her in the afterlife. Exactly how he would accomplish that now he didn't know, but he had decades to figure something out. The truth was, even if he hadn't met Lily and fallen in love with her, he still would have given up his calling. It had been so many years. Too many. And death wasn't the worst thing he could imagine.

His brief sojourns into the realm of mortals were no longer enough. If he had reunited with his brothers before the judging, they would have known what he was up to, would have talked him out of it. That was why he leapt before he saw them again. He wanted more. He needed more than just a pale shadow of a life.

So he had forsaken his duty. Forsaken his brothers. And now he'd forsaken the gods themselves. There would be a reckoning, but he didn't care. Lily was the only remaining tether linking him to the path he walked. The only reason he didn't give himself over to the next plane of existence. Wherever that might be. So, he fought to bide his time as he waited.

As the days passed, he tore asunder every gnarled and frightening beast of the netherworld that challenged him. Some came at him because he was reckless. Some, he suspected, were sent as punishment from the gods. Others were drawn to his melancholy state. The brief moments of respite he earned were too short. No matter where he went or how evasive he was, the demons always found him.

Though he'd left his mortal body behind, his wandering soul still felt the pangs of the flesh. Fortunately his needs were markedly less than they were in the human world. When Amon thirsted, he begged the spirits who lived in the trees for gifts. When Amon hungered, he stole provisions from the stores of the creatures he slaughtered, and, occasionally, if nothing could be found and the pains of his empty stomach became overwhelming, he roasted the bodies of the beasts he'd slain.

When he was utterly exhausted from the terrors he'd brought upon himself, and he was relatively safe, Amon slept. It was always brief. Always fitful. Dreaming was the only happiness he felt in his otherwise horrifying existence.

The worst part about wandering the netherworld wasn't the endless barrage of monsters or dangers that threatened a second and permanent death. It wasn't the separation from his brothers, his constant companions for thousands of years. It wasn't even the loss of purpose he felt, the absence of self-assurance he'd always possessed, or the knowledge that he had a place in the cosmos, one he was if not satisfied with, then one he accepted.

No. The worst part was also the best part.

He could feel her.

Lily was in another place, another world, and yet, he could allow himself to be with her. When he was certain that no attack was imminent, and he let his tired body rest, he'd close his eyes and see her. That was the part Amon loved. He could hover near her like a ghost. He couldn't speak to her or touch her, and she didn't know that he was there, at least not consciously. Her subconscious mind, though, could sense he was near, that he was watching over her, much like a guardian angel. This was a tremendous blessing. But it was also a curse.

Amon knew a connection as powerful as theirs went two ways. He had hoped that they might simply meet in their dreams. That their bond had been brief enough that their minds would brush gently against each other as they slept. But the link between them proved stronger than that. As Amon walked with Lily through New York, he knew she also journeyed with him through his land of nightmares.

His decision to leave paradise had caused terrible consequences for the girl he loved, and now that he was in the netherworld, there was no getting out. The gods would not help; he'd abandoned their cause. Death would be his only reprieve, and yet every time he thought he'd hurt her enough and would give up, give in to whatever dark creature was currently seeking his demise, he'd feel her, an unconscious appeal to keep trying. To hold on a little longer.

Amon sought answers to his dilemma by peering through the Eye of Horus, but the things he saw confused him. Sometimes it teased him with glimpses of a possible future. A way out. If he could just last long enough, survive in the form in which he currently existed until Lily's natural, mortal death, there was a chance he could find her. That their bond would draw them together once more.

Other times, he saw Lily as a different person, a different creature altogether from the girl he knew. He envisaged himself tortured and abused. His brothers jealous and angry. The gods at war with Chaos. These visions made no sense. Chaos was being held at bay for another millennium. The gods getting together for a meal wasn't even likely, let alone a war.

The uncertainty Amon felt was normal. He was used to the strange shadows of the future and past mingling together. The Eye saw all, and yet nothing it revealed ever made sense. Events were never in the proper order. It took a tremendous amount of focus and energy to direct the Eye to show him any one particular thing. To prevent himself from going crazy, Amon spent much of his time trying to ignore the visions that rattled his brain. Since he'd entered the netherworld, though, the Eye had gone into overdrive.

Still, the Eye's energy drain was worth it when he asked to see Lily's future. The things he saw gave him hope. Hope that they might be together again, that there was a possible future where he could again hold her in his arms.

There were moments when he saw himself cupping her face in his hands, tenderly kissing each of her closed eyelids, tasting the salt from the tears that slowly trickled down her cheeks. These blissful flashes were all he needed to know. The rest he'd let the universe worry about. Perhaps it was selfish of him to maintain their connection, but he just couldn't let Lily go. Not yet. Not when there was a chance.

Though Amon knew that she likely walked the netherworld with him in her dreams, there were times, however brief, when they both slept. During those occasions, it was possible to communicate with her, but Lily's mind always blocked him out, her body so exhausted from the trials of their connection that her consciousness shut down and she slept deeply.

When this happened, he didn't push. She needed to rest, and as badly as he wanted to talk to her, there was no point. He'd doomed the both of them to this fate because he was weak. If he had only loved her enough in the beginning to leave her alone or had sent her away earlier, maybe none of this would have happened.

Of course, without Lily, it was quite possible that he and his brothers would be dead and the world overrun by Chaos. Still, if he'd been a little more vigilant regarding his emotions, then she wouldn't be suffering now. She'd be just another human girl, one of billions in the world. No one of any importance, and certainly no one the gods would be paying any attention to. No one except him.

Amon sighed. The truth was that as long as Lily held his heart, Amon would fight. He was beholden to her; if she wanted him to press on, he would find a way.

1

Reprieve

"Amon!" I jerked awake, my pulse racing as the nightmare slowly ebbed. I'd taken to keeping a night-light on near my bed ever since the horrors that took over my dreams still haunted my dark room when I woke. Some terrible creature had cornered him. It had screeched in a satisfied way, its putrid breath stinging my nose as its tongue darted out to lick the blood from a gash on Amon's shoulder. It all felt so real.

Shivering, I wrapped my arms around my body and slid from the bed as I headed to my favorite spot on the balcony overlooking Central Park. Once there, I rubbed my hand over the head of the falcon statue perched on the railing.

The bird reminded me of Amon's golden falcon form, and when the sun warmed it, the heat stored in the metal carving seemed to linger, even in the late hours of the evening when I paced my room unable to sleep. It soothed me when I touched it and I could picture Amon as I'd last left him and not as the bruised and pain-filled man he was in my dreams.

He was lost to me. I knew that. I acknowledged that I should try to move on, maybe try to date someone else, but the memory of my Egyptian sun prince come to life was a hard one to beat. Amon wasn't perfect, but he was pretty darn close. Even now I could easily picture him standing near me—his golden skin warmed by the sun, the glint in his hazel eyes, and that secretive smile hiding behind his defined and very kissable lips.

Sighing, I leaned on the railing and looked out at the park. I was in love with a guy who was centuries old and currently moldering away in an elaborately decorated sarcophagus fashioned by Anubis himself. His spirit half, the half that was supposed to be in paradise while he waited for the next time he was needed, haunted my dreams.

Either he was in grave trouble or something was seriously wrong with me since I'd returned from Egypt. Still, the creatures I saw in my dreams were much more horrifying than any I could have made up. I wasn't that creative. Even worse than my suspicions that Amon was in danger was the problem that I couldn't tell anyone about it. Nobody even knew he'd existed.

Well, that wasn't exactly true. Dr. Hassan knew, but he lived on the other side of the world. I'd written to him when I got home, and his elated response made me smile even though I'm sure he'd figured it out when he couldn't find my body on the pyramid after Amon and his brothers had saved the world. I was more than a little proud to be a part of the whole thing, even though fooling Amon into siphoning off my energy had nearly killed me.

It took a month to get a reply from Dr. Hassan, though I'd fanatically checked the PO box I'd leased for our secret correspondence every day. He'd told me not to worry, that Amon had the protection of the gods, that he'd hidden the brothers well, and that I should be proud of the sacrifices I'd made to keep the world safe.

That was pretty much the extent of his letters. They got progressively shorter as time went on. It was as if he, too, wanted me to just forget everything that had happened and move on with my life. But how could I? Amon haunted my dreams. Not that I wasn't happy to see him. I was. But the horrors he faced were enough to send any girl, even one who had seen the things I'd seen, running for the nearest mental institution.

My parents were worried. My lack of sleep was starting to show, though I tried to act as though my life was simply business as usual. They had no idea that I'd nearly died, fallen in love with a drop-dead (no pun intended) gorgeous mummy come to life, and spent an extended spring break in Egypt. The fact that I'd actually made it through to the end of the school year without my grades falling was a major accomplishment.

They didn't know about my experience with Amon in Egypt and how much it had transformed me. I myself didn't know how much I'd changed until I got home. I thought it would show on my face, all the emotion, all the trauma, all the . . . death, but my parents only noticed my hair. My brown, no-nonsense straight hair was now riddled with random sun-kissed highlights of different shades. They didn't like it.

The first thing my mother said was, "What were you thinking?" Immediately she picked up the phone and lectured our hairstylist, who didn't have anything to do with it but who cleared his schedule instantly to repair the "damage." I told her quietly but sternly that I was rather fond of it and that my intention was to keep it. To say they were shocked at my little act of rebellion was an understatement.

As much as they protested my decision to keep my new highlights, they outright refused my request that they call me Lily instead of Lilliana. As a result, I began to feel like a stranger in my own home. To keep the peace, I told them I'd go to the college they wanted as long as I was allowed to spend the summer at my nana's farm in Spring Lake, Iowa. I figured it didn't matter anymore where I went, and the compromise went a long way toward assuaging the fears my new hairdo ignited.

Once I got the acceptance letter, they backed off and left me to my own devices, which meant I could mourn the loss of Amon without anyone taking notice. One month after another went by, and then graduation was upon me.

As I gazed in the mirror the morning of graduation, I was dismayed to see that my golden highlights, the last tangible proof I had of Amon's touch, were fading. At this rate, they'd be gone by Christmas. I indulged in a good cry before showering and dressing for my graduation ceremony.

If my mother noticed my too-bright eyes, she probably chalked it up to my being emotional about leaving high school. The truth was, I didn't care about high school. I didn't care about college or boys. I didn't care about much of anything anymore.

The time soon came for me to depart for the summer, and I was surprised that my parents wanted to drop me off at the airport. Maybe they noticed more than I thought they did, or perhaps they were just feeling nostalgic about me growing up and leaving the nest. Either way, the drive felt a bit awkward.

I stared at my reflection in the window.

My eyes were large and dull; my hair was wound in a perfect, tight bun at the nape of my neck; and my lips were stretched in a thin, unforgiving line, as rigid as a ruler. In fact, that was what I looked like: a schoolmarm. A smirk lifted the corner of my mouth as I imagined how much Amon would hate my hair like this. He preferred it wild and unbound.

After a few quiet goodbyes and some stiff hugs, my parents relinquished me to the chaos of the airport. Inside, a range of emotions hit me all at once. I remembered being there with Amon a few short months earlier, and how with the wave of his hand and a charming smile, he could wrap anyone around his finger.

I boarded the plane and strapped in, remembering how even the most mundane actions like buckling a seat belt were completely new and foreign for Amon. Though I actually did try not to think of him, it seemed that was all I could do, and when I shut my eyes, rocked to sleep by the plane, I found myself in Amon's world once again.

He wasn't fighting a monster, which was a relief, but he had a wicked wound on his thigh that was seeping blood onto his leggings. Sucking in a breath, he tore away the fabric around it and wrapped it in the bandages he'd created from the sand. Some kind of armor lay discarded next to him, and Amon shrugged out of a tunic before dipping it in a small, natural basin of water and scrubbing his arms and neck. I hoped the precious drops trickling down the side of a boulder were enough to both quench his thirst and clean his wound. The area was very desolate and dry.

Though the sight of his bare chest was distracting, I was more absorbed by the expression on his face. He was exhausted and hurting, and not just physically. I wondered if he missed me as much as I did him.

"Amon?" I whispered involuntarily.

In my dream he froze and looked around, eyes shining with an iridescent green light in the darkness. Though he'd never been able to hear me before, I still tried. One day he might. After a moment, the tenseness in Amon's shoulders relaxed, and he settled down with his back against a rock and closed his eyes. His bare chest rose and fell in a rhythm that slowed as the minutes passed and then something changed.

As his body continued to sleep, a gentle pressure wrapped around me.

"Lily?" I heard his familiar voice and squelched a sob.

"Amon? Can you hear me?" I asked the ethereal darkness.

"Yes. I can hear you, Nehabet."

"Is this real?"

He didn't answer right away but then eventually said, "I wish it were not."

"What's happening to you?" I asked desperately. "Why are you suffering? I thought you were in the afterlife. I thought you were at peace. Why are you tormented night after night?"

"I am no longer under the protection of the gods. I have relinquished my station."

"I don't understand. What does that mean?"

"It means that I would rather suffer than continue to do their bidding."

"But if you don't save the world, who will?"

"They will find another to replace me."

"I still don't understand. Are they punishing you?"

I felt his sigh as much as I heard it. "They did not choose this for me. I am the one who decided to walk this path."

"It's a pretty difficult path, Amon. Can't your brothers help you?"

"We are separated. There is nothing they can do for me now."

"I hate seeing you like this."

"I know. I am sorry for causing you pain. I didn't think our connection would be this strong." He paused for a moment before adding, "You are in pain, too, Young Lily."

Bitterly, I said in a shaky voice, "Not like you."

"No. Not like me. But you are hurting nonetheless. It is my fault. My loneliness has caused this."

"Your desire for human connection didn't cause this. The gods did. They don't understand. Everyone needs to be loved. It's completely natural."

He laughed sardonically. "I was human, Lily, once. But I am something altogether different now. I gave my humanity up for the greater good."

Thunder boomed in the sky above Amon's still form, roiling clouds shifting like a churning ocean. Lightning struck and his body jerked awake. I felt the loss of his presence, as if a warm blanket had been ripped away from me. As the ground shook, he staggered tiredly to his feet and summoned his armor made of sand to strap onto his form. Amon lifted his face to the wind as he closed his eyes and said, "I love you, Lily. But it is time for you to wake up."

He raced into the darkness to face whatever beast awaited him as his words echoed in my mind. "I love you, too," I whispered, even though I knew he could no longer hear me.

I felt a nudge on my shoulder as someone said, "Wake up, miss. We've landed."

2

Spirit Lake

The flight attendant gave me a strange look before moving on. I scrubbed my palms over my eyes, hoping my conversation with Amon had taken place only in my mind and I hadn't been talking in my sleep.

Making my way to the baggage claim, I couldn't have missed the gray-haired woman waving a handmade sign back and forth that said LILYPAD, my nana's pet name for me.

"Hey, Nana." I smiled as she dropped her sign and wrapped her arms around me. She was a robust woman, a rancher's wife, and her arms were strong and solid. As she squeezed me tightly, I felt the tension in my shoulders melt like a pat of butter in a cast-iron skillet.

"I missed you, Lilypad. It's been too long."

"I missed you, too."

Gripping my shoulders, she stepped away and gave me one of her scrutinizing looks. "Hmm. You're too skinny. Well, we'll take care of that." Smiling, she put her arm around me and we turned to watch the rotating baggage carousel. "I can't tell you how happy you made me when you asked to stay with me this summer."

"I'm just glad you said yes."

"Of course I would say yes. You know how badly I've wanted you to come for an extended visit."

I shrugged. "There was just never a good time."

Nana harrumphed. "Never a good time for your parents, you mean. To think, my own son is too busy to remember what's most important in life."

"You know they love you, Nana."

"If love looks like too-busy-to-call-your-own-mother, then yes. I'm sure they do in their own way."

I spotted my bag and yanked it off the spinning carousel, with Nana helping me to get it upright.

"Are you hungry?" she asked as we headed out to her car.

"Famished," I admitted with a smile. And I was. Surprisingly, my appetite had returned. I wasn't sure if it was a result of being with my nana or having recently spoken with Amon or if it was just suddenly feeling more like myself, but I was hungry enough to eat an entire cow, which wasn't too far off from the realm of possibility on my nana's farm.

After we stopped at a diner, we were back on the road and found that we both had a hankering to listen to Elvis. Since her old car didn't have satellite radio and most of the roads we were driving on were too far from any normal stations, we sang. Fortunately, Elvis recorded so many songs that we never had to repeat any. I looked up the lyrics on my phone and we sang our hearts out the entire drive to the farm.

There was something freeing about being on the road. I felt more like myself than I had in months, and I knew that was because I was embracing the same things Amon loved—laughing, feasting, and being with people who cared about you.

By the time Nana pulled up to the farm, it was getting late. She introduced me to her new dog, Winston, named after Winston

Churchill, who she swore looked just like him. I didn't see the resemblance. Winston got up from his sleeping spot on the porch, tail wagging, and sniffed my hand. Nana went to check on the other animals while I wrestled my bag into the house. I knew she'd be tired when she got back. Nana was an early-to-bed, early-to-rise kind of gal.

Still, instead of going directly to her room, she made me a cup of chamomile tea, sweetening it the way I liked with cream and honey and adding a little shortbread cookie on the side. Then she headed to the living room, as if sensing I needed to talk. I set my bags in the guest room, grabbed an old quilt, and cozied into a worn recliner while she took to her favorite rocking chair.

As she sipped her tea and rocked, her twinkling eyes studied me in the dim room. "What's bothering you, Lilypad?" she asked.

A stream of words crossed my tongue but melted away like chocolate over a flame. "I . . . It's hard to talk about," I said finally.

"Is it your parents? College?"

"No."

"Ah . . . it's a young man, then." I grimaced and then nodded once. "Tell me about him," she encouraged.

Could I? If anyone would understand or believe me, it would be her. Anubis hadn't said I couldn't tell anyone. He probably just assumed that no one would accept what I said anyway and it wasn't like sharing my story could change anything.

"Did he have a strong chin?" she asked, interrupting my thoughts.

"A . . . a what?" I replied.

"A strong chin. You can always tell a good man by the cut of his chin."

I couldn't help it. I laughed. "Nana, what are you talking about?"

"No, I mean it. A weak-chinned man is a man you walk away from." She slashed her hand in front of her as if karate chopping the man down.

"Are you sure you aren't talking about horses or cows?" I teased.

Nana leaned forward. "Your grandpa, rest his soul, had a rugged chin. He was a strong man. A good one. Never seen the like of him since."

I folded my arms across my chest and regarded her with a smile. "Is that how you picked him? Based on his chin?"

"Well, there was that and the steamed windows."

"Steamed windows?"

"Every time we got to kissing, we steamed up the windows."

I choked on my tea and set down the cup. "I did *not* need to know that about Grandpa."

"You didn't answer my question."

A little embarrassed, I shrugged slightly and admitted, "There might have been a few steamy windows and he does have a rather rugged chin now that I think about it."

"Aha!" Nana's eyes gleamed. "Now we're getting somewhere."

When I didn't volunteer any further information, she prodded again gently. "Did he break your heart, Lilypad?"

I rubbed my hands together and despite a valiant effort to control myself, tears spilled onto my cheeks. "Well, my heart *is* broken but it wasn't his fault."

"What do you mean?"

"He . . . he died, Nana."

"*Oh.* Oh my dear. I'm so sorry." Nana rocked herself forward and moved to the couch, holding out her arms for me. Without even thinking, I got up and collapsed against her, letting the tears flow down my face in a torrent as she rubbed my back and murmured, "It's okay to cry, honey," and "You just let it all out now." After a moment, she added, "Your parents don't know?"

I shook my head. "They wouldn't have approved."

She nodded and squeezed me tighter. Despite knowing that Amon was alive in some way, acknowledging that he was beyond my reach for the rest of my mortal life sat heavily in my heart. The grief was hot and packed into my chest like a too-full suitcase. Sitting with Nana, allowing my emotions to flow in such a free, open way, helped. The sadness ebbed out of me slowly, deflating until I felt spent.

We sat quietly for several minutes, her hand softly patting my shoulder until I finally lifted my tearstained face. "How did you get over it, Nana? With Grandpa, I mean."

She let out a heavy sigh as her hands moved to my hair and stroked it lightly. "You don't. Not really. I know that's not the thing most of your friends would tell you but it's the truth in my experience. Other people don't really want to hear about it either, so prepare for that. Oh, they leave you alone for a while. Give you a certain amount of time, but then they expect you to pull yourself together and move on."

"So, you're not over him?"

"I don't think I'll ever be. Your granddad was an integral part of my life. Don't misunderstand me. The grief changes over time. You keep busy. Sometimes your mind even forgets the pain for a little while. But when someone you love dies, there will always be a hurt inside you, like a splinter, and when you give yourself over to thinking on it, the ache comes back."

My lip trembled as I considered that the splinter in my heart was more like a jagged tree trunk.

"Aw, honey. I hope I haven't made it worse."

"I'm not sure it could be."

"I know it seems like there's nothing left. That life won't go on without him, but it does. As much as you allow it to, anyway. I like to think that he's not gone forever, that he's just in a place I can't be yet. I've thought about death a lot since the day he departed this world, and I've decided that it's like a long business trip. It's a separation that neither of us wants but it's a normal part of life. And someday, I'm not sure when, that business trip will be over and we'll be together again."

"You really think you'll see Grandpa again?"

"I don't think it. I know it."

"I never took you for such a romantic, Nana."

"Never underestimate the power of the heart, Lilypad."

I blew out a long breath. "So what do I do? Until we can be together again?"

"Keep busy. Work. Laugh. Learn. Love your family. Enjoy your life the best way you can."

"I think he'd agree with you, Nana."

She smiled. "You'll have to tell me more about him tomorrow. He must have been very special to have made such an impact on you."

"He was." Sniffling, I said, "I think I'd like to sleep now."

"Of course. Let me just get you another quilt."

As she rummaged in the closet and I moved to the guest room, I turned and said, "Sometimes I have nightmares. I don't want you to worry if you hear anything."

She pressed the thick quilt she'd made into my arms. "Don't you worry about that. I'm a deep sleeper. Besides, Bossy will be bawling to be milked before the sun comes up, so neither of us will be getting much sleep tonight."

"Okay." She turned to head up the stairs to her room. "Nana?" I added.

"Yes, honey?"

"I'm glad I'm here."

"So am I, Lilypad. So am I."

The bang of pots and pans in the kitchen woke me up way earlier than my body would have woken naturally. I wrapped a worn robe Nana kept for me in the closet around my body and headed into the kitchen. Nana was already dressed and wore a sturdy pair of work boots. "Would you rather make breakfast or milk Bossy?" she asked without turning around.

"I'll take Bossy," I answered with a yawn.

"All right. The pail is hanging on a hook by the door. Give her a good amount of hay. It distracts her while she's being milked."

"Sounds good." I quickly pulled on the work clothes she kept for me at her house. If I'd ever tried to take them home, my parents would have burned them immediately. Also my nana insisted that my regular clothes were entirely too "froufrou" to work on a farm, so she'd bought several pairs of sturdy pants and thick, long-sleeved shirts that were stored in the guest bedroom drawer. They should have been a little tight on me by now, since the last time I visited was my sophomore year in high school. The pants *were* too short, but I'd lost weight in the last few months, so the clothes still fit passably well.

Stifling another yawn, I made my way out to the barn and groped in the darkness for the hanging chain to switch on the light. "Hey, Bossy," I responded when the cow mooed in my direction. "Hold your horses."

After filling her trough with fresh-cut hay, tying her to the stall, and positioning the pail and stool, I washed my hands and then sank down next to the cow. Pressing my cheek against her soft side, I steadied the bucket, hoping I remembered the right technique. After an irritated bawl and a few mistaken attempts, I figured it out and got into a comfortable rhythm.

Half an hour later, my fingers felt a bit stiff but I had two and a half gallons of milk and a happy cow. I patted her back, fed the horses, gathered the eggs, and headed toward the house with my prizes. After I set the pail and basket of eggs on the counter, Nana grunted her thanks and pointed her spatula to the table. "Hope you're hungry," she said. "I did the fancy one you like."

"Crème brûlée French toast?" I asked, my mouth turning up in a hopeful grin.

"Of course. You've also got cheesy eggs and bacon, so eat up."

There was something to be said about a hearty breakfast after manual labor. I managed to wolf down three pieces of French toast, a giant portion of eggs, a full glass of frothy, fresh milk, and four slices of bacon before I groaned and pushed away from the table.

We washed the dishes together, and when I asked what was on the agenda, Nana handed me one of her famous lists. I was a list maker, too, and while perusing hers, I wondered if I'd picked up the habit from her or if there was something in our genes that made us feel a sense of satisfaction when we checked off the little boxes for the day.

Nana's list included weeding the garden; harvesting the tomatoes and zucchini; bathing the dog; exercising the horses; making a cake for her brother Melvin's birthday; and visiting Grandpa's grave.

When the farm chores were complete, we made Melvin's cake. He preferred strawberry and Nana not only made his cake from scratch but she also filled it with her own homemade strawberry jam. Somehow she thought it would be a good idea to kill two birds with one stone and ride the horses over to deliver the cake.

When I asked her why we were making a cake for Melvin and not both Melvin and Marvin, she said that when the twins were younger, they insisted that their parents celebrate their birthdays separately just in case they got any wild ideas about combining birthday presents. Marvin's favorite cake, a lemon treat so sour nearly no one could stand it but him, had been dropped off the week before.

Nana inexplicably determined that I, the less experienced rider, should be the one to hold the confection on the trip. Though the cake was pretty much bombproof, tucked safely into her old-school plastic, hand-me-down cake container from the 1950s, I still worried that I'd, at best, mess up her frosting or, at worst, drop it in a pile of cow patties.

Somehow I managed to keep my hands on both the reins and the cake and we made it all the way out to Melvin's house on the far edge of the property without incident. After the inevitable hour-long visit with Melvin's family, the polite inquiries about his kids and grandkids, Nana's proud displaying of her newly graduated granddaughter, and the exchange of various seedlings and return of a few salad bowls, we were finally on our way home.

When I asked Nana if she wanted to go directly to Grandfather's grave, which was close enough to the house on horseback, she shook her head. "He likes it when I get dolled up," she said.

We headed home and returned the horses to their stalls and since it had been a hot, sweaty, dog-bathing kind of day, I headed to the shower when I got back, too.

After saying my hellos to Grandpa and replacing the dead blooms with the new ones we'd cut that day, I left her alone and stood under the shade of a nearby tree to wait. Once in a while I caught the sound of her quiet voice in the breeze as she spoke with her late husband. I wondered what she was talking to him about. Was she sharing what had happened in her life since she last visited? Was she telling him how much she missed him? Or just that she loved him?

I ran through the things I'd said to Amon and regretted that he hadn't heard me say I loved him. He should have. It should have been the first thing I'd said. Instead I'd just asked if what I was seeing was real. What a waste. I'd squandered an opportunity to really talk to him and instead I'd just pestered him with questions. What was happening and why it was happening wasn't as important as telling him how I felt. Next time, if there ever was a next time, I'd tell him I loved him first.

As I climbed into bed, I knew that Nana was right. Living your life as best you can and working hard could help numb the sting of losing a loved one. I dug the heart scarab Amon left me out from my bag and rubbed my fingertips over it. The green stone twinkled as the light from my lamp reflected off it. It was warm and there was a slight pulse, like the faint beat of a heart, emanating from within. I pressed my lips against the stone, wishing it were Amon's golden skin instead, and then placed it over my heart, the position Anubis would have left it on when preparing Amon's mummy.

Yanking the covers up to my chin, the bottom tucked in tight, I folded both arms across my chest, palm over the precious jeweled piece, and wondered if this is what it felt like to be mummified. Despite my morbid thinking, it wasn't long before I drifted asleep, fingers clutching the scarab, but instead of meeting Amon in my dreams as I hoped, I was startled awake by a bright light and a deep, resonating voice. "It is time for you to arise, Lilliana Young."

3

Heart Scarab

Jerking awake, the scarab still clenched in my fingers, I scooted all the way back against the headboard and scanned the room. With the blackout curtains drawn, it was darker than the inside of a sarcophagus. I couldn't see the intruder but I felt his presence as surely as I felt my heart slamming inside my rib cage.

"Who's there?" I hissed in an alarmed whisper, knocking the book I'd been reading before bed off the nightstand.

"Have you forgotten me already?" The man chuckled quietly.

As I groped for the light switch, I heard a dog's whine and froze. If I hadn't already guessed who was in my room, the dog would have given him away. Winston did not sound at all like this dog. Actually, there was only one dog I'd ever met who had a reverberating sort of power behind his woof.

My trembling fingers finally managed to switch on the light, and there, standing before me in all his godlike glory, yet still looking like he fit in at a farmhouse in Iowa, was the Egyptian god of mummification, Anubis. In the museum, he'd worn a modern business suit. This time he was dressed in a fitted pair of jeans, a white button-down shirt that was perfectly tailored to his broad shoulders, a pair of dark cowboy boots, and a denim jacket.

He looked like *GQ* gone country. He even had a very appealing dark shadow of stubble on his face. Anubis appeared to be a man's man who could toss a bale of hay, ride a bucking bronco, hang with the guys at a grill, and still knock every farm girl from eighteen to eighty off her feet without breaking a sweat. I wondered if that was something uniquely Anubis or if it was a sort of godlike power to blend in and yet command attention at the same time.

Though he was still as undeniably handsome as the last time I'd seen him, there was something in his eyes, something grave, that belied his casual, devil-may-care expression. Whatever his reason for visiting me, I was sure it wasn't a social call.

Clutching my covers to my neck and sliding Amon's scarab under my pillow as inconspicuously as possible, I tried to look a little more regal and in control than a mortal girl could hope to look wrapped up in her nana's country quilt with thick mismatched socks peeking out from under the covers and a pair of dusty overalls hanging on a hook by the door.

"Anubis. Why are you here?" I asked, distrusting but somehow hopeful at the same time. "Did something go wrong with the ceremony? Did you decide to do a memory wipe on me after all? Are you here to make me a mummy, too?"

The places my mind went to were a little scary, but at the same time, the knowledge that this man had the power to allow me to see Amon again trumped every frightening scenario. I didn't dare ask the question I really wanted to know. The inquiry burning on the tip of my tongue was related to Amon's safety, and I was fearful that in asking, I'd be giving too much information away.

Anubis gave me a bemused look that diminished the solemnity in his eyes as he folded his arms across his wide chest. "It is only on very rare and very special occasions that I am called upon to do actual mummification, Lilliana Young. And as you are not dead, it would seem your supposition is unreasoned. Nothing went wrong with the ceremony. Seth is safely contained for the foreseeable future. And the last thing I want to do is take away your memory. If that were my intention, you wouldn't be seeing me now."

"Okay. Then what are you doing in my bedroom in the middle of the night?" The black dog nudged my hand and I reached out to stroke his head. When the dog hopped up beside me and wriggled his head under my arm so I could scratch his back, Anubis moved closer and took a seat at the foot of my bed. He regarded me with a mixture of curiosity and bewilderment.

Finally, he said, "I . . . we . . . need your help."

I sputtered, "Y-you, as in the Egyptian gods, need *me,* a powerless human girl, to help you? What could I possibly help you with?"

Anubis glanced at his dog when he thumped him with his tail, licking my arm. "He does not usually enjoy being around mortals."

"He seems to like me well enough."

"Yes. He does."

"What's his name?" I asked.

"Abutiu."

"Huh. That's an interesting name for a dog."

"Abutiu is not *a* dog—he's *the* dog."

"Is that the same kind of thing as *the* horse, as in Nebu, the golden stallion found by Horus?"

"They are the same in that they both have power beyond that of a mortal animal, but Abutiu was the first of his kind, whereas *horse* is much too simple a concept to apply to Nebu."

"So Abutiu's like the original dog?"

"Something like that."

Anubis shifted away from me on the bed and continued. "We need you to find Amon."

"Find him? What do you mean find him? You lost him?" I folded my arms. "Does this have something to do with Amon quitting the mummy business?"

The dark eyes of the god of mummification pierced me, rooting me in place. I swallowed, suddenly uneasy, and berated myself for showing my cards. *Nice one, Lily.*

"So. You know," he said. "I must admit I'm not surprised. How often have you seen him?"

At that point I wasn't sure I should be saying anything more. I gave him a noncommittal shrug and zipped my lips.

"It does not matter if you tell me or not. I know that your connection is still viable. In fact, I'm counting on it being so."

"What difference does it make either way? He's not going back."

Anubis caught my wrist and squeezed it slightly. "He must, Lilliana Young." Startled, I gently pulled away from his grip. He looked down at his hand as if surprised that he had touched me in the first place and then rose and walked the length of my room, pushing the curtains aside to look out my window at the moonlit night.

"Why do you need him so badly?" I asked. "Isn't there someone else you could charm into serving Egypt for a few eons?"

Still facing the window, he shook his head. "The three Sons of Egypt are bonded. To break that bond is to render the three of them powerless. Without all of them, the cosmos is vulnerable."

"So you're saying Seth could possibly find a way to get back in."

"Yes."

"Well, why didn't you share this information with Amon before? He thinks you can just find someone else to take his place."

Anubis turned, and a scowl flashed across his handsome face. "He never had an issue with his work, never wavered before. We only tell the Sons of Egypt enough so that they may do their duty. Frankly, I thought if any of them would give over their immortality for a woman it would be Asten."

"No. Asten would never abandon his brothers. Not even for a woman."

Frowning and running a hand through his hair, Anubis said, "It's worse than I feared. You've bonded with all three of them."

"Wh-what?" I sputtered incredulously. "I'll have you know I'm not that kind of a girl."

He waved a hand in front of himself, showing his irritation. "I am not speaking of the physical, although there are manifestations of the bond on the physical plane." He peered at me in the dim room. "Isis was right. You are unique, Lilliana Young. It's fortunate for you that you are. It gives me hope that you might survive the journey."

"Journey? What are you talking about?"

"The journey you must make into the netherworld to rescue Amon and bring him back to the afterlife."

"Aren't the netherworld and the afterlife the same thing?"

"I really don't have the time to explain this."

"I think you'd better make the time if you expect me to help you."

He peered at me, eyes narrowed, for a moment before giving in. "Very well, but you will get the abbreviated version."

"Fine."

"I govern the afterlife. It is a type of staging area where the hearts of the dead are judged."

"Okay."

"Part of it is a paradise where those with good hearts live out eternity in a state of bliss and happiness."

"Right. So it's heaven."

"Yes. Of a sort."

"So then that would make the netherworld . . ."

"The closest thing you might compare it to is hell or purgatory."

"I see. And this is where Amon is trapped?"

"Yes."

"Well, why didn't he go to the afterlife instead? Didn't you judge his heart worthy?"

Anubis turned away and fingered a straw hat hanging from one of my hooks. "The Sons of Egypt were not supposed to be judged. Not until their duties were complete."

"I take it something else happened, then."

"The goddess Ma'at decided that his bond with a human warranted a"—he seemed to search for the right word—"a checkup."

"She wanted to weigh his heart."

"Correct. Amon was asked to place his heart upon the Scale of Truth and Justice. Instead, he leapt to another realm. As you know, he is in possession of the Eye of Horus and he used its power to gain entrance to the netherworld."

"Was there any risk that his heart would be found . . . uh . . . evil?"

"There is a certain amount of darkness in every human heart. What is weighed is the balance of a person's life. If they have learned from their mistakes and have more frequently given heed to what is right, then they are judged worthy."

"Then that shouldn't have been a problem for Amon."

Tilting his head, Anubis considered me. "Your assumption is not incorrect."

"Then why did he run?"

"I suspect he ran because he was no longer in *possession* of his heart."

My body went cold, and though I tried to channel a poker face, I was sure Anubis could see right through me. Swallowing nervously, I said, "I don't understand. I mean, how could he live?"

"He doesn't. Not in the way you are thinking. He has no need for a physical heart. You might believe that a heart is merely an organ, used to circulate the blood and to beat quickly when one feels love for another, but in truth a heart is much more than that. It is the place where memory and intelligence are stored. It holds that which is most sacred—the true name of its owner."

"Um, I'm pretty sure you're talking about a brain, not a heart."

"No. I am talking about the essence of a person, what makes an individual unique. You can call it a soul, a heart, a brain, or any number of things. In Egypt we call a fully united soul bearing his true name an Akh. Without his heart, Amon cannot merge the different aspects of himself. Each part that defines him drifts apart like a broken boat out at sea. It makes him . . . vulnerable. In the afterlife, such a thing might have gone unnoticed if he had not been asked to produce his heart, but in the netherworld . . ."

"It puts him in danger."

"Yes. To the point where he might experience a second and final death. Something we cannot allow to happen."

"A second death?"

"Amon died his first death many centuries ago. He was granted a sort of immortality because he was willing to serve the gods, but heading into the netherworld without his heart was the most dangerous thing he could do. It would seem he courts an end to his existence. If he dies a second death, he is lost to us forever."

I remembered then how tired, how weary Amon looked in our dream. Maybe Anubis was right and Amon didn't want to live any longer. I knew for sure he didn't want to serve the gods, but giving up his life? What was worse was a part of me knew his dissatisfaction with the status quo was my fault. Distracted, I asked, "So Amon is now . . . what, exactly?"

"A wandering shadow. A facet of his former self. And without uniting the shadow with his true name, I am afraid he will be lost."

"I thought you said it was no big deal if he was missing his heart scarab jewel when you mummified him."

"It isn't. The amulet only leads his Akh back to his body, which he will not need for another thousand years. With the Eye of Horus in his possession, he will be able to find it on his own, but a shadow cannot return to the mortal realm." Anubis paused, then rubbed his fingers together, looking at them instead of me. "Do you want to know my theory?"

I swallowed and said weakly, "Sure."

"I believe . . . Amon left his heart containing his true name with you. Such a thing has only happened once before, and Amon would well know that using magic of that kind is strictly forbidden. In truth the knowledge of it has been hidden from all but the gods. Of course, in Amon's case, having access to the Eye of Horus, he would be privy to such spells."

"A sp-spell?" I stammered, a cold sweat spreading across my skin.

"It was used once before by Isis and Osiris. Isis enacted a spell so that she and her husband could never wholly be separated. Even death could not keep them apart."

"But Seth killed Osiris."

"He did. Since death is natural and Isis used unnatural means to enact the spell, there were, shall we say . . . complications. A terrible price was paid, and the balance of the cosmos needed to be adjusted. Such a thing has been prohibited since that time."

"It worked, though. Didn't it? I mean the two of them are still together. Amon told me about how she tricked Amun-Ra so she could visit her husband."

"Yes. It worked," he admitted.

"Even so, I don't see what all that has to do with me and Amon. We broke the bond, remember? I had to kill him."

"You did. But if such a spell linked you prior to Amon's death, it would still be in effect upon your separation."

"Well, he didn't do a spell that I recall," I hedged.

"I have not come to judge either one of you. What has happened, has happened. My purpose is to rectify the important issue at hand."

"Finding Amon," I murmured thoughtfully. He bowed his head in affirmation and I said, "I get it. I do. But I'm afraid you don't understand. Amon doesn't *want* to pick up where he left off. He wants to quit his job."

"No, Lilliana. It is you who doesn't understand. Amon *must* be rescued. If you will not do it to save the cosmos from the worst kind of darkness and evil you can imagine, and if you will not do it to save the lives of Asten and Ahmose, who will die a permanent death the same instant that Amon does, then perhaps you will do it to save Amon from endless torture and pain, for that is what he experiences right now.

"What I fear the most is not his death or knowing that he suffers. It is that he will be found by the Devourer of the Dead, who resides in the netherworld. She seeks out those lost souls who wander the Paths of Desolation and sates her endless appetite by consuming them. If she gets her hands on him, Amon's suffering will be eternal, for she can feed off of him continually.

"His connection to you will make him especially desirable to her. It is not often that she has the opportunity to feast upon a heart like Amon's, a heart that is filled with love. The blackened souls we send to her are never satisfying enough and any remaining energies they retain are consumed too quickly. Her power is held in check simply because we starve her. A juicy heart such as Amon's, fueled by your bond, would grant her enough energy to escape the confines of the netherworld."

"I thought you said his heart was missing."

"That is my . . . theory."

"Then how can she eat it?"

Anubis sighed. "The link between Amon and his brothers and between the two of you makes all four of you susceptible, for she can sense you through him. Whatever piece of Amon's heart remains, whether it's his memory or his soul, it will be as enticing to her as fresh blood is to a shark."

Holy Egyptian heaven. My hands shook. I wasn't sure if I actually understood everything Anubis was explaining, but I couldn't deny the seriousness of the situation. "Assuming all of this is true, and I believed it and wanted to do something about it, why couldn't I just use our vision connection to tell him to get out?"

"Because even if you were able to tell him, the netherworld is designed to trap a person once they enter."

"Then what's to prevent me from being trapped along with him?"

"We will tether you to the afterlife. The tether will only work with one still living. Once you locate Amon, the tether will become active and you will follow it to an exit point where we will wait to retrieve you."

"We?"

"Yes, the five of us—Isis, Osiris, myself, Nephthys, and Ma'at."

"And Asten and Ahmose?"

"They are busy performing their assigned duties."

"Okay, then what about Amun-Ra or Horus? Don't they care about what's going on?"

"Because Amon is imbued with the power of both Horus and Amun-Ra, they cannot intervene directly. To use their power in Amon's retrieval would alert the Devourer to his presence. Also, Amun-Ra was not fully convinced that the Sons of Egypt were necessary in the first place. It was only with great reluctance that he agreed to share his power. I imagine he considers Amon's betrayal of their gifts as confirmation that he was correct regarding his original position and likely blames me for selecting a faulty vessel."

"Good for you. Well, at least the gods won't throw any thorns in my path, right?" Anubis looked suddenly uncomfortable. "They wouldn't, *right*?" I encouraged him to answer.

"All I can tell you is that to enter the afterlife, which is the place you'll need to begin, you must convince Amun-Ra to allow you to ride his celestial barque."

"You mean the same one that Isis rode on when she tricked him?"

"Yes. And he's not likely to fall for the same trick twice."

"And he won't just give me permission outright?"

"No. Like I said, he doesn't see things in the same way we do."

"How generous of him. So to sum everything up, I need to convince or trick the most powerful god of Egypt to give me a seat in his boat, head into the netherworld with a rope tied around my waist, and fight various monsters and demons, including one that wants to eat my heart, all in the hope that I can navigate a world of traps, locate Amon, and convince him to come back and resume the work he hates without either of us dying a permanent death. Is that about right?"

"The rope is figurative." I folded my arms across my chest. He winced. "It is a crude, yet not imprecise, summation."

"And why exactly aren't you doing all of this yourself?"

"His heart speaks only to you, Lilliana Young. If I were to enter the netherworld, I could spend an eternity seeking him. Then who would fulfill my duties in the centuries it would take to find him? I'd have to cast light upon every bottomless crevice, every dank hole, and every monster-filled bog in the place. The netherworld is so vast, so . . . distracting . . . that the likelihood of me finding him before the Devourer does is slim. You, my dear, with a direct line to Amon's heart, will save us time. You are our best chance."

I sighed, rubbing my temples. "What if . . ." I paused. "What if I find him and he doesn't want to come back?"

Anubis came around the bed and placed his hands on my shoulders. "You will explain it to him."

"But—"

"Lilliana, Amon left the afterlife for you. And for you, he will return."

Would he? How could I do this? I was no Egyptian heroine. I could barely wield a knife against an apple, let alone a sword, against a monster, assuming I was even given a sword. Considering the folded-arms-wait-and-see approach Horus and Amun-Ra were taking, I wasn't guaranteed to make it into the afterlife in the first place, let alone the netherworld. Even if I did, how would I figure out where Amon was holed up?

"How am I supposed to find him?"

"Your heart will lead you to him," Anubis answered quietly.

There were so many questions. Too many. *Even if I knew where the netherworld was, wouldn't I have to die to get there?* I guess my decision boiled down to my level of trust in Anubis. Did I believe what he was telling me?

My gut told me yes. I tried to reason it out logically, but logic in this situation failed me. When dealing with a world of gods and goddesses, figurative hearts and spells, supernatural powers and monstrous creatures, you didn't follow your brain; you followed your heart. And my heart whispered that Amon needed me. If I was honest with myself, I'd admit that I'd known that fact for a while.

If everything Anubis said was true, then the consequences of my failing were more than I could comprehend. I'd lose everything and Chaos would destroy the world. No matter what, I couldn't stand back and let this tragedy unfold. If, for some reason, Anubis was misleading me and he was using me only to keep Amon in line, then I'd deal with that later.

Moonlight filtered in through the window and slanted across the god of the afterlife's face. The night was quiet. I couldn't hear the crickets chirping outside or even my nana's snoring and I wondered briefly if Anubis had wrapped us in one of his time bubbles where the outside world ceased to exist.

Energy and anticipation thrummed through my limbs, and my mind was soon able to focus on only one thing. I wasn't thinking about the danger, the uncertainty, the million questions I had, Seth, the gods, or even the Devourer. The only idea that I could reflect on was the possibility that I'd be able to see Amon again. A steely determination filled me.

Anubis seemed to sense this and searched my face hopefully. "Will you go, Lilliana?" he asked.

Hesitating for a single heartbeat, I answered quietly. "Yes."

Anubis gifted me with a rare, heartfelt smile. "You are truly a brave girl. I can understand why Amon has such affection for you. But, Lilliana, there is one thing you must do first. If you cannot accomplish this task, then you will not be permitted entry to Amun-Ra's realm at all, let alone ride his celestial barque or enter the afterlife."

I frowned, uncertainty flooding over me. "What is it?" I asked.

"You must transform yourself."

Choking back my fear, I posed, "Do you mean I have to die first?"

Anubis shook his head. "Not die. No. For the tether to work, you will need to be alive. But your mortality will be altered somewhat. It's an inevitable thing with this type of transformation. And you must understand that once this is done, you will never be just Lilliana Young again. You will be something altogether different."

"What do I have to do?" I asked, terrified of his answer.

"You'll have to become . . . a sphinx."

4

Hassan

"A . . . a what?" I asked, unsure I'd heard him correctly.

"A sphinx."

"Like the one near the pyramids?"

"No." He gave a frustrated sigh. "There is so much you do not know."

"No kidding."

"I will send you to the vizier. He will assist you."

"The vizier? You mean Dr. Hassan?"

"Yes. Hassan. Come now, Lilliana. We have wasted too much time already."

"You want me to go right now? Let me at least get dressed and come up with something to say to my nana."

"There is no need to bother her. If you are successful, you'll be returned to this exact time as if nothing had happened at all."

I was almost scared to ask. "And if I fail?"

"If you fail," he murmured softly, "your nana and the rest of mankind will have much more to worry about than your disappearance."

"Right," I replied with a queasy knot in my stomach.

"Now. Regarding your attire . . ." Anubis tapped his fingertip to his chin as he studied my form. My cheeks burned. With a twitch of his fingers, tiny particles of sand and dust sped toward him and twirled in a path around his hand. They coalesced and brightened, twisting faster until I could no longer distinguish them.

Anubis directed the swirling mass toward me, where the gleaming substance surrounded my limbs. Nervously, I darted from the bed just as the light burst. It melted down my body, becoming a flowing gown of green the exact same shade as Amon's heart scarab. Golden scales that looked like the scarab wings were attached to the dress at the top, forming a sort of jeweled collar that softly wound over my shoulders, my back, and underneath my arms like a shoulder harness.

The segments lengthened and continued down the sides of the gown where they crossed my abdomen like a winged corset of glistening armor. A gleaming emerald scarab sat at the center of my waist where the wings met. The bottom of the dress flowed out in delicate gossamer and ended at my ankles. On my feet were golden sandals that sparkled like the hooves of the desert horses who were descendants of Nebu, the famous immortal stallion.

"It's beautiful," I admitted.

"Yes. It should serve adequately for the present." He watched me inspect the armor and added, "I used the scarab you hid beneath your pillow to create it."

Startled, I raised my eyes to his. "You knew?"

"Of course I knew. I am a god, after all. The fact that his scarab went missing when I mummified Amon was not lost on me." Stepping forward, he stretched out a finger to the emerald but stopped just short of touching it. "The gemstone is nothing, a trinket. It is the power Amon instilled within it that is important. A piece of him resides there. Only you have the ability to draw it out and return him wholly to himself."

"Is it normal that I can feel his heartbeat when I touch it?" I asked without making eye contact.

He didn't respond for a few seconds, and I reluctantly drew my eyes to his. Anubis was looking at me with a sort of puzzled expression. His eyes slowly traced a path from my face down to the jewel at my waist.

"It means your connection is stronger than we all thought. Even Isis couldn't feel her husband's heart upon his death. It shouldn't be possible for a mortal at all and yet . . ." His words trailed off as he closed his eyes and inhaled deeply. "Yes. I sense it. Though it is faint for me. If I wasn't aware of it, I doubt I would have discovered it on my own."

When Anubis opened his eyes, he took a step forward and reached out a hand to trail his fingertips down my bare arm. I stopped breathing, confused about what was happening. Anubis murmured in a honey-rich voice, "The yearning you feel for one another is"—he paused and tilted his head—"it's heady, addictive. A potent enough elixir to tempt even a god."

His warm gaze locked on to my lips and he lowered his head as if to kiss me. I shifted minutely since his hand cupped my arm in a powerful enough grip to prevent me from doing much of anything, and he froze, apparently shocked by his own actions. The intensity in his expression, the emotion behind his eyes was quickly reeled in.

Before I could ask him what he was doing, he moved several feet away and said, "It will certainly be an enticement for every dangerous immortal being in the netherworld."

"So you're saying the scarab will make immortals want to . . ." I couldn't complete the sentence.

Anubis replied frankly, "They will want to devour you. In one way or another."

I touched my fingertips to the scarab. "That's fantastic," I murmured wryly as I pondered the ramifications of my connection to Amon.

"The potency of the spell creates an aura about you. All of those you come into contact with will be affected by it in varying degrees. The pull becomes more powerful the longer a person is exposed. The stronger the immortal is, the more he will be able to resist its lure, but those of a weak mind will scarcely be able to control themselves. They'll be bewitched. Becoming a sphinx will at least afford you the ability to protect yourself more fully."

Not knowing how to process all of that, I focused instead on the sphinx thing. "Right. About that—"

He held up a hand. "The vizier will explain everything." Ignoring my grunt of frustration, Anubis rubbed his jaw and said as he considered me, "It is unfortunate for you that Amon offered his heart. I'm not certain he understood all the ramifications of gifting you with his heart scarab. If I'd known of his plan, I would have prevented it."

"Isn't it right that he should have someone to love?" I questioned with an underlying edge to my voice.

"Love is fleeting. It's a brief spark that flares in the heavens, bursting forth in a cascade of glory only to be snuffed out in the darkness of space. It is not something worth risking the cosmos over."

I folded my arms across my chest and frowned. He was wrong. There were some kinds of love that continued, even after death. Like a ripple on the water, love moved. Long after the plunge, its effect could be felt. All that was required was someone to remember it, to see what it left behind. Then it existed, it lived. If anyone offered to sever the ties between me and Amon, I'd outright reject it.

"Wars have been fought over love, you know," I murmured.

"That observation just served to prove my point even further."

"Perhaps you shouldn't speak of something you haven't experienced for yourself."

Anubis stared me down. "You are quite bold for a mortal."

"And you are quite narrow-minded for a god."

"I find it interesting that you feel brave enough to speak your mind to me and yet you cower before your so very mortal parents. Perhaps Amon's rebellious nature has rubbed off on you. Both of you court danger like a pair of monkeys wandering too close to a crocodile-infested river."

"My relationship with my parents, like my relationship with Amon, is none of your business."

"On the contrary. Your relationships such as they may be are indeed my business. If there was a way to save Amon myself, giving me leave to destroy the connection between you, I wouldn't hesitate to do it. And despite what you are so obviously thinking, I do not say this to be cruel or to unfairly punish you. The benefits of such a thing as falling in love with an immortal are not worth more than what you are losing."

I drew myself up, jutting my chin in the air as haughtily as I could muster. "That's my choice to make, though, isn't it?"

Anubis raised an eyebrow. "For now, young one. For now."

My hands fisted at my sides, anger boiling through my veins. What I felt for the boy imbued with the celestial power of the sun was precious to me. I'd never voluntarily give it up, danger or no. He didn't understand that before Amon, nothing mattered. I'd been drifting through my life letting other people decide the path I would take. But Amon lit a spark that I'd nurtured these last few months.

Maybe Anubis was right about my parents. Maybe I'd taken the coward's way. The easy way out. Perhaps I did hide the flame from them, but it was there. I could feel it. My soul had awakened, and I wouldn't turn away from the one responsible for filling my world with purpose and light. If I had wandered aimlessly since returning home, it was only because I'd lost sight of the one thing that mattered to me. The only way I'd let Anubis destroy our bond was over my dead body.

"When it becomes necessary for you to fight—notice I said when, not if—the amulet will become your shield, your armor, and even your weapon."

I touched the green gem. "So it's magic?"

"In a way. Despite what I think of its so-called benefits, love *is* a sort of magic. A trick of the light that not even the gods can replicate. The heart scarab is fueled by Amon's feelings for you. As long as his love for you remains, the protection his heart offers is assured." Anubis called his dog to his side. "Are you ready?"

I sucked in a breath and glanced around my room, convinced that there was something I was forgetting or some question I hadn't thought of. "I suppose I am," I answered after gathering my courage.

Anubis nodded. "Abutiu," he addressed his canine companion, "return home and await my arrival." With a small snort, the dog disappeared and we were alone. The god of mummification frowned, took a step closer, then reached out and drew me into his arms. He was warm, and the sensation of being held by him wasn't at all unpleasant.

I pressed my cheek against the rough fabric of his denim jacket. "Close your eyes," he encouraged while cradling me as if I were extremely fragile. Maybe to him I was. I closed them, expecting to hear the familiar release of sand just before I felt the brush of grains against my skin, but then I remembered that travel by sand couldn't happen over large bodies of water.

I wondered for a moment if Dr. Hassan wasn't in Egypt after all and if Anubis traveled in a different way from Amon. Just as I was about to ask him, I felt the floor disappear beneath us and we sank into a blackness so complete, I was sure that there was nothing left of me.

Though I was conscious, I felt like I had no form. I couldn't feel my limbs. I wasn't breathing. I was just . . . aware. Like a disembodied spirit. If I could've screamed, I would have. It felt like an endless sort of suffocation.

Panic set in, though there was no way to physically express it. If this was the way Anubis returned me to New York after he'd mummified Amon, I was glad that I couldn't remember it. We popped into the light like a bubble rising from the ocean, and a burst of sensations came at me all at once. I had form and substance. I could feel. I could see and hear. Actually, I was so grateful just to be alive that when the journey ended, I held tightly to Anubis with trembling limbs.

Anubis wrapped his arms around me in a way that had nothing to do with keeping me upright, his lips grazing my temple, when he suddenly growled and set me aside. Though I wobbled, he made no attempt to come closer and glared at me like I'd tricked him somehow. Recovering somewhat, I leaned on a nearby table.

We'd materialized inside a room full of dusty artifacts. It was a place I didn't recognize. "Vizier!" Anubis called impatiently while keeping a careful distance from me. "Vizier, come here at once!"

I heard the unmistakable sound of pottery shattering on the packed dirt floor. "Oh my!" a familiar voice exclaimed as shuffling footsteps came closer. A figure rounded the corner. He lifted his white fedora and wrung it in his hands as he looked at Anubis with wide eyes. The man wet his lips. "Can I . . . can I help you?" he asked warily.

"Do you know who I am?"

Dr. Hassan tilted his head, narrowing his brown eyes. "I hesitate to guess," he finally answered.

"Perhaps you need a refresher course in your own studies, *Doctor.*" Anubis threw out his arm, gesturing to me as if in accusation. "If you don't know me, then surely you remember this one."

Anubis moved and Dr. Hassan turned his startled gaze in my direction and gasped. "Lily?"

"Hello, Oscar," I addressed him with a warm smile. "It's good to see you."

"And you." He moved a few steps closer, unwittingly inserting himself between me and the tall, intimidating man glowering at us, perhaps a means of protecting me, though both of us knew there was no protecting either of us if Anubis wanted to cause harm. Attempting to placate the irritable god, I decided to help.

"Oscar, meet Anubis. Anubis, this is Dr. Hassan, one of your most devoted followers."

Anubis folded his arms across his chest and harrumphed. "You'd think someone claiming devotion would at least recognize the one he professed to worship."

"Just ignore him," I said to Oscar. "He's a little testy today. Besides, he's all bark and no bite, just like his dog."

Dr. Hassan glanced up at the god, more than a little worried about my choice of words. "Lily, I don't think—"

"It's all right," I interrupted. "We're doing him a huge favor. So he owes us. Right, Anubis?"

The god frowned, but his lip twitched in a way that made me think he wasn't really as upset as he professed to be. "Are you familiar with the Medinet Habu Temple in Luxor?" he asked Oscar.

"Of course." Hassan took a step forward and placed his hat back on his head.

"Hidden within the court depicting the Seven Scenes of War with the People of the Sea there is a secret doorway located just beyond the second pylon. Seek the mark of the sphinx and turn the stone counterclockwise. Follow the passageway to the Room of Riddles. There you will find inscribed upon the walls all the information you should need to complete the transformation ritual known as Rite of Wasret."

"Wasret? What do you need of her?" asked Oscar.

At the same time I whispered to him, "Who's Wasret?"

Speaking louder to regain control of the conversation, Anubis explained, "Lilliana Young must complete the ritual to take on the mantle of Wasret in order to breach the netherworld and rescue Amon, and you, my good doctor, will serve as her tether to mortality should she succeed."

"Breach the . . ." Dr. Hassan paused, confusion evident on his face. "I'm not sure I fully comprehend your purpose," he said respectfully.

Anubis sighed, his impatience obvious. I tried to clarify. "Anubis wants me to become a sphinx so that I can save Amon, who escaped his duty by heading into the netherworld. It's a dangerous place, where he's suffering, and if he doesn't return, Seth could breach the barrier and destroy the world."

I turned to Anubis, with eyebrows raised, to see if he wanted to add anything. He was smiling at me like a proud parent. "There, you see?" he said. "I am no longer needed."

"Before you depart, great one, might you indulge me a moment as I ask two questions?"

"Very well. But make your queries brief."

Nodding vigorously, Dr. Hassan asked his first question. "Do you mean that you want Lilliana to become the matriarch of the Order of the Sphinx such as the pharaoh Hatshepsut?" A gleam had lit his eyes and I could see that he was excited about the prospect.

"No. Though that title will naturally fall to her once she goes through the rite. Lilliana will in actuality become a sphinx, something only a few mortals have ever attempted." Glancing down at his fingertips and running his thumb over them, he added in a more hushed voice, "None of which have lived through the process."

I didn't like the sound of that. But the idea of my extremely untimely death didn't seem to faze Dr. Hassan, who took an eager step forward.

Anubis folded his arms across his chest and frowned when he saw my startled expression. "Of course, they didn't have the help of the gods," he added almost as an afterthought. "Now, what is your second question?"

"Ah. Yes. Why Wasret? She is a goddess so unremarkable that I can count on one hand the number of recovered stelae depicting her likeness. There is not one temple dedicated to her. Most Egyptologists believe she was so inconsequential that her name was rubbed out entirely from the annals of history and that any deeds that might have possibly been done in her name were assigned to other deities."

"The reason all of your companions who spend their lives digging in the stone and dust of the past have found very little regarding Wasret is because she doesn't exist. Yet."

"What do you mean?"

"That is your third question, Doctor. I am afraid I'll have to leave you to discover the rest of the story on your own. It is time to say goodbye, Lilliana Young." Anubis snapped his fingers and my balance shifted. Before I could do anything except gasp in shock, my body lifted off the ground and sped toward him.

When I was stable, he skimmed my cheek with his fingertips and cautioned, "Do not trust anyone in the netherworld, even those you may consider friends." His eyes raked over my face and he leaned closer, his lips grazing my ear. "I do very much hope I will see you again. Good luck."

With that, he took a step back and a black vortex opened beneath his feet, sucking him down before re-forming into a solid surface.

All was quiet for a moment until I heard Oscar exclaim, "How remarkable!"

Spinning around, I headed back to him and wrapped him in a hug. "I missed you."

He patted my back and shifted his hat so it wouldn't fall off. "I missed you, too, young lady."

"So do you understand what it is he wants me to do?" I asked as I pulled away.

Oscar's eyes lost their gleam and as he looked away, he rubbed his forehead. "I really won't know all the details until we find this hidden room. But I can honestly say, I have never, in my long life of studying the stories of the gods and serving as the grand vizier, felt more frightened."

5

Room of Riddles

"I suppose it's as good a time as any to get under way," Dr. Hassan stated flatly. He glanced in my direction but quickly rose from where he had sat down to rest and focused his attention on the hat he was kneading with his hands. Now I was even more worried. Dr. Hassan's hat was sacred to him. He would never abuse it. "Unless you need to rest first?" he inquired kindly as he replaced the twisted fedora on his head.

"No. I think I'm okay. Besides, who can sleep after a nighttime visitor like Anubis? That kind of end-of-the-world gloom-and-doom announcement would give me nightmares, I should think."

"Yes," he mumbled distractedly, and gave me a weak smile as he began to gather his things.

"There's something you're not telling me, isn't there?" I asked as I began helping him stuff his tools into a bag. "You think I'm going to fail."

"No. *No,*" he emphasized unequivocally when I gave him a knowing look. "You will not fail. I simply won't allow it."

"But you don't really know, do you? There aren't any guarantees."

"Let's just worry about one thing at a time, shall we?" When I reluctantly nodded, he blew out a breath and said, "First things first. We need to get to Luxor."

"Right." I hoisted one of his bags over my shoulder and waited patiently for him to finish up.

When he finally turned toward me, he did a double take as if he hadn't really gotten a good look at me earlier. He pushed his hat up higher on his forehead, dropping his bag on his makeshift office table, and stretched out his fingers to touch the winged harness on my shoulder. "What is this that you're wearing, Lily? I'd assumed it was your nightdress, but obviously I was mistaken."

I smoothed my hand down the dress and felt the heat rise in my cheeks. "It's a bit much, I know. Anubis made it for me."

"It's lovely," Dr. Hassan said in a clinical sort of way as he peered more closely at each segment of the band. He walked around me slowly and didn't stop until he found the scarab at my waist. I got the sense that he knew it was there all along but he'd purposely saved the best, most interesting discovery for last.

Dr. Hassan dug through his bag and brought out a crazy pair of glasses with protruding lenses. Flipping a switch as he adjusted them over his eyes caused a brilliant beam of light to hit my waist. I stood as still as I could manage while he twisted the lenses until he was satisfied and then bit my lip as he mumbled to himself. Finally he stood and pronounced, "It's authentic."

"Of course it is," I said. "What did you expect?"

"I'm not sure. The gem is a genuine emerald of the highest quality as far as I can tell. Did you know that it is a heart scarab?"

"Yes." He took off the glasses and thumped them in his palm, calculating something. His perceptive and all-too-sharp eyes searched my face. "Before you ask, I'll tell you. It was Amon's. Anubis said a piece of Amon's heart is tied to it. I can actually make out his heartbeat if I listen carefully."

Dr. Hassan's jaw actually dropped. "Astounding." I couldn't tell from the tone of his voice if he was excited or concerned but suddenly *astounding* seemed like a word I didn't want to inspire someone like Dr. Hassan to say. *Astounding* in this case couldn't be a good thing. In my mind it translated to all the words he didn't say. Words like *perplexing, unheard-of, baffling, shocking,* or maybe just *what-the-heck-have-you-gotten-yourself-into-Lily.*

I tried to squelch my nervous thoughts and launched into an explanation of everything that had happened as best as I could recall it. He listened quietly, asking only brief questions for clarification, and when I was done, he sat heavily on the edge of the table. "I've never heard of any of this. The story of Isis and her husband, Osiris, is one of the most well documented of all the various tales of Egypt, and never have I found a hint on any of the engravings that Isis held a piece of his heart. Though now that I think on it . . ."

Oscar stood up and quickly sketched a very accurate depiction of the heart scarab on some rubbing paper, then carefully folded it and stuffed it into his one of his many vest pockets. "Of all the couples in the Egyptian pantheon, the two of them are the most connected, the most written about."

He blew out a breath. "Even so, the two of them were immortal. I have no idea how this connection of yours works, but I should think it would pose great danger to a mortal, which is why I suppose Anubis needs you to go through this ceremony. Lily, I won't lie to you and say that I have no concerns. The sacrifices you will be called upon to make coupled with the dangers of the journey . . ." He rubbed his neck as if he could already feel the tension mounting. "I just hope that I can serve your purposes well."

"If anyone can help me, Dr. Hassan, it's you."

"Let's pray that you are right. Come, Lily. Let's get you to my car."

As we headed up a dark and dusty stairwell toward the Egyptian summertime light, I asked, "Where are we?" Heat rose from the sand and rocky hills in waves.

"Saqqara. It's the ancient capital of Memphis." When he saw I was at a loss, he added, "We're about thirty kilometers south of Cairo." As he led me to his vehicle, he explained, "I've been working on this dig site for the last three months. This is the tomb of the Witness Who Fed the Flesh of the God, in other words, Maia, the wet nurse of King Tutankhamun. She was discovered here in the late nineties and I am officially overseeing the excavation of her chapel."

"Are there pyramids in this area?"

"Several, including the famous stepped pyramid of Djoser."

"Did you, you know," I continued in a whisper, "hide any of the brothers here?"

"Not here. But the body of Ahmose is not too far from this location. I never choose a site where there is active digging going on, lest the Sons of Egypt be discovered."

"Oh."

It disturbed me to think of Ahmose rotting away in a hidden tomb. I couldn't bear thinking of him in that way, let alone Amon. Instead of dwelling on it for too long, I asked, "So how far is it to the temple of the . . . ?"

"Medinet Habu."

"Right. That. It's in Luxor?"

"Correct. It will take eight hours or so."

As we drove, Dr. Hassan spent the majority of the time trying to make sure I understood exactly how perilous this plan would be by listing every bad thing he knew about secret rites gone wrong, clueless humans who wandered into god-created traps, and the netherworld in general.

But Amon's heart called to *me*. There was no one else who could do it. Not Anubis. Not Asten or Ahmose, and not Dr. Hassan. I, Lilliana Young, an average mortal girl, would end up being either the hero or the tragic victim—the first in a long line of casualties in the war between good and evil, if I couldn't prevent the unthinkable from happening.

It was late when we arrived and the temple was closed to tourists, but after a few words with the night watchman, Dr. Hassan was able to gain us entrance, and the guard swung open the short wooden gate that would have been almost pathetically easy to climb over. "Why don't they protect the temples better?" I asked as we moved away from the small guardhouse.

"Don't get me started," Dr. Hassan answered dryly as he handed me a flashlight. "Now, if I remember correctly, the second pylon should be in this direction."

We passed under the gateway of the first pylon and Dr. Hassan gave me a quick lesson on the architecture. "Pylons look much like the hieroglyph depicting the horizon. Do you see the shape there? It looks like two large hills with a sun rising between them."

"I remember that Horus got his name from the horizon."

"Close. It's the other way around. When you enter the temple, you enter the realm of the sun, or sun god in this case. Each pylon is a doorway into the next realm and each section can have different purposes. Remember that shape in case you see it later. Don't forget, Lily, the sun always leads to life. To see the sunrise is to embrace life. The sunset is where you will find death."

"Is that why you used the sunrise at the worm cave to see through the adder stone?"

Oscar smiled. "I'm pleased that you remember."

"I've learned that it helps when you're in love with a mummy to pay attention to little things like curses, adder stones, and long-winded archaeologists."

"I'll have you know, young lady, that I am one of the most sought-after lecturers in Egypt. I am hardly long-winded," he said with a wry grin. "Now. Where was I?"

"Pylons."

"Ah, yes, pylons can also serve as more than decoration or symbol. Ancient stairways and rooms have been found in some. I am thinking that this room Anubis described may be one of these."

We entered an open courtyard guarded by massive statues and columns. "Who's he?" I asked, pointing to the statue.

"Ramesses the third as Osiris."

"What do you mean by 'as Osiris'?"

"Pharaohs often depicted themselves as gods in an attempt to either gain the favor of the god or to increase the likelihood of their own immortality."

"But none of them actually were immortal, were they?"

"Not to my knowledge. Though by creating statues of such immense size, these ancient kings and pharaohs are remembered long after their deaths. That is a sort of immortality, I think."

Passing the statues, we entered the opening through the second pylon that led to a hall. As I studied the carvings that told the story of the invasion of the Sea Peoples, Dr. Hassan searched the pylon for a symbol representing a sphinx. He told me what to look for, but after ten minutes or so, all the images seemed to blur before my eyes and blend into one giant incomprehensible puzzle.

I was ready to give up when Dr. Hassan called out, "Lily! I believe I've found what we are looking for."

My footsteps echoed in the long-abandoned hall as I made my way over to him. I shivered and glanced around me, but all I saw were dark shadows and the stirred-up dust particles reflecting in the beam of my flashlight.

Dr. Hassan had his light aimed at an image carved into the wall that looked nothing like the one I'd heard him describe. When I pointed this out, he shook his head. "I understand your confusion. The symbol I described to you, the one that looks like a lion reclining, was the Egyptian version of a sphinx. This one is different. Closer, in fact, to the concept the Greeks have for a sphinx."

"I don't understand. What's the difference?"

"The most notable variance would be wings seen here. Though there are similarities between the two versions such as gender, superior strength, acting as a guardian for sacred sites, having the body of a lion and the head of a human, and so forth, they also retain some qualities that make them unique."

"Then a sphinx is . . ."

"Female. You might recall that powerful women such as Hatshepsut were often shown wearing the false beard of a man. This was not meant to cloak or deceive but was a sign of her power. In legend they are always female in origin, at least as far as I'm aware. Hatshepsut and Queen Hetepheres II were both depicted as the sphinx."

"So this Greek version has wings."

"The wings of an eagle. The other major difference between the Egyptian version and this one is that the Greek variety is much more treacherous."

"How so?"

"Are you familiar with the concept of the sphinx's riddle?"

"Wasn't it something like if you didn't solve the riddle you couldn't get past the sphinx? Is that what you mean?"

"Yes. But in this case, to fail would be deadly. She devoured those who didn't solve her riddle. Since Anubis called the place we're seeking the Room of Riddles, I would assume that the Greek version that I found here is the one we're looking for."

"It couldn't hurt to give it a try, I suppose," I said as he gave me a dubious look.

"Let's hope your assumption is correct."

I took his light and aimed it at the hieroglyph while he placed his palm on top of the image, pushing against it and twisting his hand as he did so. The unmistakable sound of stone grinding against stone told us we had indeed found what we were looking for. There was a clicking noise and then a snap. Dr. Hassan stepped back and a circular section of stone rose out from the wall, the symbol of the sphinx carved right in the middle of it.

"Hmm. Now what do we do?" Dr. Hassan asked.

We stood there for a moment, flashlights aimed, but nothing was happening. "Maybe push it back in?" I suggested.

He wiped his brow, adjusted his hat, and nodded. I stepped forward to place my hand against the stone and pressed. It stuck at first, but then it moved and I felt the stirring of something weighty behind the wall. A hiss followed by an almost painful grating noise revealed a passageway, and a heavy stone door that had been virtually indiscernible in the pylon before swung open.

When all the movement stopped and quiet descended on the temple again, the sounds of our nervous exhales seemed louder than the moan of a thousand ghosts rising from the grave. Together we stepped up to the opening and shined our lights inside. It was dark, blacker than a tomb, and I wondered for a moment if that was what it actually was and if somehow it was meant to house *us*. Dr. Hassan must have sensed the same thing, as even he seemed edgy.

We could just make out a series of steps leading downward and as I descended the first one, an act that made me appear to be much braver than I really was, Dr. Hassan put his hand out to stop me. "Please allow me to go first, Lily."

I nodded gratefully and moved aside. I thought it would be much easier to walk behind than in front, but being the last one wasn't fun either. Little prickles of anxiety trickled down my back like skittering beetles, and I kept turning around to make sure no one was going to attack us from behind or lock us in the creepy pit of darkness.

We descended until the stale air felt cool, and I realized we must be deep underground. I kept my hand on Oscar's shoulder even when he reached the bottom and stepped into a passageway that was more open than the stairwell had been, but the flashlight only showed dirt walls.

I didn't know how Dr. Hassan could do this for a living. I was seriously frightened. My imagination conjured a large sphinx sleeping in the cave that was going to rise up, rip us apart with her claws, and devour us before we even figured out what we had to do. The idea that I might become such a creature filled me with a dread I couldn't even describe.

"One thing at a time," I mumbled quietly to fortify my courage. Slowly, we moved forward, my sandaled feet sinking into soft sand.

When he found an old torch at the entrance to a room and lit it, my fear melted away and was replaced by a sense of wonder.

"Oh *my,*" Dr. Hassan whispered as we walked farther into the space.

This time I knew he was excited. We stood in a golden room full of treasures. The wealth displayed in even the small section lit by our torch was overwhelming. What was even more amazing was that the room was in pristine condition. The ruby necklaces, gleaming swords, and large golden statues were glistening as if they had just been polished and were on display in a museum. An impossibility, based on the amount of sand underfoot.

"Anubis must have dusted in anticipation of our arrival," I said.

"This is the most amazing find since Howard Carter and George Herbert discovered the tomb of King Tutankhamun in 1922!"

"Right. Except technically we didn't discover it. We were sent here."

"Oh, but, Lily. If I could explore this room with my colleagues. Share it with the world. What these wondrous treasures could represent for Egypt. How tragic that it must remain a secret. These things are not meant to be brought forth into the light of day."

"Maybe Anubis wouldn't mind if you took just one or two."

I stretched out a finger to touch a cat statue with emerald eyes when Dr. Hassan grabbed my wrist to stop me. "Do not touch anything, Lily, at least not yet. My policy is to read first and only disturb an object after careful cataloguing and photo documentation."

I nodded and Dr. Hassan shuffled a few steps forward, moving the torch higher up so he could read the wall carvings. "Ah, here is what we're looking for."

"What is it?"

"A message from Anubis."

"What does it say?"

"It essentially says that we are to only take the items we are instructed to and then copy the spell to perform the Rite of Wasret. The rest of the room should be left untouched, and when we leave, we are to seal it up the way we found it."

"Right. A spell. Doesn't sound too difficult."

Dr. Hassan hesitated. "Oh dear. This is going to take some time for me to translate."

I smiled a little nervously. "I thought you were an expert," I teased.

"Oh, I am. It's not that I cannot read what it says; it's that I must decipher the message behind the message."

"The message behind the . . . What do you mean?"

"As a grand vizier, I was taught a secret code that has been passed down from generation to generation. Where another Egyptologist might read this passage simply as 'The treasure of she who is powerful,' I can see there are certain phrases or words that are emphasized. The hieroglyph symbolizing the concept of *treasure,* here"—he pointed to a carving—"also has the sign of the Sons of Egypt over it. Therefore that word in particular is of great importance."

I listened to him mumble as he traced his finger across the wall. Nothing he said provided me with any reassurance and instead my imagination conjured all types of horrors. I heard *The scepter of she before whom evil trembles; the jewels of she who defeated the sphinx; the first wife of Amun; the crown of the Mistress of Dread; the spear of the Lady of Carnage;* and *the claws of she who mauls.* None of those things sounded particularly good. One thing was certain—I definitely didn't want to cross paths with whatever woman was being described. Then I realized something.

"It sounds like an inventory list," I said, interrupting his ruminations.

"Yes. There does seem to be some reference to the treasure here."

"What's with all the names anyway? Why can't a person just be called by their normal name instead of a lengthy descriptive title?"

Dr. Hassan blinked. "Two reasons. First, a title of such vivid description is more likely to induce the masses to show respect and to worship. But the second reason is more important. In the name lies veritable power. To know a person's true name is to control them. This is the main reason why true names are hidden."

"Then do you know who it is they're talking about here?"

"On the surface I would assume Sekhmet, since many of those names are used to describe that goddess, but if I was to pull out only the terms bearing Amon's symbol, I get *treasure, sphinx, Amun,* and *lady.* If I group only those and rework them, it says, *'The treasure of Amun is his lady sphinx.'* "

"Interesting. So what's next?"

"Can you take notes?"

"Absolutely."

Dr. Hassan handed me a small notepad full of his archaeology notes. *At least one of us is prepared.* Carefully, I turned the pages until I found an empty section, and jotted down phrases as he read. It took an hour to finish the first wall, though he worked very quickly. By the time we neared the end, I had scrambled phrases on dozens of pages. Tiring out, I was about to ask Dr. Hassan if we could return the next day when he exclaimed, "It's here! I've found the key to the rite."

I was watching him closely as he mumbled incoherently, enough that even though he tried to hide it, I caught a glimpse of the cold dread cross his face.

"What is it?" I demanded. "Tell me."

Dr. Hassan rubbed his hands over his tired eyes and blew out a breath. "It's a riddle, and we'll have to solve a number of them before we gain access to the spell."

"A riddle? How do you know?" I flipped back and forth through my pages, trying to piece together the circled words. It was all Greek—er, Egyptian—to me. If there was a secret question hidden in them, I couldn't make it out.

He patiently explained, "It is the most commonly known riddle of the sphinx. Perhaps you've heard of it: 'What goes on four feet in the morning, two feet at noon, and three feet in the evening?' "

"Oh, I know this. I read about it in school."

"Yes. Well, the typical answer is man, or a human. A babe crawls in the dawn of its life, walks upright during the middle of it, and uses a cane near the end. This is not, however, the correct answer here."

"Then what is?"

"In this case the answer is Amon."

"Amon? How?"

"In his first death, he fell to his hands and knees; then Anubis raised him into the next life, where he walked on his own two feet. Now he is at the end, where he hobbles through the netherworld, leaning upon his sword."

"But how did you know the answer?"

"It's backwards. Anubis gave us the answers first. Remember that Amun was in the very first group of terms?" I nodded. "Amon is an incarnation of Amun. That is the answer to the first riddle."

"The first riddle?"

"Yes. There will be three more. And the answers will be *treasure, sphinx,* and *lady.* This is the symbol of Amun, the sun god. If I am correct, this will lead us to the next question." Using two fingers, he pushed on the hieroglyph and pieces of stone began to shift like a giant puzzle box. When it settled, some of the stones had turned upside down while others moved lower and some disappeared altogether.

"Oh, wow."

"Let's get started, shall we?"

This time it only took him ten minutes to figure out the riddle. "This one I know as well. The key is to reinterpret it in a different way."

"What's the riddle?"

"Who are the three sisters who give birth to each other? In the standard question there are two sisters and the answer is Night and Day. I do not see how the answer could be *treasure.* Perhaps it is *lady.* But the number three is not something I've come across before. I'm not sure how it applies."

"I think the answer is *sphinx.*"

"Why is that?"

"That's what I'm to become, right? I have to go through this rite or whatever and it will change my mortality. I'll be reborn . . . in a way. It's the only one that makes sense."

Dr. Hassan looked at me thoughtfully for a moment. "I do believe you are correct. We will try it."

He found not one but two carved symbols of the sphinx, one the Egyptian version and one the Greek. Hesitating only briefly, he chose the winged version. Apparently, it was the right choice. Again the walls groaned and shifted and now we could see glimpses of a room behind the stone barrier.

"We're halfway there," I said. "We've got a fifty-fifty chance of getting the rest of it correct."

Twenty minutes later, he'd deciphered the next riddle.

"I've never heard of this one."

"What does it say?"

"It is by man considered most valuable. It sparkles in the light of the sun. Provides for all his needs. His life is wasted in the pursuit of it, and yet if he takes hold fast and true, it will never leave him." He paused for a moment. "It could be *treasure.*"

"It could also be *lady.*"

"You are right." Oscar rubbed his jaw and glanced at me. "Might I propose a theory?"

"Of course."

"The last two riddles were specific references to you and Amon."

"Yes. That's true."

"That means this one is likely applicable to you as well. If that is the case, I believe the answer is *lady.*"

"Really? Why?"

"Assuming Amon is the man in question, you are what he pursues. Not treasure. And when you are together, I see the light in his face. It reflects upon you."

"Oh. Yes. I suppose it does."

Confident in his theory, Dr. Hassan selected the symbol for *lady.* Nothing immediately happened and I held my breath for a few seconds. Then the whirring clicks began and the wall shifted, opening pockets large enough that we could thrust our hands through the openings but still not big enough for us to scramble through.

"You were right," I mumbled.

"Yes."

As he worked on the last group of carvings, I thought about the words of the previous riddle. Was Amon wasting his life in pursuit of me? How could I, a mortal girl, provide for all his needs? Even if I found Amon and saved him, Anubis would never let us be together. He'd been pretty clear in explaining that Amon needed to do the work he'd been called to do. This last section, though, gave me a bit of hope. Perhaps if we did hold on to each other there would somehow be a way for our paths to meet again.

Dr. Hassan interrupted my thoughts. "We have a problem."

"What is it?"

"The riddle is fairly straightforward this time. It says to state your purpose and find the thing we seek."

"Right, but we already know the answer is *treasure.*"

"Is it? It could be a trick. If our answer is *riches,* we will most likely be cut off. The last thing the gods accept is the theft of their precious relics, and we were explicitly warned not to take anything but the items we were instructed to."

Dr. Hassan's finger hovered over the symbol for treasure, but he hesitated. I wasn't sure what else to do.

"I suppose we have no other option," he said, ready to push the symbol.

But in that moment I noticed something.

"Stop!" I called out.

"What is it, Lily?" Dr. Hassan said, lowering his hand.

"I recognize this. It's the sign for Amon, isn't it?"

"Yes. But Amon wasn't one of the four options."

"But he was, remember? Amun was there."

"Yes, but we used that name already."

"But don't you see? You were the one who said this was all about me and Amon. It's not treasure I'm seeking, but Amon. He's my purpose."

Dr. Hassan seemed torn. "Are you certain, Lily?"

Was I? It was a gut reaction when I first spoke up. But now that I was thinking about it, I wasn't so sure. What would we find on the other side of the wall—the treasure of the sphinx or a path to Amon? Before I could second-guess myself any longer, I took a step forward and pressed the symbol for Amon.

A heartbeat later the whole wall started to shake. Stone crashed down on either side of us, and I was worried that I'd made a terrible mistake. I stumbled against the quickly shifting wall and my arm disappeared in a new opening. Fearing that I'd be crushed, I fell away from it and was caught by Dr. Hassan, who barely remained standing. With a final, terrible grating, the last stones shifted out of the way.

We stood clutching one another and breathing hard as the dust settled, and when it did, we both gaped at the sight before us. The treasure of the first room was nothing compared to what had been hidden behind the wall.

Sparkling, jewel-crusted opulence covered every surface. Life-sized statues of a cat goddess stood as lines of sentinels, eternally guarding the overflowing treasure in the room. My eyes lit on everything and nothing, unable to focus on any one object when surrounded by such splendor.

Then something moved.

Before us, seated on a golden throne with radiating beams of the sun lined with sparkling diamonds, was the most beautiful woman I'd ever seen. At first I thought it was a trick of my eyes. She seemed frozen in place, a dazzling centerpiece in an indescribably magnificent space, and I wondered if she was a painted image or a very lifelike statue. Then I heard a laugh and the woman lifted her hand and beckoned us forward.

Her silky, dark hair was as straight as an arrow and just brushed the small of her back. She wore a diaphanous white dress that gathered at the waist and then draped down her body in the style of an Egyptian goddess. Bands of gold encircled her arms and wrists, and golden sandals that looked very similar to my own adorned her feet. She smiled at me and I was transfixed by her ruby lips and her thickly lashed eyes that seemed alight with the colors of a churning nebula.

I couldn't speak or even manage to walk when she again summoned us closer. Dr. Hassan seemed to be suffering from the same affliction. We were both rooted in place. Utterly transfixed.

Since we weren't coming to her, she must have decided to come to us, because she then stood up and I realized that the golden beams of sun radiating from the throne were no such thing. They shifted and moved with her, lifting higher, stretching to encompass her entire body.

"Isis," Dr. Hassan breathed in a reverent whisper, and I knew he was right. It was the goddess herself. The one who inspired Amon's spell that connected our hearts.

And she had . . . wings.

6

The Spell of Isis

Isis didn't seem to care about my desultory stare or my absolute lack of coming up with anything even remotely appropriate to say. I was thunderstruck. All I could do was stand in place and squeak. There was something special about her and it wasn't simply because she was an immortal. She had a very different vibe from Anubis, who was dark and mysterious and with his inflated ego could come across as a temperamental sort of rock god. He was much more . . . human.

Isis was every inch the goddess. Power emanated from her. It was in her eyes, her bearing, and in every lithe flick of limb and wing. Maybe it was because she was more than a goddess. She was a sorceress, too, able to wield a kind of magic that intimidated even someone as powerful as Anubis. As she approached me, I felt a terrible, almost heady mix of awe and fear.

Her gossamer dress whispered around her form, her wings shifting before they folded up. When she spoke, her rich voice echoed in the room as if the wind were a jealous lover who desired to capture her words for himself and proclaim to all that she belonged only to him. A woman such as Isis could intimidate even my mother, and that was saying something.

"Hello," the goddess said. "You must be Lilliana."

"Lily," I corrected her, and then bit my lower lip, realizing that was a terrible first impression I'd just made. I knew better than that. I'd spent my whole life being trained on how to speak to VIPs, even when I was nervous.

She didn't seem to mind, though, and smiled. "*Lily,* then. Anubis has spoken of you frequently." I wasn't sure if that was a good thing or a bad thing, and my mind began to make a list of the possible stories he could have told her. "Come," she said. "Let me look at you."

Immediately she stretched out her hands and I allowed her to take mine. Up close, her eyes were even more interesting. From afar, I'd noticed how they sparkled and the colors within shifted. But now that I stood within arm's length, I could see the pinks, purples, and blues swirling like a storm cloud with an ominous, potentially deadly, menace hidden just behind the surface waiting to be unleashed. I'd hate to be the object of her wrath. Those unique eyes were fixed upon my face so intently that I wondered what she was looking for and what it was she was able to see.

"Hmm," she said. "It is as Anubis thought. Amon did use my spell to connect the two of you. I must admit that I had my doubts. Between you and me, Anubis occasionally has a tendency toward exaggeration. But now I can see that he was correct and there is indeed no other recourse than to allow you to attempt the Rite of Wasret."

"So that's what will turn me into a sphinx?"

"If you are successful, then yes," Isis answered.

"Will you be the one to give us the spell?"

"You've been able to pass through the test of the riddles, so you have earned the right to it."

"And what will the spell . . . do to me exactly?"

The goddess brushed a lock of hair over my shoulder in a very motherly manner. "It will change you utterly, I imagine—that is, if you survive the transformation."

Isis patted my cheek, turned, and headed back to the golden throne.

She must have sensed that I found her answer unsatisfactory because she waved her hand and then added, "You will still be you . . . *mostly.* And if you wish it, you can reside among mortals without any of them being the wiser, if that is what concerns you. But make no mistake, this is the one and only way for you to save the one you love."

I frowned, rehearsing the words *attempt* and *mostly* and *survive* in my mind. It wasn't my vanity that prompted my question. The idea that I would become a beast, a monster, something . . . inhuman was frightening. But the minute she'd mentioned that it was the only way to save Amon, I knew I would go through with it regardless of the possible outcome.

Thinking of Amon meant that my awe and natural caution when engaging in conversation with someone who could bat me away like an irritating pest was replaced by uncertainty and frustration. This whole process was taking too long. Now that I'd decided I was going to do it, every moment we delayed made it more likely that the Devourer would find Amon and consume his heart.

I approached the throne. "If you had to give us the spell anyway, then why did you and Anubis make us come *here*? We wasted hours driving to Luxor and even more trying to figure out your cryptic riddles when you could have just given us the stupid spell in the first place." I folded my arms across my chest. "It seems like all of you don't really care that much about the possible end of the world, and you certainly don't seem to be concerned about Amon or his suffering."

"Lily!" Dr. Hassan stepped forward and put a hand on my shoulder, his face showing the panic he felt. "Don't forget to whom you are speaking."

The goddess, settled once again, had listened to my accusations without a visible reaction of any kind. When I was finished, she raised an eyebrow and said, "Of course the possibility of the end of mankind concerns us. We have watched over the world for millennia and will continue to do so. It is our duty. It is our right. Though we have abilities that may seem omnipotent to a mortal such as you, there are restrictions placed upon each one of us. We have a procedure of, how do you say it"—she waved her hand, as if searching for the proper term—"checks and balances. Even *we* must follow the rules." She said the last with a frown.

"Astounding," Hassan murmured beside me.

"Yes," she went on. "Before such rules were instated, the gods had the freedom to do as they wished. At times, due to poor judgment, this lack of structure caused great human suffering and casualties. It is necessary for us to monitor one another. After all, how could we guide mankind when our own houses were not in order?"

"But if you had laws, then why was Seth able to kill your husband? Is it because there weren't any directives telling him otherwise at the time?" I questioned.

"Most of our laws have to do with interfering in the mortal world. Seth's actions represented the first time a god attacked another of his own kind. Seth was . . . reprimanded after killing my husband, but the council of the gods ultimately decided that because I had defied the natural order by re-creating Osiris, a mild punishment for Seth was sufficient. However, after his attempted murder of my son, Horus, coupled with his attempt to enslave humankind during the Sons of Egypt's mortal lifetime, all of the gods agreed to his banishment and entered into a pact to follow a set of guidelines we call the Celestial Laws."

Ebullient energy spilling out of him, Dr. Hassan queried, "Might there be a record of this list of Celestial Laws?"

"Not one you can access. The laws are written in the stars themselves, and as they always shine down upon us, they tend to tattle when one of the gods attempts anything considered inappropriate. Only a few of us are able to hear their whispers. No mortal has ever developed the talent for it."

Dr. Hassan's face fell. He'd looked like a child headed to an ice cream store, his eyes sparkling with possibilities, only to find that the store had closed. Still, the determined gleam soon returned and I was certain that if there was a way for a mortal to discern the language of the stars and learn the laws of the cosmos, then he would find it.

As for me, I wasn't sure what to make of stars that spied on gods and mortals alike. It didn't make sense. Then again, gods and monsters, and pretty much everything else I'd seen since I met Amon, didn't make sense either.

Curious, I asked, "So. You defied the order. How?"

Isis gave me a sly smile. "I bent the rules." She paused, as if waiting for me to show appreciation for her cleverness. "I enlisted Anubis to help remake my husband, an act that was forbidden by the council, but because I merged his form with that of the crocodile that devoured him, he was not wholly Osiris. He was altogether new. Osiris was still mine, as much himself as ever, and yet even they couldn't deny the evidence that his form was changed. And so they allowed it."

More than ready to end our conversation, I asked, "Will you tell me how to do it? How to get into the afterlife, I mean?"

Isis narrowed her eyes and shook out her wing before tucking it back behind her again. "Even should I be inclined to help you, Amun-Ra would likely cause you more grief if he knew I was on your side. Better we should concentrate on one thing at a time, don't you agree?"

"I . . . I suppose."

"You must understand that to even be able to approach Amun-Ra, you'll have to pass through the trial first."

"Trial? I thought we'd passed all the riddles."

"The riddles aren't the trial. They're merely the first of several auditions. You have now earned the opportunity to attempt the rite. Survive that, and then you can worry about Amun-Ra."

"Fine. So what exactly do I have to do next?"

"Patience. To understand the Rite of Wasret, you'll need to understand why I created it."

I raised my eyebrows. "You created it?"

"Yes. It's a spell I'm very proud of, despite its original outcome. It was one the gods hadn't anticipated. Thus all the rules and riddles that are now associated with it."

"All right. Then tell me."

As she shifted a bit on her throne, I got the impression that the goddess was uncomfortable. She smoothed her skirt and let out a sigh before continuing. "I created it to change a mortal—a handmaiden of mine—who I could not bear to part with when she was terminally injured. I conspired with my sister Sekhmet"—she gestured to the cat statue soldiers lining the room—"to gift her with immortality. Once the spell was done, the others discovered our use of magic.

"To prevent inexpert attempts at imitation and to control any future ideas of repeating the act that I might entertain, the Room of Riddles was created. Its purpose was to ascertain the worthiness of those who sought the same gift. Of course, no other human has successfully breached the room, until you. Most who stumbled upon the room were so distracted by the treasure only to find that to set hands upon it led to their untimely deaths."

"You underestimate mortal curiosity," Dr. Hassan posed as he shifted his hat between his hands anxiously. "There are those of us who seek far more than treasure."

"Yes. There are a few, but not many with your talents, Vizier. When the devoted, such as yourself, attempted to access the secret rite and failed, they were also disposed of."

"So the other gods were unhappy about your servant's transformation?" I asked.

A tinge of sadness stole over her lovely features. "They are not as open-minded about things as I am," she said. "They believe that the state we are born into is the only state we should aspire to. If it wasn't for me, the Sons of Egypt wouldn't exist. I was the one who convinced the gods to act and reward the three worthy mortals with our power. If we hadn't done so, we would be forced to intervene and manage Seth ourselves. Such an act would eventually drain us of our energies, leaving us unable to see to our duties."

Isis smiled, as if I would completely understand her point of view. The indifference I sensed from her toward the things Amon and his brothers had to endure set me on edge. "So *you* are the one who made it so that Asten, Amon, and Ahmose have to die over and over again? They can't fall in love or be husbands or fathers or have a normal life because of you? It's unfair to task them with cleaning up your messes just because it's inconvenient to you! Did you even *ask* them if that's what they wanted?"

The goddess cocked her head. The corner of her mouth was upturned either because she considered what I said funny or because she thought I was a curious sort of bug that needed to be squashed. Either way, I was offended. I could feel righteous anger pumping through my veins.

"The Sons of Egypt were given a choice. They could depart for the afterlife and await their kin, or they could return for admittedly brief periods of time to serve the gods. They chose the latter."

"I don't think they really understood what it was you were asking of them."

"Do you, Lily? Do you understand what is being asked of you? Or are you willing to change the very fiber of your being in order to save those you love?" I squirmed a bit under her gaze but kept my chin raised in an effort of defiance. "I can see your heart, young one, just as I could see theirs. They were worthy of the gift. Whether you call it a blessing or a curse is immaterial. They were willing, and we found a use for them."

"Just like you used your handmaid?"

Anger shot through Isis's features but the signs of it quickly disappeared. "You know not of what you speak. Baniti was dying. It was painful. When I made her a sphinx, I meant it to be a gift for a beloved handmaid."

"What . . . what happened to her?" I asked.

"Baniti couldn't come to accept her new life. She didn't have the heart for it. You see, a sphinx is dual-hearted in nature. Her mind fragmented, and she could not reconcile the woman she'd been with the creature she needed to embrace. The stories of a sphinx devouring men are true, though it wasn't because they couldn't solve her riddle. Hunters chased her, cornered her in caves.

"She was nearly wild, feral; any humanity remaining was eclipsed by the beast. Her only option was to lash out. And when she smelled blood, her other half took over. She was horrified by what she was and eventually sought her own end, though death, except under very rare circumstances, was no longer an option. Finally, unable to care for her on my own, I approached the council, confessed what I had done, and awaited their decision. They granted what she sought. Her own death."

"Then why keep the rite at all? Why not eradicate all evidence that it had ever been done?"

"Because," she answered simply, "the stars said we'd need it."

"What are you saying?" Dr. Hassan asked. "The stars knew about Lily?"

"Not about Lily, no, but we dare not question what the stars have seen. That might mean Lily is the reason. It might mean something else or someone else. It might mean nothing. The things the stars whisper are not always clear. But whatever the case, the gods opted not to erase all evidence of the spell, just in case the stars were right."

"Yeah. Well." I kicked a pebble with my golden sandal. "All that matters to me is saving Amon. I don't appreciate that all these little rituals of yours take so long."

"Ah, Lily. How little your mortal eyes see. If we were to forsake the rituals, we would be sending you unprepared toward a certain doom. Each step you take is necessary. Every hurdle makes you stronger. Tempered steel is not easily broken. You must believe we are giving you your best chance. Remember that even in the netherworld, there are certain rules and limitations."

"Like the one that says you aren't allowed to go and intervene."

"Correct. Try not to worry much; if the Devourer had him in her clutches, we would know. And even so, the process of draining him is not a quick thing. She would take her time. Because of this, I want you to understand the importance of what you are undertaking. This spell is not an easy one. You will be tested, and even if you are successful, you will need some time to acclimate to your new self. You must be firm of mind. Fix your gaze on your goal. And above all else, you must open your heart. Otherwise you may lose yourself, much like my handmaid, Baniti."

"And you're sure this is the only way to save him?"

"It is the only way I know."

Swallowing, I nodded. "Then let's see if we can do something to help him."

The wings of the goddess fluttered and she smiled. "Vizier, are you ready to receive the spell?"

"Yes," he answered. "I have one question before we get started, though."

"And what is that?"

"Why Wasret? Shouldn't the rite be named for your handmaid, Baniti, instead?"

"What do you know of Wasret?" Isis asked.

"I know she was a goddess of Egypt with most of her worshippers centered at Thebes. I know she was charged to protect your young son, Horus, and that she's rumored to be Amun-Ra's first wife."

"Hmm. It's interesting how the truths get mixed together until they become almost unrecognizable. The reference to my son was indeed Baniti. She was his nursemaid as a boy. He considered her a second mother and was nearly inconsolable at her death. The reason Thebes is a part of the story is because that is the city where she was born and it is the city where I honored her death, creating a temple guarded by sphinx statues. But these references are for Baniti, not Wasret.

"You see, Wasret, the person rumored to be Amun-Ra's first wife, the person for whom this rite remained on earth, is a person who hadn't even been born at the time her name was inscribed on the wall. It is the name the stars have whispered to us over the eons."

"Then the inscriptions we've discovered that speak of Wasret are about two different people," Dr. Hassan murmured.

Isis admired a sparkling ring around her finger as she inquired of Dr. Hassan, "You found two versions of the sphinx carved upon these walls, did you not?"

"Yes. We did," he admitted.

"They do not represent two different types of sphinx but two different individuals. One was Baniti, born and died thousands of years ago, and the other, Wasret, stands next to you now. Assuming, of course, that Lily is indeed the one we've been waiting for."

I held up a hand. "Wait a second. You're saying *I* am, or could be, Wasret? The goddess woman Dr. Hassan described?"

"That is exactly what I am saying."

"So have you suspected this about me all this time? Known who I am and what I was supposed to do?"

"Like I said, we've known that there would come a time when the spell might be needed. We just didn't know when until the circumstances presented themselves. Until the moment Amon entered the netherworld, we did not expect you to be anything other than a mortal dalliance."

"Amon and I didn't"—I waved my hands in the air, flustered—"dally."

"Irrelevant. We knew one such as you would exist, and the diviners and seers able to understand the whisperings wrote what they gleaned from the stars, which wasn't much. The stars are very fickle when it comes to sharing their secrets, even with gods."

A little shiver ran through me. I'd likely never look the same way at the stars again. Now I could only picture them as gossiping busybodies with a billion eyes who wagged their silver tongues, whispering riddles to anyone who would listen. All my life they'd been looking over my shoulder. The feeling was unsettling. "Okay, then you're saying that I'm somehow destined to do this, assuming that you all are right."

"A rudimentary, yet not inaccurate declaration."

"Fantastic. Well, then let's shuffle off this mortal coil and do what needs to be done. There's no point in bemoaning my poor little woe-begone human end. Apparently, a destiny has been written in the stars for millennia. Let's just hope it's mine. Otherwise, we're all in for a world of hurt. Me especially." I was babbling to cover my fear and, when I was done, ended up wandering the room in a trancelike state, running my hands over the statues as if they were bald-headed Buddhas I was rubbing for luck, while Isis taught Dr. Hassan the spell and gave him instructions.

All too quickly she seemed to wrap everything up. My thoughts were a jumbled mess and seemed as audible to me as a buzz saw on wood. I bit my lip as Isis turned her stormy eyes on me, afraid she could read the trepidation in my heart. If she did, she said nothing but held out her arms as her wings stretched to their full length.

Dr. Hassan had been stuffing various things into his bag, the most prominent of which was an oiled black bow that protruded from the opening. It was obvious that there were many other heavy items now contained in it than there had once been. He could barely get it over his shoulder. Dr. Hassan stepped into the circle of her arms and the two of them reached out, pulling me in with them.

"It might help if you closed your eyes," Isis advised as her heavy wings began to beat. With that understated warning, my stomach lurched as we rose into the air and shot toward the ceiling. I screamed as we slammed into the rock, but we passed through it as if it were merely a dark cloud and rose into the sky. I continued to look until the sting of the wind and the brightness of her form became unbearable.

Isis was an angel. A terrifying, brilliant streak of lightning that crossed the sky with a crack of thunder so loud, the heavens quaked. Like a fleeting ghostly comet, fiery, dazzling, and evanescent, we passed cities and farms, deserts and mountains. It was all I could do to hold on to her tightly and wonder what was to become of me.

7

Huntress

My stomach lurched again as we dropped down, down, down, and my breath was knocked out of me when she shifted me like a rag doll in her arms as she positioned us to set foot upon the ground. With a few more heavy beats of her wings, our toes made little furrows in the dirt until our shoes found purchase on a grassy knoll. Sand stirred around us, peppering our skin with little stinging prickles, until Isis finally tucked her shimmering wings behind her.

"We are here," she pronounced.

"Here, where?" I asked as I brushed dust from my arms and shook out my dress. When I slid my hands into my hair, I grimaced. It was wild, tangled, and needed a serious shampoo and conditioning or, at the very least, a hairbrush. I threw the mess over my shoulder and looked around. There was nothing but sparse trees, circling birds, and the sounds of insects for miles.

"In the mortal world, this is a part of what you would call Africa, though you would never be able to find this exact location again should you seek it. We are on the sacred grounds of the sphinx. The place where you will find your heart."

"Don't I already have one?"

"You need a second heart. Remember, a sphinx is dual-hearted."

"Okay, so I need to find a heart, then?"

"Oh, you do not find it. She finds you."

"Right. *She* finds me." Nervously, I shuffled my sandaled foot in a patch of grass. "So, who is looking for me, exactly?"

"No one yet. First, the vizier must speak the words of the spell. As its power settles over you, she will scent your intention and come for you."

"*Scent* me?" The whole conversation just took an uncomfortable turn. "If the flight hadn't already made me feel anxious, then your cryptic explanation surely did."

"You needn't feel distressed. If she deems you worthy, she will gift you her heart."

"And if she doesn't?"

"Then she will devour you."

"Oh. Is that all? Yeah. No reason at all to feel distressed." I lifted my fingertips to my mouth to nibble nervously on my nails. They still hadn't returned to their meticulously manicured shape since my last adventure with Amon.

Seeing my sorry state, Dr. Hassan intervened. "The next step is the spell, then, is it not?"

"Yes. Once the spell is pronounced over her head, she will become both the huntress and the hunted. You will wait for her here. If she survives, you will bestow upon her the weapons taken from the Room of Riddles. Remember, Wasret is a sphinx, but not all sphinxes are Wasret. Even if she is not the one the stars spoke of, she might still be able to save the one she loves. But if she does not return—"

"Then we are all lost," Oscar finished.

"Yes," Isis replied quietly. Her stormy eyes shifted to me.

"How will we know if she is the one foretold of?" Dr. Hassan asked.

The goddess smiled. "Time will tell. May luck be with you, Lily. For your sake, I wish you success."

I could only nod in return as I tried to squelch the grimace that crossed my face in place of a smile. Isis shook out her wings, but just before taking off said, "Oh. I almost forgot."

Stretching her wing around her body, she blinked rapidly, her beautiful eyes filling with tears, which she then caught with the edge of her wing. The motion seemed purposeful and not at all emotional. When she was done, she grabbed hold of a glistening feather and yanked, pulling it out and whispering an enchantment over it.

"Hold on to this," she said, before handing it to me, "while the vizier pronounces the incantation. I've made a little improvement over the last time the spell was used. The tears will protect you from any creature I am able to command, but once they are used up, you'll have my shield no longer and will need to depend upon your own strength. Use the tears sparingly. As for the rest . . ." She smiled. "I'm saving it for a surprise."

She then turned to Dr. Hassan. "I assume you will be fully able to instruct her in the ways of the sphinx. Let us pray that her mind proves steady."

"I will do my best, Goddess."

"See that you do."

With that, Isis raised her arms to the east, where the sun was just peeking over the horizon, and her entire body filled with light. I felt a stiff breeze stir the grass around us as her form rose into the sky. Though I shaded my eyes to watch her, her path aligned with the sun, and soon I could no longer tell the difference between them. She was gone.

I twirled the gleaming feather she'd left behind between my fingers. "There are a whole lot of *ifs* before I get to Amon, aren't there?" I asked.

"Yes. This journey does seem somewhat complicated, doesn't it?"

"You can say that again."

Dr. Hassan cleared his throat. "Shall we begin?"

"I suppose we should. There's some terrible beast of an unknown description out there waiting to hunt me." Oscar made a sound as he ran his palm over his neck. He was worried. "Hey," I said. "Despite my obvious levels of discomfort, I volunteered. Remember? I *want* to do this. I'll be okay. Especially if you're the one training me."

He gave me a doubtful look but dutifully picked up his notebook and began the spell. As he chanted, he walked in a circle around me:

"Here on the Sacred Grounds of the Sphinx we offer a petition.
Lilliana Young comes by day after walking in the footsteps of the gods.
Her feats are mighty and have been recorded in the annals of the cosmos.
She is the Hunted and approaches armed with strength and purity,
Seeking the Huntress who awaits with tooth and claw bared,
The one who Dances in Blood and Takes Hearts for Food . . ."

This wasn't sounding too good. Why couldn't Egyptian spells talk about puppies and chocolate and unicorns? Every spell I'd encountered since I met Amon had to do with blood and mummies and death. Granted, I was technically in love with a mummy, so some of that was to be expected, but why couldn't any of my Egyptian Indiana Jones adventures be fun? Something I could write about in a college essay.

Dr. Hassan droned on and I managed to refocus my attention.

"The one who will be her escort to the beyond,
Now is the time for your paths to cross.
Both are worthy.
Both are ennobled of the gods.
Both have accomplished deeds to prove their valor.
Huntress let your soul come forth and be not driven away.
Hunted, clothe yourself in your companion's power and do not fear her embrace.
Merge your yesterdays. Share your tomorrows.
Two fighting souls dwelling in one body.
Neither will be forgotten.
Today they are bound.

Today they are washed clean.
Today they die and are reborn."

Wait. Did he say die?

"Breathe together. Hunt together. Battle together.
Silent one, find your inner voice.
Sightless one, find your true vision.
Come find your match, O you warden of the plain!"

When Dr. Hassan finished the last line, his voice echoed with power. I could actually feel the spell settling upon me like a tangible thing. As it found its place in my heart, it sank. Like a heavy stone in a lake, the weight of it caused ripples of aftershocks that ran across my skin and shot outward as if I were the epicenter of an invisible earthquake.

The feather I held in my hand jumped free as if it had a will of its own and floated in front of me. Then the wind found it and, alarmed, I reached out to grab it, but it eluded me. It only took a moment for me to realize it was moving purposefully. It gathered speed and whipped around my body faster and faster until I felt a sharp pain in my back. Tears stung my eyes, my vision tinged with red. I spun around.

"Where is it?" I asked Oscar. "Where did the feather go?"

"It . . . um . . . disappeared," he answered.

"Disappeared? What do you mean it disappeared?"

"The feather of Isis was absorbed into your back."

"Into my . . ." I stood frozen for a moment waiting for the fallout. My back throbbed along with my pulse. Suddenly desperate, I whipped in a circle, reaching around to my back and trying to peer over my shoulder, but my fingertips didn't find anything. Again I wondered why I had to go and do something as dumb as falling for a mummy.

In a normal relationship, I'd only have to loan the guy some cash, give him a ride, or help him do his homework when he got into trouble. With Amon I had to fly around with goddesses, fend off amorous deities, and be hunted by über-beasties. Still, in my heart I knew I would risk anything for him. The chance to be with Amon again was worth every sacrifice I was being asked to make.

As I lifted my hand from my shoulder blade, my gaze narrowed on my fingertips. The swirls and lines on the pads snapped into sharp focus and I could see the pumping of my blood in the tiny veins just beneath the surface. "What is this?" I whispered, suddenly ultra-aware that my senses had been heightened by the spell. The call of birds startled me. I felt the weight of a termite colony more than a mile away and smelled a river full of wild creatures. I closed my eyes and inhaled deeply.

Something was out there.

Something powerful.

Something dangerous.

I could taste the metallic bite of it as I ran my tongue across my teeth. Turning to Dr. Hassan, I flexed the muscles of my back and shoulders, warming them, for what purpose I did not yet know. "What am I supposed to do now?"

Even though I'd asked the question, a newly awakened desire was already tugging on me with invisible strings. There was something, someone, I needed to find, and it wasn't Amon.

Oscar gave me a hesitant smile. "You must go, Lily. I will wait for you here as long as I am able."

"Yes," I responded, though my voice seemed entirely unlike my own and my thoughts felt muddled.

"Follow your instincts," he said finally. When I reached down to take a bag, he shook his head. "You are not meant to take anything with you. Even water. You are to be tested."

I swallowed, already thirsty at the idea that I'd be wandering the African savanna without any supplies. Despite my determination, tears filled my eyes. It was by sheer will alone that I didn't allow the tears to fall. Amon needed me. I could do this.

Lifting my face to the sun, I inhaled deeply both to steady myself and to try to get a sense of the direction I needed to go. The light was rosy behind my closed eyelids and as I opened myself to the sounds and scents around me, something caught my attention, a distinct thud like the beat of a distant drum.

"Lily?" I heard Oscar say.

"Yes?" I replied, chin raised with eyes still tightly shut.

"It's time to run."

In an instant, every nerve in my body snapped to attention. Angling just my head toward him, I gave a small nod and then I was running. I staggered for just a moment when my legs got tangled up in the billows of my dress, but then I caught hold of the hem mid-leap and pulled the material up, tucking it firmly into my belt.

Air filled my lungs, and I inhaled and exhaled in deep gusts, my legs and arms pumping in a steady rhythm. Soon Oscar was just a speck on the horizon, and I was surprised to find I was able to jump and balance as well as a deer. Even though I'd never considered myself particularly athletic and had never run at any speed faster than a jog, my fast pace didn't wind me. I was bursting with energy and relished the feel of my warmed muscles and the dust that coated my sandaled feet.

My hair streamed behind me, the breeze whipping through it like a horse's mane, and though I was human, and fragile, and very much in danger, I can honestly say I'd never felt more alive. My limbs hummed and all my worries fell by the wayside as I traversed the terrain. I was a creature with nothing to prove and no one to answer to. I was free.

I didn't stop for hours. But when I finally tired, I instinctively headed toward the distant river. In one section, there was a small drop that created a stream of water where I could easily drink. I crept into the undergrowth by the river, exhaling in hot pants as I peered through the sparse trees and high grasses looking for danger. The cover was thick and I was well hidden, but I waited and watched until I was sure that no one and nothing larger than a squirrel was near before venturing out.

At first, I cupped my hands in the cascading stream and poured the droplets into my mouth, but I found it vastly unsatisfying. I looked both ways and, still seeing nothing, plunged my whole face into the trickling stream, opening my mouth and taking in water in big gulps.

A part of my mind nagged me about the bugs, worms, and diseases of various kinds, but that Lily, the New York City girl, was no longer in charge. I was thirsty. I needed to drink. The river was full of water. I liked the simplicity of it. There was no doubt. No hesitancy. There was only need and the fulfilling of need. The pesky echo of myself was a girl distracted by too many thoughts, and as I drank, I allowed all of my worries and niggling fears to slip into the river and float away.

Satiated at last, I stepped back and plucked at the bodice of my wet dress. The water felt cool and refreshing on my hot skin, and I tossed my heavy hair behind me, irritated by the weight of it on my shoulders. I heard a noise and crouched down, barely noticing that my golden sandals were now mud-stained and the edges of my dress and bare legs were filthy.

A trio of small rodents had come to the water to drink and my belly rumbled. I wondered how long I would be expected to wander the savanna. Would I have to catch my own food, kill and cook it? How would I even start a fire? Perhaps there was some edible vegetation or maybe some kind of fruit.

I stayed by the river, hidden for several more hours. There was no way to explain it, but it felt like the right place to be. After an hour of vainly attempting to catch a fish for a meal, I finally gave up and resigned myself to spending the night not only alone in the middle of the wilderness, but also hungry.

After digging a small crevice in the rocks near the river, I lay down in my little earthen womb, stared up at the stars, and listened to the creatures of the night until the steady sounds of the insects lulled me to sleep.

"Lily! Lily? Can you hear me?"

The urgency in his voice dragged my dreaming self to consciousness, though my exhaustion kept trying to tow me back down to oblivion. "Amon?" I whispered groggily. "How are we able to do this again?"

"Lily? Good, you can hear me. We can only communicate like this when we are both in the dream world."

I cracked open my dream-self's eyes by sheer determination alone and saw Amon's form sleeping with his head resting on his arm. A large purple bruise decorated the exposed side of his face and the light from a fire danced over his skin. I longed to run my hand up his arm and press a light kiss to his temple and even attempted to reach out to him, but it was no use. Our dream selves couldn't touch. The mental effort exhausted me, and I was about to slip back into my happy dream world when I heard Amon speak again.

"You must try to stay awake and listen, Young Lily. I know you're tired, but this is important. You cannot do this. Do you understand me? I will not permit you to endanger yourself for me. Not for any reason."

Amon's intensity dispersed the darkness that offered sweet respite. I sputtered, "But Isis said—"

"Trusting the gods is a foolhardy endeavor. They only want to protect themselves. I will be well enough off, and I promise I will find a way to wait for you and will meet you again when it is time for you to pass on to the next plane of existence. That will only happen after you have lived a long life filled with love and mortal experience. You must not think of me or of this. This path that you are attempting is too dangerous."

"But it's the only way to save you. The Devourer will come for you, Amon. She will consume your heart and destroy the world. I won't let that happen."

He was silent for a moment. "Tell me everything they said," he urged.

I rehearsed to him all the details I could remember, and when I was done, I asked, "Amon? Are you still there?"

"I am here, Nehabet."

"So do you see? This isn't just about us anymore. This is about protecting the world."

Quietly, he asserted, "It would have been better had the two of us never met. Perhaps then I would be, if not happy in my calling, then at least compliant."

I swallowed. "Do you really regret meeting me?" I asked, almost afraid to hear his answer.

"Lily." His voice broke and there was such longing, such despair attached to my name that the weight of it crushed my heart.

"I love you, Amon, and I have no regrets either," I declared. "That includes doing what I have to do now. I will find a way to you. I promise."

"If you are determined to walk this path, then there is nothing I can do to stop you."

"But you would rather I didn't."

"The loss of the whole world holds less meaning for me than the loss of one lovely hair on your head."

"Amon." I sighed his name, wishing he were holding me in his arms. "I've got to do this."

"Then I will watch over you and advise you when opportunity permits."

"Just stay alive until I get there. Otherwise, this will all have been for nothing."

"I will make every effort."

"So do you have any advice for me now?"

"Embrace your instincts."

"That's not very specific."

"You will understand when the time comes." I sensed there was more he wanted to tell me but he couldn't bring himself to. Finally, he said, "I wish I could be with you. Protect you. I am pained to know that danger stalks you."

"I think danger stalks you more than it does me."

"There is no beast, no demon, more ferocious than the fear I feel knowing there is nothing I can do to help you."

"Isis did give me her tears. That is supposed to protect me from at least some of the monsters."

"Yes." He sighed. "But only those that fear her wrath. And in the netherworld, those are not many."

"If it makes you feel better. I wish you were with me, too."

He said nothing for a moment as he thought, and then murmured, "Perhaps I can be."

"Really?" I asked, excited by the prospect. "How?"

"To be clear, it won't be me. Not really. But since we are linked, you can use my power to call upon Nebu."

"Nebu, the desert stallion?"

"Yes. There is the possibility that he might not heed your call, but seeking his protection is worth trying."

"Okay."

Amon and I practiced the spell to call Nebu until his words changed from warnings and instruction to soft promises and whispered wishes that warmed my heart.

At some point, our minds drifted, but the memory of our entwined thoughts sustained me in my sleep. I took comfort that at least this time I'd told him I loved him. I didn't know how many hours passed, but when I sensed a change in the environment, I woke instantly and saw that a crescent moon was high in the sky, spilling its waning light over the landscape as dawn approached.

It was time. My skin throbbed, the anticipation jarring my bones.

I rose from my earthen bed, not even bothering to swipe the clumps of dirt from my dress and hair, and brushed the back of my hand against my mouth. The night creatures had settled into their beds and the day creatures had not yet risen. I was alone.

After sating my thirst once again and adjusting my skirts so I wouldn't trip, I briefly contemplated which way to go, but as I searched my instincts, I knew I needed to head toward the rising sun. The sun brought life.

I ran.

The sun was not quite at its zenith in the sky when I stopped. Panting lightly, I scanned the horizon in all directions, but it appeared the plain was deserted.

I knew it wasn't.

The brush of tall golden grass tickled my fingers and the dry stalks snapped under the heels of my golden sandals. On the left I scanned a copse of umbrella-shaped trees with thin leaves. On the right there was a sepia-toned outcropping of rocks that looked as out of place on the grassy plain as if a giant had dropped them there accidentally.

After I started toward the rocks, a strong breeze rose, causing the grass to rustle and echo the voice of a thousand whispers. I was halfway there when I realized something was wrong. The rocks were not the place I needed to go. Stopping, I closed my eyes and inhaled. A sweet sort of musk tickled my nostrils and I turned the other way. Each step I took felt portentous.

The swaying grasses were sparser the closer I got to the trees. The thin leaves shook wildly and then stilled, the breeze seemingly holding its breath. A hum rose like the sound of a million cicadas and the wild noise distracted and confused me.

My heart beat heavily in my chest, as if it were signaling to whatever waited for me that I was there and I was vulnerable. Then, suddenly, the reverberating hum ceased; the only sound was my soft breathing. I was rooted in place, completely unable to move back or to the side, and I dared not take another step forward. I could only shift my feet nervously. All my senses were alive and trained on the thing hidden in the trees that I couldn't see.

A flicker of movement on the left caught my attention.

Mustering all the bravery I could, I clenched my fists and called out, "Why don't you come out, then? I know you're there."

A rumble so deep it echoed in my chest startled me. A hiss came from behind with the crunch of dried brush. A tawny tail disappeared behind a tree. Another growl came from my left and I realized there was more than just one creature.

I ran.

Fear ate through me like acid and yet every sense was heightened, alert. Beasts, no longer attempting to be stealthy, circled me and kept pace, creeping closer with each footfall. The nearness of them sent tingles all along my back, but I dared not turn and look. That would make them real.

I made it into the circle of the trees before I skidded to a stop. If the creatures behind me were frightening, they were nothing compared to what waited beneath the large tree in the center of the grove. Not thirty feet away was the largest cat I'd ever seen. His sleepy eyes suddenly opened to a state of alertness. He flicked his thick-tufted tail in annoyance as he rose from his shady napping place.

As he shook out a dense, impressive mane several shades darker than his tawny fur, I was momentarily distracted by the dust floating away from him into the afternoon sunbeams.

The huge lion moved forward, gaining speed much more quickly than I expected an animal of his size to be able to do, and slid to a stop just in front of me. When he roared, the power of it nearly burst my eardrums. My whole body shook with panic, the aftershocks of his warning sound rippling over my skin.

He twisted his head back and forth as his mouth opened, flashing his impressively sharp teeth. Another rumbling growl told me we'd been joined by not one, but several cats that together formed a lethal assemblage. At least two dozen females had materialized from the tall grasses around the trees, and two more males, albeit smaller than the one facing me, approached the group also.

Once the entire pride arrived, they paced back and forth, growling and hissing, waiting for the signal to strike. The circle of death was frightening enough to make the devil drop his pitchfork and run, but all I could do was tremble in my golden sandals and wait for something to happen.

Nothing did.

I was expecting an attack, but the lions seemed to be waiting for something else. The male lifted his head and roared before stepping aside, signaling it was time for me to go. I took one hesitant step forward and then another.

When I reached the tree line nearly a quarter mile away and passed the tallest of them, I heard the crack of thunder. Although there wasn't a cloud in the sky, a hum of electricity made the tiny hairs at the nape of my neck stand on end.

I turned to peer at the group, shading my eyes from the sun, and heard the male bellow loudly. He repeated the action three times before all the females sat down. All except one. She strode forward, nuzzling him, but kept her eyes focused ahead. On me. With a final earsplitting roar, the male stepped back and the female answered. Before I could blink, she was headed toward me at full speed.

A gasp of horror escaped my lips, my heart quickening. Spinning, I raced over the crest of a looming hill and across the terrain as fast as my legs could carry me. I leapt over a fallen tree and a few seconds later heard the scrape of her claws on the bark. Ducking through underbrush, I twisted and turned, desperate to escape the lioness chasing me, but I was a clumsy sort of prey.

If I'd had a weapon, I could perhaps have fought her off. She was nearly on top of me. As I stumbled over a rock, her claws raked down the length of my dress and the ripped fabric trailed behind me, catching on branches and bushes. When I darted across a shallow stream, she leapt quickly to the other side, turning to face me. She crouched down, her golden eyes assesssing me, her powerful limbs flexing.

If I was going to be dinner for a hungry pride of lions, then at least I could give them a good run for it.

After kicking water in her face, I spun and ran back in the direction I'd come from. My breath came in heavy gusts and my stomach clenched; I knew that at any second I was going to feel her claws sinking into my back and her teeth kissing my throat. I despaired, knowing that I'd die here. I'd never find Amon and never save those I loved.

I wondered how long Dr. Hassan would wait for me. Would he find my gnawed bones and give me a proper burial? Would he even know what had happened to me? If only I could see Amon again before I died. Stand in his embrace once more. Thinking of Amon made me remember what he'd said the night before. He'd cautioned me to embrace my instincts. So what was my gut telling me?

I was scared. Was it possible that this lioness was the one who would judge my worthiness? I'd been expecting an actual sphinx or a monster of some kind. Not an average, everyday lion. Perhaps I'd been thinking about everything wrong. Isis had said that if I was judged unworthy, then my heart would be consumed. What was I supposed to do?

It was soon obvious that the lioness was toying with me instead of finishing me off. As the sun sank in the west, I knew I wouldn't have the energy to continue much longer. Oscar's words returned to me then about how death was found in the sunset and life in the east. I was headed toward death.

Finally coming to a stop, I turned to face my pursuer. The lioness paused and growled softly, as if disappointed that the mouse she'd been playing with was no longer interested in the game.

"Look," I said. "I'm not sure if you're the answer to this riddle. I don't know if you want to just wear me out or if you really mean to eat me, but either way I'm making the choice to live. I don't want my heart to be eaten.

"I've got to save the world, and I need to find the creature that lives out here somewhere who will share her heart so I can become a sphinx and get the job done. If that is you, then fine, let's get the show on the road. If it's not, then I'd very much like to be left alone so that I can go and find the huntress."

The lioness sat on her haunches, her tail flicking back and forth. Then, all at once, she leapt.

8

The Heart of the Sphinx

Lifting my head, I whispered, "I'm sorry," hoping the wind would carry the sentiment to Amon. I knew that my hopes and dreams for the future no longer mattered. I was unworthy. It was time to accept my fate. I opened my arms and embraced my death.

When the large cat hit my body, I felt like a bowling pin knocked over by a speeding ball. It wasn't the kind of gentle tap, either, where the bowler was unsure if the ball would even make it all the way to the end of the lane. I didn't wobble back and forth, undecided over whether I'd tip or not. She was heavy, and the blow meant that I was the type of pin that smashed into anything and everything in my wake.

I ended up on my back, her bone-crushing weight on top of me making me struggle just to inhale. Overhead, the afternoon sky had darkened and I heard the heavy boom of thunder. My arms were wrapped around the lioness, and I clutched the tawny fur of her heaving sides in a death lock, praying for it all to be over quickly.

Her sharp claws pierced the skin directly over my heart, and I felt her moist breath on my cheek. As she shifted, draping her body across my own, her left paw settled at the top of my shoulder, and I somehow managed to take in a tiny pull of oxygen. The lioness settled her head next to mine, tucking it into the gap between my shoulder and neck, and though I waited for the sharp bite that would rip open my jugular, it didn't come.

She burrowed closer. So close it felt as if I were caught in quicksand once again, but this time with a creature three times my size dragging me down. I couldn't understand why I wasn't dying. Why she wasn't eating me. I knew cats tended to suffocate their prey by crushing the windpipe, and even though I could barely inhale or exhale, she didn't seem to be in any hurry.

Minutes passed, and I wondered if she'd fallen asleep. Tentatively, I brushed my fingertips over her fur, but there was no response. The weight didn't seem as bad as it had been just moments before. I was finally able to catch my breath and groaned at the pain I felt in my torso. Her head lolled and I twisted mine to peer up at her, but her golden eyes were glazed over with a sheen of unseeing moisture.

It wasn't long before I was able to begin twisting out from beneath her, but before I thrust her limp body aside, I heard an irritated voice in my head. *Remain still until the transformation is complete.*

I stopped moving and wondered where the voice had come from. Was it Isis? Some other Egyptian goddess I'd yet to meet? What kind of transformation was going on, exactly? I tried to pry the paw away from my chest but couldn't. The claws were sunk into me so deeply, I marveled at how fortunate I was that she hadn't ripped my heart from my chest. Giving up, I lay there quietly until something happened, something even stranger than the body of the lioness dissolving before my eyes.

My heightened senses alerted me to a stranger I couldn't see. I wasn't alone. The more the lioness disappeared, the more tangible and real the ghostly presence became.

The voice that had spoken to me wasn't Isis. I was sure of it now. What was even more alarming was that the being I sensed was with me. Not next to me, and not on another plane of existence, like when Amon was with me in my dreams, but actually *with* me, in my mind. I could feel her like I could feel the shoes on my feet or the hair brushing the back of my neck.

You can feel it now, can you not? said the voice.

"Who . . . who are you?" I asked.

That is not the right question.

"Then what question should I be asking?"

The correct phrasing would be "Who are we*?"*

"*We*?" I swallowed. My mouth was suddenly as dry as a desert, and I licked my lips in a vain attempt to moisten them.

Yes. We. You are no longer Lilliana Young and I am no longer what I once was.

"What . . . did you used to be?"

I was the creature you hold in your arms.

Glancing down at the form of the dead lioness becoming more and more transparent, I asked, "This was you? I mean, the voice I hear now is from the lioness?"

Not exactly. In my corporeal form I was an animal bound by instinct. My thoughts were simple. My purpose was survival. I have given up my physical body to become something new, saving the best parts of myself to bring to this union of minds. I am, no longer. You are, no longer.

We are reborn.

We are sphinx.

"Okay, assuming that's true, then why am I having a conversation with myself?"

The merging of our minds occurs over time. Eventually, there will be only one voice and one mind. If this does not happen—

"Then I'll go insane."

Yes.

"Right. So how long do I . . . do *we*," I corrected myself, "need to stay here?"

Until my former body disappears completely. The process should only take a few more minutes.

She was now so translucent it was like trying to touch a dream.

The voice was silent for a moment, and then she added, *You do not need to address me vocally, you know. I can hear and understand your thoughts.*

"Is it okay if I speak to you verbally for now? At least until I get used to this?"

As you wish.

"Will you miss it?" I asked, curious. "Being a lioness, I mean?"

She didn't answer right away. Finally, she said, *Individually, our forms were mortal, fragile, weak. And the weak must make way for the strong. If we are to grow together, this is something you must come to understand.* As I considered her words, she added, *It is time. You may arise.*

I hadn't even noticed that the nearly invisible form of the lioness had completely disappeared.

"I'm sorry," I said as I got carefully to my feet, groaning at the ache in my body.

Sorry? For what? the voice asked in surprise.

"Sorry for what you've lost."

I have not lost. I have gained.

"You might not feel that way if this thing we're doing doesn't work."

She was quiet for a moment, and then said, *If we fail, at least we strived to break free of the bounds set upon us. No one can disparage us for the attempt we've made to become something more.*

"I suppose not."

I . . . no, *we* lifted our head and inhaled. The sharp tang of water called to us and we began running in the direction it wafted from. On the journey, the voice of my inner companion pointed out the tracks of animals and identified scents that I could discern but couldn't categorize.

When I caught my wild appearance in the reflection of the pool and despaired over the state of my dress and hair, I sensed her confusion.

If you do not like your mane, then you should remove it. We can move more stealthily without it and the scent of it warns your enemies you are coming.

"Most of my enemies can't smell me coming."

Perhaps in your world they cannot, but in the realm of the gods, anything is possible.

"I'll think about it," I said insincerely. "In the meantime, I'd take a bath in the stream if I had something to change into."

Why would you do that? The biting insects are not in season at this time.

"Yeah, well, I enjoy being clean."

But the dust of the plain hides your scent. Ah, I see. You likely use your scent to attain the attention of potential mates. I suppose that is an acceptable rationale, though it will prove inherently dangerous on our journey. We should proceed with caution in that case.

I was unable to formulate a response, but she addressed my shock.

You do realize, of course, that you cannot hide your thoughts from me.

"That's . . . that's just wrong. It's like having my mother watching over my shoulder."

You do not like your mother.

"No. I do. It's just that she's—"

My inner voice interrupted. *You do not. She does not notice your uniqueness. She wishes for you to conform to her standards and choices.*

"Isn't that what you want as well?"

She was silent for a beat.

Conforming is a reality for both of us. There was a long pause, and then she added, *You are imprudently proud of this mane, and I sense you do not intend to follow my counsel.*

"Right."

Very well. You may keep your overly long mane, and if it causes you grief in the future, we will deal with it at that time.

"Thank you." Under my breath I muttered, "Next thing you know, she'll have me throwing out all my scented lotions, too."

I could feel her incredulous bewilderment. *You purposefully scent your skin so that any predator tracking you can locate you as easily as they would a rutting buffalo?*

"Hey! I'll have you know that my very expensive shampoos and lotions smell nothing like a rutting buffalo."

She sighed. *This merging of our minds is, I fear, going to be a lengthy process. If the cleansing and perfuming of your body holds a higher priority for you than our safety, then I would suggest that you have a tongue for a reason.*

I started laughing. "You," I gasped, "you want me to give myself a tongue bath?" A moment went by when I was trying to catch my breath and enjoying the sensation of giddiness alone, and then I could sense her wishing she could join me.

"What is it?" I asked as I tried to stifle the giggles. "Don't you laugh?"

My kind experiences a quiet sort of satisfaction, but we do not act like monkeys bouncing up and down in a ridiculous manner.

"Don't knock it if you haven't tried it."

I will admit that the sensation of it is not unpleasant.

We found the niche where I'd slept the night before and I felt strangely comforted by her presence as I settled down, not nearly as bothered by the unforgiving surface beneath me as I'd been the first time. The warm light from the setting sun bathed my skin, and I basked in the feel of it. Part of me enjoyed it because it reminded me of the heat from Amon's touch, but there was another part of me, the brand-new part I suspected, that relished in the residual warmth found in the stones surrounding my makeshift bed. A longing stirred within me that made me wish I could drowse in the heat of the day instead of bedding down for the night.

"You miss sleeping with the group, don't you?" I said, reading her thoughts.

Yes, she admitted. *You, on the other hand, prefer isolation.*

"In most cases, yes."

She seemed to be dissatisfied with my answer. After a moment, I added, "But I like having you with me now. Especially during the night."

Nighttime is when we hunt. I'll have to adapt to sleeping in the evening.

"Maybe we can try mixing it up a little. I don't mind daytime catnaps."

Catnaps. I like that word.

"So do I. Good night."

Good night, Lilliana.

"Lily." I shifted, finding a more comfortable spot. "Hey, what should I call you?"

As we are to become one, you do not need to have a name for me.

"I'd feel better if I could call you something, even if it's only temporary. For the time being, why don't you think of me like a sister."

I could almost hear the soft catch of her breath. *My twin sister was named Tauret.*

"You had a twin?"

It is not uncommon with lions.

"It's a pretty name."

She was my hunting companion until she was slain. We were like two shadows in the night. Tauret was faster, but I was cunning, sharp, especially at rousting prey.

"What happened to her?"

We were at a kill. She was standing guard while I was eating. Hyenas finished her before our protector could drive them off. At least she'd been able to get out a warning before they overpowered us.

What would it have been like to lose a sister? A twin?

Do not waste your emotions on my former life. It is but a shadow of what I will become. Of what we will become.

"You can't convince me that you truly believe that thinking about your sister is a waste of emotions. You loved her."

Her thoughts danced away from me.

Having a lioness in my brain was confusing. I could see through both her eyes and mine at the same time. It was like splitting myself in half and trying to communicate ideas via tin cans connected with string. I could see how the servant Isis saved by gifting her with the powers of a sphinx lost her mind. All at once, with the very real presence of a lioness in my head, I understood what it was to live free and wild. No deadlines, no expectations, no distractions.

I wondered if it was going to be easier for me to adapt to her way of viewing the world than for her to make sense of mine. The human perspective was irritating to her. The rules were ambiguous. There was no sense of connection to others. She felt as if we buzzed in dizzying circles like gnats on the surface of a river—aimless, accomplishing nothing of substance, and bumping haphazardly from one obstacle to the next. Never seeing beyond the small habitat where we were born, lived, and died, never sinking into the depths of the river of life, content to exist only to cause our fellow creatures discomfort.

Rest now, Lily, she said, trying to shush my thoughts.

My mind quieted immediately and I knew that was purely thanks to her. When she decided it was time to sleep, it was time to sleep. She didn't feel guilty about it. She took advantage of quiet moments when she could. Without rest, she wouldn't have the ability to hunt effectively or feed her young or be alert when danger struck. We needed to refresh ourselves for what was to come. It was logical. It was simple. And it was possible, because of her.

As my eyes closed, I smiled, pleased at how easily she'd accepted me as just Lily. "You never told me *your* name," I said as I yawned.

She replied so quietly, I wasn't really sure she was answering my question. But then, as I felt the weight of the word settle in my mind, I knew that what she'd said was indeed her name and that, in a way, her name now belonged to me as well. The name she'd whispered was *Tiaret.*

Tia, I thought. *How lovely.*

Tia sensed something was wrong before I did. In fact, I had a difficult time rousing my mind enough to pay attention to what she was seeing.

What is happening, Lily? she asked, petrified. Every instinct she had said we needed to bolt.

It's okay, I whispered, sending comforting thoughts. *We're in my dream and seeing what Amon sees in the netherworld. This is where we'll eventually be.*

A shadowy creature with talons and batlike wings circled Amon overhead and, with a screech, plummeted toward him. At the last moment, Amon darted up a series of rocks and leapt, sand daggers materializing in his hands as he fell, and with a slashing motion, he disabled the creature's wings and then raised the daggers high in the air. He brought them down, sinking them to the hilt in the neck of the beast.

With a feeble, final flap, the netherworld beast succumbed and a tired Amon slid from its back, found his leather pouch, and walked away, his armor dissolving into the sand. As he continued his journey, a thick bog appeared and the stench of decay assailed his nostrils. My eyes closed of their own volition, and I felt my mind sinking away from the vision, but Tia's attention was riveted.

The mate you have chosen is brave.

Mmm, he is, I mumbled.

Your connection to him gives us an advantage. We can see the paths he wanders. I will track him more easily that way.

That's good, I murmured, my words slurring and melting away like ice cream spilled on a hot sidewalk.

You sleep now, Lily. I will watch over him.

Okay. My body was feeling the effects of having nearly been crushed, though I now knew the lioness tried to be as gentle as possible in the process of our merging. Bruises covered nearly every square inch of my torso. There was no way I had enough energy to stay with Amon in my dreams. I was glad that she could, though, and I hoped I would be able to replay everything she'd seen while I was asleep.

When I woke the next morning, my tongue felt glued to the roof of my mouth and my body felt as sore as if I'd stood all night in one of those old-school vibrating-belt machines. I wasn't sure if everything I'd experienced the day before had been one crazy dream. It certainly felt like a hallucination.

But then I felt her. Tia was . . . purring. There was no other way to describe it. It was a juddering sound that produced a contented hum in my mind. Her presence was a soothing weight I could feel in my chest, almost as if a house cat were cuddled up next to me.

I soon figured out the reason why she was so happy. She was content sleeping, yes, but there was something more. Something she was replaying in her mind. Images flashed, as real as if I'd been witness to them, of the dreamscape she'd been in when Amon fell asleep. "What? What did you do?" They hadn't had much time before the connection was dissolved upon his waking, but the moments they did have together were . . . startling.

"You . . . you kissed him?" I exclaimed in shock.

To be perfectly accurate, he *kissed* me. *A rather pleasant thing, actually.*

"Why? Why would you do that? Didn't you tell him it was you?"

I thought such a revelation might best come from you. The young man suffers enough as it is without us adding to his worry. Besides, I was curious. And once he learned we could make physical contact, he was so happy. I didn't wish to do anything to dispel his good humor.

While I stood rooted in place, my mouth opening and closing as I tried to figure out what to do, Tia sleepily yawned. Her mind was open to me completely. I sensed she felt no shame or guilt regarding what had happened either. Unable to continue the conversation with the snoozing cat taking up space in my brain, I used our connection to replay it all.

In the dream I saw Amon's sleeping body the same as always, but when he fell asleep, another version of him appeared. His real form was battered and bruised but his dream self was whole, strong, and just as handsome as I remembered.

His hazel eyes sparkled as he looked at me, and when he said my name in an almost reverent whisper, stretching out his fingers to mine, I could see his pulse quicken. He swallowed and took a step closer.

"How can this be?" he asked as I wrapped my hand in his, an expression of awe cross his face.

I was about to answer when I realized I couldn't. Tia had. I heard my voice sounding cold and distant. "It must be the power of the sphinx that grants us the ability to see one another and touch."

"I didn't know this was possible."

"Nor did I," my voice said.

Amon slid his hands up my arms carefully, tentatively, as if touching me might break the spell.

My head tilted. Tia enjoyed the sensation of Amon's touch but her heart didn't leap as mine did just upon seeing his face. I felt the pull of my lips as Tia offered Amon a half smile. "That is enjoyable," she said.

I laughed through a sob and pressed my fingers to my lips. Though what she'd said was strange, Amon didn't seem to care. He blinked and I noticed an intense expression in his eyes that made them just a shade darker.

"You don't know how much I missed you," he said, sliding his hand up my neck to cup my cheek. Amon closed the distance between our bodies, and there was a brief moment when Tia stiffened, but the moment quickly passed. I felt the hum of Tia's contentment as he stroked my—no, our—cheek with his thumb, and little tingles of sunshine from his touch both soothed and warmed our skin.

"I don't know if I'm hallucinating or if some blessed miracle of the gods caused this to be, but I don't care."

And he kissed me. The press of his mouth against mine actually made me gasp. I was utterly transfixed, and seeing it through Tia's memory was thrilling and yet upsetting. That he had kissed her and hadn't known it wasn't me stirred niggling feelings of jealousy, but seeing Amon and being with him in body if not in spirit was a gift. I felt his embrace as surely as if he held my heart in his hands.

The kiss became more passionate as Amon drew me close, fitting us together so tightly, it seemed as if nothing could tear us apart.

But something did.

Jerking his head up, he spat out a word I didn't understand, and that was when I heard the screech of an animal nearby. Amon disappeared from my arms and the battered version of himself woke. Hurriedly, he got to his feet and spun around in a circle. "Lily?" he called. "Lily!"

The ground shook as a monster, all tooth and fangs, emerged from a chasm. Tia watched until morning, but he didn't sleep again. I wondered exactly how this dream connection worked. The lioness was no longer awake herself, and yet I could not see any vision of Amon. *The connection must only work when* I *sleep,* I thought, *and then only if I'm able to dream.*

Tia had not lied when she'd said that Amon had been the one to instigate the kiss, and I found it interesting that I no longer felt jealous. Of course I wished it had been me and not Tia he was kissing, but being with Amon in any way was wonderful. A miracle. And Tia was the reason it was possible. I couldn't resent her for that, or for liking the kiss. What girl wouldn't enjoy being kissed by a gorgeous sun god like Amon?

Feeling grateful for her warm presence, I murmured, "You sleep. I'll find breakfast."

I didn't feel Tia stirring until I was halfway back to the place where Isis had left us. I hoped Dr. Hassan was still there, and kept up a steady pace despite the ache in my body that was surprisingly less than it had been when I'd fallen asleep the night before.

We heal faster together was the first thing she said to me after halting my run and luxuriously stretching my arms and back, arching it like a cat before I was able to regain control of my limbs.

"Wh-what was that?" I stuttered as I tried to find my stride once again.

Did you not comprehend my meaning the first time?

"I heard you. I just don't understand why I suddenly felt the need to stop and stretch when my muscles have been warm and loose from running."

Oh. That.

"Yes. That. Are you taking over my mind?"

I assure you that your mind is just as intact and within your control as it ever was.

"Then how did you do that?"

I didn't. You did.

"No. It wasn't a conscious thought."

It was. We thought it.

"What do you mean, we? I didn't think it. You did."

Perhaps it began that way. But your mind agreed and accepted. Do not be overly concerned. It is a good sign. It means we are becoming one. Our minds wanted us to stretch. Therefore, we did.

"Maybe to you it's a good sign. To me it feels like I'm being possessed."

On the contrary. You were feeling secure. Relaxed. You were content with me. Your mind was free and at peace as you ran. That is how running feels for me. It was only natural that you felt more in tune with me during such an act, and your body responded to my mind smoothly and easily.

As harmonious as my run had been before, it now felt disjointed. Like I was in a three-legged race and couldn't find my stride. To distract myself, I said, "I'm not mad. About Amon, I mean."

I know.

"Just . . . wake me up next time that happens, okay?"

I will try, Lily.

"Thanks." As I ran, I began to wonder what other things had changed about me now that I was a sphinx.

What is it? Tia asked.

"It's just that, well, I kind of thought becoming a sphinx would mean I would, you know—"

Look like a monster?

"No. Yes. I guess in a way."

The images you have of a sphinx in your mind are largely inaccurate, though I must admit I would have preferred to keep my fangs and my claws.

"Claws would have been a nightmare for my manicurist. So other than having you in my head, what about me is different?"

Heightened senses, for one. This began when the spell was enacted, though it became permanent when I accepted you.

"Hold on. You . . . accepted me?"

Yes. All the lionesses were aware of the spell the moment it was cast. We gathered in the clearing to assess our compatibility. Each cat was given the choice to cast off her form and merge her consciousness with you, but I was the one who could hear your thoughts the clearest. My sisters bowed to my claim and I began the hunt to assess your worthiness.

"So even then you might have killed me?"

If I deemed you undeserving, then yes.

"What were you judging, exactly?"

Many things. Your quick thinking. Your level of courage in the face of death. Your determination. But most of all, your heart.

"You could sense all of that?"

Yes. Your heart is a good one. The strength that centers it is love. There is no ambition or greed in you. From my perspective, the only thing holding you back is the limitation you put upon yourself. You cage your desires and your passions and willingly live in captivity. You know what you want but are afraid to reach for it. That you were able to come this far speaks to the depth of feeling in your heart. When I discovered these things about you, I thought I might be able to help you embrace that side of yourself and unlock the things you keep most hidden. This is why I accepted you and gave up what I was to help you become your most powerful self.

I didn't know what to say. Having Tia with me was like having a guardian angel who understood everything. Who accepted my strengths and weaknesses and was willing to stick with me and loan a supporting hand regardless of whatever trouble I found myself in. And I was about to find myself in a mess of trouble.

"Thank you. For believing in me, I mean."

I am not the only one. Your mate has an abiding trust in you as well.

"How do you know that?"

He spoke to you last night as he wandered the netherworld.

"He did?"

Yes. You didn't see that part. The young man wasn't aware that I was listening in, but he hoped you'd understand his message just the same.

"What did he say?"

Flowery things. Most of his words were insignificant, meaningless emotional professions of various lengths. The only time I really paid attention was when he spoke words of encouragement and of how he looked forward to your reunion, as dangerous as such a thing may be.

I slowly let out a breath I didn't realize I was holding.

You . . . you wish to hear his words of devotion?

"They mean everything to me," I admitted.

Then next time I will make an effort to pay better attention. To me he sounded much like a lovesick bullfrog in mating season, croaking in an ever-increasingly flamboyant manner to capture the attention of his intended female.

I laughed. Especially when I realized that her thoughts contradicted her words. Amon's words of devotion had touched her, though she didn't truly understand the purpose of it. "Just you wait until it happens to you, my friend," I said. Then I sobered when I realized she was no longer going to get the chance to fall in love if lions even did.

Quietly, I asked, "Do you love your male counterpart? He was a rather handsome lion."

Our notion of love is different. I am bonded to my family, not to one lion in particular. We function as a cohesive unit. Each one is important. We do not seek to isolate ourselves from the others like you do.

"We bond with our families, too, but when we choose a partner, a mate, we want that relationship to be special, different. Something magical that exists only between the two of us."

I am not sure that your way is better than mine. As you can see, your exclusive bond with this male means you mourn when he is removed from your immediate proximity.

"That's true," I admitted. "I feel broken without him. A bit lost."

You sacrifice much for a slim chance at happiness. A steady, productive life might be more fulfilling.

"That sounds too much like the life my parents have planned for me."

I did not mean you shouldn't explore and do the things that please you. I meant that it is important to find moments of joy in the here and now, not to set all your hopes upon one dream, upon one man.

"I'll take it under consideration."

Thank you.

It wasn't that she was wrong exactly. I never wanted to be one of those girls who pined her life away for a man. But I never imagined someone such as Amon either. I ran my palm across the heart scarab at my waist and felt a little flutter jolt through me. My heart was tied to his, and until it wasn't, I'd do anything in my power to be with him.

I could now smell Oscar but I couldn't see him. It was noon and the sun was directly overhead. Cupping my hand over my eyes to shade them, I turned in a circle. A sound behind me caught my attention and I spun around quickly, crouching down, ready to attack.

Dr. Hassan dropped a full canteen, the water gushing out in thick waves like a heart that had been stabbed. He stood there, the shock registering on his face as he scrutinized me.

"Lily? What have you done?"

9

Calling Nebu

Slowly, I straightened, rounding my shoulders, the bones cracking from the release of my tense muscles. "What do you mean, 'What have I done?'" I said. "Haven't I accomplished what you sent me out to do? You should be pleased that I didn't die on the journey."

Oscar's mouth was gaping open as he took in my appearance. "You . . . you," he finally stammered, "have the huntress with you now."

"Yes. We are here," Tia replied using my voice, which irritated me and downright shocked Dr. Hassan.

"But . . . Lily. You have merged your forms."

"Wasn't that what we were supposed to do?"

"Yes. No." He shook his head. "Not exactly."

I put my hands on my hips and watched as he removed his hat and ran a hand through his short white hair, making it stand on end. He then pulled a handkerchief from his pocket and wiped the sweat from his face. "I don't understand what you're so upset about," I said. Then, seeing him continue to dab at his forehead, I added, "Maybe you need to sit down."

Guiding him over to a fallen tree and retrieving his canteen, I bade him to drink a long swallow before I sprinkled the remaining water over his handkerchief and pressed it against his slightly sunburned cheeks. I allowed myself to briefly marvel at how my very pale skin had not been sunburned at all, considering how much sun exposure I'd had. Actually, the heat didn't bother me nearly as much now as it did when we'd first arrived.

"There," I said. "Now, tell me what we did wrong."

"We?" He wrung his handkerchief in his hands. "That's just it. There shouldn't be a 'we.'"

I frowned and then realized what he must be talking about. "Oh, yes. Tia told me that it would take time for our minds to merge. She assures me it's normal."

"Tia? Normal?" Dr. Hassan squeaked. "Now, listen to me, Lily, and do not withhold the truth," he admonished, taking my hands into his. I nodded, the confusion likely evident on my face. "When you"—he paused, as if searching for the right word—"*joined* with the huntress, did her body disappear?"

"Yes," I answered frankly.

"And did you . . . kill her?"

"No!" I exclaimed, aghast at the very notion that I could cause harm to Tia. "She gave up her physical form."

"Oh dear." He sighed and glanced at my eyes as if searching for something and then looked away, as if he couldn't stand what he found. "That is what I feared."

"I'm afraid I don't grasp what all the fuss is about."

"Yes! Speak your thoughts clearly, old one. What do you accuse us of?"

I clapped my hands over my mouth, then hissed, "Tia! Let *me* do the talking."

In my mind she responded, *You do not say the words you wish to say for fear of hurting his feelings. I prefer directness.*

Noted, I shot.

I proceeded to ask the next question she really wanted to know but managed to rephrase it in such a way as to be a bit more polite. "You're acting a bit like a harbinger of doom," I said with a half laugh that dried up in my throat as quickly as the water from his canteen disappeared into the sand. My feeble attempt at lightening the mood failed miserably. "Tell us what we did wrong, please."

"Lily," Dr. Hassan began. "You were supposed to *slay* the huntress."

"*Slay* her? You never said that!"

"It was implied."

"Not really."

Why is he upset about this? Tia asked, an edge to her thoughts that I couldn't identify.

I don't know. Out loud, I asked, "What difference does it make? Her physical form is gone. She gave it up."

"You don't understand. She was supposed to try to kill you, and you her. One of you would die, and the one who survived would absorb the energies of the fallen."

"The spell said we'd both die."

"Yes, in reabsorbing the power of the fallen, the old you would die and be reborn. The huntress is not supposed to sacrifice her own life. At least, not in this manner."

"Okay." I waved my hand in the air, flustered and altogether unhappy at the cryptic meanings and ambiguous instructions I'd received thus far. Tia was right to ask for more direct communication. "So she did. It is what it is. What difference does it make?" I asked.

"The difference, Lily, is that irrepressible changes will start to happen within you."

"Clarify," Tia said, and this time Oscar was upset enough that he didn't seem to notice that she was the one who'd asked and not me.

"If you had slain the huntress as you were supposed to," Dr. Hassan explained, "then you would have absorbed her energies, her power. You would have earned the right to harness them. Her awareness of herself would be gone. Only her instinct would remain. Because she sacrificed herself, and you allowed her to merge with you rather than take what was hers, the two of you will share a body along with the power of a sphinx. Essentially, you will no longer have complete control over yourself. This phenomenon is already evident, as you have spoken without meaning to."

"Isis should have told me what I was supposed to do."

Oscar shook his head. "You were meant to discover your purpose on your journey."

"Well, I did a bang-up job of that, then, didn't I?"

So now I was going to lose myself to the mind of the lioness? How could Oscar and Isis let me go without telling me something so vital? They'd said to embrace my instinct, and my feelings had never once told me to kill. How could I have messed this up so completely? And an even more startling notion entered my mind—what if this mistake I'd made could somehow hinder me from saving Amon?

I searched my memories for the moment when I'd let the whole thing fall apart, but I couldn't pinpoint any one error. Could it be possible that I wasn't meant to kill her? That my instincts had been correct after all? I tried to cling to that hope, but it was hard to do when Dr. Hassan seemed so sure that this wasn't going to end well. Tia had withdrawn so completely that I could barely feel her presence. Stunned, I sat down next to Oscar and cupped my head in my hands. "What's going to happen to me?" I whispered. "And what does this mean for Amon?"

He blew out a breath. "There is no reason to believe you will not be able to wield the power of the sphinx, and that is what you will need to access the netherworld. As far as your unique problem goes, I don't know everything about the lore of the sphinx, but I will share with you all that I can and hope you will find something therein of value.

"The best case I can think of is that the two of you will accomplish your purpose and will somehow find harmony and be able to reside peacefully in the same form. But I must warn you, there is a very real possibility that the huntress will overpower you and the person you are will be lost. The path you walk, you must walk together. If not, the tug-of-war for the right to control your body will begin."

I breathed in and out slowly. Focusing on each inhale and exhale, feeling like the presence that had become a part of me had utterly betrayed me. I wanted to claw her away from my mind, but it was impossible. A tiny whimper escaped from my lips instead as I realized the depth of what I'd agreed to do.

You knew this? I accused. *That I was supposed to kill you?*

In a small voice, Tia admitted, *I did.*

How could you?

For a long moment, she didn't answer, and when she did, the words were not what I expected.

I am not a coward, so put thoughts of that nature far from your mind. I do not fear death. At first when you entered our territory, I wondered if you were even strong enough to defeat me. As I chased you, your redolent stench of fear was disappointing. You smelled like prey. Not a worthy adversary at all.

But then you called out to me. Challenged me. The sign of a worthy heart. A heroine's spirit. You'd passed the test and had the right to your boon. But the boon you sought was not what I expected.

Your heart spoke of love and family. I was surprised to discover that you hadn't come seeking my death at all, though I knew that was supposed to have been your purpose. I focused on your heart, trying to sense what you were going to do. Your deep loneliness was nearly unbearable, and that emotion was echoed within me. Since the death of my sister I'd felt alone even in a pride as large as mine was. I decided to give you a choice and offered myself up to you. If you killed me, then I would have accepted it.

You had incentive and had the means. There were jagged branches nearby that could have easily been used to thrust into my neck or eye. You could have had a knife on you as well, for all I knew. The choice was entirely in your hands. My life was yours for the taking. My heart was ready for the sacrifice.

I hadn't even noticed the branches. She was right that killing her was not on my mind. My instincts had told me to give myself over to her, and it appeared that drive had been echoed in her as well.

When enough time had passed, I assumed then that you wanted what I wanted. The secret wish of my heart. To have a sister once again. If this was not your desire, then I am sorry, Lily. I assure you that it was never my intention to draw you away from your course or to eradicate your essence to assert my own will. If you doubt this, you have the ability to read my heart as well as I can read yours.

When her thoughts quieted, I closed my eyes and felt for her warm presence inside my mind. At first I was only aware of a heartbeat, and I wasn't sure if that was merely the beat of my own corporeal heart or if there was a part of her that still existed on another plane. Stretching beyond the physical, I went deeper and Tia bared her soul to me. I wasn't sure how long we were inwardly communicating, but when I opened my eyes, I had the answer I was searching for.

"Tia is a part of me now, Dr. Hassan. You don't need to worry about us. We'll work well together. The only exception being her craving for raw meat. That's going to have to change. A rare steak or some sushi every so often is all you're going to get."

Oscar looked at me for a long time and then nodded. "I hope for your sake you're right, Lily."

Reaching over, I took his fingers and squeezed. "We'll be okay. I promise."

He gave me a worried nod and then said, "Well, I suppose the first thing we need to do is show you your weapons."

As I followed him over to his dusty bag, which he'd left in the shadow of a large boulder, I said, "We will miss our claws."

He seemed uncomfortable by my use of the plural, but he recovered quickly, coughed, and said, "About that. You have claws."

I could feel the sudden thrill in Tia. "Wait. Do you mean we have a weapon that *looks* like claws?"

"No. You'll have to draw on the power of the sphinx to make them appear."

"How do we do that?" Tia asked through me, but then apologized and took a mental backseat again.

He replied, "Normally, I'd say you have to channel the huntress, but since she's there . . ."

"I should just let her take over?"

"That would be my guess."

When I nodded and figuratively turned over the keys to Tia, it was a strange feeling. I became smaller somehow. It was as if I was seeing things from a distance. It wasn't a frightening thing. In fact, I felt protected, as if I'd been shrouded in a warm blanket and I could just sit back and let someone else take the reins for a change.

In a sort of fog, I half listened to Oscar instructing Tia on how to channel her power, and when she called upon it, an electric burst of energy surged through my body. I was suddenly very alert but my own senses were numb. With fascination I watched my hands change.

There wasn't any pain, only a fiery sort of warmth that burned, but not in a bad way. The bones lengthened, a liquid heat tingling toward each of my fingertips, until an extra knuckle formed. Power rushed down my arms and silver light emerged from the tips and flowed out from each digit until finally solidifying into steel claws. I twitched my fingers and lifted them in fascination.

Holy Egyptian Heaven, I thought. *I'm Wolverine!*

Tia didn't understand my reference, but the exhilaration she experienced was indescribable. She felt invincible, more like her true self. She waved the claws in the air before testing them out by scratching a large boulder. A chunk of stone carved completely off the rock. *Oh boy. We'd better be careful with those,* I warned her.

"They are perfect," she murmured aloud, causing Dr. Hassan to wince yet again.

Uh, how do we get back to normal? I asked, not as comfortable with my new set of claws as Tia was. Tia voiced my concern to Dr. Hassan.

"You retract them," he said. "Reabsorb the power into your core."

Before I could even ponder what to do, the claws had disappeared and I was staring at my own pale hands once more.

Easy, Tia said to me with a smirk that I could tell was showing on my face.

"This is not the only power you will have at your disposal," Oscar added, twitching as he glanced my way, as if uncomfortable to be addressing my inner lioness instead of me. "There are other powers that Isis hinted at that you will discover on your journey. They will manifest only when you're ready to wield them. I am aware of some legends that may lend inspiration but they could be complete fabrications as well. You are the only one, er, ones who will be able to determine the reality of your gifts. Calling forth your claws is the easiest to master since the huntress is well versed in how to use them."

He gave us a sheepish look and said, "I wish I'd had more time. This is everything I could remember off the top of my head. I hope some of it helps." He ran his fingertip down the notebook and began. "'A sphinx is said to have the power to manipulate the wind, find the truth in a man's words, and kill by strangulation.'"

"That much is likely true, though I do not see how I may strangle my prey with teeth duller than a newborn cub's."

We're not biting into the jugular of anything, I warned her.

Dr. Hassan went on. "'She is a fierce hunter, has ferocious strength, and is typically depicted with the head of a woman, the body of a lioness, and the wings of an eagle.'"

At least two of those are accurate, Tia said to me inwardly.

Shhh. I'm listening, I chastised.

"'She is a protector and a shield. The guardian of the eastern and western horizon. She walks the paths of yesterdays and tomorrows. She's associated with death and rebirth, which is entirely obvious at this point, and once her wrath has been unleashed, only her mate can cool her blood.'"

Interesting, Tia said. And the places where her thoughts took me made me blush.

Stop it and pay attention.

He's taking too long, she complained.

This is important!

"'She stands between mankind and the Dark One of the cosmos, absorbing the tides of evil he rains down upon the world.'"

Oscar glanced up at me when he said it, and I knew we were both thinking the same thing. "Seth," I whispered.

He gave a brief nod, acknowledging he'd heard me. " 'In one myth, the sphinx is thought to be responsible for the destruction of mankind, but another says she sees through the eyes of Amun-Ra and uses that power to save the universe.' " Sighing, he closed his little notebook. "As you can see, the conflicting stories and brief descriptions won't be of much assistance. But I will endeavor to obtain everything I can on the legends of the sphinx while you are away, and hopefully I'll find something that will . . . help."

Dr. Hassan looked at me with raised eyebrows and a meaningful nod. I knew what he meant. He wanted me to know that he'd try to find a way to get me back to normal, to separate me from Tia. What he didn't know is that Tia caught, if not the full meaning, then the gist of the idea, and the concept made her . . . not angry as I would have believed, but sad.

Don't worry, I assured her. *We're in this together. It's unlikely this is anything but permanent, and even if it could be reversed, I wouldn't do it if it meant you'd die.*

She hesitated before speaking. *There is no need to dwell on the likelihood of it at present, but should such a thing ever be possible, I would move on.*

That I was shocked at the firmness of her resolve was an understatement.

Dr. Hassan interrupted our inward communication. "I apologize that this is all I was able to come up with while you were gone, Lily."

"Thank you," I said, attempting to take control of my body again. I found it interesting that I nearly had to push the words out through my lips. Tia wasn't feeling grateful at all. "It is more information than we had before," I said with a voice that felt stilted and unnatural. "It will have to be enough."

It isn't really enough, though, is it? Tia countered mentally as she reasserted control and raised my arm to study her too-human hand, wishing once again to release the dangerous claws.

Though I knew the claws made her feel more like her old self, they freaked me out. What worried me more was what would happen if she decided to stay in control of my body. Could I get it back? Would I be relegated to watching her live a life, my life, and not be able to do anything to prevent it?

Stop. Please? I added. Asking her to withdraw.

After a tense moment, she did. But I felt her resentment and the loss she experienced as I relinquished her to a lesser role again. Now I knew how it felt being a passenger in someone else's body.

She'd either hidden the worst of it from me or it didn't bother her as much. If my little taste of having claws was any indication, I would go insane if the situation was reversed and I was the one confined in the body of a lioness. Tia sensed my panic at being mentally caged and her disgruntled feelings disappeared. They were replaced by a soothing sort of empathy. She understood. And that was when I knew she was a stronger . . . soul than I was.

Perhaps that was the reason, if the opportunity presented itself, she'd rather disappear than be locked in the same form with me for eternity. Assuming, of course, that we were now immortal. Which I guess we weren't, since the other sphinx was no longer around. I wasn't sure what all this meant for the two of us, but we both thought it better not to dwell on it for too long.

Dr. Hassan stood. "Isis instructed me to give you these weapons. They are the ones I recovered from the cave."

He lifted a sort of harness that fit over the shoulders, and there was a long metal stick in each of the two pockets. Reaching out, I took one and pulled it free. The weapon was sharpened on the end that had been resting in the scabbard.

"Ah," Tia exhaled the sentiment as she stretched out my other hand and took hold of the other weapon. There was an awkward moment of scrabbling for control as my body was literally pulled in two places at once. Both of us froze.

I apologize, Tia said. *I did not mean to assert myself.*

It's okay, I replied. *It has to be hard to always be a passenger.*

I will watch for now.

I'm sure you're the better fighter, though.

There is no one to fight at the moment. Take this opportunity to learn.

Dr. Hassan watched us with a barely concealed expression of alarm. "How are you feeling, Lily?"

"I'm good," I answered while giving him what I hoped was a reassuring smile. "It's just going to take some getting used to."

"Indeed."

"So, tell me what this weapon is for."

"Ah!" He seemed excited and in his true element then. "This is a very rare and ancient weapon used by the gods. Much like Amon's scimitars, these spears can be used in close combat, but they are also distance weapons."

"Spears?" They looked more like long sai knives than spears, but the tines on the side were nearly as long as the shaft, like three-pronged machetes. The three elongated blades on each weapon were wicked-looking and came to a sharp point at the tip. "Aren't they a little short for spears?" I asked.

He held out his hands and I dropped the heavy handle into his palm. When he touched a raised knob in the center, a kind of hidden spring caused them to elongate into full-sized spears. Inside my head, Tia was almost purring with happiness. With a quick press of the button, the weapon compacted back into a size that would fit into the scabbard.

Oscar helped me put on the leather harness and buckle it across my shoulders. "You can use them for both slicing and stabbing at close range or to impale at long range," he said.

Experimenting, I reached up behind my neck and drew out the spears. They seemed to fit my hands perfectly. I rotated them in my palms, relishing their weight, and was surprised at the natural agility I displayed when wielding them.

I threw one and the head of the spear sank almost liquidly into the thick trunk of a tree a good distance away.

I was about to ask how I felt so comfortable with the weapons when Tia explained. *It is likely our instinct. Your senses have been heightened, including your sense of space and touch. Just as I am able to calculate the speed and distance between me and my prey.*

But surely it's more than just the abilities of a lioness, I replied. *You've never handled a weapon like that before, and it was like I already knew how.*

She answered matter-of-factly. *We are sphinx. You drew upon the power inside us. I felt it. Did you not?*

Now that she mentioned it, I had felt something. A kind of current that ran through me the moment my intention to draw the weapon entered my mind. Distracting me from my thoughts, she asked impatiently, *The other one?*

I gestured to the other form protruding from his bag. "You have a bow, too, I see."

"Yes," Dr. Hassan said as he snapped out of his awe-filled stare and crouched down next to the boulder.

He brought me a gleaming bow carved with images I didn't understand. I ran my fingertip along each groove, wondering what they meant. When I showed them to Oscar, he shrugged and said, "I have never seen them before and I hesitate to guess. I would imagine this is what Isis meant about learning along the journey."

The quiver was full of arrows tipped with gleaming white feathers edged in gold. He saw me fingering one. "They are the feathers of Isis," he explained. "Their aim is always true, but as you can see, there are a limited number of them. Use them wisely."

With my weapons strapped on, Dr. Hassan paused. He looked at me with a strange mixture of sympathy and as if I were one of the gods he revered. Finally, he sighed. "I wish I knew how to better assist you." He paced a few steps off. "If only I could accompany you."

"If it helps, I wish you could go with me, too."

He crushed his fedora in his hands. "It's simply not possible. I asked Isis. I begged her to the point of risking her wrath as I waited here for you, and the only answer I received is that I'd never make it through.

Only you are meant to do this. Only you can save Amon. All I can do is prepare you for your journey to the beyond, and to do that I must seal upon you the Heart of the Sphinx, the final piece of the spell." When I nodded, he said, "Repeat after me."

As he spoke, each word seemed to latch on to my being, as if each piece of me that he listed in such a way manifested itself physically.

"My hair flows as a lion's mane. It is my shield.
My face is comely and shines with the brightness of the sun
My eyes see into dark places and open secret caverns
My ears can locate a scarab buried in a desert
My nose can scent a flower petal sunk in the depths of the ocean
My voice is mellifluous and imperils all who listen
My lips are drawn wide to swallow the souls of the evil
My teeth are sharpened weapons aimed for the cruel and crookbacked
My muscles are warmed and ready for battle
My belly is not soft but is as rigid as a boulder
My body is lissome; my form dangerous and enticing
My feet are ready to carry me past hidden doorways
My claws seek your demise and will unravel you utterly
My wings will ward off evil and triumph over my enemies."

As he finished the last part of the spell, a sharp pain shot up my back that nearly ground me into the dust at my feet. Slowly, I arose and knew that I would never be the same person, the same woman, the same creature again. I was not human. I was not lioness. I was sphinx. I lifted my arm, and though it looked the same, I knew there was an increased hardness in my muscles. My skin tingled from the roots of my hair down to my toes.

My being, the core of who I was, had changed, and yet, from what I could see, I still looked like me. I wondered if I stared into a mirror would I see the same eyes staring back at me or would I see a stranger? Would Amon even view me the same when I saw him? Could he learn to care for the being I'd become? I steeled my shoulders, knowing that it didn't matter. He needed to be saved and I—no, we were the only ones who could do it.

Dr. Hassan, who now looked at me with even more veneration, quickly explained, "The place you are seeking is called Duat. It is the home of Amun-Ra. You can only access it during the day and discover the entrance to it through a tomb. I can take you to one that's only a few hours away."

I lifted my nose and closed my eyes. Tia's mind joined with mine and we spoke as one in thought. It felt right and seamless somehow. If my voice was the wind, then hers was a deep tide pool stirred by the wind. "There is a forgotten tomb belonging to a lost traveler much closer. We will find the way ourselves."

Fretfully, Oscar nodded, as if he'd expected such an answer. And because he seemed pained to leave me in the state I was in, we left him instead. We journeyed across the landscape until I could no longer make out the rise where Oscar stood; then, knowing what I needed to do, I raised my hands and called upon the power of the sphinx, bidding the wind to expose the hidden tomb I sensed below. Grains of sand started to shift, and then thousands of stinging granules rose, guiding us toward our destination. After the wind died down, we stepped forward.

The dark cavern that the wind had exposed held the skeleton of a man who'd died in the desert long ago. Though it wasn't an official tomb like the one Oscar had been considering, it would do for our purposes.

Channeling the power residing inside us, we blew out a soft breath. It ruffled the worm-ridden clothes of the dead man and punched a hole in the darkness of his deathbed. The hole grew, stretching like a fragile bubble until it was nearly big enough for us to step through.

It was a path to another realm, a dimension unlike either of our worlds. My mind interpreted it as a wormhole, but Tia didn't understand this. To her it was a whirlpool in a black pond leading to a place she had no knowledge of or wish to discover. We both sensed the problem at the same time.

We're going to need help, she said.

Yes. I contemplated the obstacle and then a memory surfaced. *I think I know what to do,* I murmured.

Closing my eyes, I chanted the spell Amon had practiced with me and imbued my words with all our energies. A short time later, the dune next to us shifted and roiled.

What is it? Tia said, fearing a large serpent or a pack of jackals.

A friend, I answered with a small smile.

A moment later, a huge figure burst through in an explosion of sand. The great beast nickered softly and trotted toward us, his coat sparkling in the sun like mica. He was beautiful. Much larger than the horses Amon had called before. Stepping up to him, I ran a hand down his silky neck and tried to calm Tia, who was frantic at being near him.

I have answered your summons, Sphinx. Where do you wish to go?

"We are headed to Duat," I answered.

That is a long journey, and a dangerous one.

"Will you not be able to take us?" I asked.

The stallion stomped his golden hooves and flicked his tail in irritation. *Of course I am able to take you,* he declared. *I am Nebu!*

10

The Place Where Dreams Are Born

I held out my hand and Nebu stepped closer, pressing his nose into it. Just as his moist exhale tickled my sensitive palm, Tia took full possession of my body, snatched my hand away, and reached for the blades at my back. In a flash she raised the sharpened edge of a mini spear to the great neck of the golden stallion, touching the spiky point of a second to his chest.

"Stay away from us, *Unadorned One,*" she spat at the gleaming horse.

Tia! What are you doing? I hissed as I tried to reassert control over my own body. *He's here to help us!*

"He is *not* here to help us!" she cried. "This . . . *unicorn*"—she hissed the word as if it were something hateful and ugly—"is here to steal you away. You obviously do not understand what he is capable of."

What on earth are you talking about? He isn't a unicorn. He's a horse. Granted, he's a magical-Egyptian-pretty-much-indestructible-possibly-made-of-sand-immortal horse, but he is a horse. Haven't you ever seen one before?

"Of course I've seen horses before. I'm not a cub, Lily. And he's as much a horse as I am a house cat. Can't you see it?"

See what?

"The place where his alicorn used to be."

I looked more closely at Nebu, and there was a sort of muted glow coming from a spot in the center of his head, but his whole body gleamed enough that I'd assumed it was an especially bright section of his coat.

What's an alicorn? I asked.

"It is the symbol of his power. He has been stripped of it, like all of his kind. That is why I called him *Unadorned.* It is an insult to all unicorns. They don't like to be reminded of their shame."

Shame?

The stallion bobbed his head and stomped his feet. *What is this? Who are you?* he mentally shouted, flicking his tail in irritation.

Tia ignored his question and shouted, "Lily is not the fragile virgin you are seeking!"

What I'm *seeking? I seek nothing!* he sneered. *I might have expected riddles from you, Lady Sphinx, but your words cut to the quick, and I have done nothing to deserve the heaping abuse you've piled upon me. I only came here as a favor to the young man wielding the Eye of Horus. It would have been much easier to send one of my children, but he pleaded in such an eloquent manner and expounded upon the virtues of the one he loved so movingly that I decided I wanted to meet you myself. Suffice it to say, I am disappointed. And Zahra, my daughter who carried you to the oasis, spoke so highly of you, too.*

"We don't need you or your special brand of assistance. Seek an innocent elsewhere, for you won't lay your head in this virgin's lap!"

Nebu eyed us as if we were a creature he'd never seen before and trotted a distance away.

Tia! First of all, I don't appreciate the hostile takeover of my body, especially without even a tiny warning. Second, you have no business talking about my virginity or lack thereof with anyone, especially a guy, er, horse. I'd rather not have the fact that I am still a virgin, because my mummy boyfriend pretty much kept his hands to himself right up until his untimely death, advertised everywhere. It's not that I'm ashamed or anything. It's just that there has to be some kind of boundary established between us. We need to come up with some rules about what we will and won't share publicly about each other. Third, what is your deal? Why are you acting like this? What's your problem with horses and/or unicorns?

"I will not talk about this here. Especially in front of *him*. He's dangerous, Lily. You do not understand how monstrous his kind can be."

Nebu circled around us now, bobbing his head up and down. I suspected the only reason he hadn't left yet was because of Amon, and I knew to the depths of my soul that we needed him. Seeing that Tia was happy about driving him off, and brandished her knives to give him further motivation, only made matters worse. I needed to manage the situation.

Tia, I pleaded. *We need his help. If he doesn't take us where we need to go, Amon dies. The world ends. Chaos reigns. You don't want that. I know you don't. You've got to trust me. I promise I won't do anything without consulting you first.*

"I do trust you," she murmured quietly, much more at ease now that the stallion had moved farther away from us.

Good. Then give me back control.

She hesitated only a moment, but the instant she made the decision to give in, I felt it. Tia, feeling slightly guilty, retreated deeply into my mind and hid like a kitten under a bed.

"Wait!" I cried out, in charge of my own voice again. I quickly stowed the blades at my back and held out a hand to the retreating horse.

He approached cautiously, doubtfully, like a reluctant colt after a treat, and then backed away quickly, nearly sitting on his haunches. Neighing, he shook his head as if something was bothering him.

I do not know what game you play, young sphinx, but I am not in the habit of offering my services to just anyone.

"I know. I'm sorry." Taking a few slow steps in his direction, I stretched out my fingertips, and he, almost reluctantly, closed the distance. When he seemed comfortable enough, I patted his cheek and he pressed his head against my shoulder in response.

He blew a soft breath through my hair. *You may speak,* he said in my mind quietly.

"I have a passenger with me," I explained. "And she seems to be concerned and somewhat fearful regarding your intentions."

Tia hissed, sulky and unhappy about my saying that she was afraid.

A passenger? What do you mean by this?

Clearing my throat, uncomfortable, I wrung my hands and said, "The spell to make me a sphinx worked, but the consciousness of the lioness that merged with me so we could achieve this power is still a part of me."

The stallion bounced and I quickly backed away as he reared up on his hind legs and pawed the air, nickering loudly. His hooves gouged the sand, kicking it up until it was as agitated as he was. *You have brought a lioness here? This is unacceptable. Remove her from your form immediately.*

"Remove her?" I laughed uneasily. "Even if I could, which I can't, I wouldn't."

The horse twisted his head to peer at me. *Now I understand why you said the things you did.* He sighed deeply. *I am sorry, then, Innocent One, but as much as I crave your association, I cannot take you on your journey.* He turned to leave, flicking his tail.

"Don't go!" I called out, and placed a hand on his back. "Please," I begged. "We both know that we cannot accomplish our goal without you."

I sensed that he wasn't as eager to leave us as he had been a moment ago.

I do not like lions, the stallion said finally, obviously torn at the idea of stranding us there. *But if she will remain quiet on the journey, I will agree to take you to Duat.*

I patted him happily and kissed his warm cheek.

If you agree to grant me a boon, he added as he knelt before me.

At the same moment I murmured, "Of course," Tia screamed in my mind, *No!*

But it was too late. The bargain was already made. She knew it and broke down into torrential sobs. I prayed my own instincts were right.

As I climbed on the back of a unicorn, I thought how silly I'd been to think I was prepared. There was no anticipating something like this. My life was now beautiful, marvelous, unanticipated, unscripted madness. It's one of the things that attracted me to Amon. There was a loveliness to the unexpected, and the more I was a part of it, the more I craved it. I would never be the same girl again, and it didn't bother me as much as I thought it should have.

Nebu got to his feet and I held tightly to his mane as he headed over to the uncovered tomb. Though there was uncertainty and danger ahead, I felt ready for it. I didn't look back. Not at Dr. Hassan. Not at the African landscape. Not at the world I knew. And not at the girl I used to be. Lilliana Young was gone. I was someone, some*thing* altogether new.

He will betray your trust, Tia said, interrupting my thoughts.

But Amon promised he'd send help, I replied. *He wouldn't have sent someone who would hurt us.*

Unicorns only help themselves to the vulnerable and innocent, she muttered moodily.

Are you sure he's really a unicorn? I asked, still doubtful.

She sighed impatiently. *I will tell you their story when we are alone. I do not want him to hear my thoughts.*

All right, I said to her secretly. *We'll be careful.*

Hold to me tightly, said Nebu, *lest you fall and are lost in the Land Between.*

"The Land Between?" I questioned, but there wasn't time for him to answer because he reared up and leapt into the dark bubble we'd opened in the tomb. And just like that, the world we knew was left behind. With a snap, the bubble closed around us and I could see nothing, hear nothing but the powerful breathing of the stallion as he ran.

I squeezed my eyes tightly, threading my fingers through his silky mane as I pressed my thighs against his sides and prayed that I wouldn't fall off. The last place I wanted to end up was lost in the abyss we were in.

After what felt like an hour, I saw a light ahead and we sped toward it. The brightness grew and rocky soil materialized ahead. We dashed forward as fast as lightning, and with a crack of Nebu's thunderous hooves that echoed in the sky above us, we struck land. Beams of pink and purple, orange and yellow filtered over the stony landscape, lighting it softly, serenely, with the barest touch of color.

The terrain reminded me of the great rock canyons of the Wild West. Pink pinnacles rose over horseshoe-shaped plateaus made of sandstone and shale that must have been formed by ancient rivers and colorful lake sediments. Pale stripes of minerals in different colors graced each peak and mound of stone. We passed wide arches and impossible rock formations that had been so eroded it was a wonder they still stood.

I saw no signs of wildlife or people, but there were plants and trees that peeked out from crevices and behind arches. The fresh scent of a desert just after a thunderstorm wafted over me. Though the landscape was bathed in soft light, the sky was dark, illuminated only by the thousands of stars overhead, and I realized then that the dreamy quality of pastel light on the sepia terrain had been created by them.

"It's beautiful. Do you live here?" I asked.

No. This is a part of the Land Between. We have passed through the first barrier and have entered the second. This is the Place Where Dreams Are Born.

"Interesting. Will we fall asleep here, then?"

No! To sleep in the Place Where Dreams Are Born is to forfeit your life and become a dream. You will cease to exist unless a mortal conjures you in his slumber.

It didn't sound too bad when I thought about it. It was a good way to die if you had to. Plus, I could rely on Amon dreaming about me at least once in a while.

It is imperative that you remain awake while we are in this realm, he warned.

"Then perhaps you should tell us a story," I suggested as I patted him.

Okay, I will tell you one of my favorites: the story of Geb and Nut.

As he regaled me with the familiar story, I heard Amon's voice instead of Nebu's. I closed my eyes and pictured his handsome face, his lips next to my ear, as Nebu narrated the story of a god and goddess and of a love so strong it took tremendous power to separate the two beings. Even then, with the vast heavens between them, they clung to each other by their fingertips and their gazes remained always fixed upon the one they loved. I wiped away a tear leaking from the corner of my eye, and before I knew it, Nebu stretched out his legs, lengthening his stride.

"What's happening?" I called out.

We have reached the far side of the Place Where Dreams Are Born. We've passed the second barrier and are about to embark upon the third and final one. We're at the drop-off.

"The drop-off? What do you mean, 'the drop-off'?"

Before he could explain further, I saw exactly what he meant. The hard sepia dusted terrain abruptly ended and beyond it was nothing but star-studded night, like we'd reached the end of the world. A place where ships would sail right over the edge of the earth and into the unknown.

"Nebu!" I cried.

Tia screeched inside my head, and if she'd had claws, she would have dug them into my spine.

All will be well, Lady Sphinx. Hold on tightly, the unicorn said.

With that, the muscles of the stallion's back shifted beneath me, and great golden wings sprouted behind my legs. With an immense thrust, Nebu's hooves left the ground just as we reached the edge of the cliff. He leapt into the sky, legs pumping and heavy wings beating against the wind, taking us higher.

I was on the back of a broken unicorn, an immortal desert stallion. I felt not unlike Bellerophon, who'd dared to ride his beloved horse, Pegasus, up Mt. Olympus to confront the gods. He had failed and was struck down on the journey, but I wasn't going to let that happen to us. With eyes wide-open, I scanned the sky. Our destination loomed somewhere ahead, just beyond the stars.

11

Heliopolis

The ground fell far beneath us, and I had to soothe and calm Tia as best I could even though the height caused me alarm as well. Thankfully, Nebu ascended slowly, keeping us as level as he possibly could. The higher we rose, the colder it got. Tia cowered inside me, trembling, even though it was *my* arms that were prickly with goose bumps and *my* nose that had lost feeling.

When I asked Nebu if we were going to freeze and die due to lack of oxygen, he replied, *You are a sphinx now. You cannot perish from something as simple as frostbite. Besides, you will be warm again soon enough. Remember, our destination is the home of the sun god.*

If Amun-Ra's home was anything like being near Amon, I had nothing to worry about. Amon generated warmth like a space heater. Just thinking about him made me feel like I'd wrapped a thick blanket around my shoulders. The little shivers in my muscles subsided. *Perhaps my fears are more of a mental thing than physical,* I thought.

And regarding your question about oxygen, you misunderstand when we are.

"Don't you mean *where* we are?"

I mean when. *To you this must feel like the atmosphere of your own Earth. The stars surrounding us would represent something like space. But we are not in the place your mind tells you. Just because you inhale and exhale does not mean there is oxygen, and we are not in the when we left.*

"Then what am I breathing, exactly? And if we're not a where, then when are we?" I asked.

You are breathing in the light of the stars, and I don't mean the stars in your universe. Stars have a different meaning here. To answer the second part of your question, we are Between Time.

"That's why you called it a Land Between. You didn't mean between places; you meant between times."

Yes. That's right.

I sensed Nebu was pleased with my ability to understand what he was saying.

Tia was no longer listening. Her brain couldn't process metaphysical discussions such as this. She was a huntress. A warrior. Her instincts told her something was very wrong and she didn't belong in the place we were. A cat needed to feel the ground beneath her paws. She needed to tread known paths and terrain. She had no desire to discover anything about the realm we'd found ourselves in.

Curious, I asked him, "Is this how Anubis travels as well? He journeys between time?"

Yes. All the gods travel in this manner.

"But not the Sons of Egypt, right?"

The Sons of Egypt do have the ability to manipulate time, but to travel in the dark space Between takes a physical toll on them. The gods are not affected in the same way.

"That brings up a question I've been meaning to ask for quite a while. Why don't the gods do their own dirty work? I mean, why give Amon and his brothers the responsibility for something that the gods caused to happen in the first place? They're the ones who banished Seth. They should clean up their own messes."

Nebu's wings twitched and he shook his head as if he were uncomfortable. *I dare not speculate on the why. I have my theories on the subject, of course, but it's not my place to say anything.*

"Well, you can bet I'm planning on saying something. It's unfair what they expect. Their so-called gifts are really just cop-outs."

Feeling chilled again, I rubbed my hands together and blew on them to warm them up.

The discomfort you feel at this time is nothing compared to the physical challenges you will face in the netherworld, you know, Nebu said.

"Now you tell me," I murmured.

Surely you didn't think this journey would be easy.

"No. I guess my human side is showing, isn't it? I'm feeling a little too much like Lily Young and not enough like a sphinx at the moment."

Perhaps you should ask your lioness for help.

"What? How?"

She can help you regulate your body temperature.

"Really?"

Tia heard his suggestion and her presence bubbled up to fill my frame. A blessed warmth came with it, as if she'd wrapped me in the fur coat of a lion. I was still in charge of my body, but she stayed with me now, right below the surface, despite her fear of being airborne.

Thank you, I said to her silently.

I apologize for allowing your suffering to continue. I was not aware that I could stop it.

It's okay. We're learning as we go.

"Thank you," I said to the stallion. "We're feeling much better now."

You're welcome. Just remember that anytime you need to access the power of the sphinx, you will need to do it together. To harness it requires you to be unified in your desires.

"That's good to know."

Are you ready, Lady Sphinx? Nebu asked.

"Ready? For what?"

To enter Duat.

"Oh, that. Umm, sure?"

The unicorn banked and then pressed forward slowly. It looked as if we were entering a horizontal black pool of water. The stars remained fixed but the space between them shimmered like liquid vinyl. Nebu's head and chest disappeared, encompassed by the opaque sludge. It reminded me of being absorbed into the giant worm's mountain where Dr. Hassan had stored Asten's sarcophagus.

As the liquid closed over my legs and flowed up the rest of my body, I couldn't help taking a deep breath and closing my eyes. I'd been absorbed and/or crushed by one too many things since I'd met Amon. Between quicksand, a suffocating lioness, mountains, a stone box, and now the gateway to Duat, I was surprised that I didn't have a worse problem with claustrophobia than I did. Each experience felt like a tiny death. And now that I was a cat, at least partially, I wondered if this was going to use up one of my nine lives.

It's a myth, Tia's inner voice said.

What is? I answered, desperate for a distraction as the blackness closed over my head.

That cats have nine lives. They don't. They get one, just like every other creature. The exception being your mate, of course.

Finally the darkness lifted away and we beheld a paradise arrayed in all its glory. We'd entered a new world—one more beautiful and lush than I'd ever seen. A vast ocean shimmered beneath us with the soft golden rays of a perfect sunset. It reflected Nebu's thick wings, my bare white legs on his back, and the green of my dress.

Strange seabirds called out to each other as they dove, trying to catch dinner in a school of fish with scales that flashed brightly under the water's surface. Other, larger animals I couldn't see spouted thick mists of water, then quickly disappeared beneath the ocean surface. The balmy breeze carried on it the scents of a turquoise ocean, golden sands, bright citrus, and tropical flowers, all baked by a summer sun.

The unicorn dipped lower, dragging his feet in the wake; the water, so warm it could have been from a hot spring, splashed over my sandaled feet. Ahead of us was an island surrounded by low tangerine clouds, and jutting up from the billowing mass was a golden city. Carved obelisks, arched bridges, gleaming towers, massive statues, and impressive pyramids with gilded capstones that shone in the waning sunlight dotted the landscape. Though it was sunset, the light generating from each building was easily enough to rival a full moon.

"Is this Duat?" I asked.

Nebu nickered lightly. *No. The city before us is only a part of Duat. It is the Heart of the Sun—the home of Amun-Ra—otherwise known as Heliopolis. To gain entrance to the afterlife and the netherworld, you'll need to travel to the far side of Duat, to the place where the sun sets in the evening.*

"The sun is setting now. Can we get there before nightfall?"

We cannot. Even if I could manage to get you there in time, you would not be allowed to obtain passage on the Cosmic River without first calling upon Amun-Ra. He must grant permission to ride on the celestial barque. Without the leave of He Who Came Into Being by Himself, the Protector of the Untraveled Road, you would not be allowed to even remain within the borders of Heliopolis.

Nebu beat his wings and flew above a great wall that surrounded the city, and I could see the movement of people between the buildings down below.

"Who are they?" I asked.

Some are lesser gods. Some are servants who have pledged an eternal devotion to Amun-Ra. Others are his creations.

"Creations? You mean like children?"

In a manner of speaking, yes. Like the unicorn, there are a vast number of creatures formed by the cosmos, and even a few created by Amun-Ra or the other members of the pantheon. Many of them live here in Heliopolis in peace.

"So they're not human, then?"

Some are. Some were.

I dared not ask for more details about that. At least not yet. It was all a little too much for me. "So where are we headed? The capitol building?"

We will attempt to gain entrance at the gateway to Amun-Ra's palatial home. Can you see it there at the top of the hill?

The area of the city where we were headed held the most exquisite, most dazzling buildings I'd ever seen. A colossal temple crowned with an obelisk, carved in the form of a great bird, rose from a mountainside, capped with a sparkling miniature pyramid.

Nebu explained, *The pyramidion on the top of the temple represents the highest point in the city.*

"Pyramidion?" I asked.

Yes. It's the peak of the Benben obelisk. Amun-Ra's image has been carved into the large diamond you see there, and all who live in the city look to it at sunrise and sunset to remember that Amun-Ra is the first to be welcomed by the sun each morning and the last to honor it before dusk falls.

"Hmm. I wonder if he's trying to compensate for something."

Nebu whinnied and shook his mane. *I would be careful what I say in the Golden City,* he warned. *Amun-Ra is not a god to be taken lightly.*

I smiled and patted Nebu's neck. "You worry too much. Believe me, I've been trained in the social graces since the time I could talk. We'll be fine."

It's just that it would pain me to learn that your journey ended before it began. Perhaps I should remain at your side when you meet him.

Threading my fingers through his mane, I held tightly as he gracefully descended to the flagstones below. His hooves hit the sparkling tile, and the air he stirred up as he balanced his weight blew my hair in every direction. He tucked his wings into his side so tightly that they disappeared even from my view, and we trotted down the long bridge leading to the gate, where guards stood with long, dangerous-looking spears crossed between them.

Perhaps, if all goes well, you could pass along a message for Anubis to give to my woman. I do not know if he will deliver it, but it couldn't hurt to ask.

"I could do that," I offered, wondering about this woman who was loved by a unicorn. "Anubis owes me anyway. What would you like me to say?"

Tell her . . . tell her that my heart still burns for her.

Even more mysterious. "If I can, I will share your message." I slipped off his back and teetered for a moment, trying to gain my balance. Nebu pressed his nose into my hand and I patted his muzzle in gratitude.

Come. Let me guide you as far as the inner chamber if I cannot convince you to allow me to remain by your side while you're here. The stallion walked beside us as we approached the guards, and he addressed them himself. *This sphinx wishes to gain an audience with He Who Came Into Being by Himself. We request entrance.*

A stone-faced guard answered. "Tonight he has business elsewhere, but perhaps Horus might like some entertainment."

Entertainment? Tia hissed, bristling at the idea. *They wish to make sport of us?*

Tia was interrupted by one of the guards opening the gate and ushering us inside. We were given some vague instructions and left to our own devices, which I found strange for a fortification as large as Amun-Ra's temples. I suppose that spoke to the power of the gods. There must not be too many who wished to challenge them.

Since Nebu walked confidently beside us and seemed to know where he was going, I wasn't overly worried.

I wondered how best to approach Horus. Surely he would help us. Amon did carry his Eye, after all. What we were doing would affect everyone, even the people who resided in the golden city of Heliopolis. If Seth broke free, they would be in just as much danger as the mortal realm, wouldn't they?

As we walked through the temple, all I could do was gape at the splendor and opulence of Amun-Ra's home. Servants passed us bearing golden pitchers and trays full of ripe fruits, sweets, and cheeses. After the fifth one nodded demurely, giving us not even a second glance, I finally noticed something. "They're all women," I observed.

Who are you referring to? Nebu asked.

"The servants. And they're all gorgeous."

Both Amun-Ra and Horus like to surround themselves with beauty and the riches that their stations afford.

I rolled the idea over in my mind for a moment and then said, "Ah, I understand."

What is it? Tia asked me.

I've been around guys like this before, I explained. *They show off their money or power by only associating with those they consider worthy.*

And are we not . . . worthy? she asked.

In our current state? Not really. I ran a hand through my wind-tangled hair. My dress was mud crusted, ripped, and bloodstained from where Tia had sunk her claws into me. I brushed my hand across the heart scarab at my waist, searching for some comfort to get me through our current situation.

Ah, Tia said in my mind. *You wish to bathe and*—she searched for the word—*condition your mane.*

Yes.

And if we did this, we would be worthy enough to gain an audience with Horus?

I'm not certain of that, but at least we wouldn't embarrass ourselves.

Are you sure baring our claws and teeth, even dull ones such as yours are, wouldn't impress him more?

I'm sure.

After a beat, Tia said, *Very well. May I address the unicorn?*

Tia's presence bubbled to the surface, and the switch of control felt as natural as merely stepping out of the way. "Unicorn," Tia said. "It is I, the lioness. Lily feels ashamed to meet a god adorned in this manner. We require your assistance."

Nebu cocked his head, studying us with an unblinking eye. *Lioness,* he said, and inclined his head respectfully. *You've been quiet. I nearly forgot you were there.*

"I did as you asked," Tia said simply with a shrug.

You did. I appreciate your patience on the journey.

"And I appreciate you for not dragging Lily off to be your virgin sacrifice," she said with a smirk.

Nebu nudged her shoulder softly and she froze, but at my urging, she was soon able to relax again. She even awkwardly patted his nose in a stiff sort of way. I was proud of her.

You don't need to be so rough, the stallion remarked with a jerk of his head.

Tia dropped her hand. "I apologize. I've never petted a unicorn, or any other creature, for that matter. My type of caress usually ends in death. But from your reactions when Lily does it, it would appear that you enjoyed it. Perhaps I was mistaken."

I normally do enjoy it, he said as he took a step closer. *You may attempt it again, Lioness. If you wish to,* he added.

Stretching out her fingers once more, Tia gently cupped the unicorn's cheek. After a moment, she said, "I find it strange that you endure a human's touch."

You would like it, too, he answered, *if you were in your old form.*

"Perhaps," she said. "But that is never to be again." There was a hint of sadness in her voice, and it was the first time I noticed that when she spoke, my voice sounded different. It was throatier, rougher, a bit like she'd swallowed sandpaper and was trying to speak around it. I thought about all that she'd given up to make me what I was. It seemed to me that sharing my body with her was a little thing to give.

After a moment, Tia asked Nebu again, "Is there anything you can do to help us?"

No, he replied. *There is nothing I can do. But there is something* you *can do.*

"I? What can I do?" Tia asked as she took a step back.

You are sphinx, he answered simply. *Focus on what you want together.*

"But I do not know exactly what Lily needs."

Then let her take the lead, but open yourself to allow the power to flow through you.

Tia nodded, and in the blink of an eye we switched places.

Whether Nebu knew the switch had happened or not, he patiently guided us. *Close your eyes and think of what it is that you want.*

I obeyed, envisioning clean and appropriate attire to meet Amun-Ra and Horus. At first I didn't notice anything was happening. I thought the warmth on my arms was from being inside the gleaming temple, but I soon felt the sting of sand. I opened my eyes and found I was surrounded by a little storm cloud of dust. It whipped around me in a circle, beating softly against my limbs, scrubbing my skin until it shone.

The rags of my dress disappeared in the cloud and the grains settled against me, forming a new dress. This time, instead of the jade green of the heart scarab, I was clothed in cream and gold. A tight bodice beaded in sparkling gems wrapped around my torso. Strands of gold cinched my waist. The scarab was now a brooch attached to the right shoulder of my gown where the bodice met the sleeve, and starbursts of tiny green beads shot from it and tapered off, disappearing altogether when they reached my belt.

The floor-length skirt was adorned with gold-tipped feathers sewn into the fabric, the tips angled out in such a way to make me look like a bird. As I touched one, I realized that the feathers were identical to those of Isis. Comfortable slippers adorned my feet, and bands of clinking gold bracelets wound up my arms. Reaching up, I was comforted by the feel of the spears on my back and the tips of the feathered arrows still sticking out of the quiver.

My hair was tossed in a cyclone of sand that pummeled through the strands until they were soft and smooth. The grains tickled my scalp, and my hair was soon swept up in loosely pinned curls. I touched the top of my head, which still tingled, and glanced into a polished shield that was mounted on the wall. The last bits of sand above me solidified and created a golden winged headpiece that crowned my face in such a way that it was reminiscent of a lion's mane.

Tia was pleased with that effect and bragged that the last part had been her doing. I ran my hand over the beaded bodice, smoothing the fabric over my hips, fingers lingering on the silky feathers. "Well, how do I look?" I asked Nebu.

Like a queen, the stallion replied. *Shall we proceed?*

I nodded and strode ahead confidently, knowing I was now prepared to meet a god on equal footing. The noise of people laughing, tinkling fountains, and soft music guided us, and it wasn't long before we found the source of it. It was a party.

Putting on my best I'm-so-pleased-to-make-your-acquaintance smile, I stepped inside the large atrium, my hand on Nebu's back for moral support. The room was full of beautiful things—fountains, statues, long, richly oiled tables full of delectable foods—and women. There were women everywhere.

Redheads, blondes, brunettes. Women who looked like they were from Africa, Asia, South America, Native America, Alaska, Russia, Polynesia, and some who looked . . . otherworldly. It was like a Miss Universe pageant of the tall, poised, and lovely. Some of the women lounged. Some served. Some conversed in small groups. But there was one thing all of them had in common other than their staggering attractiveness.

They were all giving their attention, whether fully or partially, to one thing—one man, to be specific—a man who lounged on a white chaise and exuded power. He was a man richly dressed, and seemed accustomed to getting what he wanted. He was a man as handsome as any Hollywood actor, and he was well aware of his charms. He was a man surrounded by fawning women, and the most beautiful things in the world. And he was a man who was staring directly . . . at me.

"Hello," he said warmly as he flashed me a winning smile, one that had probably enchanted every woman he'd ever encountered in his long life. Though he hadn't moved from his reclined position, I got the sense that his relaxed appearance was a front, and that in the blink of an eye he could either have a knife at my throat or throw me over his shoulder and carry me off. I wasn't sure which one he was more inclined to do at the moment, but either way, I knew that this man, this . . . god . . . was dangerous. The dimple on the side of his mouth and the mischievous twinkle in his eye were disconcerting.

Instead of answering him, I merely nodded deferentially and tightened my grip on Nebu's mane. The unicorn spoke up. *Allow me to introduce Lily. She is a newly made sphinx who seeks an audience with Amun-Ra.*

Horus heard what Nebu said, but his eyes never left mine. It made both me and Tia uncomfortable. *The god stares us down*, she murmured. *He challenges us!*

No, I said. *He is taking our measure. Be patient.*

Smoothly, Horus rose from the chaise. He was tall, lean, and muscled but not overly so, and as he approached, Tia remarked that he moved like a jungle cat, purposely, slowly, his eyes never leaving his prey. *Horus stalks us,* she hissed.

I ignored her and narrowed my eyes, taking in his rakish expression and his handsome, angular face. My fingers itched for the weapons on my back, but I forced a smile to my lips while placing my hands on my hips, showing him that I wasn't afraid. I was perfectly capable of defending myself.

When he stopped a few feet away and the air between us became thick with expectation, I finally inclined my head and said, "It's nice to meet you."

A small laugh crossed his lips as he tilted his head to study us. "Yes," he murmured, a rich tone to his voice that told me each word he spoke carried a thousand possibilities. "Very nice." Without looking at anything but me, he raised his fingers in the air, twisted them with a flourish, and said, "You may leave us. I've found my . . . distraction for the evening." He shot me a smile warm enough to melt the sun.

At those words, every woman in the room faded away as quickly as an ice cube in the desert. I swallowed, suddenly nervous, and spent the next few seconds dissuading Tia from calling up her claws.

"You too, Nebu," Horus said.

I think not, the stallion answered, causing the god to finally glance in his direction. *She is not here to sate your appetites,* Nebu warned.

Horus grinned and turned back to me, boldly taking my hand and kissing my fingers. "Perhaps I am here to tend to hers, then." Horus raised his head and gave me a meaningful wink. At that, I lost control of Tia. One second my hand was being kissed by a god and the next, I'd raked my claws across his palm, causing instant and deep cuts, then pulled my hand far away from his. Instead of blood, light pooled at each of his wounds and then quickly healed.

The attack didn't bother Horus. Actually, it appeared to do just the opposite. Seemingly beguiled, he took a step closer, slid his hand up the still-extended claw to my bare arm, and murmured enticingly, "How refreshing. There's nothing I like more than a woman who offers a challenge."

As fast as Tia emerged, she retreated and I was in control once more. I took a step back and moved around him, putting Nebu at my back so that the god had to turn around to face us. "The unicorn is right. We haven't come here to"—I searched my mind for a word that would be clear and yet not insulting—"bask in your glory." He raised an eyebrow but his lips twitched with humor.

"Then, please, enlighten me as to the reason you've decided to gift me with your company."

"I'm here—we're here," I corrected, "to ask permission to ride the celestial barque into the netherworld."

"Ah, I see." Horus walked over to the table and filled two golden goblets. After presenting me with one, he raised the other in my direction and lifted the cup to his full lips. "Why are you still here, Nebu?" he asked, a slight tinge of irritation to his voice. "I thought I asked you to leave."

You did. I simply wish to assure the young lady's safety first.

"You doubt my abilities to function as a proper host?" he asked with a roguish wink in my direction.

On the contrary, I have no doubts as to your abilities. I have doubts as to your intentions.

"I see. Then what can I do to persuade you that my intentions are entirely honorable?"

You can swear on your golden falcon.

Horus spun to face Nebu. "You should know better, *Unicorn,* than dare a god to swear by the very piece of himself that has been cut off. Should I have you swear on your alicorn and the powers you have lost? You go too far, Nebu."

Is he speaking of Amon's golden falcon? I wondered. *If so, he doesn't sound happy that Amon has it.*

I apologize if I have broached a tender subject, Nebu addressed Horus. *It is merely that I know how very precious the falcon is to you and I know that if you made a vow by it that you would not break it.*

The wide shoulders of Horus lowered slightly but the handsome man finally nodded and waved his hand in dismissal. "Very well, I swear on the wings of my golden falcon that I will not harm the young sphinx or use my powers to influence her in any way."

Thank you. Nebu took a few steps toward me and nuzzled my arm. *I must depart now, Lily. I do not have the leave to deny a request of Horus. But should you have need of me at any time or in any place, use your young man's spell to summon me. I will come if at all possible.*

"Thank you, Nebu," I said quietly.

You are welcome. Do not forget, young sphinx, I will someday return to collect my boon. The unicorn pushed his head into my arm for a final time, then stretched his great shimmering wings and leapt into the air. He rose higher and higher until he reached the domed ceiling of the atrium, and with the twitch of Horus's fingers, the roof opened up to the night sky and he disappeared.

When Nebu was gone, Horus approached me, walking around to the other side of the chaise I'd just sat upon, and draped across it once again. He captured my hand in his and trailed kisses from my now human fingertips up my arm to my shoulder.

Nervously, I said, "You promised Nebu you wouldn't use your powers to influence me."

"I'm not using my powers," he said, lips tickling my skin. "I'm seducing you with my all-too-human magnetism."

"Be that as it may, I already have a boyfriend. Besides, your mother, Isis, said you'd help me."

Horus sighed and lifted his head. "Don't you know it's never a good thing to mention a man's mother whilst he is in the middle of rendering you mindless with passion?"

"I'm hardly mindless with passion."

"Yes," he said with a frown. "Why is that? I usually don't have this much difficulty convincing a woman to succumb to my charms."

"Maybe I'm just not as susceptible as the women you generally associate with."

"No. That's not it."

"I'm pretty sure it is."

He peered at me closely, his chiseled jaw inches from my face. If he'd wanted to, he could have closed the distance between us as easily as a thought, but instead his eyes narrowed, as if searching for something beneath my skin. For a moment, I thought he was looking for Tia, that he might sense her within me, but had he found something else.

Shaking his head lightly as if confused, he touched a fingertip to my chin, tilting my head one way, then another. He pressed his fingertips against my heart; then his eyes widened as he looked down at my brooch. "What is this?" he said with a tiny note of alarm. "How did this come to be?"

Horus backed away from me and stared at the heart scarab as if it were a deadly scorpion. Pointing at it, he asked, "Did you do this on purpose to trick me?"

"Trick you?" I said with a small, worried laugh. "No." I placed my hand over the smooth scarab and felt the little tickle of Amon's heart. Then, under my breath, I whispered softly, "Anubis warned me that immortals would react to it."

"Of course we react to it!" Horus spat, anger coloring his handsome features as he sprang to his feet. "You nearly had me trapped under the same spell as this poor fellow who you've obviously tied to you unawares. Was he not enough of a conquest for you, Sphinx? Did you need to add a god to your list of supplicants?"

"Now, wait just a minute!" I shouted, angered by his allegations and feeling the need to stand up for myself, even if my accuser happened to be an all-powerful god. I stood, jabbing a finger into the air. "Amon wove this spell, not me. If anyone was unaware of it, I was. You have no right to blame me for anything. Especially when it was the action—or inaction, I should say—of you and Amun-Ra that caused Amon to do what he did in the first place. If anyone is to blame for this, it's you and your fellow gods!"

Horus stood on the other side of the chaise, chest heaving, hands balled into fists. Roughly, he ran a hand through his thick brown hair, and then he froze, a spark flashing in his dark eyes. "By the netherworld's darkest pits," he muttered huskily as he vaulted over the chaise and took me into his arms. I struggled against his grip but was unable to move. He brushed his lips against my throat and groaned softly. "Even now, knowing it isn't real, I find I cannot resist you. The sweep of your neck, the curve of your cheek, the scent of your skin, all of it is heady, evocative. You must not deny me, Lily."

Bending me over his arm, Horus swept me up in a dramatic, knee-buckling kiss. It was passionate, drugging, and powerful, and even though I pushed against him, he wasn't deterred in any way. In fact, my movements seemed to add more hunger to the fire fueling him.

I was struggling, trying to figure out how to slide my hands out from between our bodies and over my head to grab my weapon, when a voice rang out in the atrium, effectively cooling the ardor Horus was overwhelmed by.

The authoritative voice carried behind it the strength of a thousand suns. "What do you think you are doing, Nephew?"

And as Horus finally lifted his head, the deep pools of his eyes glazed with passion, a crack of thunder echoed in the sky above us.

12

The Waters of Chaos

"Uncle! I was . . ." Horus looked like a little boy caught with his hand in the cookie jar. As he hemmed and hawed, trying to find an answer to Amun-Ra's question, there was absolutely no doubt in my mind that the man who stood before us was indeed the sun god. I continued to try to wriggle loose from Horus's grip.

"I know perfectly well what you were doing. Unhand the maiden at once."

A blush stained the cheeks of the god who'd been ardently kissing me a moment before, and he let me go. Horus stepped back, but his eyes kept flicking toward me as if it pained him to be even an arm's length away. I steeled my shoulders, straightened my disheveled clothing, and curtsied to the golden god who stood before me.

Why did you let him kiss us? I asked Tia in my mind. *That would have been the appropriate time to pull the claws out! I'm not good enough at it yet to do it on my own.*

I enjoyed his caress, she replied simply. *He was very . . . ardent. I admire a male who goes after what he wants. Perhaps I love this man.*

Seriously? Trust me when I say you don't. You hardly know him. And let me remind you, we aren't open to the attentions of other males. We have Amon.

You *have Amon,* she reminded me. *I have no one.*

Well, you can't have him. *He's a god, and a very lusty god, at that. He'd conquer you and move on to the next pretty face within a week at best, a day more likely.*

I no longer have a pretty face. I borrow yours, remember? Speaking of pretty faces . . .

We'll talk about this later, I warned her.

Amun-Ra was easily over six feet tall, and he was handsome, but not in the same pretty-boy sort of way Horus was. Amun-Ra's attractiveness lay more in the strength of his form and the confidence of his bearing. His eyes were the lightest shade of brown I'd ever seen—nearly golden, like amber—and his skin was slightly darker than Horus's, but there was a light that emanated from him. I could feel his warmth fill the space, the air nearly humming with it as he approached. Sweat beaded at my temple and began trickling down my cheek, and Amun-Ra took notice as I wiped it away.

"I apologize for making you uncomfortable," he said. He closed his eyes and the light visibly leeched from his skin. His eyes changed from the palest sand color to a rich caramel to a chocolate brown. I realized I'd been squinting, and blinked as if seeing him for the first time. The shape of his face was angular. His chin pointed. And there was a dimple in the center of it. From out of nowhere a servant girl brought him a goblet glistening with condensation. He drank deeply from the cup and then gazed at his nephew, eyebrows lifted. "Well?" he asked.

Horus sprang to attention. "Uncle. Allow me to introduce Lily, a newly made sphinx who seeks an audience."

"Ah," Amun-Ra said. "And who is the other one?"

"Other one?" Horus mumbled with an expression of confusion. "There is no one else here."

"There most assuredly is," Amun-Ra answered. "Perhaps your hands were too busy to notice that you held not one woman in your arms but two."

Oh I like him even better than the first one. He notices me. Can we kiss him next? I'd like to feel the muscles of his arms. I will choose him.

What? No! I channeled back to her.

"Two? How is that possible?" Horus asked in bewilderment.

Ignoring him, Amun-Ra asked, "And who are you, my dear?"

I knew he wasn't talking to me and reluctantly nudged Tia forward. "I am Lily's lioness," she purred in the gravelly, more luscious version of my voice. "My name is Tia."

"Welcome, Tia," Amun-Ra said as he inclined his head. "I have been told that the two of you have traveled far to see me."

"We have," I said, quickly gaining control over my body again before Tia tried to lick Amun-Ra's earlobes. Figures I'd get stuck with a lioness in heat.

I heard that, she said. *I am* not *in heat. It's just that your unicorn was right. I find I enjoy the sensation of being petted by a human. Speaking of warmth, though, this one makes me feel as if I'm basking on my favorite sunning rock.*

I shushed her as the newly arrived god addressed us.

"Please, won't the two of you join me for a late meal?" he asked, and I knew he meant me and Tia, not me and Horus. "I find I am famished after a tour of Duat."

It has been long since we've eaten, Tia reminded me.

"We'd love to," I said, and took his arm when he extended it, gritting my teeth as I exerted strenuous mental control to stop Tia from squeezing his bicep. Horus followed behind us, sulking but unwilling to let me out of his sight. His busy hands kept stroking my arm, and when I pushed them away, Tia took the opportunity to move closer to the sun god. She also kept sending me impulses to turn my head and admire the cut of Amun-Ra's frame. His curly head of hair reminded her of a lion's mane, and she liked the way he smelled. *Stop it!* I said to her, and focused on the rushing of servants instead as we walked through the long hallways.

"Your home is beautiful," I remarked, attempting to ease into some small talk.

"Thank you."

We entered the dining room, and though Horus made a stumbling attempt to sit next to me, Amun-Ra bluntly told him that his seat would be on the opposite side. Though many women bustled around bringing dish after dish to the table, the three of us were the only diners. When our goblets had been filled with a golden liquid Amun-Ra called ambrosia, the servants lifted the domes off the dishes as one.

Fragrant steam wafted from platters filled with orange duck, creamy mashed root vegetables, a salad dotted with edible flowers, and a sort of pudding dessert that snapped with fire, and my mouth watered. I hadn't realized just how hungry I was. Amon would have appreciated Tia's zest for feasting. Having long gotten over my need to maintain my New York City svelte figure, it wasn't too hard for Tia to convince me to enjoy second and even third helpings. I ate until I was so stuffed I could barely move.

"Thank you," I said when I was done. I dabbed the corners of my mouth carefully with my napkin, even though Tia would have preferred that I sweep my lips with a fully extended tongue. Seeing Horus groan in near pain as he watched me do something as simple as patting my lips was bad enough already. If I had done what Tia wanted, he'd likely expire on the spot. I threatened her that I would happily never eat meat again if she continued sending me her brazen thoughts, and she sulkily retreated to the back of my mind and listened moodily.

Since, thanks to Tia, it was at the forefront of my mind, I asked Amun-Ra, "Why are you not as affected by me as Horus is? Even Anubis seemed to be having problems with my heart scarab."

Amun-Ra leaned back, his eyes twinkling. "It affects me as much as the next man, but I have more self-control than my nephew. He hasn't practiced the discipline of self-denial much over the years. To put it frankly, he's weak."

Horus finally broke eye contact with me and glared furiously at his uncle. "You shame me."

"You shame yourself," Amun-Ra replied with a sigh and a shake of his head that indicated he wasn't angry with his nephew at all but more frustrated. "If you exercised self-control, you would find the temptation easier to bear."

"Is it that painful, then?" I asked.

"It is the worst kind of pain," Horus exclaimed. "I see you sitting there so close and yet I feel every fraction of distance between us as if each is an unbreachable, unending chasm. I am undone by it."

Amun-Ra rolled his eyes at Horus. "Do I need to banish you from the room?"

Horus gasped as if someone had punched him in the gut. "Please do not jest with me like that. I cannot leave her."

"I am entirely serious. If you wish to remain, then you will keep your overtly swooning comments to yourself. Lily and Tia do not need to bear your insufferable fascination."

Grinding his teeth, Horus nodded pertly and went back to his quiet staring.

"Is everyone in the netherworld going to react that way?" I asked. "Or does it only apply to immortals that are more . . . human?"

"It will have an influence over every immortal. The form doesn't matter. Even Nebu was charmed, though he is in love with another, which generally protects one from the scarab's pull. Then again, perhaps he simply likes you. That's always a possibility. You'll never know, really. Besides, you're assuming I'll allow you to enter the netherworld in the first place. And I'll warn you right now, I'm not inclined to do it."

"What? After all I've . . . we've done? I've come so far, and Tia, well, Tia has given up everything!"

Amun-Ra held up a hand. "Please do not misunderstand me. I am not unsympathetic to what you've gone through; it's just that I do not hold with the theory that the universe will come to an end should Seth return."

"Uncle!" Horus exclaimed.

"What do you mean?" I asked at the same time.

Scrubbing a hand through his dark, close-cropped curls, Amun-Ra said, "Seth was not always the incarnate of everything evil that Horus believes him to be."

"He's had too many chances at redemption. He is beyond hope," Horus declared.

Giving his nephew a meaningful look, Amun-Ra said, "No one is beyond hope. You especially should know that."

Horus sank in his chair, a scowl marring his handsome features. "After all he's done to me, I'd like to think you'd take my side."

"I did take your side. Time and time again I took your side. Even when it might have changed the outcome if I hadn't." Amun-Ra turned to me. "Horus makes Seth out to be a horned devil with a forked tongue and cloven hooves, and perhaps in some instances, he depicts himself in such a way, but that is not the boy I knew him to be."

"You knew him when he was young?" I asked.

"Has no one told you the story of Seth?"

I shook my head.

Amun-Ra frowned. "Perhaps it will be better understood if I start at the beginning."

I sat back in my chair and basked in the warmth of Amun-Ra's presence. Tia dozed like a sleepy cat—half of her listening and aware while the other half stretched out lazily in perfect serenity.

"I was the first god who came into being," Amun-Ra began. "At one time there was a space in the cosmos where matter collided, a sort of primordial jumble of thriving energy. We called it the Waters of Chaos since the matter ebbs and flows there like a multifaceted ocean. It remained confined in one place as well as if the fluid material comprising it were trapped in a colossal ball of glass. When one of our stars—not a sun such as you know, but the magical orbs that ring our world—fell, it collided with the Waters of Chaos and I was born.

"For a long time I wandered from place to place, discovering the limitations of my strength, but as the eons passed, I found I was lonely. I determined to make myself companions and used my power to hurl two more stars into the waters. Shu and Tefnut emerged from the Chaos. They married and Tefnut gave birth to Nut and Geb. Do you know of them?"

"Amon told me about Nut and Geb having to be apart."

"Yes. That was my fault. By the time Nut and Geb married, we realized—let me rephrase, *I* realized—what we had done. And as a result, I forbade them from having children."

"What do you mean? What did you do?" I asked.

"You see, we were never meant to be. When I rose from the Waters of Chaos, I took something from it. The warmth and life-giving heat of the stars went with me. I did not know it at the time, but my creation left it lesser, and when Shu and Tefnut were born, they rose with the power of the wind and of the water. When they did, those elements went missing from the Waters of Chaos.

"I was alarmed by my discovery, to say the least. The others didn't believe me, and Nut and Geb were far too enamored with each other to listen to my warnings. Even though I sent their father, Shu, to keep them apart, they managed to find a way to be together. They gave birth to Isis, Osiris, Nephthys, and Seth, and when their children came into their various powers, my theory was proved correct. After that, there were only small fragments of life-giving energy left in the Waters. It was undeniable. The rest of my family finally agreed with my theory."

"So what did you do?" I asked, fascinated by the story of his origin despite the distraction of having to repeatedly kick Horus's foot away from mine. Finally I shifted my chair far enough out of his range that he would have had to get up to reach me. Vexed, he shot me a tormented look so full of wanting, heat crept up my neck.

"Nothing at first. We weren't sure what we *could* do. But ultimately we decided to finish what we had begun. Through eons of study, we learned that the Waters of Chaos had been, at one time, the birthplace of all life in the cosmos. The circumstances of our creation had left it nearly bereft, sterile. The nine of us came together in a great council called the Ennead, and even though the children of Geb and Nut were still too young to understand fully, we made a pact.

"We fashioned lesser gods from the remaining traces of the Waters of Chaos. Anubis, Ma'at, Thoth, Khons, Bastet, and several others came into being at that time. We carefully distributed the remaining powers of the Waters of Chaos between them and then that once vast, fertile sea was gone. Each new god was constrained to make an unbreakable vow to join us in taking upon ourselves the burden of caring for the cosmos.

"A set of laws was established, and we turned our attention to fashioning mortals. Worlds more numerous than you can conceive have been shaped and nurtured by us. Your Earth became our most cherished achievement. When we were satisfied with the work we'd done, I built Heliopolis and settled here to watch over the many worlds and the beings that inhabited them.

"Now our duties include being the champions of the poor and fostering truth, goodness, and justice. Our aim is to use our powers to attain perfection and harmony. We took the ankh as our symbol, for it represents life and it reminds us of what was sacrificed so that we could come into being.

"We move through the universe like a great wind stirring the fires of progress. Though we are unseen by mortals, our presence can be sensed in every dawn, every sunset, every brush of scented air on your cheek, and every raindrop. We are a part of everything and everything is a part of us."

"So Seth was one of you, then?" I asked.

"Yes," he replied. "Seth was a happy, curious child. He loved his family, was fascinated by the way the worlds were made, but the day he was imbued with his powers, everything changed. At the time, I thought we were being punished. That there was nothing left for him to inherit. I didn't see it for what it was."

"What happened? What powers did he get?"

"He received the most terrible and mightiest power of all of us. One that had the potential to destroy everything we'd created—"

"Wait. If you made an unbreakable vow to protect the Earth and pretty much everything else in the cosmos, then why was Seth trying to destroy the ancient Egyptians? Didn't he have control over his new power? Why did you have to recruit Amon and his brothers to stop him? Why is he in a cosmic holding cell, and why was Sebak so adamant about wanting him loosed?"

I knew I was rushing him and asking too many questions. It was obvious. But I felt the weight of saving Amon pressing upon me, and Tia's directness had influenced me to push for answers that we weren't getting. I was growing impatient with the process of learning what we needed to know.

"Seth didn't technically break his vow," Amun-Ra said. "He just sees things a little differently."

"A little differently?" Horus exclaimed. "He seeks our demise!"

Amun-Ra sighed. "Seth has a different definition for caring for the cosmos. You see, he came into his powers much later than his siblings. Isis was a powerful spell maker. Osiris ruled over things unseen and could call upon the elements to do his bidding. Nephthys's power was quiet, subdued. She could see into the very heart of a person and understand them fully, truly, in a way no one else could. This is why she became Seth's wife."

"But he didn't love her," I said. "He wanted Isis."

"Yes. He wanted her but he didn't love her. At least, not in the way Osiris did. Seth was obsessed with Isis and her power. He wanted to use her to make his spells. His wife, Nephthys, became intensely jealous, not because she didn't love her sister, for she did, but she needed and craved the love Osiris shared with his wife. She wanted that with Seth. Unfortunately, he was not in the correct frame of mind to offer that."

"He never will be either," Horus interjected.

"I'm afraid I still don't understand," I said.

"That's because I've gotten ahead of myself. The only reason I even bring up Seth's relationship with his siblings is balance."

"Balance," I echoed.

"Yes. Each god was given a gift, every one of them important in a different way. Seth's gift was perhaps the most important of all because he is how the universe maintains balance."

"How so?" I asked.

"He's evil," Horus explained. "He balances out our goodness." Amun-Ra frowned but he didn't contradict his nephew, who, emboldened by his uncle's pause, continued. "Seth was created to stir up trouble. The cosmos needs that spark of dissonance, that cord of uncertainty to create. Without it there is only perfection. How do you understand up if there isn't a down? Or comprehend love without hate?"

"So let me make sure I'm getting this. Seth's job was to cause contention, purposely, so that . . . what? Mortals don't get too complacent? Too happy?" I asked.

"It's a bit more complicated than that," Amun-Ra said. "There is a place for chaos. Humans understand and appreciate peace only if they know the horrors of war. They can only grow if there is an obstacle to overcome. The cosmos is only balanced if there is a way to experience the bad along with the good."

"Okay." I folded my arms across my chest. "Then what went wrong? Why is he locked up?"

Horus seemed unwilling to answer this time and deferred to Amun-Ra, who sucked in a breath. "Seth is imprisoned not because of causing chaos but because he wants to unmake *all* that we have created."

"Including us," Horus added.

"What? Why would he want to do that?"

"He's jealous," Horus said pettily. "He wants to rule it all."

Amun-Ra narrowed his eyes at his nephew. "Seth seems to have determined that the only way to truly bring balance back to the cosmos is to attempt to refill the Waters of Chaos."

I tilted my head. "But I thought you said they'd been completely drained."

"They have been," he answered.

"Then how would he refill them?"

"He'd destroy us all in the hope that when we died, our energies would return to the place they originated from," Horus said. "The only exception in his mind would be him and his chosen mate, Isis. With Isis at his side and the Waters of Chaos filled with our life energies, he believes that the balance would be restored with one perfect god and one perfect goddess to rule it all."

"That's a long shot. Isn't it?" I asked. "I mean, there's no guarantee that your life energies would refill the Waters of Chaos, is there?" Horus glanced at Amun-Ra and a long, meaningful look passed between them. "What?" I pressed.

"When Seth made his first move, the attempt that took Osiris's life, a part of the power that Osiris had been endowed with returned to the Waters and another portion, we are unsure as to how much, remained with the one who murdered him."

"Seth," I declared, blowing out a breath.

Amun-Ra nodded. "Isis stopped the process before it was fully realized and used a powerful spell to remake her husband, but he was not the same as he once was. He was lesser somehow. Isis made it clear to all of us then that she wanted no part of Seth's plan and that she considered him her enemy."

"Yes, Osiris, her husband, was the first mummy. Right?" I shifted forward in my seat and sipped from my goblet.

"Correct," Amun-Ra said. "When Isis became pregnant, a thing that was forbidden, there was very little energy in the Waters of Chaos to create a god. I had to bestow their child with some of my powers so that he might live.

"Because of this, we learned that our powers could be freely offered to another. That is how you became a sphinx, after all. Isis gifted her lions with a portion of her power, and now that energy resides in the two of you."

I folded my arms. "I'm surprised you didn't punish her for creating the sphinx spell like you did when she tried to save her husband. It's cruel to keep them apart."

"Isis misunderstands my intentions. What you see as cruel, I see as necessary. Isis broke the law and a consequence had to follow. Despite the law, I am merciful. They are allowed to see one another. As often as her duties allow, I grant her permission to visit the afterlife."

"Still, it seems wrong to separate two people who love each other like that."

Amun-Ra steepled his fingers and considered me. "Sometimes sacrifices must be made and we must give up the thing we want most in the world so that others might live contented and happy. Isn't that right, Nephew?"

"Wouldn't he actually be your great-grandson, not a nephew?" I asked.

"The life I instilled within him called for a reevaluation of our relationship," he said with a frown. "He is actually closer to a son to me now than anything else, but Osiris chafes at the mere suggestion of it, so I took on the role of his uncle instead. Willful though my charge may be."

Horus righted himself in his chair with as much dignity as he could muster. "I had to grow up quickly and try to protect myself. Seth came after me at a young age," he said with a yearning look in my direction.

"You fought with him. Amon told me," I said.

"Yes. Seth saw me as the weakest of the gods and therefore the easiest to destroy. He knew Amun-Ra was much too powerful to come after him directly, so his plan was to siphon off the energy of the lesser gods first, starting with me. I also represented his defeat, for I was the product of the union he failed to extinguish. He declared my birth an illegal act willfully realized by my corrupted parents, and one that deserved the ultimate punishment. I was the embodiment of the very thing he despised the most, and he was determined to kill me until Amun-Ra intervened."

"Isis became naturally distraught after Seth made several attempts to kill Horus," Amun-Ra added. "She poisoned me in an effort to learn Seth's true name so that she might destroy him before he killed her son."

"Hold on. Amon told me that Isis poisoned you so that she could find out *your* true name so that you would help Horus. He said she wanted Horus to be your heir."

"Either one would have served her purpose," Amun-Ra went on. "If she obtained Seth's true name, she could put an end to him, and if she had mine, then she could control me and make me destroy him for her. I am the only one powerful enough to do it, not having given birth to any children of my own. And being the first god to come forth from the Waters of Chaos afforded me the opportunity to learn the true names of all the members in my family. Isis wanted to stop Seth once and for all. If any of us survived the unmaking Seth was attempting, she wanted it to be Horus. When I refused to give up either of our names, she asked me to take Horus under my protection instead, and I did."

"So you made him your heir?"

"I don't see my relationships with my family members in that way. We are all equal in my mind. Even those gods who have more limited powers have duties that are vitally important in the creation and maintenance of the universe."

"I disagree, Uncle."

"I know you do. But I cannot help loving Seth as much as I love you or your mother." He turned to me. "To soothe her, I told Isis that Horus would receive the opportunity to win a special gift, one that would make him powerful enough to ensure that Seth could not destroy him, but that Horus would need to pass a series of challenges before winning it. It was not a gift I gave away lightly."

"You're talking about the Eye of Horus, aren't you?" I asked.

"Yes. When I presented Horus with the three trials to test his worthiness, Seth appeared and demanded that he be included. I thought a supervised competition between the two gods might go a long way toward helping Seth return to the fold, to give Seth a chance to prove himself and show the others that he was not the man they thought he was. But Seth used his powers to unmake Horus's eyes. In losing his vision, Horus saw clearly for the first time. His suffering helped him to understand the needs of others. And I knew then that he was truly worthy of the prize."

"I found Nebu," he said. "Even blind I was able to defeat Seth, thanks to the falcon who kept me alive."

"Wait," I interrupted. "Amon told me you never found Nebu, that the one who did would become the heir of the sun god."

"Nebu and I disagree on the matter of who found who," Horus answered with a cocky smile. "Even so, Seth didn't like what happened next."

Amun-Ra grunted. "Seth was angry, but even he could not find fault with my decision. Horus was given new eyes, including my most powerful gift, currently in use by your young man, Amon. Despite outward appearances, Horus does make sacrifices for the greater good from time to time."

"Amon is currently in possession of my golden falcon *and* the Eye," Horus groused. "That's why I've been grounded here for so long. Without the Eye, I'm vulnerable. Perhaps the company of a beautiful woman—women," he corrected with a wave of his hand to indicate both me and Tia, "will help me forget my troubles."

I completely ignored him while Amun-Ra twitched, clearly at his wits' end with Horus's lovesickness. "Insufferable as your manners are, you have earned the right to live under my protection for as long as I have the power to keep Seth at bay. And I would remind you that he is contained. Your exile in Heliopolis is self-imposed."

I spoke up. "So when did that happen? Imprisoning Seth, I mean."

"Despite my feelings on the subject," Amun-Ra said, "the gods rallied against Seth after he nearly killed Horus, and he was cast out from our home. For a while, he left us in peace. But then Seth realized that if he destroyed the things we'd wrought, the energies of our designs, as feeble and as mortal as they were, would also return to the Waters of Chaos. Those energies would then be refashioned, and a portion, regardless of how minuscule it was, would remain with him. Wars erupted. Murderers thrived. Bloodthirsty men took power. We did what we could to counteract it, but the vow we'd made to use our powers for the benefit of others kept our hands tied. We were unable to contain him. All we could do was try to fix what he destroyed. But he became so skillful at wreaking devastation that there was often nothing left to repair.

"This was when Nephthys presented the idea of imbuing humans with our powers. She sought out three worthy young men who were willing to sacrifice themselves to protect their loved ones, and we gifted the striplings with the power to keep Seth contained. Because they were not limited by our vow, they were able to do what we could not."

"Not all of the gifts were willingly given, I'll remind you," Horus murmured.

Arching a brow, Amun-Ra said, "Some were reluctant, and I'll admit I was one of them. I was certain we could talk to Seth and figure out a way to resolve his concerns."

"That's why I had to step up," Horus said. "The Ennead approached us for help, and when Amun-Ra wouldn't comply, I had to offer my powers, as well as the golden falcon, to your Amon."

I reached across the table and took his hand, and so incredulously happy was his expression, you would think I'd just agreed to marry him. "I've ridden on the back of the falcon," I said. "He's beautiful. I can see why you miss him."

Horus wrapped his fingers around mine and squeezed lightly, giving me a genuine smile for the first time, and not one glazed by lust. "He's been my truest companion since he saved me in the desert," Horus said earnestly.

I half smiled in return and slowly removed my hand from his. "So Amon and his brothers keep Seth locked up for you, then, by performing the rite they do every thousand years?" I asked.

"Yes. They are the . . . How should I put it so that you can understand? They are the gatekeepers, the guardians of the prison," Amun-Ra answered. "But they did not create its walls. A bigger sacrifice was necessary before we could contain him."

My fingertips tightened on the table edge. "A bigger sacrifice than the Sons of Egypt giving up their lives time and time again? Not being able to live or love freely? Never being able to find happiness for themselves or having a family of their own?"

"Yes," Amun-Ra answered frankly.

"What's a bigger sacrifice than that?" I demanded.

"We lost our grandparents," Horus murmured.

"What?"

"Our grandparents, Shu and Tefnut, willingly gave up their corporeal forms and created a place in the cosmos, a prison made of wind and water that confines Seth. Every millennium, bits and pieces of the beings they once were siphon off and return to the Waters of Chaos. The Sons of Egypt provide reinforcement but it's really only a matter of time until the prison is weakened enough that he will break through," Horus said.

Stunned, I asked, "Well, what will you do then?"

"Amun-Ra thinks we should just let it happen. Let Seth come for us."

"But that means he'll kill you all," I said.

"Probably," Horus answered. "What's worse, though, is that he'll destroy everything we've created. Including your world."

"Anubis said he'd enslave us if he got free," I murmured.

"That's likely," Horus said. "Either that or he'd just unmake the entire planet."

"Look, if there's one thing in the universe worth living for, worth fighting for, it's love. I love Amon. He's suffering and I want to stop his suffering, plain and simple. If that helps the world, even better. If that means Seth stays incarcerated for another couple thousand years, then I'm good with that. I consider him your problem, not mine. Now, the two of you can either help us find Amon or we'll figure out a way to do it ourselves.

"I'm not asking for you to watch over me, lend me power, or even protect me from what awaits us. Odds are we won't even survive, but we've got to try. All I want is permission to travel to the netherworld. Nothing more. I appreciate your story. I understand your dilemma. But we've been sitting here rehashing the past long enough. It's time to take action.

"So I guess the real question is, Are you two gods going to stand up and act like the omnipotent, omniscient beings you're supposed to be? Or are you going to sit here and wallow in the past until it's too late to accomplish anything meaningful and, as a result, relegate the innocent who have done nothing to deserve your disregard to a fate worse than death?"

13

Turquoise Trees

Amun-Ra tapped his lip with a forefinger, contemplating what he was going to do with me, while Horus smiled broadly. "Oh, I *like* her, Uncle. Please say I can keep her."

The sun god ignored his nephew and instead studied me. Finally, he shook his head. "I cannot help you." When I opened my mouth to protest, he held up his finger. "It goes against everything I believe to assist any member of my family in the overthrowing of another. If Seth escapes, he escapes, and I will use the opportunity to guide him in the correct path as I did before. I must remain neutral, no matter the consequences, no matter the cost."

"But—" I managed to get out before he cut me off.

"However, I will make no attempt to stop you should you wish to travel to the netherworld."

"You know he'll never agree to take her without your approval," Horus protested.

"Lily and Tia have a pronounced ability to talk immortals into supporting their agenda. I have no doubt they'll convince him."

"Who's him?" I asked, but both gods disregarded my question.

Amun-Ra rose from his chair and a servant girl immediately

appeared. "Please escort this young sphinx to a sleeping chamber," he instructed her, "and do not allow Horus to know which one."

The girl nodded and indicated I should follow. Horus cried out in surprise, making a fumbling attempt to jostle his way around Amun-Ra to join me. "Relax, Nephew, you shall see her again before she departs on the morrow."

After we turned down several hallways and smooth-tiled corridors, the girl came to a stop.

"Here is your chamber," she said. "I'll return just before dawn to help you with your ritual bath."

"Ritual bath?" I echoed.

"Yes. You do wish to enter the netherworld, correct?"

"I do. I just didn't know there was a special bath involved."

"To enter the afterlife as a mortal, you must first cross the sky river and present yourself for judgment. If accepted, you will then be granted access to the netherworld."

"Judgment? Who will be judging us?" I asked.

"Ma'at, of course. Your heart must be weighed. That is why you must prepare yourself ahead of time."

The object that was now the subject of our discussion began thumping wildly. *Are they going to rip it out of my chest? Was I going to have to die before walking the pathways of the afterlife and the netherworld?*

After she left, I paced the room until Tia reminded me that I needed to rest. She was right; I wouldn't have enough energy to convince the gatekeeper to the afterlife, let alone save Amon. Obediently, I washed my face and put on the nightgown the servant had laid out.

I settled into the bed, closing my eyes and attempting to sleep, but several hours passed until rest found me. Even then, my dreams took me to the netherworld.

Amon was awake and traveling through a forest, unlike any I'd ever seen before. The blue trees shimmered, moving in the breeze like wind chimes, their leaves coated with what appeared to be sparkling minerals or sugar.

Though it was raining and he turned his open mouth to the sky, Amon caught nothing. His lips were chapped and he tried continually to wet them. That was when I saw her. A tiny sprite with translucent wings sat in the crook between the trunk and a branch of the tree watching him.

Finally, he spotted the little tree sprite. "I won't hurt you," he said kindly. "Please, don't be afraid."

"I'm not afraid," she said with a touch of an accent I couldn't place. "There are beasties who come to the Turquoise Forest who are much more frightening than you are. You're a strange sort of monster." She put her hands on her tiny waist.

"Am I?" he responded with a tired smile.

"Oh yes. Are ya going ta try ta sting me like the ol' scorpion? Perhaps ya can't. It looks as if yer tail is missing."

"I don't have a tail."

"Pity. His tail is rather impressive. There's not much about ya that's impressive as far as I can see. Are ya a dosser, then?"

"I'm not sure what a dosser is. And I'm much more impressive with my weapons."

"A dosser's a fella up to no good. I don't see any weapons."

"No, then I'm not a dosser. My weapons are magical. I call them from the sand."

The sprite frowned. "We don't trust magical folk, but seeing as how yer knackered nigh ta death, ya don't seem to pose much of a threat. Been gawking at ya for the last two days."

"Oh. That's . . . good, I suppose?"

"Depends. I see your thirst is somethin' terrible."

"It is. I feel like a desiccated corpse left to dry to a husk in the blazing sun."

"Awful for ya, then, isn't it?" She scowled and then muttered, "I heard ya! Stop interferin', ya thick excuse for a tree. I suppose we can help," she said reluctantly to Amon.

"Can you?"

"Yes." Then a mischievous twinkle lit the fairy's eye. "Must be hard ta be so thirsty when it's been bucketing down like 'tis." She smiled mysteriously and lowered her voice. "I know how ta ask the tree ta give up her water. And ya

can't tell anyone that we helped ya, either," she warned. "It's my job ta guard this tree. If all the creatures in the netherworld knew how ta take her water, well, there wouldn't be any left for the trees, then, would there?"

"No, I suppose there wouldn't be."

The tree sprite crooked her finger at Amon to call him closer. "The secret," she whispered, "is in the wantin'. You can't want it."

"Not want it?" Amon questioned with a bewildered expression.

"Right. If the tree knows ya want it, then she won't let ya have it. She doesn't trust men very much."

"I see." Amon nodded soberly and took a step back, examining the great tree that stretched wide limbs over his head. "Well, Tree, I'm not thirsty. Nope. Not needing a drink at all, though I just crossed the desert of a thousand burning suns, where it was hot enough to make even a hell demon sweat and beg for relief."

Slowly, a thin limb crept closer to Amon and a broad blue leaf unfurled, showing that it held nearly a cupful of water.

Drinking deeply, Amon licked the last wet drops from his lips and smiled warmly. "Thank you. I wonder how it is that you and your tree ended up stuck in the netherworld."

The sprite said sadly, "We were tricked into coming here."

"Tricked? How?" he asked.

"This is a fairy tree and she used ta be on the top of a lovely hill in Ireland."

Now her accent made sense. She spoke with a lovely lilt to her voice—an Irish brogue I could listen to for hours. "An' I loved her even before I even knew she was magical," she said. "I'd sit beneath her and dream about far-off places. Climb her branches and gaze up at the stars. It was a grand thing.

"One day a stranger eyed me at the market. Full of ill intent, he chased me until I found myself near the tree. She must'a known I was in danger, because the trunk opened and I leapt inside. It was dark, but it was better than what the man had planned for me."

"What happened then?" Amon asked.

"The man began chantin' a spell and the tree shook. The trunk cracked and great drops of sap trickled down over my hands. I heard the crash of one heavy

limb and then another. The man said she had to give up either me or her heart. Ya see, when a fairy tree gives up its heart, it releases great power.

"But she loved me and refused. Instead, she did something forbidden. She pierced the man's heart and killed 'im. She was struck down for it, died with me inside, and was sent here to the netherworld. When she was planted in the Turquoise Forest, my form changed ta this. Now it's my job ta take care of her, just like she took care of me."

"And you do a good job of it. Do you mind if I rest here awhile?" he asked.

"Do what ya like," the sprite said.

Amon put his back to the wide tree trunk and sank down to the forest floor, resting his arms on his knees and pressing his head against them.

"Amon?" I called. The sprite didn't react to my voice, but I sensed someone else was there watching me while I dreamed. "Amon?" I cried again.

"I'm here," a voice behind me answered.

"Amon!" I spun around and was in his arms before another second passed. I took his face in my hands and kissed his lips, his cheeks, never wanting to let him go.

He laughed and then groaned. "Lily, you're crushing me."

"Oh! I'm sorry." I took an awkward step back, but he offered me a sweet smile as he took hold of my shoulders and drew me close again.

Tilting his head, he studied me, the happy expression mixed together with one of curiosity. "You're stronger," he said. "Different."

"I know, I—"

"Wait." Amon ran his fingertip down my cheek. "Let me look at you first."

As Amon peered into my eyes, I got the sense he was looking for something specific. There was no sense of romance in his gaze.

"Are you using the Eye of Horus?"

"Yes," he murmured distractedly.

"What do you see?" I whispered, almost afraid of the answer.

He opened his mouth but paused, his eyes widening. "There's . . . there's too much." His glazed eyes focused on me once again, and the corners of his mouth turned up. "I'm just glad you're here," he said finally.

"Amon." Gripping his hand, I looked around and pulled him back to the

tree where his sleeping body rested. Biting my lip, I purposely moved to the other side of the trunk and sank down to the thick grass at its base, pulling him along with me. "We need to talk."

He nodded and stretched up to tuck a lock of hair behind my ear. His hand lingered there briefly, and then he captured both of my hands in his, as if afraid that if he let go, I'd disappear.

"First of all, you should know that I'm currently in Heliopolis."

Amon started. "You've made it that far already?"

"Haven't you been watching me when you dream?"

He shook his head. "Not in the last few days. I haven't been able to sleep as often as I'd like. Besides, I don't need sleep as much as a mortal, and this place affords very few safe places to rest."

I let out a breath, half relieved that he hadn't seen Horus's advances. "Right. Well, I've asked Amun-Ra for help, but so far he's not too interested. Horus, on the other hand . . ."

"Horus's hands will be tied if Amun-Ra refuses aid."

"Oh."

"It's still a long way to the netherworld, Lily. You should go back. You'll be safe. Nebu will take you."

"I can't. Not when we're so close."

Amon cupped my face in his hands. "This is enough, Nehabet," he said, gazing into my eyes. "What you've achieved is more than I could wish for. Being able to touch you, to hold you in my dreams, will carry me through endless torments."

Grasping his hands, I pulled them to my lips and kissed his palms tenderly. "It's not enough for me," I said softly. "I'm coming for you, Amon, whether you wish it or not."

He sighed softly and collapsed against the tree trunk. "I suppose I'm not surprised. You always were stubborn."

"Not stubborn," I said. "Determined."

His mouth twitched. "A determined sphinx. The gods must be shaking on their golden thrones."

"Not all of them," I sighed, tracing the lines on his palms. I glanced up at

his handsome face through lowered lashes to find him watching me. "What is it?" I asked.

"Are we going to talk about it?" he murmured.

"About what? There are a lot of things we could talk about."

"Yes. But there's one thing in particular you're avoiding."

"There is," I whispered, and couldn't help feeling a swell of emotion. A small stir in my mind told me Tia was listening. She'd been so quiet that I'd barely remembered she was there. It was likely she was giving me time to be with Amon.

Amon waited patiently, slowly rubbing my hand between his palms.

I sucked in a breath. "There's sort of someone in here with me," I said.

"The lioness?" he asked.

Nodding, I removed my hand from his and tugged at the grass, yanking it out and making a little pile next to me.

"I couldn't let her die. She knew I didn't want it and now we're both in here and . . ."

"What is really bothering you?"

"What do you mean?" I said, keeping my eyes locked on his for the first time since the topic came up.

"You're at peace with her. At least, as best I can tell. The Eye of Horus showed me that you will come to love one another if you don't already."

I blinked and realized that he was right. Having Tia around was disconcerting, but I did care about her.

"I do. I mean, I'm happy that she's alive. She . . . she's special." Tia's consciousness spread out a bit further, and I felt the contented brush of her mind touch mine. It was almost as if she was curled up next to me, offering her supportive companionship. Licking my lips, I wiped my sweaty palms against my thighs and got to my feet, nervously pacing. "I guess I've just been wondering if I . . . if we . . . I mean, if you . . . could still love me this way."

My back was to him, and I rubbed my hands along my arms. He didn't answer. Why? Was he taking a moment to think about it? Was he unsure? I heard him get to his feet, and his palm grazed the crook of my elbow as he gently turned me around.

The expression on his face carried so much pain, so much confusion, that tears sprang to my eyes. "You . . . you don't, then," I sputtered. "You can't. It . . . it's okay. I understand."

"No, Lily. You don't," he said as he grabbed hold of my upper arms.

Fat teardrops spilled down my cheeks, blurring my vision, but Amon's warmth as he touched his thumbs to them dried them instantly. "It's not a little thing," he began, "to gift another with your heart, let alone a heart scarab."

"Yes, but . . ."

"Please allow me to finish." I nodded weakly and he went on. "When I first met you, there were certain things the Eye of Horus allowed me to see. I knew what kind of person you were, what motivated you, what things made you happy, and what things caused you sadness. Your qualities were what sustained me during my time on Earth. Our bond went beyond the physical. We were stronger together than we were apart.

"I don't know what the future holds for us, exactly. Terrible dangers and struggle lie ahead, but I've also been given tiny glimpses of such exquisite happiness that I cannot feel anything other than hope. I'd do anything to make them come true. My heart is fused to yours, and there's nothing in this universe that can divide us. Not Seth. Not the netherworld. Not death. And certainly not a lioness, especially one that kisses as well as she does."

Amon winked and I laughed amid my sadness. "You knew it wasn't me?"

"Let's just say when a lioness kisses you, it's unforgettable."

"Hey!" I slapped him lightly on the chest as he wrapped his arms around me.

He sighed, pressing his cheek against mine as he murmured in my ear, "I love you, my sweet Young Lily. Nothing will ever change that."

Hugging him tightly, I teased, "How'd you like an unforgettable Lily kiss?"

"I thought you'd never ask."

Amon trailed his lips down my cheek until his mouth met mine. The warmth and heat of a thousand suns filled my frame. Amon's kiss burned and teased and promised me things I never even knew were possible. Experiencing the real thing was so, so much better than reliving the memory. My fond recollections hadn't given Amon the credit he deserved.

He traced a path with his fingertips down my spine to the small of my back, cupping my hips and tugging me closer. Everywhere he touched he left tingles of energy behind, reminders that he'd branded me his. When I sensed he was being careful with me, as if I were still a mere mortal girl, I returned his ardor with an intensity that surprised and delighted him. I'd just run my hands up his powerful arms and into his hair when, abruptly, the vision of Amon was wrenched away from me.

I cried out, just as Tia and I found ourselves in a dark enclosed place.

"Where are we?" I asked her. "Heliopolis?"

We are still in the world of dreams, I think.

Using my enhanced vision, I was able to make out the distant shape of stars above and behind me but they felt beyond my reach; I was bound in a thick nothingness like a black hole. Suddenly, I realized that I wasn't alone. The huntress within me sensed another presence, a predator, and a dangerous one.

I spun in circles, trying to locate my enemy, but their scent or sound eluded me. They watched me, and the feeling was invasive, like they could see into the depths of my soul and could easily detect every weakness. My heart raced as I tried to suppress the scream building up inside me.

Then a voice spoke in my mind, and it was unlike Tia's or Amun-Ra's. It was a voice full of power, one that terrified me and left a chill reverberating through my bones. I knew then who it was.

We meet at last. I've been waiting for you for a very long time. My servant got a taste, and the scent of you has been tickling my nostrils ever since. You don't know how happy I am that you've begun this journey. You're so much more . . . interesting now than you used to be.

When I couldn't speak out loud, I communicated with him using my mind. What do you want? And why am I here? I asked.

Do you mean to unmake us? Tia demanded.

I heard a laugh and the harsh din caused my body to shiver.

Unmake you? No. Well, perhaps not yet. Before I can capitalize on unmaking anyone, the impossible triangle must be fully formed. You're nearly there.

What are you saying? I challenged, not wanting to understand but also knowing I needed to.

All will be revealed in time, young ones. Perhaps you should focus on your current priorities. Speaking of which, I hope you enjoy your visit with the Devourer. She's a greedy hostess, *he said, almost fondly,* but I'll make sure she welcomes you appropriately when you enter her home.

The wisp of an ice-cold breeze tickled my cheek and I suddenly got the impression that I'd been touched. My skin crawled.

It would appear as if my mind-numbing . . . confinement has finally proven interesting. Watching your dreams will offer me a most pleasant diversion until such time that my release is assured.

What? How is that possible? I demanded.

Fortunately for me, your new powers coupled with your bond of love with the carrier of the Eye of Horus made my eavesdropping on and, I'll admit, appropriating, your dreams, a reality. Destiny draws us closer, my dear. *He paused and chuckled.* Come now, don't fret. This is a good thing . . . for me, *he added.* I look forward to meeting you again. Next time, I hope to introduce myself more . . . fully.

Next time? I thought.

Goodbye, Sphinx. *Laughter echoed around me. Though I knew it was happening more in my head than in the space I was in, I turned in circles, pressing my hands to my ears, imploring it to stop.*

A knock at my door jolted me awake. I sat up suddenly, pressing my hand against my racing heart and then my flushed cheeks. "Just a moment!" I called out as I padded to the door to open it a crack. The servant girl was back. Had it really been several hours? I rubbed my hands across my face, trying to wake myself up from the terrible dream that I desperately hoped was just a bad nightmare. "What time is it?" I asked her.

"It is nearly dawn. You must finish the bathing ritual and then be on your way. If you do not arrive at the pier by sunset, you will miss your opportunity."

"Okay. Let's get this show on the road, then," I said nervously.

She lowered her eyebrows in puzzlement but asked no questions.

The only things I took with me to the bathing room were the weapons we'd been given and the leather shoulder harness. As I walked, it struck me again just how totally unprepared I was. I had no food. No canteen for water. No backpack full of supplies. My phone had been left with Dr. Hassan. I knew next to nothing about where I was headed or how I was going to get there. If I didn't have Tia with me, I was sure I would have freaked out and run screaming all the way back to New York. I was in way, way over my head.

Tia tried to reassure me. *The only way out sometimes is to move forward. The path is not always clear, but your instinct will guide you.*

I don't have instinct. Not like you do, anyway, I said.

We *have instinct,* she corrected. *We can hunt when we hunger. We will find water when we thirst. We will save your young man. And we will* stop *the Unmaker.*

I wish I were as confident as you are.

A lioness cannot indulge in doubts. She must kill or be killed. Hunt or be hunted. Hesitation makes us weak. It is a human trait.

And if we make a mistake? If we die?

If we die, we leave this world knowing we tried. There is honor in that.

I fell silent. There was something comforting in looking at the world through Tia's eyes. Everything was so clear to her. It was black-and-white. She was brave in a way I wasn't sure I could ever be.

It was easy to be brave when Amon was with me. I relied on his abilities. His knowledge of the world he moved in. Now I knew he understood very little about the assignment he'd been given. He was being used by the gods. I was, too, of course, but at least Amun-Ra and Horus had summed things up pretty well. I now knew Seth's agenda and the reason the brothers had to do the things they did.

I wasn't sure if that information would change his perspective or not. Whatever that understanding brought, at least he'd know. He and his brothers. They could make an informed decision. Recognize their true place in the Egyptian pantheon. They'd see Seth for what he was.

At the very least I needed to make sure they were made aware of everything Amun-Ra and Horus told me. For a moment, I wished I'd had more time with Amon to tell him everything I'd learned, but then I thought perhaps it was better that I hadn't. Especially now that I knew Seth could spy on our dreams together.

We soon entered a large bathing chamber with a sunken tub. There were three women already in the room. One stirred fragrant oil into water that was so warm, steam billowed out. When she looked up at me and smiled, I saw her blink sideways, like a crocodile. Another, whose short-cropped hair resembled something more like fur than hair, set candles on the tiled corners of the tub and lit them with a wave of her hand. The third, a beautiful blonde who could have graced the cover of any NYC fashion billboard, spread white flower petals on the water, and the girl who entered with me began tugging on the ties of my robe.

I gathered the edges tightly in my fist. "Um, is this ritual something I can do by myself? I'm not entirely comfortable with getting naked in front of a bunch of strangers."

"You do not wish us to be present?" She frowned.

"Maybe you can just teach me the spell and I can do it on my own?"

She shook her head. "It is too complicated and requires all four of us to speak. Perhaps if we leave while you enter the water and then return to begin the incantation?"

"I guess that would be okay."

The women left and I hurried to disrobe and slip into the steaming water before they returned. As I sank down onto the seat, the fragrant liquid lapping my chin and shoulders, I realized Tia was shocked.

What is it? I asked.

It is . . . pleasant. I did not think immersing yourself in water would be. Will we wash our mane now? she asked.

I was about to answer, but just then the girls came back. I was nervous about them being there, but I soon let go of my inhibitions when they began chanting, raising something in the air. Each girl stood at a corner of the bathing pool and lifted a lump of muddy clay shaped like a brick.

The first girl spoke:

"Lands of the south, keep the stinging sand at bay."

When she finished speaking, I let out a gasp as she tossed the softened brick into the water. Dirt rose and billowed out from it. I drew my feet up closer to my body and wrapped my arms around my knees.

"Fires of the east, repel the raging beasts that mark her path."

The second servant concluded her statement and also threw in her clump of mud. This was repeated two more times, but the next girls were even closer to me, and the splash from the bricks soaked my face and hair. One said,

"Waters from the west, flow over the darkness and reveal the hidden faces,"

while the last one added,

"Winds of the north, overthrow those who would stand in her way!"

Flotsam and dirt coated the surface of the pool, and I felt the grit flowing between my flexing toes.

My once relaxing and soothing bath was now full of filth and muck. When I lifted my arm from the water, bits of dirt clung to my skin. "This isn't really going how I expected it to," I said. As I sat there in the cooling water, my soaked hair dripping onto my neck and shoulders, the girls disappeared.

I wasn't sure if the bath was over or if they were getting ready to add some rotting meat and discarded trash to the water as well, and I was almost ready to get out and look for a shower when they returned. The mud-stained tunics they'd been wearing had been discarded. This time they were dressed in pure white. The material was so bright it almost gleamed.

Frowning, I stared at my dirty hands and compared them to the girls' clean, pale arms. "So what now?" I asked.

My guide pressed her finger to her lips, gesturing that I should be silent. As one, the four girls took their positions at the edges of my now filthy bathing pool and raised their arms in the air, chanting:

"Amun-Ra, lend your power this day.
Cast aside that which is old and unseemly
Renew this woman and prepare her for judgment."

The tiles around the edges of the sunken tub grew hot. They burned red, then shifted to bright orange, yellow, and brilliant white. The water surrounding me grew hotter as well and was now beginning to bubble and boil. I cried out, not because it was burning me, though it was pretty much as hot as I could stand, but because my entire body was tingling and the water began to glow.

"Like Horus, make this daughter bright.
Take her on your primeval wings
As she departs, a soul of Heliopolis,
To walk with the gods and see them in their true glory.
Transform her on this, the day of her death."

Wait . . . what? Tia and I both thought at the same time.

"Accept the offering of her invocation.
Let her see the true and only sun.
Vindicate her. Sustain her.
Allow no evil to have power over her.

Benu Bird, he who leads the blessed to the afterlife,
Protect her heart in the judgment,
Help her find her spirit's desire,
And take her to her celestial home."

The room grew so bright I could no longer see my hand in front of my face, but when they ceased chanting, the light dimmed incrementally until I could begin to make out shapes and the outline of myself. When my vision finally cleared, the girls were gone. So was all the water in the tub.

My body was warm. My hair dry and clean. The tiles of the tub were pristine. There was no trace of the muddy residue. No outline of filth around the edges. My skin smelled like flowers and I felt utterly relaxed and refreshed. At the bottom of the tub, I noticed a symbol. It looked like a golden bird, and it gleamed and pulsed as if it had been the source of the heat.

I wasn't sure if it had been there before and I'd simply not noticed it or if it had appeared as a result of the ritual. Uncertain, I stood up and climbed out of the tub. On a table nearby was a stack of white material and an ornate full-length mirror. I palmed through the clothing first and found a pair of white sandals next to the dress. My short spears and bow as well as my harness were next to that.

Picking up the dress, I held it up to my body and gazed at my reflection. There was something blue around my eyes. I leaned closer and touched my finger to the edge. Blue smudged my fingertip. Paint. My face had been painted to look like an Egyptian goddess's. I wasn't sure how or when that happened and was contemplating the idea that I might have passed out in the tub or frozen while the girls did my makeup, when I felt the brush of silk against my neck.

A deep honeyed voice, dripping with desire, said, "You are the most fetching and exquisite creature I've ever set eyes upon." A pair of hands, very strong male hands, smoothed fabric over my shoulders.

I gasped, my eyes darting to the reflection in the mirror. "Horus!"

I screamed, and grabbed for the robe he'd placed around me. Quickly, I shrugged my arms into the sleeves, wrenching the tie to draw it closed, and spun around. "What right do you have to enter my bathing chamber!" I yelled, jabbing my finger into his muscled chest.

A bubble of rage rose inside me and I raised my hand, tightening my fingers into a fist around his neck. It had been an instinctive move, and Horus grabbed his throat briefly, his eyes widening. But then, just as quickly, the power waned.

You will not hurt him, Tia said.

I wasn't consciously trying to, I explained. *It just happened. It must have been the strangle-your-enemies power that Dr. Hassan told us about.*

Out loud, I said, "I'm sorry, Horus. I didn't intend to injure you."

"I know that at least a part of you didn't want to. Not truly. It's why your power faded."

"What do you mean?"

"When you and your lioness are not of the same mind about something, your power doesn't work. The only time you can act as individuals is when the other acquiesces or sleeps."

"Interesting. But it still doesn't excuse your behavior. Why are you here?"

He winced as if my words caused him pain. "Forgive my audacity, but I remain in your thrall. Please know that I couldn't even conceive of causing you harm. My only desire is to be close to you."

I found my gut response to slap his face, stomp on his instep, and knee him where it would hurt him the most being nullified by my alter ego. *What are you doing?* I mentally hissed at Tia.

Horus would make a powerful mate, she explained. *You have Amon. What does that leave for me?*

I realized then that Tia's feelings for Amon might not be the same as mine. Were we destined to have an emotional tug-of-war over control of our heart?

"I beg you not to go," he said, interrupting my thoughts. "The netherworld is dangerous. It's unlikely you'll survive, let alone rescue your"—he frowned—"boy. Stay here with me. You'll grow to cherish me over time, just as I do you. There are so many things I can show you. Teach you. I can take you to a world where we can swim in a purple ocean and float on pink clouds. I can keep you warm on a planet of sparkling ice that casts prisms of light so high into the sky that the world is encased in rainbow hues. With me you'll never experience pain, sorrow, or death." Horus took a step closer and touched his forehead to mine. "Stay with me and be my love. Or, if that is not something you can do, then . . . just stay."

This time Tia wasn't the only one moved by his words, and I knew that was inherently dangerous. His promises stirred the air, wrapping around us, brushing against our defenses. The wispy tendrils seemed to touch the tender spots of my consciousness. It was tempting. How easy it would be to just let everything go and remain in the golden city of Heliopolis. Not worrying about the complications of being a sphinx. Not feeling the weight of the world on my shoulders. Just heading off to the far reaches of the universe and seeing the amazing wonders these gods have created.

Tia was the one to pull back this time. She'd wanted to experience the passion he offered, to perhaps find a mate of her own, but she wasn't willing to give up our quest. Flashes of our prior dream filled my mind. *We must stop the Unmaker. He is not what we . . . what I . . . need at this time.*

Closing my eyes, I nodded. Grateful for her acquiescence, and giving Horus a tight smile, I determinedly pushed against his chest and stepped away. Turning to the mirror, I looked up at him in the reflection. "We must fulfill our purpose," I said. "We are flattered . . . no . . . we are privileged," I amended, "to have one such as you find us interesting. Honestly, we don't know what awaits us and we are frightened, but we must try. Do you understand?"

Horus didn't reply immediately but ran his hand around to the back of his neck. His eyes were wild with fear, and he was desperately seeking something, anything to dissuade us. I gazed at him steadily, confidently, and he finally straightened and nodded. "I do." He lifted a hand toward me and then stopped as if he thought better of it. With his head lowered, he said, "Will you allow me to help you prepare?"

I turned, surprised. "I thought everything was done."

"Not quite."

He picked up a small jar and poured some of its contents into his hand. The scent of perfume wafted around me. "What is it?" I asked.

Indicating I should turn around, he rubbed his palms together and stroked his fingertips down my neck. "It's a mixture of oil and myrrh, the purest oil in the cosmos. It's taken from a flower that grows in the snow at the upper altitudes of a mountainous planet a great distance away." Horus moved to my side and took my hand, then pushed the sleeve of the robe all the way up my arm. Slowly he massaged from my shoulder down my arm, over my elbow to my wrist and then down my hand all the way to my fingertips, making sure to get oil between each finger.

As he moved to my other arm, he asked, "Do you know how Anubis prepares bodies at the time of their death?" I nodded. "You must be adorned in a similar way."

"Do I have to wear mummy wrappings?" I asked.

He smiled. "No. But you will need to wear white. You must be dressed in fresh clothing of the purest shade. If you cannot remain barefoot, you will wear sandals of the same color that wrap around your legs."

Speaking of legs, Horus had now crouched down and taken hold of my foot. As he ran his oiled palm under the sensitive arch and then up the back of my calf, I danced away nervously.

Horus let me go and looked up at me. "I won't hurt you."

"I . . . I know. I'm just not used to getting a massage standing up," I stammered, trying to come up with something less embarrassing than *nobody has ever touched me like that before*. Tia wasn't helping either. She was enjoying his ministrations too much to protest.

Frowning slightly, he asked, "Would you prefer to lie down?"

"No. Let's just . . ." I wrung my hands and shook them out. "Let's just get this over with quickly. Okay?"

"As you wish," he said softly, and held out a steadying hand.

I leaned against the table, fingering the soft fabric as his palm found my leg again. He swiped the oil up and behind my knee, to halfway up my thigh, only lingering there for a fraction of a second before he did the same thing to the other one. Relief spilled out of me in a shaky breath as he stood up and turned me to face him once again.

Ignoring my obvious discomfort, he dipped his fingertips back into the jar and stroked his thumbs across my eyebrows. Asking me to close my eyes, he touched each eyelid, leaving a whisper of moist, tingling oil behind. The lobes of my ears were next, and then he traced the edge of my jaw on both sides. The last thing he did was touch the pad of his thumb to my bottom lip.

His gaze fixed on my lips and his expression became hungry and hot. Lifting his eyes to mine, he whispered, "You are ready."

I swallowed, the sensation thick and searing my throat. "Thank you," I murmured languidly.

"You're welcome," he answered with a warmth that spoke volumes. We stood, unmoving for a few more heartbeats, until I noticed he was smiling. "Lily," he said.

"Yes?" I answered, my eyes now drawn to his mouth.

"If you keep looking at me like that, I'm not going to let you go anywhere."

I inhaled and realized I had stopped breathing for a few seconds. Turning away from him felt torturous, but somehow I did it and stepped toward the little table containing my weapons and my dress. That was when I noticed the heart scarab peeking out from under the folds of white. I brushed my hand against it and the passionate fog that I'd been enveloped in dissipated, my mind completely clear.

Narrowing my eyes, I turned, and my suspicions were confirmed when I saw the self-assured grin on Horus's face. "You tricked me, didn't you?" I accused.

He shrugged like the popular boy at school who knew he could get away with naughty behavior if he flirted with the teacher. "There's no way you would have paid any attention to me at all if you had that on your person. Catching you unawares while bathing was the only way I could try to steal you away from him."

"You're despicable," I said, though my skin was still too warm from his touch to lend any weight to my words. "I knew we should've strangled him, Tia."

Horus raised his hands in surrender. "I've lost. I'll admit it. And rightfully so." He sighed. "It's been centuries since I've had to work so hard to gain a woman's interest." When he saw my irritated expression, he added, "Take heart. You rejected me all on your own." Leaning closer, Horus stretched out a hand to find something on the table behind me and brought his very tempting mouth to within inches of mine. He smiled when he found what he was looking for and added, "Mostly."

Straightening, he dangled a necklace with a dark blue stone between his outstretched fingertips. "Maybe when I present you with my gift, you'll deign to give me that kiss we both so very much desire."

I folded my arms across my chest. "I don't think so. What is that?" I asked.

"It's an amulet. The stone is lapis lazuli, not precious as far as the value mortals assign such things. Its worth, instead, lies in what it can do."

"So what does it do?" I asked, unable to resist stepping closer to touch the stone.

"This side"—he indicated the carved emblem—"holds a lotus plant, the symbol of Upper Egypt, and the other is a papyrus plant, which is the mark of Lower Egypt. These markings"—he indicated the silver ring around the stone—"hold the three signs of the gods—power, endurance, and life. A portion of my power is contained in this. It is the Healing Stela of Horus."

"And you're giving it to me?"

"I'm lending it to you," he corrected. "It will heal you on your journey but you must still be careful," he warned. "If you lose a limb, the Stela cannot regrow it. If your head is removed from your body, you will die. I do not wish to recover my Stela from your bloated corpse," he said ferociously.

"I understand." My mouth twitched in a smile.

Horus turned me around and clasped the necklace around my neck. "While you wear it, no path will be hidden from you. One side turns to the sky and the other to the earth. If you ever have a problem telling which is which, use the stone. It will help you right yourself."

As I was pondering what kind of a place I would be in where I couldn't tell the land from the sky, he spun me back to face him and cupped my shoulders with his strong hands.

"I'm serious about the peril, Lily. Your journey is a hazardous one full of ancient menaces and dark paths."

I nodded. "I know. We'll be careful. I promise." I touched my fingertip to the blue stone hanging from the silver chain around my neck and said, "Thank you." Looking up at the worried god still holding on to me as if his sheer willpower alone were enough to keep me safe, I stood on my tiptoes and pressed a kiss against his smooth cheek.

He smiled warmly, but his expression immediately changed to something darker. "That's not exactly the reward I was seeking, Lily." Wrenching me against his body, Horus kissed me again, and this time it went beyond passion. It was anxious and desperate, hungry and clutching. It was as if I could save him from drowning. When he began to lift his head, I pulled him back, and I wasn't sure if it was me or Tia, but I kissed him more deeply, only dimly aware that the heart scarab was still on the table. In that moment, the beat of Amon's heart was as distant to me as a speck of sand on the beach an ocean away.

Horus groaned, running his hands up my back and burying them in my hair. Tia trembled with delight, and her thrill filled my mind until I could no longer remember who I was or what I was doing. Horus held me tenderly yet firmly. I felt like his air, his life, and nothing could make him let me go. That is . . . until the room exploded.

14

The Celestial Barque

I stumbled, and if Horus had not been holding me so tightly, I would have fallen. Waves of power washed over both of us as the room filled with light. It undulated in a steady rhythm, one that was very familiar. It was the flapping of wings.

My heart thrilled for a moment; I thought Amon had somehow gotten free and was here. That he'd found me. But even as I allowed my eyes to adjust, I recognized that it couldn't be him. The gleaming orange and red bird that hovered in the air above us was much too small to be Amon's golden falcon.

Still, the creature was resplendent, regal. And as it regarded me, Horus inclined his head in respect, though his expression seemed sulky. "It would appear your cause has influenced the great benu bird to come out of hiding," Horus said.

"Benu bird?" I asked out of the corner of my mouth as the gorgeous winged beast moved to a protruding beam and settled there. He danced on his crimson legs, flapping his wings and preening the feathers that flickered like fire. Two long tail feathers stretched all the way to the floor, and when they brushed against the tile, little sparks rose.

"Yes. Many have confused him for a phoenix. Unlike a phoenix that rises every five hundred years, the benu bird is immortal. He was likely watching our"—Horus paused and narrowed his eyes at the bird—"exchange and chose the perfect moment to reveal himself."

"Reveal? Meaning he was already here?"

"He can make himself invisible. He was probably here all along. It's a rare thing to see him, as he hasn't revealed himself in centuries." Horus frowned. "It's interesting that he does so now."

"Does he mean to help me, then?"

"It would appear so."

"He's very beautiful."

Horus snickered. "I'm sure he likes to think so."

Slowly, I approached the bird and held out my hand. "I'm Lily," I said. "Thank you for coming to help us."

Opening his beak, the benu bird twisted his head so one eye peered down at me, and then he sang out, the notes haunting and beautiful and like nothing I'd ever heard before.

"How lovely!" I exclaimed when the song was finished.

Horus cupped the back of his neck and stared long and hard at the bird. "He's unique, all right."

"Did you create him?" I asked.

Chortling almost uncomfortably, Horus answered, "The benu bird came into being by himself. If Amun-Ra is the sun, then the benu is the sunrise."

I glanced at him in puzzlement, but then the benu bird flapped his wings, rising, and turned into a streak of light that disappeared through the high window. Rematerializing on the other side, he tapped the glass with his beak and circled.

"He wants you to follow him," Horus said.

"Right." I turned toward the pile of clothing and picked up the white dress. Horus stood behind me with his arms folded across his chest, an eyebrow lifted, the corner of his mouth tilting upward. "Would you mind leaving while I dress?" I asked.

Glancing up briefly at the window the bird had disappeared through, he muttered, "I suppose that's for the best."

"Thank you."

"I'll wait for you outside and escort you as far as the city wall. The benu bird will take you from there."

I nodded, and when the door closed behind him, I quickly doffed the robe and stepped into the white dress. The gleaming material was gathered at the empire waist and flowed down my body, ending just above my white sandaled feet. The beaded top covered the entire bodice like a yoke and encircled my shoulders. I twisted my hair up in a knot and secured it with the white tie from the robe; put on my shoulder harness, adjusting it to fit over the dress; secured the strap of the quiver across my body; and took hold of the bow.

As I looked at myself one last time, I felt Tia's discomfort. "What is it?" I asked. She didn't answer, so I cocked my head and tried to access her thoughts. "Ah," I said finally. "It's the dress."

I just don't know how we are supposed to run and fight with all this material encompassing our form. We would do better to go naked.

I laughed. "Maybe. But then we'd freeze. I don't have a coat of fur like you." I bit my lip. "How about a compromise?"

She caught the edge of my thoughts and I felt her acquiescence. Summoning the power of the sphinx, we shortened the dress to the length of a tunic and covered our legs with a supple pair of white leggings.

Horus met me in the hall and gave me a quick look of approval, including an appreciative glance at my legs, and then led me through a maze of hallways until we came to a door.

Once out of Amun-Ra's home, the golden god caused quite a stir. Citizens of Heliopolis stopped whatever they were doing to watch him as he led me through a bustling thoroughfare to the edge of the city. Though I looked for the benu bird in the sky above us, there was no sign of him.

"Are you sure he'll meet me?"

"Yes," Horus answered flatly as a group of merchants saw him and paused mid-transaction.

"What's wrong with them?" I asked.

He flinched. "We don't typically walk among our creations."

"Really? Why not?"

"It makes them . . . uncomfortable."

"How so?"

Shrugging uneasily, he allowed himself to be distracted when a woman dropped a bowl of purple fruit at the sight of him. One orb rolled to his feet. Horus picked it up, dusted it off, and handed it to me. "They don't want to stare into the faces of those who made them. It reminds them that they are mortal. Most prefer to worship us from afar."

"But don't you want to know them?"

"No."

"Why not? I would think you'd be proud. Like a father."

Turning, Horus took hold of my shoulders and stopped me. "Because, Lily, to know them is to love them. If I love them, then it will cause me pain when I lose them. It is the curse that comes with immortality. Do you understand?"

"I . . . I think I do," I answered quietly. He looked like he wanted to say more.

"What is it?" I asked.

"Why do you venture on this course when the inevitable outcome, even should you be successful, is to part with the boy you profess to love once again?"

"He's worth it," I said simply. "The physical distance doesn't matter because the truth of our connection is engraved in my heart. I could no more deny my feelings for him than I could deny the brightness of the sun."

Horus frowned. "You know, there was a part of *you* that responded to my kiss, too."

"No." I shook my head. "That can't be right."

"The spell I cast wouldn't have worked at all had you been

unwilling," he said. "Your lioness may have been swayed by its lure, but if you had been truly against it, it wouldn't have happened."

"I should've known you'd play dirty with a spell," I groused.

Tia tried to appease me. *It is not your fault, Lily. I was the weak one. Horus . . . tempts me. It should not damage your relationship with Amon.*

I don't want to talk about it, I said sulkily.

Perhaps someday I could love Horus, she mused.

It's not love, I responded dryly in my mind.

I wish for him to hold me in his arms and rain kisses upon my lips and face. I like it when he pets me. This is what you desire from your Amon as well. Is this not love?

No. Yes, I groaned. How was I going to explain the concept of love to a lioness? *Those things are lovely,* I told her mentally. *They feel wonderful. But they are only expressions of love. Only symbols of the emotion behind them.*

Then Horus loves me. If he expresses it so deftly, he must.

A man who does not love you can fool you with . . . physical distractions. True love takes time. It's not instantaneous. You must get to know the other person. Come to admire them. Find out what they dream of, what they hope for, and see if those things are echoed in your own heart. Only then will love begin. And you will know it's true when you are asked to give something up in order to protect the one you love. Tell me, if Horus were to meet an untimely end, would you mourn him? Would your heart break over his absence?

She was quiet for a long moment. *I would miss his kisses, but I would not feel a piece of my soul rip should he depart our company.*

I smiled. *Then you know what love really means.*

That my soul rips when we are separated?

Exactly.

Horus stopped at a wall so high I couldn't see the top of it. With a wave of his hand, stones shifted, grinding against the bedrock and on each other with the sound of a thousand millstones that made my bones shake and strain as if they would crumble to powder. Holding my arm to keep me upright, Horus finally let go when a gap appeared in the wall.

"This is where we part, young sphinx."

Pain crossed his face, and he moved in close as if to kiss me again. He seemed almost unable to help himself, but I stepped back, determined this time to keep him at bay. Fortunately, it became a non-issue, as a screech overhead stopped him in his tracks. He glared at the circling benu bird and satisfied himself with pressing his lips against my palm. "Farewell," he said as I stepped through the opening. "Follow the bird. He will not lead you astray."

"Goodbye, Horus. Perhaps we will meet again."

"Perhaps." He waved his hand and the stone wall began to seal itself shut behind me. "But it would be better for me if we did not." His bright, hungry, but worried eyes haunted me as I turned and set off from Heliopolis.

Above me the benu bird came into view. Though it was hard to see him through the trees, he always circled back to find me. If I wandered in the wrong direction, I'd hear his song echo in the forest. Sometimes I'd pass a tall conifer and find him perched on a limb watching me.

When I got close enough, I tried to ask questions, but as soon as I began he'd take off, his long tail hanging several feet below his body. Just when I started to feel thirsty, we came upon a beautiful waterfall that cast rainbows in the air. The water was cool and crisp and the pool below was full of bright, multicolored fish. I gasped when they actually rose from the depths, their fins fluttering quickly like hummingbird wings, weaving playfully through the waterfall before diving back into the pool. Of course, Tia wondered what they tasted like, while I exclaimed over their uniqueness and beauty.

We continued on all afternoon, the benu bird leading us. When he picked up speed, so did we. As we ran, I had another change in my body to ponder. I marveled at my new level of endurance, the deep inhales and exhales as my legs and arms pumped in a steady rhythm that felt at once foreign and natural. I began to second-guess myself. Each thing I did that was out of the norm for me, or that I knew was impossible for a human to do, made me face the fact that I wasn't human anymore, and the thought was uncomfortable enough to make me push my fears to the back of my mind, which was much easier to do when I ran.

Tia seemed much more accepting of our new status. She was a lioness and then she wasn't. She embraced new discoveries like kissing a gorgeous man or luxuriating in a warm bath with wild abandon and passion. The differences in her new form didn't cause her alarm so much as curiosity, and when I made a comment about it, she found my worrying over what was already done irrational.

As we ran, my thoughts quieted. Hurtling over fallen tree trunks and large rocks with the ease of an Amazon, we passed through the forest and crossed a wide grassy plain, then climbed a hilly path dotted with animals that resembled a cross between a goat and a bear. The animals merely lifted their heads as we sped by and then went back to grazing.

I gasped when we came to the other side of the hills. What stretched before us was an indigo sea. Using my powerful new eyes, I gazed out at the wide expanse of water and wondered if this was the same ocean we'd passed over when riding Nebu. The colors were surely dissimilar.

The city of Heliopolis was full of golden light and twinkling buildings but this side of Duat was the opposite. The mountains were gray. The landscape dull and muted. The trees and bushes were dark shadows against the gloomy terrain. Even though the sun was out over the water, there was no warmth, no sparkling waves.

"What is this place?" I asked Tia.

I do not know. But I scent death.

Shivering, I rubbed my arms as a spine-chilling breeze lifted the fine hairs on the back of my neck. The tickle of winter encircled me and I got the impression that I was surrounded by all things decayed and petrified, hidden just beneath an icy layer that I couldn't see past.

We followed the benu bird to the water's edge, where a rickety dock stretched forth its leprous arm into the sea. Next to it sat a thatched bungalow made of rotting beach wood. It might have been painted once. At least I hoped the dried red flecks, which resembled dead, thorny blooms, peeling from the sides of the home, were paint. But if it had been once, it was now so weathered it was barely noticeable.

There was an air of abandon to the building, as if the only thing that might choose to reside in such a place would be a ghostly sailor who haunted the beach looking for victims to drown in the murky waters. But then there was a gorgeous boat, looking as out of place as an NYC socialite at a hillbilly competition.

Like a sleek show dog bound to a homeless man's cart, the vessel sat poised and unmoving, its mast rising high as if it looked to the heavens for rescue. It was tied securely to the dock, which didn't assure the boat's safety so much as the dock's, and I hoped its presence meant that someone likely did live here, or at least visited once in a while.

The vessel's gleaming ebony paint shone in the weak light of the setting sun. A pair of intricately carved oars rested against the hull, and the sturdy mast with a thick sail was bound with tight ropes as well. At the bow of the ship was a carved figurehead of a bird, which looked suspiciously similar to the benu bird, which was now perched atop the broken dock post.

The bird stared down at me expectantly, as if it was waiting for me to do something. It danced on the top of the post, ruffling its feathers as it softly sang for me. One of its feathers brushed against my arm and warmth seeped into my skin briefly before it was lifted away once again.

When the bird's song ended, the pieced together door of the hut swung inward, revealing an interior so dark, I could make out nothing inside, even with my enhanced eyesight. It swung shut again with a reverberating bang.

"You . . . you want me to go in?" I asked the bird.

The bird answered me by flying to the falling-down shack and perching on the roof.

"I guess you do," I said. "Okay, then. Here we go."

I knocked on the door that clung to the side of the home on broken hinges. It hung at such a slant it couldn't even close properly. As my knuckles rapped against it a second time, it swung drunkenly, giving me glimpses of the dark space within. When nobody answered, I shrugged and pulled open the door. It didn't squeak so much as groan with debilitating pain as it hung open and stayed exactly where I left it.

"Hello?" I called out, my voice echoing in the space. The dying sunlight cast long lines of pale light through the gaps in the boards of the house, the gloomy streaks making it appear to be more of a prison cell than a home. "My name's Lily," I announced in the space as I took a tiny hesitant step inside. "Is anyone here?"

There was a rustle to my right. It sounded like shifting paper or perhaps the scattering of a nest of vermin. A dark shape disentangled itself from an even darker corner of the squalid home, and I heard the rumble of a deep voice.

"What do ya want?" the voice demanded, the question followed by a toxic-sounding round of phlegmy coughing and a snort.

"Horus sent me," I responded quietly, the tone of my voice rising at the end as if I'd been asking a question instead of making a statement.

The coughing escalated, and the person hidden in the darkness finally stopped and spat. Glistening yellowish pus landed on the sandy, warped boards by my feet. I moved a step back into the frame of the door, suddenly ready to bolt.

A scraping noise indicated the figure was moving closer. "Horus?" the voice questioned suspiciously. "What do I care for him?"

"Isn't he your master?"

"My master?" The person started cackling, which soon turned into coughing again. More shuffling, and then I heard the jingling of a box. A tiny flame burst into life, growing larger as a lamp was lit. The person in the shack lifted the gas lamp and turned toward me.

Seeing it was a man and not a monster should have offered me a semblance of calm, but instead, I grew more nervous. He was hunchbacked, and though his frame was thick with flesh, his cheeks were hollow, haggard, and his feverish gray eyes were as leeched of color as the boards of his home. Thick blue veins stood out on his heavy arms. Large lips protruded from a wiry black beard that was so unkempt and long, I wondered what creatures might be nesting in its depths.

"Ya woke me from my sleep," the man accused as he stared at me with heavy brows low enough to impede his vision. He pulled a handkerchief from his pocket that was so filthy the only good thing to do with it would be to burn it. I stared speechless as he lifted it to his hooked nose and snorted loudly enough to rattle the floorboards. He must have noticed the grimace on my face because the next thing he said was, "Get out!"

My hands tightened into fists. "No," I answered, and lifted my chin defiantly. "I need to get to the afterlife, and apparently you have something to do with that."

The man took a few steps closer and stared down at me from an imposing height. He was much bigger than he'd originally looked. "I don't ferry the living, girlie." His pungent breath washed over my face, and even though I felt slightly nauseated, I wasn't going to back down.

"You will this time," I replied as confidently as I could.

He tilted his head, considering me, then turned around and busied himself at a table. I heard the sound of liquid sloshing into a cup and the man took a deep draught. With his back turned, he said, "It's a one-way trip on the barque of the sun and it's not safe, even for those with nothing to lose."

"I don't care. I've come this far and I need to keep going."

Refilling his cup, he glanced at me out of the corner of his eye. "Did ya bring an obol?"

"An obol?" I echoed.

"An *obol*." He sighed. "An offering?" He stared at me expectantly, his heavy brows drawing together, and then his shoulders fell and he moved back into the darkness. "I'm not taking ya anywhere without my obol."

An object fell to the floor at my feet. It rolled around in circles before stopping. The glint of gold shone in the darkness. The man froze as I leaned down to pick it up. It was a golden coin stamped with the image of the benu bird I'd seen carved on the boat and on the tile of the tub in Amun-Ra's home.

"Will this do?" I asked, and tossed it in his direction, still unwilling to step out of the bright light of the doorway and into the dark space of his home.

Though he didn't seem agile enough, the man stretched out his bulbous, vein-covered hand and snatched the coin out of the air. He looked at it, turning it over carefully, and then his eyes darted over to me. "Who *are* ya?" he asked suspiciously.

"I told you. I'm Lily."

He frowned. "I don't mean yer name. You need to tell me who ya are."

"Well, I'm a mortal, a human, or I was once. Now I'm a sphinx. Horus has arranged for me to meet you so that I might travel to the afterlife. My boyfriend, Amon, is one of the Sons of Egypt, and he's stuck in the netherworld. I need to save him so Seth doesn't break free of his bonds and rain chaos down on Earth. Does that suffice?"

The man blinked. Once. Twice. Then he spat another gob of mucus at his feet. "A sphinx, is it?" He rubbed the coin between his fingers, studying me, as if trying to figure out if I was speaking the truth. "And when exactly would ya be wanting ta leave, girlie?"

"Immediately."

He shifted, grunting, and stroked his beard. "Are you sure ya wish ta go?"

"Yes."

Shuffling closer, the man looked up at the darkening sky. "Then I suppose we'd better make haste. Best you board *Mesektet* immediately. I'll join you shortly. It's going ta be a long night, girlie. Ya have no idea what you're in for, but I accept ur payment." His brows lowered. "And it's too late ta back out now that I've accepted the job," he warned. "Yer just lucky this obol is of such high value. Otherwise I wouldn't even consider takin' a kicker at all, let alone one so late in the day."

"A kicker?"

"A living soul. A lion/girl like you who's still alive and kicking. Now stop distracting me and get a move on or we'll miss the gate and make this conversation as pointless as a dead man begging ta live."

"Right."

Spinning, I headed outside and glanced up at the house to see the benu bird singing a final mournful tune before he flapped his wings and headed back to Heliopolis. The sun was nearly down. Only a sliver of it still remained above the water. I'd just climbed on board and found a place near the back of the boat that looked secure enough that I wouldn't simply fall overboard, when the large man stomped down the dock.

Our boatman released the knot securing the boat and as we began moving away from the dock, I noticed a carving in the wooden post.

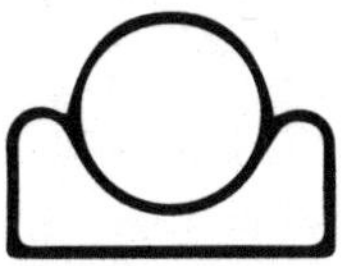

"It's the sunrise," I murmured. "Dr. Hassan said to watch out for it. It leads to life."

"Close," the man said as he plucked an oar from it fastenings and threaded it through the oarlock. "That image has a dual meaning. In this case, it's the sunset, not the sunrise."

Where does the sunset lead? Tia asked.

Dread filled my frame as I clung helplessly to the ropes of the ship. "The sunset," I said, "leads to death."

"Now," he warned as he unfurled the sail, which immediately caught the wind and billowed out, "best hold on for yer life." He stopped what he was doing and let out a wry chuckle. "It's not very often I get ta say that."

15

The River Styx

The wind picked up and the boat bounced over waves, which were rougher with each passing second. Angling the boat toward the setting sun, we raced ahead faster and faster, chasing the dying orb as it sank below the sea. Within moments the only thing I could make out was the large man on the tiller just behind me. My stomach lurched as gravity shifted. I felt like I was on a terrifying roller coaster that had just left the tracks.

Seeing through the darkness was something I had begun to take for granted after inheriting Tia's powers. But I wasn't able to see the white of my clothing and, that disturbed both of us.

"What's happening?" I cried out as a large wave crashed over the edge of the boat.

"This area's choppy, girlie," my peculiar companion hollered. "Best hold tight for the transition!"

"What transition? What do you mean?"

He didn't answer, and as the ship lurched upward and then fell with a heavy crash into the sea, I decided I needed to hold on to something more substantial than a rope. Stumbling to my feet, I shuffled closer to the boat captain and grabbed the rail of the ship, wrapping my arms around it and locking onto my wrists. It was a good thing I did because as we crested the next wave, the ship became momentarily airborne and my legs lifted out from under me as we dropped down once again. My body bashed against the deck with a painful blow.

"One more wave oughta do it!" he cried, and I braced myself as the ship angled up the next swell. A dark wall of water rose before us and gravity shifted again. We climbed higher and higher, and I knew once we crested the wave, we'd fall to our deaths. There was no way we wouldn't sink. It wasn't possible. We'd either flip over backward or break into a million pieces on the other side.

"Hold on!" he shouted. "Here it comes!"

Up and up the boat climbed until it was nearly vertical on the column of water. I wasn't sure how my companion had been able to remain standing. Surely he wasn't strong enough to hold up his own bulk. Freezing water sprayed us from every side. Even with the power of the sphinx, I knew my arms couldn't hold out much longer.

Tia was terrified. Death by drowning was not the way a cat should die. Of course, a human-turned-sphinx on a mission to save her mummy boyfriend shouldn't die that way either. Tia's fear echoed my own, reverberating through my body as we clutched the railing desperately.

Just when I was ready to give up, to let go and allow my body to be swept away, I heard a triumphant cry and the shaking of the boat eased, pale light washing over us. Slowly the craft realigned itself, and when I was at last able to unlock my trembling arms from the rim of the boat, I cautiously looked for the source of the light.

We were encompassed by stars. Heavenly bodies so bright and close I felt like I could reach up and catch them. I'd never seen so many. When I looked over the side, I was shocked to find the rocky ocean gone, and stars beneath us as well. They shifted and moved in a pattern that looked almost fluid.

In wonder, I asked, "Where are we?" I stretched my hand down and felt the tickle of the sparkling substance below. It was cold but not freezing, and when I lifted my hand, a pattern of lights ran over my fingertips before dripping off my skin and rejoining the starlit stream beneath us.

"The Cosmic River," the large man behind me answered. "In your world it's called the Way of Milk or some such rubbish."

"The Way of Milk? Do you mean the Milky Way?" I stared out at the expanse around us, marveling at the colors swirling among the stars and the ink of the sky.

"Yeah. That sounds 'bout right," he said. "We're lucky we made it, seeing as how we left so late and all. Wasn't sure a kicker like you would survive the transition. O' course, we still have a ways to go. You could die at any time." He almost sounded happy at the prospect.

"Well, we didn't. Lucky for you, I suppose. You get to keep your payment."

"Get to keep my payment whether I ferry you alive or dead. Makes no difference to me."

Something he said triggered a thought. "You're Charon the ferryman, aren't you? And this is the river Styx!" I added excitedly.

He snorted and then hocked a ball of spit over the side of the boat. "Don't know too much, do ya?"

I frowned and folded my arms. "Well, if you're not the ferryman, then who are you?"

"I got no reason to tell you nothing. Not like talkin' with the passengers is a part of my job description."

"Well, would you be so kind as to at least tell me your name? Please? I'd like to know who to thank for getting me to the afterlife safely."

"Name's Cherty and this here's my boat *Mesektet*. And just so's we're clear, I didn't decide to take you because *he* wanted me to. Don't need him telling me how to do my job. I reckon I can choose for myself who rides with me and who doesn't. Even if he is my boss."

"Who tells you how to do your job? Horus?"

"Not Horus. Your bird friend. Amun-Ra."

"Amun-Ra? You must be mistaken."

"No mistake. Only one person takes the form of that particular bird and that's Amun-Ra."

I mumbled, "So Amun-Ra's the benu bird?"

"Haven't seen him in that form for quite some time."

"Horus said he hasn't appeared in a while. It makes sense, I guess. But why would he guide me as the benu bird instead of as himself? And why would he help me when he explicitly told me he wouldn't?"

Cherty shrugged. "I don't pretend ta understand what motivates gods. They're all too busy arguin' and courtin' and generally makin' a mess outta things. Most of which means extra work for me."

"So am I the first kicker you've taken across?"

"Not the first." The boat rocked a bit when we hit a rough section of the Cosmic River, but Cherty deftly adjusted the rudder and we moved past it. "Took a lad once. Heart was near torn from him. He'd lost his lady love and was determined to get her back. I warned him it was foolish. He paid well, though, and I figured it was his life to lose. Still remember the grand music he played while we sailed the night sky. He almost made it back with her, too. Nets got her and then Apep got him soon after. Real shame. Oredes or Oreptos or Orpheass was his name, I think."

"Orpheus. I've heard that tale."

"Have you? Not too surprised. Your human world likes their bedtime stories."

"Is that why you won't admit who you are? You don't like what humans say about you?"

His mouth pursed as his hands tightened on the tiller. "Don't hardly matter none what people say. I know the truth."

"I was frightened of you at first, you know. I'm not now. It must be lonely and sad doing what you do."

"Don't forget dangerous," he added.

"Well, that goes without saying."

He shrugged. "Needs to be said. What with the odds of you dyin' and all. Reckon you won't be meetin' up with your boyfriend. Least with your scarab jewel, ya know how he's feelin' about ya." He nodded at the jewel on obvious display. "Most people I take across the river don't even get that much. I hafta listen ta their whinin' and bellyachin' the whole trip. Most days I'm more like a psychiatris' than a grim reaper. They make it seem like I'm the one that causes death when in mos' cases they bring it on themselves."

We journeyed on in silence for a time, and I was enjoying the gorgeous night view when the breeze suddenly died, the billowing sails gradually falling against the mast. "What's wrong?" I asked.

"We're enterin' Apep's territory. Best be silent, girlie. I'll try my best to get you to the other side of his waters alive, but I make ya no promises."

Quickly, he took down the sail and deftly bound the length of it against the mast. Positioning himself on a bench between the two long oars, he dipped them into the Cosmic River and we began moving ahead again. Every once in a while, he'd stop, lift the oars, and listen. A few minutes later, I heard a ghostly moan, like the song of a whale and Cherty froze, whispering, "Hand me my river sticks."

"River Styx?" I mouthed. "Aren't we on it?"

He rolled his eyes and directed my attention to the two sticks with sharpened points. I nodded and handed him the weapons. After tucking them into a gap by the bench, he gestured to the hammer. I gave him that, too, and he set it by his feet. He picked up the sticks and listened carefully, peering into the stars that surrounded us.

I thought I saw a flicker off to the side and I tapped his arm to show him the spot. He fixed his piercing eyes on the section of river I'd indicated but after a moment shook his head. It was a long time before he set the oars into the water again, and we soon moved forward without incident, a breeze picking up a few hours later.

When he settled behind the rudder again, I said, "I would imagine you stay very busy. Aren't there like thousands of people who die every day? If it takes this long to get to the afterlife, how do you get all of it done?"

"Luckily the disembodied take up very little room; as long as a piece of them touches the ship, they go. If it's crowded, the dead hang off the sides by their fingertips. Sad thing is, makes it real easy for Apep to swallow 'em."

"So who or what is Apep? Or do I even want to know?"

"Even Amun-Ra don't fool around with Apep. Seth made him. Of course, that was back before when he was actually makin' things. He was just a child in those days, at least by the way you'd reckon it. Apep is a . . . well, I guess the closest thing you could compare him to would be a snake. Or a dragon, maybe. No. Snake is better. Giant snake. Like a monster anaconda. He makes his home in a certain place in the cosmos right on that piece of river we passed. His favorite snack is—you guessed it—the disembodied. Not much else to eat around these parts, I suppose."

"Has he tried to eat you, too?"

"Would if he could catch me. I guess you could call him my archnemesis. There's nothin' he'd like better in the world than to sink *Mesektet* and enjoy the feeling of me in his hot little belly."

"Does he, um . . . eat the living?"

"Oh, I'd imagine he'd enjoy gobbling up a tasty little treat such as you. I'd think you'd be real nourishin' and scrumptious to one such as him. Might be able to feed off'n your flesh for a decade or two. He nabbed a right proper number of the disembodied on my last trip. Likely he's still a bit gassy from that. Otherwise he would have been on us like a fly that found a capysaur turd."

My nose crinkled up at the thought.

"First time I ever ferried a sphinx. Centaurs, unicorns, even a testy dragon, but not a sphinx."

"Didn't you take the other sphinx? The one Isis made?"

"Never met her. Happens sometimes. Especially if the dead are unhappy when they pass. They wander. Tryin' ta find something to give their death meanin'. Probably what happened to her. They never make it ta my shores. The embalmin' rituals Anubis created help guide them here, but even then there are those who get lost. Mortals, especially modern ones, don't know too much about navigatin' the Cosmic River. They mess it up. Some burn their dead and throw the ashes in the river. Some float bodies out to sea or down the Nile. They mistake their mortal rivers for mine, but the only way ta get ta the afterlife is ta cross here." Cherty held out his hand, indicating the expanse around us.

A whirlpool of the stars in the river caught my attention and I shivered. "Will Apep chase us?"

The ferryman shrugged. "Anythin's possible. But like I said, we got lucky. Not so sure that would happen on a return trip, assuming, of course, that I'd be willing to consider making an exception to my one-way rule and that you survived. . . ."

"So do you fight him?"

"Can't kill 'im. All I can do is drive 'im off and hope he don't make off with too many of my passengers."

"But he sticks to his territory?"

"Mostly. Every once in a while the devil surprises me. Though I'd think by now he's exhausted all of his tricks. That's the bad thing about immortality. Work gets monotonous. Apep keeps it interestin'."

"Yeah," I grunted. "I guess that would be a problem." Talking about immortality made me ponder my own. Was I truly immortal now, like the other sphinx, Baniti? Did I want to be? There was so much I could do and learn as an immortal. I could be with Amon forever. It was an intoxicating notion. But if I could only see him for two weeks every one thousand years, that would be extremely lonely. Could a relationship like that work? Maybe I could stay with him in dreams.

The truth was, the sphinx I'd become frightened me. I didn't know how to wrap my mind around it. Maybe Dr. Hassan could figure something out. Of course, seeking a way to recover my mortality might mean something unpleasant for Tia. She meant more to me every day we were together. The lioness was like a sister to me. I'd always longed for one.

But then, could I even go back to a normal life? Attend college? Or schmooze at my parents' various functions when I had a lioness for a mental roommate? Even worse, how could I change my state knowing it might kill her or that she'd disappear forever?

The rocking of the ship was soothing, and I laid my head back against the rail, letting it lull me to sleep. The tinkling sound of the stars faded and was replaced with the crackle of a popping fire.

"Lily?" I heard the soft exclamation.

"Amon?"

I groped in the darkness, unable to make out his shape. Finally, my hand brushed against his arm.

The sound of soft weeping filled my mind. "Oh, Lily. Why have you come?"

"Amon? What's wrong? Are you hurt?" Immediately, I knelt down next to him and wrapped my arms around his neck. He clutched me close but I pulled away, keeping a hand on his shoulder as I attempted to use my sphinx vision to find his true form. "Tell me," I demanded, unable to see anything. "Is your body injured?"

"I am beyond pain. I am a man tormented. Especially knowing how close you are. You must turn back. Ask—no, plead with Cherty to take you back to Heliopolis."

"I can't. You know that. Besides, I'm too close."

"There's still time. Go back. Forget me. I beg of you."

His quiet sobbing made my heart quiver, and tears sprang to my own eyes. "I have to find you. I won't give up. Don't ask me to." Amon didn't answer. "Please tell me what's wrong."

"Everything," he murmured. "Nothing. I am in the Field of Fears. Here I am safe from everything and everyone but myself."

"Oh, Amon, I'm so sorry. Just wait for me. I'll find you. I promise."

It was as if he didn't hear me. "It's almost easier facing a monster," he said. "There's nothing for me to fight here. My darkest despairs have surfaced to torture me. And you are at the heart of it. In offering you my heart, I have destroyed the one thing in the universe I wanted to protect. I am the one who's sorry, Young Lily."

I took a deep breath and tried to speak calmly, rationally. "Your heart is all

I ever wanted. It's the one thing that keeps me going forward. Try to remember that and know how much I want to be with you."

"You should have taken Horus up on his offer," he said morosely. "He would have been a much better choice."

"I don't want Horus."

"A part of you did. I . . . I heard him say it."

I bit my lip. "I apologize if seeing that added to your pain. But I don't love Horus. I love you. Besides, I don't believe everything Horus says, and you shouldn't either."

He ignored my sad attempt to explain. "You need someone strong like Horus. I don't blame you for choosing him."

"I didn't choose him. In fact—"

"Just turn around, Lily," he interrupted. "Go home. Live as normal a life as you can. There's nothing here for you anymore."

"I'm not leaving you."

"It doesn't matter. Even if you're stubborn enough to try to find me, I won't be here. You'll never find me."

"You'll be there, Amon! If you do something stupid, I'll . . ."

Tell him you'll sink your claws into his back.

"Yes, I'll sink my . . . Tia!"

It is becoming difficult to remain patient with this human sentiment. Step aside, Lily.

Tia! *I suddenly found myself locked behind a mental door where I could hear but not speak.*

"Young man, you will cease lamenting immediately," Tia said. "Lily is in love with you. She has selected you as her intended mate. So far I have not protested this decision, but if you continue to bemoan your fate in this manner, I will encourage her to find someone more worthy. I advise you to muster the same courage she has shown.

"This journey has been arduous for her, and it is not made easier by your casting her aside. In her mind there is no man as pleasing or as perfect as you are. From the soles of your feet to the crown of your head to the depth of your soul, you are all that she desires. Be thankful that I do not influence her other-

wise. Now, you promised that you would advise us. I suggest you do so and make the most of the very few moments you have to communicate."

Suddenly I found myself back in control and Tia retreated, turning her back to me and giving us as much privacy as she could.

"Amon? I'm sorry about that," I said.

He was quiet for a minute and then he replied, "No. Don't be. She's right. It still doesn't change anything, but you've given up everything to save me. I can at least acknowledge that and love you enough to do what I know has to be done before I'm out of options."

"What does that mean?" I asked nervously. "Amon?"

"She asked for my advice," he said, "and here it is. When you meet up with the guardians, stay close to them. They'll protect you. If somehow you do make it to the netherworld, avoid the Mires of Despair at all costs."

"The Mires of Despair. Got it."

"If you can get there, there's sanctuary in the trees."

"What are you going to do?" I asked, almost afraid of his answer.

"I'm going to use the Eye. I've only drawn on its power when absolutely desperate. The Devourer will be able to find me when I access it fully, but if I can use it to figure out a way to leave here, I'll take it. Hopefully, I'll be back in the afterlife by the time you arrive. You'll know if I've been successful if I'm waiting for you on the dock. No matter what happens, Lily, know that I love you and wouldn't trade one second of our time together for anything."

"I love you, too. Be careful."

"I will. I'll try to—"

My body lurched to the side and I was jolted awake. "Try to what?" I cried. "Amon?" I called out, but he was gone. Cherty stabbed at something over the side of the ship, then jerked his arm up. In his hand he twirled his river sticks before jabbing them at something again. Glancing over his shoulder, he hollered, "Girlie! Grab my rucksack and fish out the coin. Be quick about it!"

I ran to the pile of loose rubbish he'd had on board and grabbed a bag, then headed over to him. Quickly I dug through the items in the bag, but I couldn't find the golden coin with the benu bird stamped on it.

"I don't see it!" I yelled.

"It's in the secret flap. Feel aroun' with yer fingers!"

I gasped as a slime-covered arm with webbed hands tipped with razor-sharp claws grabbed on to the ship. The skin was black and filled with a dark fluid just beneath the surface. It looked like ink trapped in a thin balloon. With a howl, Cherty impaled the arm to the side of the ship; blue-black fluid burst from the skin and dripped down the side of the boat. An inhuman screech filled the air, and when he pulled out the sharpened stick, the arm slipped over the side.

"I can't find it!" I shouted.

"Here! Hand it off!"

I tossed him the bag and reached behind me, grabbing my shortened spears. I twirled, then jabbed them into the soft bodies of two creatures crawling up behind him. He tossed them overboard and then dug through the bag. "Got it!" he called out, a smile on his face, but before he could pull out the coin, an arm snaked up, wrapped around the strap, and yanked it over the side of the ship.

"Varlet!" Cherty cried as he shook his fist in the air. "Gotten more than you deserved with that one!"

More of the vile creatures attempted to clamber aboard. "What do we do now?" I cried.

"Hold 'em off while I make for the nets!"

"The nets?"

"Keep 'em pugnacious prima donnas off as best ye can, girlie!"

"Right," I murmured, and spun into action. As Cherty worked the tiller, rocking the ship back and forth and letting out the sails until they were nearly ready to pop, I did my best to keep the boarders at bay. With deadly accuracy, I sliced throats, stabbed torsos, and chopped off arms. Tia was able to sense when one of the intruders was sneaking up behind us, and I was grateful for her instincts.

We soon found that when using the power of the sphinx, we were able to strangle our victims, but it was a slow process and required concentration. Also, it only worked on one enemy at a time. Fighting with weapons became sloppy when we tried using them while spearing the beast, but strangulation was an effective power to use from a distance.

Soon Cherty joined us and we worked as one, felling the enemy. I was surprised when a dark creature collapsed at our feet. She was beautiful. Her inky black hair fell to her waist, and she held up her hand in an imploring gesture. Instead of legs, her bottom half reminded me more of an eel. Shiny scales covered her long form that ended in a fin like a shark's.

I hesitated only a moment, and when I did, she sprang forward, using her powerful tail to propel her up; bared an open, wide mouth of sharpened teeth; and sank them into my shoulder. White-hot pain exploded and a stinging sensation rippled from the wound out across my body. I screamed to see that she had wrenched a hunk of flesh from my shoulder. Cherry-colored rivulets dripped down her chin as she spat and smiled triumphantly.

"Bloody viper!" Cherty cried as he brought the hammer down on her head. She slumped to the deck and the ferryman viciously kicked her limp body over the side.

"What are they?" I asked as I leapt into the fray again, trying my best to forget my stinging shoulder.

"Cold-blooded, voracious serin. And we've navigated into a cursed school of them."

"Serin?"

"They're usually not so active. Greedy carps!"

"Are they mermaids?" I asked as I dispatched a trio in quick succession. "'Cause they look like evil mermaids."

"They're distant relatives. If a mermaid is a blue jay, then the serin are vultures."

"Are they immortal?" I asked, hoping they might be swayed by my scarab.

"No. But they breed quickly. I report infestations so's Amun-Ra can keep their numbers in check. Usually I can distract 'em with a pretty coin, 'specially one from Amun-Ra. I throw it overboard and they leave me alone ta fight over it. Sometimes killin' each other in the process, the voracious vixens. Now that they's gotten a taste a you, they's unlikely ta give up on us."

"Fantastic."

Stowing my short spears in the harness on my back, I summoned my claws and vaulted onto the back of a serin. Ten minutes later the creatures mysteriously disappeared.

Pressing my hand against my bloody shoulder, I hissed, but moments later, I felt something hot against my chest—the necklace Horus gave me, glowing. It warmed my skin, and a tingling sensation crept from my throat over to my shoulder. I watched in shock as my wound began to heal. Soon there was no indication at all that I'd been injured other than the tear in my white tunic and the spots of blood that darkened it.

Cherty was so focused on the Cosmic River that he didn't notice my miracle healing. I moved up next to him and gratefully took the skin of water he offered, drinking deeply.

He pointed ahead. "There. Do ya see that ripple? Like reeds in a river?" he asked as he looked over the side.

"Yes. What is it?"

"When a large animal, like, say, a crocodile, moves through 'em, it scatters the reeds and draws up mud."

I stared hard at the river and finally noticed that not all the lights flowed. Some clusters stayed in one place, like glistening plants.

"What's hunting us?" I asked.

"Menfishers. Horrible beasties that stink of corruption. Pierce one and ya are drenched by his foul water. Their flesh is decayed and their bones are soft. They weave their nets of sinews ta catch those unawares."

"So they're like water spiders?"

"Yeah, but they look more like giant silk grubs. Their nets are like aspen trees. They grow from a single root sucker. The queen creates the net and her little minions perch along the web in different spots, waitin' ta pounce upon those that get caught in it. Once there, they devour your flesh, then swim down ta their queen ta regurgitate the nutrient-rich bits of ya, which are then divided up between the colony's larvae. They'll eat pretty much anythin'—the disembodied, serin, kingjacks, and anythin' else that lives in these waters."

"Charming."

Cherty was somehow able to navigate through without much trouble until we neared the end and the ship suddenly reeled to the side.

"We been snagged!" he cried. "Quickly! Bring me my hammer!"

Glistening, ropy arms had fastened on to the front of the ship. At the tips of the beasts' long tubes were sticky bulbs that sucked noisily, creating mucous slicks everywhere they latched on. They looked like the limbs of a thin, albino octopus. When Cherty bashed one of the tips, it slunk back into the black water. Soon another and another burst out and hit the ship, the impact rocking the vessel back and forth like a toy boat.

"Grab the rudder," Cherty shouted. "We've got ta do this quickly or we'll be grub meat for sure! When I drop the hammer, shove the tiller all the way to the right!"

"Got it!"

"Now!" he cried as he dropped the hammer on a bulbous limb. From out of the depths a giant white slug had reared its head and began to climb along a slick line of its own web. The line was now no longer attached to the ship, and the creature, along with its sticky trap, slipped beneath the surface of the star-filled river once more.

"That'll teach ya! Ya abominable beasties!" Cherty shouted as he brandished his weapon in the air before making his way back to me. "We make a good team," he said. There was an appreciative gleam in his eye that hadn't been there when I'd boarded.

"Yeah. I don't envy your day job," I said.

Cherty laughed. "No. I imagine ya don't. Should be smooth from here until mornin'," he added. "Rest now."

Hours later, which to me felt like minutes, the ferryman nudged my shoulder.

"We're here."

"The afterlife?" I asked.

"Not quite. We're at the Isle of the Dead. Just passed the pillars a while ago. When we dock, we'll be greeted by the guardians of the gates and they'll take you on to the Porch of Judgment."

"I see," I said, standing up to crane my neck and search for a sign of Amon. If he'd been successful, then he would meet me on the dock. Maybe it wasn't this dock. Maybe there hadn't been enough time. My heart sank, but I tried to keep the nugget of hope alive. Amon just had to make it.

The Isle of the Dead was a dark place. There was an almost tangible stillness to it. Ancient trees dotted the mountains, and I saw the ruins of old stone buildings. We docked and two men in armor sporting helmets and swords approached. One man's armor was tinted bronze, while the other one wore silver. After Cherty tied off the ship, he turned to help me down.

"Thank you," I said, and took his hands.

He squeezed them back, a watery sheen in his gray eyes, and then quickly dropped them and glared at me as if I'd tricked him into displaying the gesture. "It's me job," he said gruffly.

Reaching into the ship, he grabbed a bag of food and handed it to me, then turned around to address the guardians.

"This one's a kicker, a sphinx. Amun-Ra sent her. You need to take her in."

"A kicker?" the tallest guardian said from behind his helmet.

"A sphinx?" said the other one.

I grabbed my bow and quiver from the secure place I'd left them on the boat as the guard continued. "There hasn't been a sphinx in—"

The larger man grabbed the arm of the other. "Lily?" I heard his muffled voice say.

The guardians stepped forward and each of them tore off their helmets. My heart leapt in my throat, unbidden tears filling my eyes. The two men came toward me, and when Cherty tried to block them, they easily pushed him aside and knelt at my feet.

"It *is* you," the larger man said.

"How did you get here?" asked the other.

I wrapped my arms around both of them, giving each a kiss on the cheek. "Asten. Ahmose. I'm so happy to see you."

16

Guardians of the Gates

"Girlie!" Cherty hissed as he grabbed my arm, wrenching me away. "No one touches the guardians, Dreamer or Pathfinder. Ya 'ave no idea what terrible things could happen ta ya." The ferryman put his arm around my shoulder. "The dreamer torments the wicked with the most horrible visions as he guides them to the Porch of Judgment, and the pathfinder, well, let's just say he's as adept at leading people off the path as keepin' 'em on it," he whispered.

"It's okay," I said, smiling. "They're my boyfriend's brothers."

"'Ur boyfriend? Are ya tryin' ta tell me 'ur boyfriend is the revealer?"

"I guess," I answered with a frown. "His name is Amon."

Cherty slapped his meaty palm against his forehead. "By Apep's pulsing pustules, girlie! Do ya have a deat' wish? What am I askin'? Of course ya have a deat' wish. 'Ur here, ain't ya?"

He punched the side of his boat, which told me just how upset he was.

The ferryman went on with his lecture. "Bad enough ya gotta make 'ur way here, bein' a kicker and all. Now I find out you've fallen fer one a the wanderin' three, the soulless. And the wors' one o' the bunch, too. The revealer shows the disembodied exactly what they don' wanna see.

And most o' the time, it ain't a pretty picture. Nothin' good will come o' helpin' a man such as that."

"They're not soulless. They've just been given a very difficult job that requires them to serve the gods. I'm sure that whatever it is they're tasked to do, they take no delight in it. You should know a lot about that yourself, I might add."

He took hold of my arm and shook me slightly. "Just trust me when I tell ya, it's 'ur fanny gonna be in a mound o' trouble if you head out wi' the likes of those two."

Ahmose stepped forward. "Be careful with her. She is frail."

Snorting, Cherty replied, "Shows what you know. This one's 'bout as frail as a dragon's backside."

Narrowing his eyes, Ahmose said, "She will be safe in our hands, Ferryman. I assure you."

"You should leave now," Asten added with a menacing look I'd never seen him wear before.

The ferryman stared into Ahmose's eyes and seemed to find something there because his shoulders fell and he turned away. Gruffly, he said to me, "It's 'ur choice, then. Do ya still want to go wi' 'em?"

"Yes," I answered. "I have to find Amon."

He kept his back to me, his breathing deep and ragged. "Suit 'urself, then." Clearing his throat, he spat a final greenish gob of phlegm into the water, grabbed a rucksack and a flagon from his stash, and shoved them into my arms.

"What's this?" I asked.

"Some stores from ma personal stash. Without food, a kicker like you won't last too long, 'specially in the netherworld. In there I got a bunch o' raisins, each one filling yer belly fer hours; some fig cakes that double when ya break 'em apart; and the flagon o' cider there never runs dry."

"That's very kind," I said as I took the items and placed them in the larger bag.

"And 'ere. Take this, too."

He tossed me a golden coin stamped with a man hunched over a pole riding a boat. "It's you," I said.

"When ya want ta return. Toss it inta the water. I'll come ta find ya."

Carefully, I put the coin into the bottom of my quiver, then wrapped my arms around Cherty's thick waist. "Thank you," I murmured into his chest. Standing on my tiptoes, I kissed his cheek and he turned a brilliant shade of red that traveled all the way down his neck.

"Welcome." He stepped away and kicked a pebble into the quiet water lapping against the ship, then stooped to free the rope from the dock. After tossing it haphazardly aboard, he placed a heavy hand on my shoulder. "Just promise ye'll be careful, girlie. Don't trust the soulless. They ain't the mighty men of valor ya think they are."

"I'll be cautious," I pledged.

He grunted, clambering aboard the beautiful vessel and sailing back toward the treacherous waters we'd barely escaped hours earlier.

I turned and gave Ahmose and Asten a small smile as I tightened my grip on my bow. "Hello," I said.

Their eyes burned into me. Asten was the first to speak. "Lily! What have you done?"

"What do you want to know first?" I said with a sheepish look.

"How did you get here?" Ahmose asked insistently.

"By boat," I said as I jerked my thumb over my shoulder and smiled cheekily. "But I guess that was pretty obvious."

"This isn't funny, Lily," he replied.

"No," I sighed. "It's not. Long story short, Anubis recruited me. He needs me to find Amon."

"Amon?" Ahmose repeated, his eyes shifting nervously to Asten. "Why would he want you to do that?"

"I guess it's because I'm the only one who can." I repositioned the bag over my arm so they could see the gleaming green scarab pinned to my shoulder.

Both brothers' eyes widened, Ahmose taking a step back while Asten took one closer. He removed his bronze chain mail glove and brushed my hair back before stretching out his fingertips to the scarab. On impulse, I touched my fingers to his. "I can touch you," I said. "I wondered if I'd be able to."

"Of course," Asten replied, his warm gaze lifting to mine. "What did you expect?"

I shrugged. "I don't know. I thought you'd be spirits, I guess. I couldn't touch Amon at first, but now that I'm a sphinx . . ." I trailed off and saw the brothers give each other a pointed look. Asten examined the scarab and then announced, "It's his," with finality to his voice.

"Why would he do it?" Ahmose asked.

"Isn't it obvious?" Asten answered. "He loves her." Asten looked at me as if seeking the elusive emotion on my face. He seemed puzzled but fascinated by the idea at the same time.

Ahmose muttered, "Yes. But to risk such a thing . . ."

"We knew he was different during the last rising. This explains it." Asten tapped the gemstone.

"But when?" Ahmose asked.

"It happened just before Anubis killed him," I answered, and let the quiver strap cover the scarab, slightly uncomfortable with the attention they were giving me. "Amon thought I was dead. I was, almost. But Anubis told Amon what to do to heal me."

"He bound himself to you," Asten murmured thoughtfully.

I nodded. "Yes, but then he was told we needed to break the bond. I was supposed to kill him. But I couldn't do it, and Anubis kindly offered his . . . *assistance,*" I said with a sarcastic inflection. "Later we found out the bond was still in effect, which actually turned out to be a good thing because now I have the ability to find him."

"Find him? So you are saying he's lost?" Ahmose took a step forward, his face clouded with concern.

"It seems he jumped to the netherworld."

"The netherworld!" The men looked at each other, then, as one, grabbed my arms and yanked me down the dock.

"We must hurry!" Ahmose said.

My feet were barely making contact with the wooden boards of the dock. "Wait just a moment," I called. When neither of them stopped, I shouted, "Hold on!" A switch flipped from inside my mind with a deep growl. Tia was in charge. She tore our arms out of their strong grips and twirled. Crouching down, claws extended, she glared at the two brothers. "You will *not* touch Lily in such a manner," she hissed menacingly, cocking her head as she stared into their eyes.

Ahmose looked horrified, but Asten's expression was curious. A cocky smile lifted the edges of his mouth and a dimple appeared in his cheek. His eyes twinkled, as if he was interested in challenging Tia. "Ah!" he said. "I nearly forgot. You're not just Lily anymore."

"That's right," Tia jeered. "You two are not her only . . . protectors."

Asten bowed, but it was in an almost mocking way. "I can see that, Lady Lioness. We apologize for . . . manhandling her."

Tia shifted our legs beneath her. "The two of you will walk ahead of us. We will follow. But you *will* tell us where you are taking us first."

"Of course," Asten said smoothly. "We are escorting you to the Porch of Judgment. Since Amon is in the netherworld, time is of the essence."

Ahmose added, "Anubis has much to answer to. We were unaware that Amon gave Lily his heart scarab and were simply told that he was on a different assignment for the time being. His disappearance was kept from us and knowing that we were purposely left in the dark is very disturbing."

"We knew something was amiss," Asten said to Ahmose.

Asten turned to us again. "Will you accompany us?"

Tia paused and looked into the eyes of both men. "Very well," she said finally. "You may proceed."

You know they weren't hurting me, I said to Tia as she relinquished control.

They have no right to force us to do anything. We are sphinx! she said. *We are worthy of their respect.*

We are. They didn't mean to harm us, though. I'm sure of it. You're taking Cherty's words too much to heart.

And you are not taking them to heart enough, *Lily.*

Hmm. I considered her words as we walked, leaving the dock and entering a thick jungle, the brothers leading us down a worn path. I watched in fascination as their loosened armor dropped to the ground, disintegrating into sand. Soon they wore only tunics, boots, and their swords. I caught them up on what had happened since we'd parted, what Anubis had told me, and that I'd shared dreams with Amon, briefly describing the connection. When I recounted my dream of Seth, they gave each other dubious looks.

I asked them why we weren't traveling by sandstorm and they explained that particular ability only worked for them in the mortal realm; however, they could still summon weapons. It explained why Amon had to fight in the netherworld and couldn't simply disappear. Then I continued to ask questions about what to expect at judgment, what they believed the netherworld was like, and why it was they didn't know about Amon, but Ahmose kept his concentration focused vigilantly on the terrain and allowed Asten to take the lead in communication.

"We only know what the gods deign to share," Asten explained. "We are as much at their mercy as you are. Actually, you seemed to have garnered more of their attention in the last few weeks than we've been able to get in centuries."

"It was because Horus desired us," Tia said before I could stop her.

"Did he?" Asten said, a roguish smirk appearing on his face. "Not sure I can blame him."

"Cut it out," I warned Asten. "I can't handle your flirting with me, too. Horus was bad enough."

He rubbed his chin. "Perhaps you just weren't swayed by his pretty face. The ferryman seemed to like you well enough. He might make a much better companion than Horus."

"*I* liked Horus," Tia said out loud. "His power and confidence make him an attractive choice for a mate. But I do not love him. At least, not yet."

Asten laughed. "I confess I'm curious as to what qualities a lioness might seek out in a mate."

It surprised me that Asten could tell the two of us apart so easily. Not even Horus had been able to do that.

"Since I am no longer a lioness in truth, I am still discovering that for myself. Being a lioness was . . . easier in many ways."

Asten sobered. "And what about Amon? What will you do if you don't feel the same way about him as Lily does?" Asten asked.

"Then I will endeavor to alter my feelings for her sake. Either that or I will encourage Hassan to aid me in seeking oblivion."

Oblivion? I spurted in alarm. *I will not see you bring harm to yourself, Tia,* I whispered to her in my mind.

"I won't cause you to doubt your feelings for your mate," she murmured back.

"How utterly absorbing," Asten said soberly, but a moment later his expression lightened. He winked, a gesture Tia quite enjoyed. "If I was jealous of Amon before, I'm doubly envious now," he teased.

I took control of my body just as Asten cupped my elbow, helping me around a large boulder.

He sees me, Tia said in my mind. *And I quite like that cleft in his chin. Those are good qualities, I think.*

Sighing, I rolled my eyes and ignored Tia's inner appraisal of Amon's brother.

Soon Asten shouted to Ahmose that we were getting close to the river.

"What river?" I asked.

"It's a waterway, actually," Ahmose said, speaking for the first time in an hour, though he still wouldn't make eye contact with me. "It's called the Waterway of the White Hippo."

"Is it dangerous?" I asked.

Asten stopped and waited until I looked up at him. "Everything in the afterlife can be, Lily. And everything in the netherworld definitely is. Don't forget that."

His expression added more weight to each word, and I again thought that there might be more to Ahmose and Asten than I knew. I nodded and we made our way to the edge of a river where a small watercraft was tied. Asten aided me into the boat and had me sit while Ahmose took hold of a long pole and pushed us out into the flowing water.

Asten became our guide as we traversed the terrain. We passed out of the trees and came upon large plains full of dark waving grain. "That's the Field of Reeds," he explained. "There are numerous crops here to provide food for the dead."

"Are the disembodied the workers I see out there?" I asked after spying several shadowy figures stooped over the grain, collecting it into large piles.

"Those are shabtis," he said.

"Really? Like the ones Amon summoned?"

"I would assume so. They are tied to certain gods or loaned out to overseers. Occasionally, when a heart is judged unworthy, a master who is willing may decide to allow the dead soul to serve until it is determined that their heart has changed and they are now humble. Unfortunately there isn't always a way to determine who the master is, as that is considered a private matter between god and servant."

"So there could be shabtis here that serve Seth," I said.

"It's a possibility," Ahmose answered.

"It's more than a possibility. It's a fact," Asten contradicted. Then he explained. "Any shabti that is raised from the dead to serve in the mortal realm must come from the afterlife. That means the shabti that tried to kill you and Amon came from here."

"So Seth has eyes and ears here, too."

"He does," Asten said.

We floated quietly for a time and then I asked, "So, what Cherty said about you two is true? Do you torment his passengers on arrival?"

Neither of them answered at first.

Ahmose admitted quietly, "The ferryman was not . . . inaccurate."

"But why?" I asked. "It doesn't seem like you to torment those who've lost everything."

"It's not our fault," Asten said. "Though the place we're going is called the Porch of Judgment, the dead are actually judged from the moment they set foot on the Isle of the Dead. That's why the journey is so important."

Ahmose explained. "When a person is in our presence, our powers make them aware of all their wrongdoing. By the time their heart is weighed, they already know the outcome. Some try to escape their fate. They run or throw themselves to monsters along the way, succumbing to a second death before a punishment is meted out. Many of them would rather meet an uncertain end than end up in the Devourer's garden. I don't purposely lead them on the wrong path, but being near me makes them aware of all the flawed paths they chose in their mortality."

"And being close to me," Asten added, "causes them to see all the bad things they'd ever done play in their minds in a never-ending vision. If it's really bad, it can cause some of them to go mad."

"And what about Amon?" I asked. "What happens when they are close to the revealer?"

Ahmose answered. "Because Amon has the Eye of Horus, he knows all things. When the dead are near him, they have the opportunity to see what their lives could have been had they lived up to their potential."

"That doesn't sound too bad," I said. "Why did Cherty say he was the worst?"

Asten answered thoughtfully. "Amon's power is the most difficult to bear because he reveals the unknown. The dead already know the wrong they've done. They remember the choices and the paths they've followed, but to see the happiness, the wonder of what they could have had, is the most trying thing for the dead to absorb.

"Seeing it and knowing they will never have it . . . well, let's just say that drives more of them into the mouth of darkness, seeking their second and final death, than either of our powers combined. Getting a glimpse of what could be is . . . at once disturbing and intoxicating . . ." Asten's words trailed off and when I turned to him, I found him intently watching me. At seeing my puzzled expression, he turned his eyes toward the trees.

"So if that's all true," I asked, "then why am I not experiencing those effects?"

"It's because you're still alive, Lily," Ahmose answered.

"But *I* am not," Tia added, slipping into control. "I am, what is the word, disembodied."

Asten smiled, but it didn't quite reach his eyes. "You are a beautiful exception to the rule. Though your body is gone, you share the living body of Lily. That means your judgment is suspended until such time as you have nowhere else to go."

"That's not going to happen," I vowed.

"In the meantime," he went on, "our powers won't affect you."

At that moment the boat rocked violently and I heard the guttural call of a large animal. A surge of water spilled over the rim of the boat, a dense spray of it shooting up in the air.

"What is it?" I cried.

"They don't call it the Waterway of the White Hippo for nothing," Asten said sardonically.

Ahmose lifted the pole and jabbed it into the ivory shape hovering beneath the water. I saw other shapes surrounding us as one large hippo lifted its head above the waterline. Its mouth gaped open, and, enraged, it bit into the side of the boat, nearly overturning us. I very quickly came to doubt the efficacy of Ahmose's pole as a weapon and lifted the bow over my shoulder, preparing to defend us.

"Stop," Asten said, and covered my hand with his. "You cannot kill anything. Not here. These animals are considered sacred."

"But how are we to cross if we cannot muster a defense?"

"It's a part of the judging, Lily. If they deem you worthy to pass over, you will. If not, they will jostle the boat until you fall out."

"And then what? They chew me to bits and spit my sorry carcass out, making the riverbed my tomb?"

"They've never consumed one who was living," Ahmose said.

"Well, that makes me feel a whole heck of a lot better."

"It's likely they cannot judge you at this time, regardless," Asten added.

"Let us hope for their sake that is true," Tia said. "I have taken down a hippo before but it was not an easy kill."

I shook my head, worried at the ease with which Tia surfaced now, and glanced at Asten, feeling the flush of embarrassment creep up my neck, but the look he gave me was not what I expected. It wasn't disgust or even pity I saw on his face. He was actually impressed.

"You must be quite a huntress to take down a beast like that," Asten said.

Tia shrugged, or perhaps I was the one who shrugged. The lines between us seemed to be blurring, especially since we'd reunited with Asten and Ahmose. But neither of us said anything as we glanced warily over the side, watching the huge white forms surging beneath the water.

Hippo heads rose from the depths to eye us. Sometimes we saw only the rounded tops, black eyes blinking as they stared at us curiously. Other times they lifted half their bodies out of the water, which made me think the water wasn't really that deep. I couldn't imagine animals of that size floating. Tia quickly assured me that they weren't able to—at least, they couldn't in the mortal realm.

"Ah," Ahmose said. "Even the bull wants a peek at you."

Off to the side, a huge male hippo blew water from his nostrils, opening his mouth as he bellowed loudly. His canines and incisors were incredibly thick.

"The rest of these are his harem and offspring," Ahmose said.

The big bull hippo he indicated sucked in a mouthful of water and spat it over us, then submerged beneath the river.

"If he's letting you pass, the rest of them will, too," Ahmose said.

"Then why are the others sticking their heads up?" I asked.

"They probably haven't seen a living being here in quite some time," he answered.

"That's right. I forgot you two don't count."

"We don't," Asten said with a twinge of sadness in his voice. "As of right now, our bodies are moldering on earth somewhere in the elaborate sarcophagi that Anubis made us."

I stretched out a hand and placed it on his arm. "But I can still touch you," I said. "That's something."

"Yes. But we can't feel it."

"You can't?" I asked, shocked.

Asten shook his head. "At least not in the way we do when we take our physical forms. I am aware of pressure and warmth but the touch does not hold as much feeling, as much sensation, as it would normally," he said.

"But Amon can feel my touch in the netherworld. Why would it be different here?"

"Perhaps it is due to your bond," Asten suggested.

"Maybe it can work with you, too. The three of you are bound together also. Can I try?"

"If you like," Asten answered, curious.

He held out his hand and I grasped it. When he squeezed my hand lightly and began to rub his thumb in small circles, I opened my mind to experiencing the touch. I felt the warmth of his palm, the little hairs on the back of his hand, the lines and whorls of the pad, and even the tiny pulse of his heartbeat through his fingertips.

I used the power of the sphinx to enhance my touch even more. Soon I felt a current running just beneath my skin. It was warm and alive and I became aware of each breath that filled his lungs, the way he bit his lip, the feel of the wind on his face, and his racing heart. The scrape of his skin against mine was a pleasure more delicious to me than even the kiss of Horus had been. It was like someone rubbing the back of your neck or beneath your jaw in just the right place so that the tension in your muscles melted. I liked it. A little bit too much.

Pulling my hand from his, I gave him a weak, apologetic smile. I could still feel the tingles from where his thumb had caressed me. Looking up, I found I was momentarily caught in his melted chocolate brown eyes. Instead of his characteristic mischievous smirk, he gifted me with a small, genuine smile.

"Could you feel that?" I asked softly.

His mouth was slightly parted and it didn't take enhanced vision to see his pulse jumping at his throat. "Oh, yes," he answered, and swallowed. "The sensation was . . . it was startling. I've never experienced such a thing in the afterlife." He paused, then added quietly, "Or any life for that matter. Thank you." He turned away.

My heart beat erratically, thoughts muddy and confused.

"We were *pleased* to touch you," Tia admitted flatly.

Asten's smile grew, his eyes darting back up to meet mine. "I'm glad," he said, not a drop of mirth in his words. "Feel free to practice on me anytime."

Shifting slightly away, I asked, "How long until we get there?"

"We must pass through the burning tree first," Ahmose said.

It wasn't long before I could no longer see the white forms in the shallow river and when we came to a wooden dock, another one where Amon did not wait for us, my heart fell. Ahmose guided us up to it and tied off the boat. When Asten got out, he turned to me and offered his hand. "May I?" he asked.

Something about the way he looked at me and wrapped his arm around my waist to steady me as I stepped onto the dock made me feel both elated and sad. He kept hold of my hand as we walked up the path and I didn't withdraw it. I knew he couldn't feel my touch unless I was channeling the power of the sphinx, but I could very much feel his, and it didn't feel like the way a brother would hold my hand.

There was a part of me that thought he could be something more if he wanted to and guilt filled me. Against my shoulder I felt the beat of Amon's heart, and I wondered if he was dreaming at that exact moment, seeing me hold hands with Asten, and if that would make him upset enough to want to give in to a second death.

Giving Asten a tiny smile, I withdrew my hand, and though he seemed to understand, I could tell he was disappointed. He wasn't the only one either. Tia's discontent filled my mind, too, though she didn't say anything. My feelings were so jumbled I was surprised I could function at all.

Ahmose led us down a path until we came to a giant tree encircled by fire, its heat washing over us.

"What do we do now?" I asked.

"You must find a way to the other side," he answered.

"How?"

"We cannot tell you. Each soul that journeys the Isle of the Dead must find its own way."

Letting out a breath, I nodded and headed to the right, but there was no end to the flames. Going left didn't get me anywhere either, and the longer we stayed close to the blaze, the more concerned Tia became.

We cannot make it, she cried in my mind. *You must ask the guardians for help.*

But they can't help us. They told us as much. I craned my neck to try to see over the wall. The tall tree beckoned with thick trunks and very green leaves despite the fire surrounding it. *Maybe we can climb over it,* I suggested.

Tia hated the idea but helped me focus my eyes to try and discover tree limbs that overshot the crackling flames. There were none.

Should we walk through it? I suggested. *Maybe it's a test.*

Absolutely not! Tia insisted.

Then what's your big idea? Not hearing too much from you. And I'd think I would, considering how vocal you've been lately.

I did not know my thoughts were so repulsive to you.

Not repulsive. And it's not your thoughts I'm having a problem with—it's the surprise takeovers. I sighed. *It's just . . . getting hard to keep us separate sometimes.*

I, too, am having a hard time remembering myself. We are . . . bleeding into one another.

Maybe that's a good thing.

Maybe.

So then let's use that to our advantage, I said.

What do you mean, Lily?

Let's call on our power.

I didn't need to hear her words to know she agreed. Closing my eyes, we drew upon the power of the sphinx and I felt Tia's thoughts entwine with mine, our purpose becoming one. We wanted to get over the wall of fire.

We called upon the wind and it banked the flames enough that we could traverse them. Backing up a few feet, we ran, leapt, and then somersaulted in the air before landing on our feet safely on the other side. The moment our feet touched ground, the flames disappeared and Asten and Ahmose approached us.

"I've never seen a crossing done like that before," Asten said, an appreciative gleam in his eyes.

"Most of the dead just walk through the flames," Ahmose added as he folded his arms across his chest. "They know they can't be burned."

"Well, we didn't know that," I replied. "Besides, it's very likely we could have been burned. Our flesh is still living."

"And we wouldn't want to scar something so lovely," Asten said.

"Come," Ahmose said. "It's not far now to the Porch of Judgment."

The dirt and pebbles of our current path were replaced with stone as the dark expanse of a stone temple came into view.

"Is that it?" I asked.

"It is. Don't wander now," Ahmose warned as if I would suddenly decide to leave them.

The Porch of Judgment looked like an ancient palace in ruins. Large blocks of stone lay broken and shattered in various sections. There were no windows, just large, carved recesses with sealed-up sections where window should have been. The pillars that stood on each side of the imposing stone door were hollowed out, and fires burned inside them, giving haunting life to the images engraved on the outside. They looked like frightening iron jack-o'-lanterns with gaping maws, waiting to swallow the dead. Braziers burned on the top, sending flaming ashes and smoke skyward.

"Little scary, isn't it?" I asked.

"It's meant to be intimidating," Ahmose answered.

"Well, it's working," I said.

Ahmose grabbed an iron ring on the door and pulled while Asten took hold of the other one. With a substantial creak, the doors swung open. Without thinking, I reached for Asten's hand. Though he seemed surprised at the offer, he didn't hesitate and enfolded my fingers in his.

Once we were inside, the doors closed on their own. Torches lined the hallway, rings of smoke sticking to the stone walls like the dark shadows of tortured souls. I squeezed Asten's hand, and though I knew he couldn't feel it in the same way, I soon felt an echoing squeeze. It comforted me and helped soothe Tia's nerves.

"What's next?" I whispered.

"We meet the gods and your heart is weighed," Asten replied.

"Do I need to do that? I mean, I'm not dead."

"Honestly, I'm not sure. If what you said is true, they're expecting you. It should go easier for you than it does with most of the souls who find their way here."

I swallowed. "That's what I'm hoping for."

We entered a large room where three thrones sat empty. In the center of the space was a large golden scale, with torches casting a dim light over the vast chamber. I felt like I was in a dungeon waiting to hear my sentence. After Asten guided me to a dais, giving me a reassuring smile, he had me stand there while Ahmose stepped forward and began chanting a spell.

"This Soul has come to the afterlife
She has journeyed the channel of the sky and the earth
She has walked with the guardians
She has trod the path of the white hippos
She has passed through the tree of fire
And she has come through unscathed
She is prepared for the judgment
She seeks to have her heart weighed
And is ready to follow the path you choose for her."

The three of us stood there, waiting for something to happen. When nothing did, Ahmose added:

"She is noble and she is beloved
Please give her audience."

This time the room shook. When it finally quieted, a storm cloud of sand filtered in from the open passageways and created a human-sized cyclone. The sand solidified and a familiar shape took form.

I lifted my hand slightly, waving at Anubis as he approached, a tiny smile transforming his perpetual glower. "You made it," he said.

"No thanks to you. Your directions were rather cryptic."

"I told you what I was able to. Did you come through Heliopolis?" he asked.

I nodded.

"And how did you get there?"

"Nebu. He asked if I would pass along a message."

Anubis took a step closer. "I already know what he asked of you."

"And? Will you tell her?" I pressed.

He sighed. "She already knows."

Asten stepped forward and placed a protective hand on my arm.

A familiar glower stole across Anubis's face. Just then, three more cyclones appeared and Anubis stepped back and took a position along the stone wall.

Three beings materialized upon the thrones. Sucking in a nervous breath, I narrowed my shoulders and looked at the three gods seated before me. Two of them were women; the other was a man. The man's skin had a greenish tinge to it. He was handsome, with dark hair and piercing eyes, and I remembered the story Amon told me about Seth and Isis. I guessed that the man seated before me must be the winged goddess's husband, Osiris.

I had no idea who the other two women might be. The one on the left had flawless dark skin and glossy lips. Her hair was wound and pinned on top of her head with an elaborate headdress, her back stiff and her demeanor regal. She reminded me of a strict schoolmarm, albeit a beautiful one. Her eyes flicked over me with a calculating expression, and I got the impression that she was extremely on top of things; she was surely the one in charge. This was despite the fact that both Anubis and the man I guessed was Osiris were pretty much as intimidating as Horus and Amun-Ra.

Everything about the other woman was soft, her demeanor sagacious and kind. Her long blond hair hung to her waist and the jewelry she wore was thin and simple—a silver bracelet, a thin belt made from different precious metals, and a tiny chain that hung across her forehead and draped down around her cascading hair. She wore silver sandals and the folds of her dress fell to the floor. She actually gave me a smile that was part encouragement and part curiosity when I glanced in her direction.

Out of nowhere, a group of shabtis materialized in a corner and began playing soft music. I recognized a flute, a harp, and a sistrum, a golden instrument that looked like a badminton racket, only instead of a net it had tiny disks that slid back and forth when shaken. The only reason I knew about it was because Dr. Hassan had unearthed one recently and described it in his usual meticulous detail in a letter.

Maybe the gods summoned the musicians as a way of soothing the dead before they ripped out their hearts for judgment, I thought.

It is *pleasing,* Tia noted.

You missed the point, I said.

What was your point?

Heart ripping.

Other servants stood by the gods, waving ostrich feather fans, holding plates of grapes and goblets glistening with condensation. Not one of the shabtis made eye contact with me. Actually, they appeared to be studiously avoiding looking at the entire judging area.

The austere-looking beauty spoke first. "What is your condition?" she asked.

"My . . . condition? I don't understand."

"Please answer the question. What is your condition?"

"Um . . . alive, I guess?"

"This will never do. She isn't ready," the testy woman complained. "Remove her from my sight at once."

Immediately, Ahmose and Asten began to protest, and a burst of power from the woman's fingertips froze the two of them instantly. Anubis took a step toward me then, but one glance from the woman made him reconsider his decision and he moved back into his former place with a wince.

The kind-looking woman wrung her hands and said, "Please, won't you reconsider?" but the first woman glared at her until she turned her head aside. Finally, my questioner took a step closer, raised her hand, and said, "She will be banished and sent back to the place from whence she came, only to return when she has shuffled off the chains of mortality."

She waved her hand in a flourish to leave, but not before the man on the throne stood. "No, Ma'at," he said. "She won't."

17

The Scales of Justice

"Osiris?" The goddess Ma'at spun, her mouth shaped in a surprised O.

"My apologies," Osiris said. "I meant no disrespect. But you know as well as I do that we need her."

"That's your opinion," she replied. "The law is—"

"The law means nothing in this case," Anubis said, taking a bold step forward, his eyes sliding briefly to me.

Ma'at glared at him like he was a naughty schoolboy ready to be punished with a ruler. "How dare you say such a thing?" she spat. "The law is everything. Without it, there is no balance, no order."

"Ma'at," Anubis countered as he gestured with his hands. "Don't you think you're being a bit extreme?"

"Me? You have allowed your mind to be clouded by the mortals you favor. You hold out hope for redemption where none can be found. Even if it were allowed, which it isn't, the likelihood of success is infinitesimal and absolutely not worth risking this one's immortal soul. Besides, it would be ill-advised for me to endorse such a foolish venture when Amun-Ra refuses to offer his support. And furthermore—"

"Um, he did, though," I interjected. "He guided me to Cherty as the benu bird."

Ma'at turned on me. "You will cease speaking immediately!" she bellowed. "You are only to answer the questions I pose to you. Otherwise remain silent."

"Shouldn't I get a say in deciding my own fate?"

"She has a point," the kinder goddess proposed.

To say that Ma'at didn't like to be contradicted would be an egregious understatement of vast proportions. She turned her back to me, ignoring me completely, as she addressed the other woman. "This is not an occasion where we should allow the influence of a mortal to color our decisions, Nephthys. I know how you love them, but you must cede to my experience regarding this matter."

Nephthys twitched her hands with nervous energy and glanced in my direction. She then nodded and sat back in her chair. I stared at her, wondering how so delicate and beautiful a creature could have agreed to marry the creepy god Seth. Amun-Ra had said she could see into his heart. Personally, I wouldn't want to get close enough to the guy to do any such thing. A shiver ran down my spine as I thought about him.

Ma'at turned her attention back to me, likely preparing to banish me yet again, but Anubis interrupted. "Wait! I will offer to be her patron."

Ma'at closed her eyes, pinching the bridge of her nose with her fingers. "You cannot, Anubis. You know this already. The law says you are only allowed to select one mortal and you have. This"—she gestured vaguely to Asten—"young . . . person was your choice. You imbued him with your powers, how many years ago was it?"

"Millennia," Anubis muttered tightly with a quick glance at Asten.

Ma'at smiled. "Exactly. You can only advocate for one mortal while they still live. And he does live . . . in a manner of speaking."

"I will sponsor her," the soft-spoken goddess, Nephthys, offered.

"Oh, Nephthys." Ma'at clicked her tongue. "You are not allowed to take part in such a thing. You know that your rights have been stripped due to the actions of your errant husband."

"I know," Nephthys admitted. "It's just that I'd like to help."

"Your help, I might remind you, is what got us all into this mess in the first place. If you hadn't been so keen on gaining the attention and approval of your husband, you would have told us what he was up to long before we had to call upon the Sons of Egypt for their assistance. Not that we blame you, dear. It is not unusual for a woman to compromise her values in order to gain the affection of a man."

"Yes," Nephthys said meekly. "Of course. I understand."

My hands tightened into fists, and I had to work to keep my claws retracted. Tia bristled along with me. So far we didn't like the goddess of justice very much.

"It is within the bounds for *me* to sponsor someone," Osiris interjected as he rose from his throne and approached the dais. "Is it not, Ma'at?"

The goddess hedged. "Technically, you have the right, Osiris. But in doing so you are allowing yourself to succumb to the powers of her heart scarab."

"That is completely false," he avowed. "You may judge my heart if you wish, but you know that I am bound to Isis. I love my wife. Our relationship offers me protection from the influence of the scarab. Anubis"—he gestured to the god holding up the wall—"may be under its sway . . ."

Glancing over at Anubis proved that Osiris had come to the right conclusion. Anubis had fixed his eyes on me and appeared unwilling to tear them away.

". . . but I assure you I am not," Osiris continued.

"That is all well and good," Ma'at said. "However, I would caution you not to waste such a precious gift on one such as her."

"Hey!" I spat.

She ignored me.

"Really?" Osiris said. "And why is that?" he asked as he folded his arms across his chest and appraised me, considering her words. But when she wasn't looking, he winked and I tried in vain to suppress an answering smile.

"First, she is still alive. We don't judge the living." She cupped her hand around the bar of the scale and raised her stubborn chin, waiting for his retort.

"Is that the only thing?" Osiris asked calmly.

The goddess faltered for a moment. "No. There is more. She seeks to enter the netherworld to rescue her love. The last time we allowed something like this to happen, there were grave consequences. And his lost love, I'll remind you, was still residing here, in the afterlife, which is inherently less dangerous. That is why we decided to forbid such a thing."

"Hmm." Osiris turned to me. "Are you looking to save your love? To bring him back from the netherworld to be with you?" When I glanced at Ma'at and hesitated, he added, "You may speak."

"I didn't think bringing him back to the mortal realm was even possible. As much as I want to be with him, we both know he has a duty to fulfill."

"There." Osiris smiled at me. "She has no intention of carrying him off."

Ma'at gave him a slight roll of her eyes. "It's a technicality."

"So is your adherence to the law," Osiris said.

The goddess's face turned purple. "Don't you understand? She will not survive the journey! Amon is lost. Everything is out of balance. To lose her, too, is . . . it's unthinkable. She's too important!"

We're important? I said to Tia. *What do you think she means?*

I am not certain. Perhaps we should attempt to wrestle some more information from Anubis. He left us woefully unprepared for this tribunal.

He didn't even mention it, I said.

Yes. It makes me wonder what else he forgot to mention.

Osiris calmly argued, "Her importance is indeterminate at best at this time. She followed all the rules to enter the afterlife and has presented herself for judgment appropriately."

"That's because she had help," Ma'at declared with frustration.

Osiris glanced at the frozen forms of Asten and Ahmose. With a wave of his hand, the enchantment disappeared and they both looked around in confusion. "Did the two of you offer this young woman help as you guided her here?"

Ahmose shook his head. "She went through the same trials as the disembodied. We did not assist or protect her in any way."

"It wasn't necessary," Asten said. "But if it had been, we would have," he added honestly.

"You see?" Ma'at jumped on his answer. "They would break the law to help her. Just like Amon did when he escaped his judgment!"

Osiris interjected, "You cannot ignore the fact that we all agree she is vital. If she fails, everything falls apart. But if she succeeds . . ."

"If she succeeds, then there's a chance to bring back balance," Nephthys said quietly. "It might turn things around. Turn *him* around."

Ma'at sighed. "There's very little chance of that. I fear you are the only one left who holds out hope for him. You wish for an outcome that is so impossible as to be almost certain of failure."

"Let's talk about what's really making you upset," Anubis said.

Stiffening, Ma'at answered, "I don't know what you mean."

"I think you do. You don't like that Amon didn't offer up his heart when you demanded it."

"No one denies me," she said sulkily while glaring at Anubis. "It is my calling, my right to weigh hearts. I am the great judge, the one who finds balance. How do you all expect me to accomplish anything when you constantly circumvent me? Even Amun-Ra—"

"Maybe you could judge his heart now," I offered.

The goddess looked up. "What do you mean?"

"I was thinking you might be able to weigh his heart based on the heart scarab he gave me. Assuming such a thing is possible, of course."

All the gods sucked in a collective breath, and I wondered if I had just committed a major afterlife faux pas. No one said anything for a moment, and when I looked to Asten and Ahmose, their backs were ramrod straight, neither of them daring to look in my direction.

Ma'at finally spoke. "No one has ever offered such a thing. You need to understand that a heart scarab is considered a very private and personal token of affection. What you propose has never been done before. I do not know if I can even weigh it or if the weighing of it will cause damage to your connection. I must also warn you that even should I manage to successfully judge it, you will be liable for anything I find."

"Do you know what that means, Lily?" Anubis warned, concern shadowing over his eyes. "You will pay the price for Amon's actions, and not just during his mortal sojourn but for his entire existence, even the time he's spent in the netherworld."

"I understand. I'm not afraid of what you'll find in Amon's heart."

"It's not just you anymore, Lily," Asten added with a frown. "Tia will pay the price as well."

Tia? I whispered in my mind as I put my hand over my chest, where my heart beat in a steady rhythm.

If you believe this to be the right course, I will follow, Tia answered.

Are you certain?

If you are confident, then I am as well. I do not fear the outcome, she said. *As we are unified of body, we will be unified in the face of the unknown. I am with you.*

Okay, I said, my heart swelling with emotion at the level of trust Tia showed me. I was so grateful not to be going through this alone.

"We will submit the scarab for judgment," I declared, unclasping the brooch from my shoulder and handing it over.

"Well, since we're all getting along so much better at present, can we dispense with the gloom and doom?" Nephthys asked shyly.

"Oh, I suppose," Ma'at said, obviously in a much better mood now that she had her prize. While she busied herself at the Scales of Justice, Nephthys rose from her throne and drew her hand in a wide arc from left to right. As she did so, the room shimmered. The dark stone became gleaming white tile trimmed in gold, and the torches transformed into sparkling sconces lit by soft candlelight. Chandeliers hung overhead. In each corner of the long hall there was an impressive statue of each of the four gods with a shrine set in the alcoves behind them. The music from earlier continued, though the musicians disappeared and tall vases were filled with long white feathers tipped in gold. They reminded me of Isis.

"Do they belong to your wife?" I asked Osiris as I pointed to the feathers.

He smiled sadly. "They are my only reminder of her during the long spans of time we spend apart."

"Can't she stay here with you?" I asked.

"The law . . . ," he started to say, and then he gave a small shrug and a smile as he turned to watch Ma'at.

"The law stinks sometimes, doesn't it?" I said.

Osiris laughed briefly. "Yes. It does . . . stink." He wrapped his mouth around the last word as if he'd never heard it said like that before. He glanced in my direction. "It is very brave. What you're doing, you know. We all think so."

"Apparently not everyone," I stage-whispered, and gestured to the goddess bending over the scales.

"She's not usually so testy," he explained. "She blames herself for what Seth did."

"Why?"

"She is responsible for separating chaos from order. When chaos began to take over, she felt it was her own weakness that caused it. After Seth was imprisoned, she decided to adhere to the law even more strictly in the hope that such a thing could never happen again. Ma'at took the loss of our grandparents hard. Attempting to find absolute cosmic harmony was how she coped with everything that happened.

"She forgot that the purpose of the law and the protection and justice it offers is often more important than the law itself. Mercy must always balance justice. Unfortunately, she seems to have neglected that aspect over the centuries. It's why she likes to keep Nephthys close. She's the voice of mercy to balance out Ma'at's unwavering adherence to rules."

Osiris smiled and then continued gesturing at the hall. "That's why this place is often called the Hall of Two Truths."

"Meaning the truth of justice and the truth of mercy?" I asked, my own power of discerning the truth coming into play.

"That's right."

"We are ready," Ma'at said. "Osiris, are you certain you want to stand for her?"

"I am," he answered.

"Very well. Then we shall begin."

Ma'at placed the heart scarab on a stand next to the large scale and then approached a golden box set atop a pedestal that hadn't been there until Nephthys transformed the hall. From inside the box, Ma'at reverently drew out the object.

"This is the Feather of Justice," she said. "Its weight is so light as to be inconsequential. When a heart is free of evil, it is not weighed down by sorrow or guilt. In this case, the scale will balance and the person may retain their heart and is admitted into paradise. This type of heart is very uncommon. When a soul has committed *some* wrongdoing but has expressed sorrow, made recompense, and learned from the experience, allowing it to mold their heart into a kinder, more empathetic one, then the scales dip only slightly and that person is also admitted into paradise. This is the most common type of heart."

"And when a person has committed evil?" I asked, wetting my lips.

"An evildoer's heart is heavy. The weight of it depends on the quantity and the depth of the crimes they've committed. In some cases such a person can be rehabilitated." I nodded, remembering the shabti workers in the Field of Reeds. "But in many instances," she went on, "such a heart has no place here and it, along with its owner, is sent to the netherworld, a place of torment and suffering, and eventually they succumb to their second and final death. Their life essence, then, if it doesn't feed the Devourer, will return to the Waters of Chaos."

Ma'at brandished the feather, raising it to the sky before placing it gently upon the scale. The feather looked much different from the feathers of Isis. It almost appeared as if it were made of glass.

"It's diamond," Osiris said, like he was reading my mind.

The glistening feather did look crystalline, almost as if it had beads of water clinging to it. Now I knew that each branch was a thin diamond with a tiny diamond drop on each tipped barb. When she picked up the heart scarab, I panicked for a second and mentally crossed my fingers, hoping that whatever happened next wouldn't hurt Amon and that I was doing the right thing.

"Let us begin," Ma'at said. Looking directly at me, she again asked, "What is your condition?"

I bit my lip, pondering the right answer, and was about to say *human* or *sphinx,* when Osiris said, "Their hearts are guiltless. They are free of every sin."

"Have you committed violence?"

This time Osiris stepped back and nodded that I should answer.

"Only when attacked."

"And to eat," Tia added.

"I have struck down innocent beasts who murdered my teacher," Osiris said. "I have punished those who hurt my subjects, but I have never enjoyed violence."

I glanced over at Osiris, my brow knit in puzzlement. He appeared to be in a sort of trance. Thinking back over his words, I realized he wasn't speaking for himself. Osiris was channeling Amon.

Ma'at nodded, satisfied with our answers, and I noticed a tiny dip in the heart. "Have you ever taken that which did not belong to you?"

"I have not," Tia answered confidently.

Osiris spoke next. "I took Ahmose's toy boat when we were young. I was jealous that his was better made and faster than mine. I sank it in the Nile and never told him, though he cried."

I glanced over at Ahmose, and his expression was one of surprise and then forgiveness.

"And you, Lily?" Ma'at asked.

I shrugged. "I never had the need to take anything that didn't belong to me. My parents gave me whatever I asked for, and I never spent enough time with other children to make friends, let alone take what they had."

The goddess turned to glance at the scale. A slight frown furrowed her brow, but it was soon gone and she asked the next question.

"Have you ever committed perjury, hidden the truth, or deceived another?"

Again Tia stated boldly, "I have always been truthful."

I grimaced, wishing I were more like Tia. "I've lied—frequently, if I'm being honest. I hid the scarab from Anubis. My parents don't even know I'm here. They have no idea I'm a sphinx. They think I'm at my nana's house right now. They don't know about Amon or what happened this past spring. I told them I was happy with the plans they'd made for me, when in truth I dread every second of my future. I've told so many white lies to their friends and colleagues I can't even remember all of them. I even lied about coloring my hair!"

Nephthys put her hand over her mouth and giggled but ceased immediately after a sharp look from Ma'at. "And why did you tell all these untruths, Lily?" she asked.

"Mostly so they wouldn't worry."

"Were you trying to escape punishment?"

"Not really. My life at home is a punishment. There wasn't anything they could do to make me more miserable than what they'd already planned for me. I just wanted to keep Amon's secret and I didn't think they'd understand."

The scarab dipped as Ma'at cast judgment, and this time it was clearly visible.

"Don't you think you're being a little bit hard on her for that one?" Anubis said, and I noted that he stood much closer to me now than he had been before.

"It is not your call to make," Ma'at answered stiffly. "And, Amon?" She gestured to Osiris.

"I lied to Lily. I made her think I didn't care about her when I was falling in love with her. I told my brothers we could successfully complete the ceremony to align the sun, moon, and stars without her, when I knew we would fail. I put her welfare ahead of my duty," Osiris murmured in his trance state. "When Asten and Ahmose asked what was wrong, I kept my feelings from them. They didn't know how desperate I was to get out. To escape. How I would sacrifice anything, including my relationship with them, even the very cosmos, to be with her.

"She doesn't know that without her, there is no hope for me. No life. Only death and darkness. She thought I was brave in sacrificing myself in the pyramid, but if Anubis had given me just a few more minutes alone with her, I would have used all the power at my disposal, even the Eye of Horus, to hide the two of us in the farthest reaches of the cosmos. If I'd known that she would have agreed, I would have gladly spent my life trying to avoid the gods just to be with her. After my death, escape to the netherworld was my only option. Since my leap, I've used every power at my disposal to prevent her from sacrificing herself for me, and yet a part of me is glad that we are still connected and that she still wants to be with me as much as I want to be with her. I'd do anything for her. Anything. This was the reason I refused the weighing of my heart."

When Osiris was done speaking, the room was silent. A trail of tears leaked down my face. If Amon *had* asked me to run away, I think I would have gone. Especially if it meant he didn't have to die. I wasn't sure what that made me that I would put my relationship, the life of one man, the man I loved, over the well-being of all the souls who lived in the cosmos, but it was something to consider. It was Anubis who finally broke the silence.

"A heart scarab usually prevents the owner's heart from testifying against him at the judgment."

Ma'at replied quietly. "In this case we are hearing the echo of his thoughts through Lily and Tia. Amon's true feelings are summoned forth through their connection. Is there anything else forthcoming that pertains to this question?"

Osiris screwed up his face like he did have something to say, but he was trying to hold it back. Beads of sweat broke out over his brow. Then, finally, he said, "Lily is in possession of my ren." The god panted after speaking those words and looked up at Ma'at with alarm. Her expression echoed his. In truth, all the gods, including Asten and Ahmose, seemed awestruck, and not in a good way.

"What does that mean?" I asked warily. "What's a ren?"

Asten was actually the one who explained. "Not even *we* are privy to Amon's ren. It is his true name. To utter a true name is to bring life to something."

"Or death," Ahmose said. "It gives you absolute power over the person."

Everyone stood there staring at me like I had just grown a third eye. "Well, I don't have it," I said, gesturing wildly with my hands. "I think I'd be aware of it if I did."

"Amon's scarab speaks the truth, Lilliana Young," Ma'at said. "It cannot do otherwise on the scales of judgment. This is a sign," she added, gesturing wildly to the other gods in the room.

"We don't know that yet," Anubis cautioned. "It could be that he just wanted to share it with her. It doesn't necessarily mean what you think it does."

"If Amon is bound by the scales, then so am I," I said. "So you know I'm telling the truth when I say I don't have it. If I do, then I'm unaware of it."

"Do you really think this might have something to do with the prophecy?" Anubis asked.

"There is no way to tell," Nephthys answered.

"What prophecy?" I asked, looking at each god in succession. They all looked reluctant to speak. When I glanced in Asten's direction, he gave a slight shrug.

"There is an ancient prophecy regarding chaos," Ma'at explained. "It says that there will come a time when chaos reigns the cosmos. Harmony will be lost. Order will fragment. The power of the gods will be trapped in a spider's web. That is the time when the Liberator will appear. But she will not be able to save all that is lost. A great sacrifice will need to be made to bring the balance back. She will use a true name to swallow the sun and it will disappear forever."

"And you're saying you think I'm this Liberator?"

"We don't know," Nephthys said. "It's a very old prophecy. But Amon—"

"Yeah. I get it. He's imbued with the power of the sun. And I supposedly have his true name," I said.

"If she did know Amon's true name, it would make all this much easier," Anubis said.

"How so?" I folded my arms across my chest and frowned.

"You could use it to summon him. He would have no choice but to heed to your call."

"I . . . I could do that?" I stammered. "That seems like an awful lot of power."

"It is," Osiris said. "As devoted as I am to my wife, I do not share my true name with her. It is a dangerous thing, for once another person knows, you are doubly vulnerable."

"I would never do anything to hurt Amon," I protested.

"Perhaps not willingly, dear," Nephthys replied. "But there is a power in knowing and those who might wish to exploit that power would come after you."

"Yes," Ma'at said. "This knowledge must remain here, with us. That Lily is in possession of Amon's ren will never be uttered by any of us. Is it agreed?"

"Agreed," each god said in turn. Ahmose and Asten also nodded.

"Very well," the goddess of judgment continued. "Shall we finish this, then?" I could almost tell from her attitude that the remaining questions were superfluous. She'd already made her decision.

When Ma'at asked if we'd ever caused others to weep or caused broken hearts, I was unsurprised by Amon's answer, and mine was easy. My parents were more likely to have a broken heart over a waning stock portfolio than about me, but Tia's answer was surprising. She said, "I fear a lioness's heart is made of material too tough to love and perhaps too strong to break." Her answer made me feel sad, especially knowing that was how she truly felt.

After a few more queries, Ma'at nodded. "This question is the most important of all. It is vital to be of a moral caliber strong enough to refrain from taking that which does not belong to you, just as it is to be truthful or to not cause physical harm, but it is the heart that speaks to the character of a soul.

"The three of you have a great concern and love for those around you. Even Amon, who admits that he ran away and wanted to hide from his duty, did so out of love for another. This wish is utterly human. It is not an evil thing to desire love and a connection with another person but a gift worthy of striving for. Each one of you spoke not of the desire to inflict your will upon others, to subjugate, or to intimidate, but of the sorrow of loss."

The goddess sighed deeply and turned toward the scale. Placing her hands under each bowl, she closed her eyes and quietly chanted. When she opened them, she picked up the feather in one hand and the heart scarab in the other and approached the dais.

"A judgment has been requested and a judgment has been made," Ma'at said. "I have judged the heart of the deceased, Amon; the wandering spirit, Tia; and the still living, Lily. Their souls stand as witnesses against them. In all sincerity, I decree that . . ."

I sucked in a breath and bit my lower lip, nibbling on it nervously. Asten looked over at me with a worried expression that made me doubt myself even more, and I shifted on my feet uncomfortably.

". . . their deeds are righteous in the balance of life. The misdeeds discovered have been absolved. Their hearts are true and they will be granted passage into paradise."

The goddess smiled and I felt the sweet trickle of icy relief in my veins, but at the same time, I wondered what her decision meant. Wasn't I supposed to go to the netherworld? How was that going to work? Amon wasn't in paradise. I stood in place wringing my hands, wondering what was supposed to happen next. Thankfully, I didn't have to wait long.

"It's a good thing, truly," Anubis said. "But she will need you to open the path to the netherworld, even so."

"I cannot do that," Ma'at said.

"How will she get to the netherworld if you don't send her?" Anubis said.

Ma'at sighed. "I cannot send a good soul to the netherworld, even if they're willing. Amon was able to make the jump because he possesses the Eye of Horus."

"So we're out of options?" Anubis asked.

"She could latch on to the coattails of one condemned," Ma'at suggested.

"That could take decades! The most vile hearts worthy of condemnation don't just appear every day," Asten proclaimed.

"And I suppose you have another idea?" Ma'at replied.

Asten folded his arms. "Yes," he said. "I've got an idea."

"And what, pray tell, is that?" Ma'at asked.

"I think you should find my heart evil enough. She can ride on mine."

18

The Heart of a Dreamer

"I want my heart to be weighed on the scales of justice!" Asten declared, his countenance as wild as a whirlwind. The spacious hall suddenly felt tight and small, as if the air were full of secrets.

"Asten! What are you saying?" Ahmose hissed in alarm.

Quietly, Asten replied, "You'll know soon enough." He paused, glancing at Ahmose briefly, regret filling his eyes, and then added, "Brother."

"Son. Don't do this." Startled, I watched Anubis pace toward Asten and place his hand on his shoulder. "It isn't the time," he said. "We'll find another way."

Asten shrugged and smiled, attempting his trademark cocky smirk, but the gesture was empty and weak, devoid of his usual wit and charm. "It was going to happen eventually, wasn't it? I've played the part long enough. The lies have eaten away at me for millennia. At least this way something good might come of it."

Ma'at had ordered a drink but before touching it, waved her servant over and hastily placed the goblet on the tray. Red liquid sloshed over the side, drops dribbling to the floor. Though the servant hastily made an effort to clean up the spill, my eyes remained transfixed on the stain. It looked like blood against the white tile. The stone was so porous it soaked up the liquid, and despite the best efforts of the girl, she could not remove the pigment. It felt portentous, an ominous sign, and my heart beat heavily in my chest with the sure knowledge that something horrible, something irreversible, was happening.

Clenching his jaw, Anubis straightened and turned toward Ma'at, pointing a threatening finger in her direction. "There will be no judging!" he announced. "Asten doesn't know what he's doing."

"I know exactly what I'm doing," Asten countered boldly. "And I understand the consequences better than anyone. How many doomed souls have I escorted across the Isle of the Dead? How many have I seen burned in the fire or swallowed by the hippos? How many have I dragged here to their judgment, where they collapsed in a heap of weeping and wailing supplication? I am more prepared than most, and I knew a day of reckoning was coming. I've been granted more time than I deserved. That was thanks to you, Anubis. You've helped me keep my secret over the years, even from my brothers. I'm not sure why you did it, but I'm grateful, regardless."

"Asten, please," Anubis said. "Won't you reconsider? There are plenty—"

"A judging has been requested and a judging will take place," Ma'at announced. She waved her arm and all the servants disappeared. "I do not pretend to know what mysterious turpitude the two of you have covered up, but we will soon find out."

"What is your condition?" the goddess asked softly.

Asten nibbled on his lip before heaving a deep sigh. "My heart is guilty. I am not free of sin."

Ma'at moved her hand with a flourish and Asten cried out in pain, clutching his chest. White particles of light as soft and yet as piercing as the stars rose from between his fingers and moved purposely forward in an undulating rhythm. They strained toward Ma'at's outstretched hand, gathering together and coalescing as they did so. Asten staggered and breathed heavily as the last of the light left his body.

The delicate material contracted and re-formed itself into what looked like a mound of gleaming clay. Ma'at blew on it almost reverently and the thing she held quivered, then stilled. When she passed me to place it on the scale, I heard the soft beat of Asten's heart, a slightly different rhythm than the one coming from the heart scarab. I glanced at him in alarm but Asten appeared to be fine, though there was a slight catch in his breath.

"Let's start with the easier ones this time, shall we?" Ma'at asked as she returned to stand in front of Asten, her sharp eyes fixed on his face. "Have you broken hearts? Caused others to weep?"

Nodding, Asten said, "There have been a few women who I've left brokenhearted at the end of our earthly hiatus. There was one in particular that Ahmose was interested in and I stole her away."

"And why were you wasting time on that?" she questioned.

Asten shrugged. "I was lonely. I wanted the companionship of a beautiful woman. But there was nothing I could do to extend my stay, so I just disappeared when the time came. They cried, but in most cases they got over me fairly quickly."

"And what happened then with Ahmose?"

"Ahmose isn't the type to love and leave a girl. When I saw he was getting serious, I intervened."

Ahmose's body was tense, his hands tightening into fists. "*Why*, Asten?" he quietly inquired.

Asten looked at his brother with regret. "Because it would have broken you. You would have done what Amon did, but worse. You would have sacrificed everything just like he did."

"Then why didn't you stop *him*?" Ahmose asked.

"I didn't stop Amon because"—Asten paused and looked at me—"because she loved him back. Tiombe didn't love you," Asten murmured softly.

"It wasn't your place to judge," Ahmose said.

"No," Asten agreed. "It wasn't. I regretted it as soon as it was done, but consoled myself when I saw your anger. If there was a risk that you would kill anyone, it was me, not yourself, and I made peace with that."

Ahmose folded his arms across his chest. "Glad someone did."

"Let us move on to the next question," Ma'at said. "Have you committed violence?"

"I have," Asten answered quietly. "I've battled the undead. I've fought the minions of Seth. I've dragged the damned to their tribunals and have ignored their pleas. And"—he sucked in a shaky breath—"I've caused the death of an innocent man."

"Caused?" Ma'at said.

"No. I more than caused it," he disclosed. Asten's eyes flicked my way and then he turned his head as if he couldn't stand looking at me. "In fact," Asten continued, "I was the one that took his life."

I gasped, completely shocked that the young man who carried me on his back when I couldn't walk, who flirted with a glint in his chocolate eyes and a knowing smirk, who showed kindness and understanding to Tia, was a murderer. I couldn't reconcile the man I knew with what he was saying.

"Perhaps you'd better explain," Ma'at suggested.

"Lily knows the story about our teacher, how we left the school that day to hunt. It had been my idea. Ahmose and Amon were reluctant to break the rules. I was the wild one of the group, always trying to lead them into trouble. They would never have attacked the jackals if I hadn't been the first to run into danger."

Jackals? Tia shook and scrambled backward inside my mind.

Asten continued. "And I only did it because I knew they wouldn't let me fight alone. The two of them have a royal sort of moral code that I don't seem to possess."

"Go on," Ma'at encouraged.

"Well, that night, after defeating the jackals, we camped and I slunk away, hoping to recover the horns of the ibex."

"And why did you need them?" Ma'at asked.

"My"—he paused—"mother was yearning for a child, a second child," he explained. "And I'd taken it upon myself to hunt down a sorceress. She told me that if I ground up the horns of the ibex, mixed it into the fresh milk from a goat that had recently given birth for the first time, and gave it to my mother to drink, that she would then be able to conceive."

"So you went back for the horns," Osiris said.

"Yes, and when I did, I found the broken body of our teacher. He was still alive. I collapsed at his side and bid him drink from my skin of water, but it was obvious to me that his chance of survival was extremely unlikely. He'd already lost most of his blood. His lower leg had been removed and dragged off. He'd made a tourniquet from some torn cloth, but there was nothing I could do. Not really.

"Anything I attempted would only prolong his suffering. In the time it would have taken to bring my brothers, he likely would have died anyway. And the idea of leaving him to be devoured alive as I sought them out was unthinkable to me."

Something broke in Tia's mind.

"Since you cannot lie when your heart is being weighed, you obviously believe this to be true, and yet you still blame yourself for his death. Why?" Ma'at asked.

Asten didn't answer at first. He had a faraway look in his eyes, as if he was replaying the grisly scene in his mind, and I wondered how many times over the centuries he'd done so.

"He tried to speak," Asten said softly. "But no words escaped his lips. Even so, I knew what he wanted. His eyes pleaded with me, begged me for help. Our teacher needed a miracle. You asked me why I blame myself?" Asten said fervently. "It was *my fault* he was out there. *I* was the one who wanted the ibex. *I* was the one who stirred the blood of the jackals. Not Amon. Not Ahmose. *Me.*

"After looking into his piteous eyes, I made a decision. Taking hold of his shoulder, I whispered, 'I'm sorry,' then placed my hand on his forehead, took my knife, and sliced his throat. What remained of his lifeblood poured over my hands." Asten lifted his hands and stared at them, tears filling his eyes. Touching his shaking fingers to his trembling lips, he closed his eyes and took a deep breath, as if he was trying to set aside the horror that haunted him.

"It didn't take long for him to die," he said when he regained control over his voice. "After that, I took my prize, hid the horns in the underbrush, and returned to my brothers. The next morning when we heard the report that our teacher was missing, all I could feel was the fear of being caught, the shame of knowing I was to blame. They'd find his body and see the cut on his neck and know it was made by man. They'd hunt for his murderer."

Asten's voice shook with emotion. "When they did locate him, the animals had desecrated his body enough that no one was the wiser." His body heaved with a powerful inhale and then he let out the mighty breath in a half sob, half laugh. "And do you want to know what I felt? I felt relief!" he cried, his expression one of outraged self-loathing.

Tears trickled down my cheeks as I imagined the young man Asten had been. My heart broke for him.

He went on shaking his head. "The sorrow over the loss of our teacher wasn't as important to me as not being caught. It's true. Guilt consumed me, but I was safe. I'd kept my secret. When I went to see the sorceress and told her what had happened, the woman cackled in glee and said the blood of the innocent that stained the horns would make her spell even more powerful."

"And did you give your mother the potion?" Ma'at asked.

"I did." Asten swiped his hands over his eyes, his palms digging into the sockets. "It was the only thing I could give her. I owed her that much."

"I sense there is more to that answer that pertains to another question," Ma'at said.

"There is," Asten confessed. "I've memorized your questions, Ma'at. The two remaining are 'Have I ever taken that which did not belong to me?' and 'Have I ever committed perjury, hidden the truth, or deceived another?' The answer to both questions is yes."

If Ma'at was impressed, she didn't show it but waited patiently for Asten to explain.

"When I was ten years of age, the old nursemaid who had taken care of me as a baby was on her deathbed. As was my duty, I went to visit her. When I came to her bedside, she dismissed all of the servants and told me her little secret. She said that when she was called upon to care for the queen's young baby, the prince had been very ill.

"One morning she rose to check the cradle of the young prince and found him dead. She panicked and prayed to the gods to bring back the life of the little one, but it didn't work. Disguised, she wrapped the babe in a cloth and tossed his little body to the crocodiles, then met with a servant woman who had a son the same age and offered her pilfered riches from the king's coffers in exchange for her baby. She did this in order to save her own life, which would have been in jeopardy had it become known that the royal prince had perished under her care. The serving woman agreed.

"I am that child.

"My old nursemaid died soon after, taking her terrible secret to the grave. Once I knew the truth, it tormented me. Over the years I became paranoid. Every servant who looked my way, every merchant who studied my face too long, was banished from my presence. Once, a self-proclaimed uncle appeared, demanding money in return for his silence. He claimed he knew who my real mother was. I threw him in prison. After starving him for months he finally told me where to find my real family.

"I disguised myself and went to see them in the heat of the evening. I spied on them and discovered that the man who was my true father was a drunkard. He abused his wife and his other children, my sisters. Soon after, the rumor was that my family had left. In a drunken rage my father had killed my mother and then sold his progeny off to various traders who paid him in drink.

"Again I felt not outrage. Not sorrow. Instead I felt the sweet joy of relief. My mother and my sisters would never try to come find me. They were gone."

"Oh, Asten," I said, and stretched out a hand to him, but he stepped away.

"I'd done nothing to help her. My real mother died as a result of my fear, my complacency. My cowardice has been my shadow all these years. The boy, the prince I was, disappeared, and in his place was a doppelganger, a changeling, who was truly loved by no one, wanted by no one, and missed by no one. When I died, my final thought was that I could finally be at peace knowing it no longer mattered whose son I was."

Asten turned to Ahmose, who stood frozen in place, his hands at his side, an expression of shock on his face. "Do you see, Ahmose? I am *not* your brother. I am not the man who was destined to do this work." He looked at Anubis. "What I am is a fraud. When I confessed as much to Anubis after he took us away from our homes to explain our new roles, he told me it was too late. He'd already imbued me with his power. There was no taking it back." Asten lifted his arms, palms up, as if sacrificing himself on the battlefield. "I was the son of a *bricklayer*"—he almost spat the word—"raised by a king and queen who, even at the end of their mortal lives, had no idea that their son was an imposter."

Glancing at me, Asten said, "That is why I was desperate to help the queen, the woman I called Mother, though she wasn't mine, have another child. Even though the witch who helped me with the potion haggled for a price that was . . . unthinkable, I felt I had no choice. At the time I thought that if she might have another son, I could quietly disappear and he could rule.

"And now you know the whole sordid tale." Asten held up his hand and ticked the list of his mistakes off his fingers. "I've lied. I've deceived others, almost all my life. I've killed. I've been selfish. I've stood by and done nothing to confront the abuse of my own flesh and blood. I've cast the innocent in prison. Banished the blameless. I've usurped the life of a royal prince, one destined to do great things. And I was paranoid about losing my position every hour of every day. I'm called a Son of Egypt, the Prince of Waset, and yet I am unworthy of those titles. Where my brothers are silver, I am a stone. They are tall cedar trees and I am the common sycamore."

I covered my mouth with my hand to stifle a sob. How could Asten have kept these things hidden deep within his heart all this time? He was good at wearing a mask. I would never have guessed how dark his thoughts were. How much he'd buried behind his self-confident grin.

"Is there anything more?" Ma'at asked, her face still fixed in a neutral expression.

Asten thought for a moment and then nodded. "We spoke of Amon's true name and I don't even know mine. What name did my birth mother call me? What kind of legacy could I have possibly had if my own mother gave me up for money and my father sold his own offspring? All that I am is a pretense. I've used my *prodigious* legacy to build up a wall of deception so high and strong there is no way to topple it."

When the echo of his words faded, the only sound in the room was the rise and fall of our breaths. The slight sound of the scale shifting caught my attention. Ma'at glanced at it and narrowed her eyes, studying the movement for a time. I held my breath as the scale rose and fell, and finally it settled with the heart a few inches lower than the feather, much lower than Amon's had been.

I was about to say something, to protest, to fight for Asten or defend him by telling Ma'at all of the good I'd seen him do, but Ma'at seemed to anticipate my outburst and raised a finger of warning that effectively shut me up. Instead of casting her judgment or asking Asten more questions, she turned to Anubis.

"Why have you kept the knowledge of who he is from us?"

"I did not consider it important."

"He is mortal."

"Not anymore." Anubis shifted and raised his eyes to Asten.

Ma'at tilted her head. "That's why you chose him, isn't it?"

Anubis stiffened. "What do you mean?"

"Amon and Ahmose were conceived supernaturally. Asten wasn't."

"That is true. It makes no difference, though."

"Doesn't it?" Ma'at asked.

"No."

"You had to know," Ma'at accused. "As a supernatural death, you must have been called to the baby's side, the true prince, to escort him to Heliopolis to help him begin his journey. You knew he was gone and yet you insisted that the Sons of Egypt would be able to bear the burdens of the cosmos."

"And I was right, wasn't I?"

"So far. You were lucky. If we had known—"

"If you had known, Seth wouldn't be contained. Only the three who were created by him but nurtured by us have the power to keep him at bay."

"But we don't have three, do we? We have two. Asten shouldn't have the ability to wield the strength of his brothers." Ma'at narrowed her eyes at the powerful god, but he stood his ground, not giving an inch. "How did you do it?" she asked.

Smiling, Anubis said, "I fashioned a boy from snips and snails and puppy dog tails."

An exasperated hiss left Ma'at's lips. "I see you plan on keeping your secrets, then."

"Just as you keep yours, Ma'at."

"I have no secrets," she exclaimed, and yet I saw a tiny hint of alarm cross her eyes.

Ma'at approached the dais. "Tell me, Asten. Have you dreamed your own dreams?"

Asten turned his head and appeared reluctant to speak. Finally, he said, "Do you speak of the Dreams That Could Have Been?"

The goddess sighed impatiently. "You know what I mean," she said.

"I don't care about your dreams of racing horses or of beautiful girls prancing around you in a meadow."

Shifting uncomfortably, Asten said, "I have seen more than one future path."

"And?" She leaned forward expectantly.

Asten shrugged. "Do they matter? Perhaps my dreams don't even apply to me. You know very well that I only see one future for each soul, one dream of a perfect life, full of happiness. Seeing that there are several potential outcomes for me proves there's something wrong. I'm wrong. My soul is broken, so what do my dreams matter? I know that all of those possibilities are beyond me anyhow."

"He could be right," Nephthys said. "Maybe it doesn't work with him. If he was the true prince, the power of dreaming would be easier for him to access. You know he struggles with calling forth the dreams sometimes."

Ma'at considered her words. "That is true. Giving powers such as we did to a mortal should have broken him long ago. It's surprising that he still functions as well as he does." She seemed to come to a decision. "Very well, just answer one question."

"What is it?" Asten asked wearily.

"Do your dreams include her?"

Ma'at pointed to me and I inhaled sharply. Asten lifted his eyes to mine, and there was something in them that seemed both hopeful and horrified.

After a tension-filled moment, he admitted softly, "They do." My heart stilled. "But that is the dream that must not come to pass," he said.

"Why?" Ma'at didn't ask this time. I did.

My skin tingled and I found it difficult to breathe. I felt as if I were trapped in a very tight space and the only thing keeping me focused on not hyperventilating was Asten. There was something tangible between us. Something warm that filled my frame and the space around me. It felt wrong and yet right at the same time.

"Why?" I repeated.

"Because . . ."

My gaze locked on to his and I found I couldn't look away,

". . . because if that dream is a true one, a real one, then it will mean that I have betrayed my brother," he said softly. "And that is not something I could live with."

The two of us were standing several feet apart, but for a brief moment I felt as if we were close enough to touch. I became highly attuned to his body and took in his broad shoulders, his generous mouth, the way a lock of his hair curled over his forehead, and how his eyes could somehow warm me with just a look. Balmy tingles trickled down my spine as if someone had just caressed my bare skin.

Osiris interrupted. "Are you going to judge the boy, then, Ma'at?"

The warmth left my skin and was replaced with spine-chilling fear. Though I knew we needed to get to the netherworld somehow, I didn't want to risk Asten's immortal soul to do it.

"Yes. Let's get this over with," Anubis said.

Placing the feather in its box, Ma'at cupped Asten's heart in her hands and raised her arms in the air. "Asten, Son of Egypt. You have submitted your heart for judgment. Your soul stands as a witness against you. I decree . . . that the deeds of your past cannot be properly judged at this time, for you have not had sufficient time to be absolved of these offenses. The intervening of a god has warped your timeline, and as such, I will grant a temporary stay of judgment."

Nephthys smiled, moving to stand, but Ma'at's next words stopped her in her tracks. "However," she said, "to atone for your crimes, I sentence you to the netherworld to serve as a guide for Lily and Tia. Should you survive the trials there, gain the forgiveness of your brothers, and learn to place others before yourself, we will reassess your placement—that is, of course, contingent upon a successful return."

As one, the gods rose and approached the dais. Side by side with sober expressions they waited while Ma'at finished. "Mercy and truth be with you, Asten. We banish your heart to the netherworld."

The air flickered, the starlit substance on the scales catching fire before it extinguished, leaving only spinning pieces of black char. The room shook and Asten fell to his knees, writhing and moaning.

I ran to him, clutching him close, just as everything stilled.

Then Asten let out a piercing scream, his heart fragmenting into tiny pieces as his lifeless body stayed slumped in my arms.

19

The Lake of Fire

Anubis took hold of my hand. "The tether is now active. When you are ready to leave the netherworld, stretch out your hand and think of me. It will lead you to an exit point and I will come to retrieve you. Ahmose will accompany you, as he is particularly suited to keep you on the straight and narrow." He looked at Ahmose. "It is up to you now, Pathfinder."

"I understand," Ahmose answered.

"What happens next?" I asked, now that the gods had disappeared and the bright hall was once again swathed in darkness.

Ahmose crouched down next to me and placed his hand on my shoulder. "We wait," he said. "It shouldn't take long now."

"What are we waiting for?" I asked as I brushed Asten's hair from his forehead. His skin was smooth and still warm to the touch. His face seemed at peace. I hoped that he'd get the second chance Ma'at spoke of, that she'd be able to somehow see Asten as I did. He'd made mistakes, but I didn't think they were irredeemable ones. My heart wept for him and for all he'd been through, but I took comfort in knowing that Anubis had seen in Asten what I had. He gave Asten his power even knowing everything. That had to mean something.

As I made a mental list of the possible reasons Anubis had kept

Asten's secret for so long, I felt the man I was holding stir. His eyes fluttering open, he slowly got to his feet. When I asked if he was okay, he didn't respond but began moving forward in a trancelike state. "What's wrong with him?" I asked Ahmose as I shifted aside during Asten's attempt to walk right over me.

"He's headed toward the gate. Stay close to me."

We followed Asten down a long hallway, and when he came to a dead end, he didn't hesitate, instead going straight through. "We won't be able to see it," Ahmose warned. "Only the doomed can feel the call of the netherworld."

"But then how did Amon—" I was about to finish the question when Ahmose took hold of my arm.

"He's going through!" he shouted. "Hurry, Lily!"

Before I understood what was happening, Ahmose grabbed on to Asten's shoulder and wound his other arm around my waist. It was a good thing he did, because the three of us were then sucked into a vortex, a cyclone of wind so powerful that it lifted my hair from my head, drawing us through the stone wall as we tumbled together in dizzying circles.

Ahmose's grip on his brother slipped and he struggled to grab his tunic and then his wrist. At the same time he yanked me close. I wrapped my arms around his waist, burying my head in his chest as the gale howled around us. Thoroughly ill from the spinning, I tried desperately not to throw up on Ahmose, an act that would be extremely ungrateful considering that he was the only steady presence in all this tumult.

Just when I thought I couldn't last another minute, the turning stopped, and we had only a brief moment of respite before it began twisting us in the opposite direction, slowly at first and then faster and faster. I swallowed and bit my lip until it bled, hoping to distract myself from the feeling of vertigo.

"We're transitioning now from the upper to the nether!" Ahmose shouted.

Even if I had wanted to respond, I wouldn't have been able to. The winds pummeled us and I got so turned around, I wasn't sure which direction we were going. My hair wound around my face like a flag in a hurricane. If I thought I was sick before, I felt ready to expire now. Even Tia with her natural cat instincts couldn't help me retrieve my balance, and she was so terrified anyway, I could barely keep her focused. I pleaded silently at first and then in desperate whispers for it to be over, and then I remembered the token Horus had given me.

Digging the fingers of my left hand into Ahmose's back, I slowly lifted my right to the ornament that hung around my neck. As I cupped it, it grew warm and the force of the squall lessened. The twisting slowed and we moved weightily, like a pair of tennis shoes in a dryer, thumping and knocking against each other as we tumbled before we finally we came to a stop.

I opened my eyes and blew the wild, windblown hair out of my face. Ahmose asked if I was okay and in response I nodded, only able to give him a weak smile. Once again I was grateful not only for his strength and his ability to keep the three of us together but also for his calming presence. We were still gradually descending, but our bodies began falling lightly, softly, like a dandelion seed. Without the wind, the sensation was almost gentle.

Ahmose grunted as he shifted his brother closer. "Can you hold on to my neck, Lily?" he asked.

"Yes." I wrapped one arm around his neck and then the other, locking my wrists when I realized that my muscles no longer strained to hold on to him. "When they said we'd be riding his coattails, I didn't think they meant it literally," I said as I looked down at Asten's back. He hadn't spoken since his collapse, and I wondered if he would be a zombie the entire time we were in the netherworld. The idea of it made me very uneasy.

"This is quite dangerous, Lily. You must stay close to me at all times."

I shifted my attention to Ahmose's face, which was a mere few inches from mine. His steel-gray eyes were filled with worry. Nodding, I answered, "I will. Believe me, you don't have to tell me twice."

"Good." His warm hand was splayed against my lower back, and goose bumps rose up my arms. I suddenly became aware of how closely our bodies were locked together. His face brushed against mine, and the sensation of his rough stubble against my soft cheek was pleasant enough to cause a shiver. I also noticed how nice his skin smelled—like a deciduous forest, all oak trees, moss, and the crisp spices of fall.

A light from below us lit his skin, causing his gray eyes to take on a silver sheen, and my breath caught, lost in them for just a moment. He glanced down and squeezed my waist. "Hold on, Lily. We're almost there."

What is wrong with me? I asked Tia.

Anubis did say you have a connection with all three brothers. Perhaps this is a result of its manifestation. In times of stress, a lioness looks to her protector and bonds with those who will defend the pride.

Well, if stress is the trigger, then we have a good excuse, at least, I thought to her, shaking away the feeling.

Tightening my grip on his neck, and ignoring the fact that I felt safe being held by Ahmose, I closed my eyes and waited for the impact. I opened them in surprise when I felt Ahmose's arms wrap fully around my waist and lower me to the ground without so much as a jostle.

Asten, who Ahmose had dropped onto the sand, was slowly getting to his feet, while Ahmose stepped away, rubbing the back of his neck and watching me out of the corner of his eye. I wondered if he had been as affected by me as I'd been by him and felt more comfortable not meeting his eyes.

Quickly moving into his line of sight, I called Asten's name, and when he didn't respond, I grabbed his hand and squeezed it. He didn't so much as twitch. I tried to swallow my disappointment and then cocked my head, wondering why I felt that particular emotion. *Did I want* his *attention, too?*

"He won't be able to answer us until we find his heart," Ahmose explained.

"Ah, I see," I said, still not making eye contact. "So, where do we begin looking?" I asked as I reluctantly let go of Asten.

"The heart seeks out the thing that pains him the most. A banished soul only recovers his heart if he fights the demons that haunt him. The worse the crime, the more sore the battle. Whatever demon has the strongest hold on Asten's heart will be guarding it. If we follow Asten, he'll be drawn toward his monster."

"Right."

Ahmose lifted his eyes, peering into the foreboding landscape around us. We seemed to be in a wasteland. A burning, sulfurous scent was carried on the wind. Large mounds of dirt and rocks were piled up haphazardly. With my sphinx eyesight, I could detect the slight pulsing of a few of them, which, if they had been on earth, would have made me think they were termite mounds. Since they were in the netherworld, who knew what kind of horrible creatures made the hills their homes.

At first, I thought the terrain similar to the Place Where Dreams Are Born with its pinnacles and rock formations, but upon further inspection, the colors that brightened the rock were garish and menacing. The mounds of stone cast dark shadows where sinister things quivered and hid or slunk through the dusky gloom. Instead of beauty, I was struck by the idea that death and decay were slowly eating away at the landscape.

The ground was rocky with sharp stones that peppered the sand. And the thick depth of the grains sucked at our feet, nearly toppling me with every step as I slogged through it. My white sandals were quickly becoming uncomfortable. The only landmarks I spied were a few barren and ugly trees that stretched out sharp, skeletal claws to snag my hair. Tia lent me her strength so I could tolerate the hellish temperature, but she could do nothing about the stench of sulfur and corruption.

Asten seemed to be headed toward the place where the sulfur smell was emanating from. Not knowing if that was a good thing or a bad thing, I checked that our knives were ready and that my bow and the quiver of arrows were still at my back and then started after him.

My heart told me Amon was in a different direction, but I feared that if we didn't follow Asten, we'd lose him. Tia agreed and we began tracking him. Within four steps, I was struggling to catch up. Asten glided over the terrain like a ghost, while I slogged as if moving through mud. "He's getting ahead of us," I called out.

"Here," Ahmose said. "Take my hand. I can find the surest path."

I placed my hand in his and it was quickly enveloped in his large, warm palm.

This feels nice, Tia said. *Not like the embrace of Horus, but it is soothing. Comforting. I understand your desire regarding this one. Your cubs would be of a good size and healthy.*

Gah! You're talking about cubs? Cut it out! This is weird enough as it is, I thought back to her. *I am way, way too young to be thinking about offspring.*

You are not capable of reproduction at your age? she asked.

This was getting uncomfortable. I explained reluctantly, *My body has the* ability, *but humans don't usually reproduce until they have settled down. They finish college, get married, and buy a house first.*

Ah, she said. *It would be appropriate, I suppose, to find the proper location for the raising of cubs first. Since you are in a transitory state, it makes sense to hold off for a time.*

Ignoring my inner lioness, I turned my attention back to Ahmose, who had been holding out his other hand, stretching it over the top of the sand. Nothing happened at first, but then the grains began to shift. Asten kept moving ahead, and I worried again that he would get away from us. The sand hardened and a crooked path formed, coming in and out of view.

Ahmose stepped up onto a section of firm sand. "If we walk this path, we will avoid the pitfalls that would swallow us up and lead to destruction," he said.

"What about Asten?"

"Asten must walk his own path. We will stay as close to him as we can and only deviate from the path if absolutely necessary."

"Okay," I said. "Lead the way."

I hoped that as soon as I saw Amon again, these awkward feelings I was developing regarding other men would disappear. Whether they were originating from Tia or not, I was apparently a willing, if reluctant, participant.

I tried not to think about it, but since she was, at that very moment, thinking about Ahmose's well-defined arms, my thoughts drifted in that direction as well. She was wondering if she could come to love either one of them, and I couldn't fault her for that. They were both good choices.

Her thoughts particularly drifted in Asten's direction and as we walked she replayed his confession in her mind. She empathized with him, for she, too, felt out of place and less than worthy. The idea that Tia considered herself not as important as I was shocked me, and I made a promise to try to give her opinions and thoughts equal weight.

Asten moved in and out of our sight from time to time, but Ahmose always reassured us that he was close, and the path did seem to follow the same general direction he was walking. Occasionally, Ahmose would stop and place his hands on the path, and he'd discover a new direction that would get us closer to his brother. After a few hours of traversing the same dull landscape, me lost in my thoughts, we finally found the source of the burning smell.

It wasn't obvious what it was at first. The horizon glowed with a golden-orange hue and I thought it might be a sunset, though Ahmose told me he didn't think that was possible. A sunset would indicate the presence of Amun-Ra, who, though he had guided me to Cherty, had never set foot in the netherworld. At least, as far as Ahmose knew.

Soon we figured out what caused the lights over the hills. We came upon a wide lake that roiled with a blazing liquid that undulated and shifted as if there were various forms writhing beneath its surface. Asten stopped as if taking in his surroundings. The light coming from it reflected off Asten's face like the flickering of a campfire, and I found the quiet power and ruggedness of his jaw beautiful. I had the overwhelming urge to run my fingertips along it.

Asten blinked as if waking from a dream, and in that moment he looked down at me and must have seen something in my expression, because his changed. His brown eyes lit with tenderness and his lips parted just slightly, as if he'd found something he'd been long seeking. I took a small step closer. For just a moment I thought he was going to touch my cheek, but then something broke the surface of the lake and commanded his attention.

When the moment passed, I shook my head slightly, wondering what on earth was going on. Maybe the heart scarab was affecting him, too. I knew it was only a matter of time before it would influence both Asten and Ahmose, but this was the first indication that one of them was bending to its power. Sucking in a breath, I vowed to be stronger and turned toward the lake.

I'd never conceived of anything like it before. Across the burning water was a waterfall of sorts that seemed to feed it, but the liquid was thick and viscous, a golden chocolate caramel lit from behind. The lake was beautiful in its way, even though I knew that Asten's personal demons must live hidden within its depths. As I thought of what they could be, Asten moved closer to the fiery water's edge.

"Stop!" I cried. "Don't go in!"

Fear clutched my heart. I was deathly afraid that Asten would drown or burn in its fiery waves.

"What is this place?" I asked Ahmose when Asten was at a full stop at the water's edge.

"I've heard of it, though it is not at all as I imagined. It is called the Lake of Fire, a place of purging. The errors one makes can be, in essence, washed away—that is, if the person doesn't drown during the process. It's interesting that his heart ended up here."

"Don't all hearts come here?"

"Not at all. Most hearts go to the Mires of Despair. That his came here means the wrongs he did caused more pain to himself than to anyone else. The bad news is that his heart sought the deepest point in the netherworld to hide, something we can attribute to how long Asten has allowed these feelings and mistakes of the past to fester. The good news is that if he manages to successfully bring his heart back to the surface, he can, in essence, be free from his demons. That's not a small thing in the netherworld."

"So you're saying that Asten's going to dive in?" I asked, hoping that I was wrong.

"That would be my guess. His heart is even now calling to him from its depths."

Just then, a large creature with gaping jaws broke the surface and dove back in. Its eye must have sighted us because it breached not once but twice more, each time coming closer. I shook my head. "It's too dangerous. We can't let him go in there."

"I don't think we have a choice," Ahmose warned.

Asten turned to look at us with a weak smile and waded in.

Ahmose caught my arm when I tried to go after him, giving me a pained look. "He has to fight his demons to win back his heart," he said, fingering a lock of my hair.

Turning, I stared desperately at the lake. The golden water clung to Asten's legs like thick goo.

I panicked. We were going to lose him. We couldn't lose him. Not when I thought I could love him. *No. Wait. What? That's wrong. No, it isn't,* my mind insisted. My heart beat swift as a roe, and before I understood what I was doing, I leapt from the path and ran toward the shore.

"Lily! Wait!" Ahmose cried out as I ran, but I ignored him and pressed on, splashing into the thick liquid just as Asten dove under.

"Asten!" I cried, tossing my knives and the quiver and bow onto the sand before plunging beneath the waves myself. When we couldn't see, I locked my mind with Tia's and summoned our power. All at once the light that filled our vision dissipated and we could clearly see Asten ahead of us. A shining rock drew him forward, downward.

I swam awkwardly, my human half and my lioness half moving like two disparate creatures fighting. I switched back and forth from the breaststroke to a doggie paddle and ended up kicking viciously, tearing through the water like I would through a large animal. Even though the Lake of Fire was viscous and reddish, the water was cold, so cold that it felt like we had sunk into a grave. My eyes closed, and Tia was the one who raised our body temperature enough for us to return to the living—at least, as living as we could be in the netherworld.

Our claws extended naturally when a scaled monster attacked, and we raked our nails down its side, black blood filling the water before the creature disappeared. I used Horus's healing stela to repair a wicked gash on my leg that the toothy beast had rendered before vanishing.

Tiny biting fish swarmed around Asten, but he paid them no heed as he swam downward. Sensing something hunting us, I turned and sought it out, swimming quickly and boldly toward it. With a quick slice of my claws, I dispatched the creature and moved on. This lake could be the end of us. Asten was now just a speck on the edge of my vision. I was barely able to see him even with our sphinx abilities.

Another monstrous creature took note of me. This was beginning to feel like an underwater Whac-A-Mole. I tightened my fist and used only the power of my mind to destroy it. The large beast thrashed violently for a full minute before going still.

I'd already been holding my breath for much longer than I'd be able to as a human, and my lungs weren't burning at all. I hoped the same thing applied to Asten. He was imbued with godly powers and he was technically dead, so that might be in our favor. If he was running out of air, his body didn't show any signs. As he swam through the school of deadly fish, his blood filled the water, and I worried that the scent would attract larger predators. I narrowed the distance.

Asten was floating above his glowing heart, the vicious creatures surrounding him, taking off little pieces of his flesh. His muffled screams as they attacked pierced me. I moved nearer, but the fish ignored me completely and swam to his other side, avoiding me when I approached.

Trying to fight them off with my claws proved fruitless, so I kicked my legs and reached for his glowing heart instead.

The object was too heavy for me to lift, though I tugged and pulled and used everything I had to try prying it up from the bed it rested in. There was nothing for me to do as Asten was picked apart. He fought and kicked but it was to no avail. He couldn't stop them. Then, suddenly, their behavior changed. Instead of attacking, they hovered, as if waiting for something.

My hair swirled in front of me and I angrily pushed it aside. *Asten!* I thought, swimming closer. *Don't give up!* But he had. Lifting his hands, grimacing at the bits of flesh that hung from his fingertips and floated like little loose pieces of sodden bread, he blinked once, twice, and then his eyes found me.

We stared at one another for a long moment, and during those precious seconds, I tried to plead with my eyes, to convey how badly I wanted him to live. Asten seemed to understand. Lips curving up in a sweet smile, he nodded and threw back his head, stretching out his arms.

He closed his eyes and gave in to the swarm. The tiny yet monstrous fish became very excited. They swam around him with increasing speed. Faster and faster they went until their forms became blurred. Then, all at once, the whole group tore into his belly, burrowing beneath his skin. Asten screamed as his entire body filled with light. It emanated from his ruined fingertips, from his feet, his mouth and eyes.

My whole body shook, my heart pressing against my rib cage like it was ready to explode. Regret and sorrow pierced me so fixedly I barely cared if I survived either. Asten was going to die a second and permanent death and there wasn't a thing I could do to stop it. What good was having the power of a sphinx if I couldn't protect the people I cared about?

Below us, Asten's heart burst into a thousand tiny particles of light, then floated back to touch his gleaming skin. They sank into it, causing his limbs to heal. The jerking of his body stilled, and when they were gone, his head slumped forward. He floated in the fiery water unconscious. At least that was what I hoped.

Retracting my claws, I slowly approached and wrapped an arm around his waist. I reached up to touch his cheek and his eyes opened. Relief poured through me, and I wished I could have both laughed hysterically and cried.

A familiar gleam lit Asten's chocolate brown eyes and he winked, the side of his mouth lifting up to his trademark smirk. The gesture was heartfelt and genuine. And yet it wasn't. He was happy to be alive and happy that I was there with him. Though he was obviously tired, he was Asten whole and complete once again. But now there was a quiet acceptance upon his shoulders.

He'd absorbed the burden of his demons. Not only had he faced them, but he'd also wrestled them and won. They would always be a part of him, but they would no longer hold him back. And, more importantly, they would no longer weigh down his heart. Asten took hold of my hand and squeezed it gently, then brought it down to his lips to press a soft kiss against my palm.

He tugged, wanting me closer, and I drifted willingly, wrapping my arms around his neck. His eyebrow lifted in question, but then he nodded as if that, too, was something he could accept. He looked up and kicked, drawing us to the surface.

I wasn't sure how long we'd been down, but by the look on Ahmose's face, it had been much too long. He was pacing frantically and didn't notice us until he heard our flailing attempts to get ashore. He raced out into the water and dragged me up, crushing me against him. "Lily," he breathed my name in relief. "I thought you were lost."

"We're okay," I said, hugging him briefly and then stepping away, the thick waves of orange fluid shoving me against him as I moved.

"I couldn't go in after you. I tried, but each time I set foot in the lake, it turned as hard as stone. When I backed out, it turned liquid again. I thought trying to get to you would kill you. Otherwise I would have come."

"That's strange," I said. "The lake stayed liquid the entire time we were down there. I wonder why it let me go after Asten and not you."

"Perhaps it sensed our link," Asten ventured.

"Yes." Ahmose folded his arms across his chest. "Maybe it's time you tell me all about this dream you mentioned and just how Lily features into it."

Asten frowned and held out a hand to me. I took his arm easily and waded ashore with him. When I looked back, Ahmose was the one frowning. Over his shoulder, Asten responded, "You know I am only allowed to share a dream with the person or people it involves, and this one"—he glanced down at me briefly—"definitely didn't involve *you*." Asten looked up, as if scanning for something, and though there wasn't a sun in the sky, he said, "I suggest we find shelter. Night is coming."

Ahmose soon joined us, and he looked at the sky as well before raising his hands and mumbling a spell. The sand around us shifted and then settled as his eyes spotted something ours couldn't. "I've found a path," he said.

"Good." Asten nodded and turned to me, touching the tip of my nose lightly, his eyes flashing. "As fetching as you look drenched in the fiery waters, you are likely uncomfortable and the picture of a poor devotee. If you would allow me to fashion you something more befitting your station?"

I dipped my head and tried to ignore the way Ahmose's eyes narrowed with a tinge of jealousy. The scarab was working its magic. I knew it was affecting Asten, too, but it didn't bother me. At all. Which was something I found disconcerting.

Asten murmured something, brandishing his hands as a familiar sparkling fog rose from the sand and surrounded me; the fiery little stars flickered around my body, warming me and settling on my skin with little pops.

Dry fabric wrapped around me, hugging my limbs tightly. But to my delight, the fabric moved and stretched as I did. When the sparkling cloud dissipated, I ran a hand down my arm, enjoying the feeling of the white silk blouse against my skin. My leather harness still sat comfortably on my shoulders, my spear-knives drew easily like they had just been cleaned and sharpened, and I wore soft khaki breeches with brown boots that came up to mid-calf.

Panicked for a moment, I ran my hands over my shirt and finally breathed a sigh of relief when I found Amon's heart scarab pinned to the harness. "Thank you," I said, marveling at the softness of the clothing. I lifted a hand to my hair and found half of it loosely gathered at the nape of my neck and fastened with a leather tie. The other, shorter sections were tossed haphazardly by the hot breeze.

"I thought you would like something practical and no-nonsense with your hair," he said.

"I do." I smiled at him. *Wait. Did I?* Tia assured me we did, but I suddenly couldn't remember. I gave it some more thought, my brain roughly wrenching memories to the surface until they finally came loose like forgotten treasures buried beneath the sand. Even so, they were tarnished, almost forgotten, and I found that I could only recall them from a distance. My mind felt sluggish. Less . . . Lily-like. But then I remembered that Amon liked my hair down and curled or my standard smooth style and I was able to relax again. Amon was the reason I was here. The reason I'd come to the netherworld. How could I have distanced my thoughts from him, even for a moment?

Ahmose took my hand but I turned back and offered my other hand to Asten. "Are you coming?" I asked.

Asten bent his head down to mine and answered with a roguish wink. "A thousand monstrous beasties couldn't keep me from your side."

I gave him a small smile, and with him on one side and Ahmose on the other, it felt like all was right. We set out together—the four of us, including Tia—and it wasn't long before I realized there was a reason I'd had a problem remembering Amon. He was distancing himself from me on purpose to protect me, but I could still feel his heart was calling out to me. Now that I had Asten and Ahmose at my side, the distance from his heart felt unbearable.

We pressed on, me doing my best to ignore the pain and the suffering that I could now feel reverberating in my body. It weakened me to the point where I found it difficult to walk. Soon, I noticed Asten and Ahmose were also distressed. Something was draining us. Stealing our energy. At some point I was carried and I finally drifted off, dreaming of something horrible, deadly. And that something knew I was there.

20

Breath of Evil

Opening my eyes didn't scare away the monsters. Just the opposite happened. My level of discomfort increased. Asten and Ahmose were nowhere in sight. The fire I could have sworn was burning earlier was gone. I was in a sort of waking dream. I stopped dead in my tracks when the crack of a whip reverberated in the darkness. Then a familiar cry made me snap out of it and I took another step forward and then another.

The indistinct shape in front of me turned out to be a rock covered with a fine powder of sand. The air was hot and oppressive, like something thick and sticky had seeped into my lungs. It wasn't long before I felt a stitch in my side from the labored inhales and exhales. Still, I knew the cry had been Amon's. I had to find him.

Amon's heart scarab beat violently against my shoulder, its rhythm erratic instead of his usual steady, strong pulse, but I could feel the pull of it guiding me, pushing me forward. My own heart began mimicking its unsteady and fearful pace. Creeping through the dimness, all I could do was hope to find the beast that caused Amon's distress.

A smoky, guttural voice carried out from the path's depths. "Yes. She approaches. Just as I have foreseen."

"L-leave," Amon sputtered, "leave her out of this."

"I think not," the voice answered before letting out a shrill cackle that caused me to shiver. At the same time, the sound of a thousand sets of wings seemed to take flight.

I could see nothing, but my imagination conjured flocks of creepy winged things all around me ready to rip out my eyes and nibble on strips of flesh. I gasped, realizing that very thing could be happening to Amon right now. I picked up my pace, one hand trailing the large stone, the other groping in the darkness. When I came upon a smooth section, I stopped and examined the structure with my sensitive fingertips.

"It's not stone at all," I murmured quietly.

An instinctive urge made me lean forward, and I closed my eyes and inhaled. Even without Tia's help I somehow knew what it was. I could almost taste it on my tongue. "It's iron. An iron wall." Wondering where I could possibly be, I moved on.

The heat continued to press against my lungs with each breath, as if the devil had wrapped his hands around my rib cage. My feeble inhales became more shallow and forced. The last thing I wanted to do was faint. Amon needed me. I panted as I hurried toward the voices, but there was no opening in the iron wall, and it soon became clear that the conversation I was eavesdropping on was happening on the other side.

Amon screamed and the desperation building up tore at me.

"There's got to be a way," I murmured.

Ascend, *Tia whispered. Almost instinctively, I allowed the power of the sphinx to flow through my limbs; the warmth running down my arms filled me with strength. My fingers tightened and elongated, the wicked claws sharpening before my eyes.*

With a grunt, I took a few steps back and leapt. My eyes sharpened on a dim point overhead that I might be able to use as a handhold. When I shot easily past it, I gasped in surprise and scrambled awkwardly on the stone until my claws actually caught. To my human eyes, the wall was smooth and impassable, but with my heightened senses I could feel tiny imperfections, thin ridges and narrow gaps.

Like a cat on a tree, I nimbly pulled myself up, supporting all my weight with just the strength of my fingers. Scrabbling atop the wall, I crouched on the balls of my feet as I utilized the combined strength that made me and Tia unique, but I knew that our strength wasn't what it once was. Our eyes narrowed and focused. I blinked, and, as if someone had suddenly flipped a switch, the dark shapes below took form.

I cocked my head to listen as a dusty open-air theater of sorts came into view. Shaped like a bowl and surrounded by an impossibly high metal wall, it was being used as a spectacle, and the main source of entertainment was the man I loved. Instead of seats, the edges of the circular stadium writhed with specters that were less than entertained. Their demeanor bordered on tortured.

Gaunt and feeble, the creatures tore at their hair and clothes as they hissed. Thrashing and shifting, their bodies blended together and moved in strange ways, almost passing through one another like ghosts. I could clearly see the edges and borders of the iron wall they pressed against through their bodies. Though their forms fluctuated between fleshy and immaterial, they seemed unable to pass through the wall and escape. There were so many moving in such a tight space that they looked more like a multifaced beast than individuals.

They are without number, *Tia said.*

I agreed, horrified. Then something triggered the mass. As one, they began weeping and rending their clothing. One woman—at least, I thought it was a woman—pressed her hands against her face and they actually melted into her cheeks as she howled.

It reminded me of the Edvard Munch painting The Scream, *which had hung in the Met for a while. I remembered admiring it, wondering what awful thing could have happened to make a person shriek like that. Now I knew. It was being banished to the netherworld.*

In the center of the circling horde, Amon hung limply from chains that bound his wrists to a large pole. His tunic hung down from his waist in tatters. A monstrous beast approached that looked very similar to an albino Minotaur, except for he had a double set of horns and a crocodile-like mouth. With arms the size of Christmas hams, he snapped a whip against Amon's back with a resounding crack.

I cried out as my breath left my body. Strips of flesh had been torn open, deep crisscrossed wounds decorating his muscular bare back. Now I knew why I was having trouble breathing.

A qilinbian, *Tia said weakly, and I hated the idea that the sting I was feeling and the weakness in my body were due to whatever was being done to Amon. That he'd kept the brunt of this pain from me for so long meant he'd been suffering immensely and, from the look of it, for quite some time.*

A what? *I asked.*

Instead of speaking through our mental connection, which seemed more difficult than usual, a picture of what she meant formed in my mind. Suddenly, I understood the purpose of the weapon and how it was utilized. It was a whip used against unicorns.

Sharp enough to gouge their flesh, which was much, much tougher than any animal in the mortal world, it did terrible damage, even to the flesh of the dead, which I imagined would be difficult to score. I shivered to think what such a weapon could do to a living being, even one imbued with power such as Tia and myself.

I choked back a sob, feeling helpless to protect the man I loved from such pain, but there was a new part of me that took in the scene with a sort of calculated indifference. My mortal, human side screamed desperately that we would save him. We had to. That was why we'd come all this way. It was the whole reason Tia was even with me.

But as I crouched there, taking note of all the variables and assessing how to overcome them, my emotional turmoil lessened. Just as I took a backseat in my own body when Tia was in charge, I felt my human self pushed aside. What took control, though, wasn't fully Tia and it wasn't fully me either; it was . . . us.

In that moment we weren't lioness and human residing in the same body. We were someone new, someone powerful—a supernatural being that was entirely . . . else. A warrior who wanted to fight and not for love or duty, not for meat or to protect cubs. But because it was our purpose.

It was the reason we'd been created. This was the reason. To put down this menace. And that new someone wanted to rescue Amon, but she didn't necessarily want to save him for the same reasons I personally did.

I . . . we . . . blinked. Something was changing. Though I made a feeble attempt to stop it and take control of my body again, I somehow knew that if Tia and I were going to be able to use our power fully in the way we needed to, we had to allow this change to happen, and we needed to embrace it. Feeling more than hearing Tia's agreement, I took a deep breath and let go, becoming more of an observer than a participant.

Our claws dug into the edge of the wall as we leaned forward, gouging deep scratches into the iron. Flecks of it shaved away and rained down upon the heads of the beings beneath us, but the disturbance went unnoticed. The bodies didn't seem to be aware of much more than their own suffering.

Just the idea of entering the same space these bodies occupied made the blood in my veins run cold. But this only impacted the tiny tamped-down version of myself. The part of me that was sphinx feared little. As I crept along the edge, looking for the quickest and quietest place to descend, I steeled my resolve, knowing I'd soon be surrounded by the lost dead.

Just then, the voice spoke again. I froze atop the wall and looked down. The Minotaur had coiled his whip and stood immobile, his head lowered. Puzzled, I looked for the source of the voice. I'd thought he was the one who'd been speaking. But then I saw her.

She was difficult to make out at first. A dark sort of cloud surrounded her, obscuring her until she wanted to be seen. It moved with screeching winged beasts that flapped leathery wings, giving me tiny glimpses of the being that stood in the center of their menacing flock.

Slowly, the writhing mass approached the Minotaur and a long and lovely limb reached out toward the pale monster. Her fingernails were painted black, her skin a greenish gray. The wings pummeled his body but he didn't flinch, even when several of them bit him hard enough to draw blood that trickled brightly down his ashen arm.

As her hand slowly encircled the Minotaur's large bicep, the creature smiled blissfully. Even from a distance I could see that he quivered in pleasure at her touch.

"Can you sense her, pretty godling?" the woman asked Amon as a long leg emerged from the winged mass. "She's very close. Perhaps if you're . . .

cooperative," she tantalized, "I'll chain the two of you together so you can watch as I suck the life from her."

Her voice seemed familiar. I'd heard it somewhere before, but at that moment, I couldn't place it.

The reddish-black bats fluttered closer to her form, eventually settling on her back and shoulders to form a flowing cape. The smaller silvery-winged beasts alighted on her head and became a gleaming headdress. The effect was chilling, especially when the minions sitting on her shoulders raised their sharpened wings in the form of jagged, spiked epaulettes that protected what might otherwise have been a vulnerable throat. My hands itched to test the edge of my spear-knives against her living armor.

She was beautiful, with long hair piled atop her head, and she was curvy in a femme fatale kind of way. Every inch of her looked like the queen of the netherworld. Dr. Hassan had shown me pictures of the Devourer in a book on the drive to Luxor. That Devourer looked like a monster hippo with sharp teeth.

The real version, however, looked more like the kind of woman who wrapped every man she met around her little finger with one glance and then took them for everything they owned. It was all too easy to imagine her chewing up her victims for breakfast, spitting out their mangled carcasses, and rounding up another dozen for lunch. She was alluring and cunning, dangerous and provocative—exactly like the black widow she appeared to be.

"Ah!" She laughed, a sound at once lovely and utterly frightening. "She brings your heart. This is even better. Now I can take my time to savor the taste of you for centuries!"

The wanton gleam in her eye or the way she licked her cherry-red lips might have been mistaken as suggestive, but the part of me that was Tia knew it for what it was. The creature was hungry. And between me and Amon, we were a veritable buffet she could feast upon. For the first time in this dream, I wondered if my presence had put Amon at further risk. If our connection while in the netherworld meant I was really there and not just dreaming.

The Devourer ran her hand over the thick shoulder of the monster enforcer beside her and then pouted. "You know, it's been such a long time since I've eaten. I've practically wasted away."

The woman ran her hands down her hourglass curves, causing the adorning little bats to screech and resettle themselves on her dress. Something within stirred me to action, only partly to put her in her place. The other side reacted to the challenge of another predator trying to steal what belonged to us. Amon was ours and no one was going to take him from us or question our claim.

I stood up and ran, as light on my feet as a bird of prey, leaping from the iron wall and somersaulting in the air as I landed in a crouch, one knee down, facing the Devourer and her supersized, whip-wielding minion. Consciously, I'd placed myself between them and Amon. I was surprised at the distance I'd covered in a single leap, but I didn't reveal it. I lifted my head and glared at the woman, who regarded me with a mixture of pleasure and mild curiosity.

Knowing she could sense my presence was disconcerting, and as her eyes locked on me, I wondered if I'd made a mistake in showing myself. When I'd walked with Amon in dreams before, none of the netherworld creatures had noticed. Now everything was different.

Standing boldly, my fingers stretched out into wicked claws, I announced, "If anything, I'd say you look a little on the plump side."

Her smile faltered. Now that I was closer, I noticed the smaller details that made her more demon than human. Her eyes had elongated vertical pupils like a reptile's. Instead of eyelashes, she had tiny plumes that fanned out around her lids like downy crow's-feet and blended into the skin above her cheeks. Her long hair that hung like feathers ended in spiny little barbs that moved of their own accord as she walked, stretching toward me like snakes ready to strike.

The little silvery creatures that made up her headdress blinked as they watched me; their black eyes were so sunken in their bony plated heads that they looked like living skeletons. And when she parted her lips, I saw a greenish light emanating from her mouth, as if she'd swallowed something radioactive.

"How delightful that you've chosen to join us," she said with a jubilant expression. "I so look forward to getting to know you better."

She stalked slowly toward me, her hair rising and undulating about her head. Reaching over my shoulders, I patted my back, seeking my spear-knives, but panicked when I realized I didn't have them. Raising her hands, her sharp black fingernails within scratching distance, she opened her mouth and gave out a hair-raising moan. The light in her mouth released a green fog that quickly enveloped me. Breathing it in, I felt like I was drowning in an icy poison, one that seized my lungs, as if liquid nitrogen had been poured down my throat.

I lifted my claws to attack, but her body passed right through mine, leaving me with a chill that crept into my bones and the taste of mildewed spearmint in my mouth. She spun, screaming again, but this time in frustration. When she did, greenish-gray veins protruded from her smooth, porcelain skin, causing it to crack and split. Green light bled through, but as she took a deep breath, the cracks sealed.

The Devourer smiled, this time slightly ruffled, and addressed me as politely as if she'd invited me to sit down to tea. "This is just a temporary setback," she assured me. "I simply need to gather my strength. I'd been wasting away," she added in an aside to the albino bull creature that stood in the exact same spot. Now that she wasn't touching him, he looked far less enamored by his benefactor. Actually, I noticed he was giving me an appreciative look. Interesting.

With the flourish of her hand, she summoned a dozen or so of the wailing multitude who stood on the sidelines. Their cries of protests intensified as they compulsively marched forward clearly against their will. When the mass of ghostly forms drew near, they trembled, and though the chosen one fought against her power, he finally wrenched his face toward her and bowed his head.

"Eat," she commanded.

Eat? *I thought she was the one doing the eating.* What's going on? *I wondered. It was only then I noticed that each ghost held a gleaming orb in their hands—their hearts.*

The specter shook violently and then screamed as if his entire body were being ripped apart. His mouth opened wider and wider, and when it hung, gaping loosely enough that he could have swallowed a suckling pig whole, his eyes changed from frightened to feral. The ghost swallowed his own heart, then jumped on the ghost nearest him and bit into his ethereal form.

The second ghost wailed miserably, and it wasn't long before he was entirely consumed; then he ate the next, each one scrambling over each other to escape the horror.

I stood there like I was trapped on a haunted house ride that I had no con-

trol over and no way to escape from. I wanted to put my hands over my eyes and scream until the nightmarish scene was done, but I also needed to know exactly what the Devourer could do so we could find a way to defeat her.

Horrified, I pushed my fear into a tiny part inside me. In the same way that my emotions regarding Amon were suppressed, my feelings about what was taking place were ignored. I wasn't in charge. Tia wasn't in charge. The sphinx was in control, and she wanted to witness this.

When only one shade remained, he stood in place, engorged and trembling. The menacing gleam in his eyes dimmed to fear once again, fat tears dripping down his face as he coughed and spat, trying to rid himself of the glut he'd ingested.

"There, there," the Devourer said with the cluck of her tongue. "It's almost over, Luscious. Let's put an end to your suffering, shall we?" She held out her hand in a gesture that approximated warmth, but a chilling menace clearly lay beneath it.

The ghost fell back in a panic, scrambling toward the invisible wall and attempting to claw his way up the side. While he did so, the evil queen's mouth fell open, and though it didn't unhinge as far as the specter's had, it still appeared unnaturally wide. Green light flowed from her toward him, folding over him like an arctic fog over an iceberg.

She reached out and took hold, wrapping the shuddering soul of the man tightly in her arms, molding his essence to hers. Her caress was almost tender—that is, until her hair rose around their forms and the barbs shot into the ghostly being, finding painful purchase. The wraith shrieked with the sound of a thousand braking trains, and it was almost a relief when the ghost began to lose cohesion before she sucked him up completely and the grating noise ceased.

Turning to us, she licked her lips, using her finger to tuck the little fluttery ribbons of gray that hung from them into her mouth. "Mmm," she said as her calculating eyes looked us over, her lips stained as crimson as heartbreak. "Delicious." Delicately, she smoothed the ruffled creatures hanging on her cape. "Now then, where were we?" she asked. "Ah, yes. Come here, little one. Put your trust in my shadow and I will devour you."

"Lily!" Amon cried. "Wake up!"

"What?" I looked in his direction, confused, but then my attention was once again riveted on the Devourer, who was creeping closer. That she could move as indiscernibly as a vampire was unsettling.

"Wake up, Lily!" Amon shouted again.

Wake up? *I echoed in my mind, my brain foggy.*

"Wake! Up!"

I fainted instead.

"Wake up, Lily!" a different voice cried.

I opened my eyes to find a concerned Asten and Ahmose hovering over me. The fire had turned to embers. "What . . . what happened?" I asked.

"We couldn't wake you," Ahmose said.

"You were crying out in your sleep," Asten added.

Nodding, I sat up and took each brother's hand in mine. "I have some terrible news."

21

The Mires of Despair

"What is it?" Asten asked as he helped me rise. He didn't let go, even after I was standing, which I found both distressing and comforting.

"Amon's been captured by the Devourer. She's . . . she's torturing him."

Ahmose took the announcement in stride, nodding, as if he'd expected as much. "We've felt it. She cannot kill him, Lily. At least not until his energy along with ours is fully drained."

"Yes," Asten echoed. "There's still time. We can save him."

I looked from one to the other. "You already knew this?"

Uncomfortably, Ahmose met my eyes. "From the moment we arrived in the netherworld," he said.

"You feel his pain. Just like when his eyes were removed."

"It's bearable," Asten said. "Dividing the pain between the three of us diminishes his."

"But . . . the wounds on his back." Quickly, I let go of Asten's hand and moved behind him. Before he could protest, I lifted his tunic to ascertain the damage. Dried blood and welts covered the smooth golden skin like someone had used his flesh to sharpen their scissors. The sight of it caused me as much anguish as when I'd seen Amon abused. The Devourer would pay for what she'd done.

"But I felt his wounds, too. Why aren't mine as severe as yours?" I demanded.

Ahmose sighed uneasily. "The three of us have been shielding you. And Amon uses the Eye of Horus to protect you from the worst of it. As he weakens, you may begin to feel the effects. Disorientation comes first and will be followed by physical pain in increasing degrees, the result of which may even lead to your death. This we cannot allow. For you to die a first death in the netherworld would mean you would be permanently trapped here."

"What do you mean by 'first death'?"

"Those who come to the netherworld, with the exception of yourself, have all died either as mortals or as an immortal whose power was ripped away. When we encounter these beings, Ahmose and I have the power to dispatch them, offering them a second and permanent death, one that sends their essence to a place even we have no stories of."

"Maybe back to the Waters of Chaos?" I suggested. "Amun-Ra told me a bit about it."

Asten cocked his head. "The gods have not seen fit to share everything with us. Apparently you know more than we do."

"I'm not saying we all go there. He just talked about energy returning when . . ." I shook my head. "It doesn't matter now. What's important at this moment is that you let me share the load—"

Raising his hand, he cut me off. "We are immortals, Lily. We can bear the pain more easily. Just as we are not as sensitive to touch, we are not as sensitive to pain. For you, a mortal, to bear it"—he shook his head—"it would debilitate you."

"But I'm a sphinx now. I can handle it. There are worse things than pain."

"That is true, but you need to understand, Lily, that your bond with Amon is much more powerful than ours. You sustain him. We need to keep you strong, if not to shield you, then to aid him. You must allow us to protect you in this way," he finished.

Gently, I settled Asten's shirt and turned to Ahmose. His lips were in a thin line as he bobbed his head to acknowledge my unspoken question.

"We'll be all right, Lily," Asten said as he took my hand again, squeezing it in reassurance. "The injuries of the body are temporary. It is the draining of Amon's life energies that is the more serious concern. We just need to rescue him before more damage is done."

I nodded, then suddenly realized that my hand was clasped in Asten's and that he was absentmindedly rubbing his thumb in little circles over the flesh between my thumb and forefinger. When I looked up at him, he let go and turned away, a flush creeping up his neck. I frowned and decided to ignore the tingle on my skin where he had touched me.

For the first time since Amon and I were separated, I wished the brothers were mortal again so they could bond with me as well and take some of my energy. Becoming a sphinx and wearing the Stela of Horus seemed to have invigorated me with energy to spare. Even though I hadn't slept, my body was strong enough to run for hours. I'd willingly give up some of my strength so they could heal.

But for now, there was nothing I could do—at least, nothing I knew of—so I decided that the best course of action was to work on saving Amon. "There's more I haven't told you," I murmured. "The Devourer knows that I'm here. If Amon hadn't warned me to wake up . . ." I paused. "It just felt like she might've had the power to do something to me, even in a waking dream."

"Is it possible, Asten?" Ahmose asked. "Can her dream connection be that powerful?"

Blowing out a breath, Asten rubbed the back of his neck. "I don't know. There's no precedent. The only link similar to this is between Isis and Osiris. And that bond is strong, even in dreams. It enables them to communicate across vast distances. But neither of them has ever come face to face with the Devourer or entered the netherworld, that I am aware of. We just don't have enough information to safely guess."

Ahmose grunted. "Then we'll just have to assume the worst and hope for the best."

Glancing over my head, Ahmose frowned slightly to Asten, then raised an eyebrow.

"I can't," Asten said. "Don't ask it of me."

Turning to him, I asked, "You can't what?"

He sighed, looking to his brother for help, but Ahmose just folded his arms across his chest and stared Asten down.

Finally, he answered my question. "It is possible for me to monitor your dreams."

"That seems like a good solution. So you could help me fight the Devourer when I see her again?"

"No. That's not how it works. You can't fight the Devourer in your dreams, not truly."

"It felt like I could."

"Well, you can't. Or, at least, you shouldn't. The dream world is full of vague possibilities and hints of what could be, but it's also colored by what we want. And sometimes, when it learns what we desire most, it snatches that very thing away from us. It's a tricky business, and one should never trust while in one's dreams. Time and time again I've seen people get lost, never to reenter the waking world.

"Even I, who has been gifted the power over dreams, have been susceptible to it. Keep in mind that even assuming it is possible to defeat the Devourer while in a dream state doesn't mean it would happen in reality. And with your connection to Amon, all you might accomplish is tipping her off to your strengths and fighting skills. Already she might have been able to access your true whereabouts by following your dream self back to our camp."

"Which means we should be departing this place soon," Ahmose said.

"Yes. We should," Asten answered, and made like he was ready to leave.

"Hold on a moment," I said, placing my hand on his arm to stop him. "None of that explains why you wouldn't want to help me." Asten glanced down at my hand and then slowly, shakily, placed his on top. When his eyes met mine, I saw hidden secrets and sorrow in their depths. Curious, I instinctively triggered my power to discover the truth, but before I could work the magic, he broke our connection.

His fingertip tucked under my chin, tilting my face to look up at him. "Don't," he said plainly. "I know you want answers but, please, I ask you not to probe further. Not about this."

The pain that filled his eyes moved me in such a way that I nodded, ashamed I'd tried to see what he clearly didn't want to share. I lowered my head, tears filling my eyes.

His warm voice stole quietly across the space between us, and though his words were simple, I knew there were layers of things left unsaid seeded between each word. "Please, don't cry. I'm sorry, Lily."

There was something about the way he drew out my name. It made me feel uneasy and hopeful and alert all at the same time. Something was happening. I became confused, but my sensitivity was heightened. My heart leapt in a staccato rhythm, and a discernible hitch in my breathing was echoed in his. At the same time, anguish swelled between us, spilling over and drowning the emotions like milk poured into a glass too full.

Asten blinked and shifted, breaking eye contact. Without a word, he turned away and headed off, leaving me and Ahmose alone, the trail of his footprints the only thing left to mark his path.

"What's wrong with him?" I asked Ahmose as I wiped away an errant tear. I should have probably asked myself the same question. When I'd looked at Asten just now, I'd felt something, and it was much more than the affection for a brother.

Am I going crazy? I asked Tia. *Do you think I'm starting to fall for Asten, too?*

There was a long moment before Tia answered. *Asten is a worthy choice. Is he not?*

Yes. But that's not the point.

Do you blame him for his past errors?

No.

I wanted her to tell me that some strange sphinx thing was guiding my actions, that I wasn't being disloyal to the man I loved. The man I wanted. The man I was here to save.

She knew what I needed to hear, but instead said something that made the blood freeze in my veins and my heart sink with sorrow.

Feelings can change.

With that cryptic response, Tia stopped talking. It was the first time I suspected that Tia was hiding something from me. I didn't like the feeling. Not one bit. Having someone else in your mind was bad enough without suspecting them of sabotaging your thoughts or manipulating your emotions.

Shaking me slightly, Ahmose brought me out of the world inside my head. "What's wrong, Lily?" he asked.

What isn't wrong? I thought.

"What isn't Asten telling me?" I asked. "About the dreams, I mean."

"Connecting to another's dreams is a very . . . intimate experience," Ahmose said, placing his hand on my back to guide me in the direction of Asten's tracks. "Your thoughts and desires will become clear to him, and his to you. I would imagine it's not unlike your relationship with Tia."

Great. It was bad enough to have a lioness with me. How would it feel trying to separate the thoughts, feelings, and dreams of three different individuals? I realized in that moment how susceptible I was to losing my identity and becoming lost, not only to Tia but also to the persona of the sphinx. If I ever got out of this, I was going to need some serious therapy.

"How would connecting to Asten like that help me, then?"

"Asten's presence would effectively replace Amon's. Instead of going to his dream world, you'd be entering Asten's."

"I see," I said, suddenly feeling very uncomfortable with the idea of sharing dreams with Asten.

"Is Asten concerned about sharing my thoughts on such a level?"

His silver eyes met mine. "I'd say he's more worried about *you* knowing *him,*" Ahmose answered softly.

That was something I wasn't concerned about at all. If I had one talent of my very own, something that was purely Lily and not something I'd acquired in becoming a sphinx, it was that I was an excellent judge of character.

"Ahmose?" I bit my lip.

"Yes?"

"Are you upset with Asten for not telling you who he really was?" I asked.

Shrugging slightly, Ahmose answered, "Asten has always been my brother. The other one, the queen's birth son, was never a part of my life. The circumstances of Asten's birth do not matter to me in the slightest."

"But what about the part where he seduced the girl you liked? What was her name?"

"Tiombe," Ahmose said with a catch in his voice.

"Yes. You . . . you've forgiven him, haven't you?"

Ahmose sighed. "In truth, I forgave him decades ago. I never told him as much. I let him suffer, thinking I still resented his involvement, but had I known how much pain he was holding on to . . . well, let's just say I regret not offering my forgiveness earlier. I've had a long time to think about what happened. If I'd had more time, I would have discovered Tiombe's true nature eventually on my own. That it was quickly revealed when Asten pursued her made the parting that much easier. At the time, I thought I'd never speak to him again. But even then I could tell that Asten wasn't doing it to hurt me. He thought he was helping."

"So you don't blame him, then? Not for any of the things he confessed?"

"All of us have secrets, Lily. That his were made public doesn't diminish my opinion of him. I know and love my brother. Also, knowing that Anubis was aware about all of it and still granted him power makes Asten even more exceptional in my eyes. What saddens me is that he didn't think he could tell us. After our first deaths, our positions as princes were no longer of import."

"Maybe he didn't want you to think less of him."

"We could have shared his burden. Asten has allowed his mistakes to weary his heart, and he fears our affection for him will shift as easily as the sand. Amon and I are made of more solid stuff."

I nodded, agreeing with him, and then asked, "If you know he's a good man and I know he's a good man, then why was his heart banished?"

"That's a very good question. I suspect it has less to do with Asten's choices in mortality and more with the need to send us here. It's a subject I plan to take up with the gods in earnest once we return."

We navigated around a large hill to a wide plain. Asten stood peering across it. Though he didn't turn to acknowledge our presence, he addressed us the moment we came up behind him. "It's the Field of Fears."

"Begone!" a wheezing voice said. A little hunchbacked man peeked out from behind a large rock. Blistering bubbles stood out on his nose and arms. One of them popped, oozing yellow pus. I noticed a screeching monkey on his back that held a gleaming orb similar to Asten's heart.

Asten raised his bow. "Who are you?" he demanded.

"Just a beleaguered ghost—weak, and not worth the time it would take you to fight me." Though he claimed weakness, I didn't miss the grinding of his teeth and the determined look in his eye. He'd surely give as good as he got.

"We're looking for our friend."

With a calculating expression, the little man said, "I know where he is. I can take you to him. *If* you'll give me something in exchange." He poked my rucksack. "You've got some powerful stuff in there."

"I . . . I suppose we could share them," I stammered.

The ghost cackled with glee and led us through the Field of Fears.

Halfway through, Asten slowed.

"He's stepped into a fear," our guide complained. "Bleeding hearts with their bleeding silly fears. He gets stuck here of all places? Ridiculous."

"What is he afraid of?" I asked.

"This is the no-one-loves-me-and-I'm-all-alone fear," he answered in a mocking singsong voice. "Who cares about blinking love? What good does it do? I'm alone every day. Don't hurt me none."

"He feels alone?" I asked, my voice huskier than usual.

"How do we get him out?" Ahmose asked.

"Easy. Give him something more fearful to think about." The little man grabbed hold of my arm. His monkey screeched and bit me, hard. A giant pustule rose on my skin. Asten suddenly moved, breaking free of the fear, and picked up the little ghost with one hand.

"What did you do to her?" he demanded with burning eyes.

"What I needed to," the ghost answered as he kicked his legs futilely.

"Asten, I'll be fine. See?" I channeled the power of the healing stela and the angry blister on my arm shrank until it disappeared.

"My price just went up," the ghost said. "I want that healing thing-amajig."

"No," Asten answered bluntly. "It wouldn't work anyway. Your injuries are your penance."

The ghost tried to stare them down, but they weren't having it. "Fine," he said, giving in. "Just don't go getting stuck in the fear of kittens or puppies. If you do, I'm leavin' you there."

When we finally passed through the field, I breathed a sigh of relief. We'd made it.

"You'll find the one you're looking for thataway. Now give me what you promised."

I offered the surly ghost my bunch of raisins, and he disappeared.

We'd only walked fifteen paces when Asten said, "I'm afraid we've been deceived."

"But the scarab says Amon is truly this way," I said.

"Perhaps the path to him lies beyond," Asten replied.

"Beyond what?"

"That." He nodded, indicating the path before us. "The worst place you can end up in the netherworld—the Mires of Despair. It's far too vast to circumnavigate. I'm afraid the fastest way is through."

"If we survive," Ahmose mumbled.

"Great, another near-death experience . . ." I paused, reaching into my bag to offer Asten a sip from the flask of cider. He was sweating. It was the first time I'd seen him sweat in the netherworld, which was disturbing. I wondered if, at that moment, Amon was being abused and they were feeling the effects and not sharing it with me.

Distracted, I dug into the gaping maw of my bag and came up with nothing. "He stole it all!" I shouted. "That scheming monkey on his back stole the cider and the cakes. Now he has everything!"

I looked back toward Ahmose and sweat had broken out on his brow, too. Both their mouths tightened into thin lines. "She's hurting him now. Isn't she?" I asked.

Asten nodded rigidly.

"Every moment Amon is in the hands of the Devourer is a moment too many," I murmured quietly.

A heavy weight soon fell upon my shoulders as well. The Devourer was draining Amon, and it now affected all three of us. I slumped against Asten. My body trembled, but I was comforted by the idea that the energy she took was shared among all of us, and that as long as we were alive, we could rest assured that Amon was, too. A shudder went through me, and though I wanted to know what had happened to Amon, I didn't at the same time. It was at least an hour before we felt recovered enough to resume our journey.

"Are you ready?" Ahmose asked. I nodded. He rubbed his hand across his jaw. "Going through could take at least a day."

"You can find the quickest path," Asten encouraged his brother.

Relieved that whatever was torturing Amon was over, I looked down past the perilous, jagged rocks descending to the valley floor below, to the countless waves of white grain. A ghostly moan sent an eerie echo, and I stared at the movement of the grain, puzzled by it. The plants moved haphazardly, and not at all like wheat on a farm. "What is it?" I asked.

It is unnatural, Tia whispered in my mind. *Not of the earth.*

"Not it. *They,*" Ahmose answered.

"They?"

"Yes. They are the undead. Those who were banished and who were unable to fight off their demons like Asten did," Ahmose explained.

"They're like our ghost guide," Asten added, "only they've been discovered and brought here. Some feel they have no reason to fight their demons. Others try but are quickly overcome and grow too weak to stave off their tormentors. Here in the mire they are plagued for eternity as their hearts are dangled like bread before a starving man."

"So they're like the ghosts I saw the Devourer consume? They weren't as solid as our guide was."

Asten's fists tightened, though I wasn't sure he was entirely aware of it. "Yes. This is her garden. Her stores of . . . food."

"That's horrible!" I exclaimed.

"There's no choice but to pass through," Asten said. "If we hurry, we can make it through before the reapers come."

"Reapers? Why does that sound even worse than the existence of an undead farm?"

"The reapers are not to be trifled with. Any soul caught in their path will be harvested. Trust me when I say we don't want to linger in this place."

"So how do we get down there?" I asked. "Can you find a path, Ahmose?"

"There is only one safe path down. We'll have to carry you," he answered.

"Carry me? Are you going to jump?"

"Not exactly," Ahmose hedged. "Come. You'll go with me."

"I'll take her," Asten said, and stepped forward, placing a hand on my arm. Ahmose gave his brother a long look but then nodded and backed away. Apparently Ahmose wasn't feeling the effects of the heart scarab as keenly as his brother at the moment. Ahmose raised his arms and levitated in the air, immediately heading over the side of the cliff and descending rapidly.

Asten moved in front of me and gave me a small smile with just the tiniest glint in his eye, reminding me of the cocky version of Asten that I was more familiar with. Taking my arms, he placed them around his neck and leaned down to whisper in my ear, "Hold on to me tightly now."

I nodded as he leaned down and scooped me up. Within the space of a heartbeat, he had risen in the air and we slowly began to float down to the valley below. Again I felt my heightened senses become attuned to the man carrying me. The feel of his strong shoulders beneath my palms, the hair that brushed my fingertips, and the way he held me enchanted me.

As I gazed up at his face, an inner part of me tried to recall Amon's, but the details I loved so much seemed to pale in comparison and I found I couldn't hold his image in my mind, not when Asten was so close. A tiny sound of dismay escaped from my lips and he looked at me.

"Are you all right, Lily?" he asked, clutching me closer.

"Yes," I managed to squeak out.

Asten studied me and seemed to see something in my expression that I'd been trying to hide. Warmth spiraled between us, and his eyes melted into liquid pools. With my heightened vision I could see the spark of little stars that glinted in them. The corner of his mouth lifted, not in a smirk but in a smoldering promise, and whatever it was he was silently promising me, I wanted, needed, to say yes.

He edged closer, touching his nose to mine and then grazing our cheeks inch by tantalizing inch until his lips found my ear. Tangling my fingers in his hair and stroking the nape of his neck, I focused on the feeling, imbuing the touch with my power, willing him to feel the caress and the contact of his skin on mine. I heard his sharp intake of breath and then his quiet murmur shot goose bumps down my neck. "Careful, little lioness," Asten said in a husky voice. "A man can only resist a woman like you for so long."

I swallowed thickly. "But I'm not . . ." I couldn't finish the thought. My pulse pounded in my throat and the warm scent of him—cedar, amber, spice, with a hint of cocoa—enveloped me. He smelled delicious. Like something I wanted to taste. Something was very wrong with what was happening, but another piece of me thought it was very right. *We want this,* a voice whispered in my mind. *We want* him.

Asten lifted his head, flames of heat flickering in his eyes. He wanted this, too; I could sense it. The space surrounding us felt feverish and frenzied. I cocked my head and pulled him closer, his lips only centimeters from mine. "Asten," I began with a sultry, pleading tone to my voice.

"Lily," he answered with an echoing hunger.

Tilting my head up, I waited breathlessly, with an almost aching anticipation, for his kiss. But it never came. I opened my eyes and found his closed.

"Asten?" I whispered, confusion smothering the passionate fog I'd been in.

"We can't do this, Lily." His eyes finally opened but what I saw was not the desire I hoped for, but regret and self-recrimination. "Though you are as pure and lovely to me as the most brilliant star in the heavens, I will not do this to my brother."

"But . . . Asten, I—"

"I'm sorry. I won't add you to my list of mistakes."

"That's all I'd be to you?" I accused. "A mistake?"

"No. That's not . . ." He shook his head. "Don't misunderstand me."

Our feet touched the ground and Ahmose approached. "Misunderstand what?" he asked.

"Nothing," Asten answered.

I put my hands on my hips, feeling the stabbing pain of rejection mingling with the sick nausea of guilt. "That's right. It's nothing," I said brusquely, and adjusted the bow across my back, automatically checking my knives at the same time. As I turned to head toward the field of ghosts undulating in an unseen netherworld wind like thousands of gray, inflatable air dancers, I pushed the thought that I wasn't at all afraid of flying when held by Asten to the back of my mind.

Ahmose took my arm. "Wait, Lily," he said. "Let me find the path first."

I nodded and folded my arms across my chest. When Ahmose crouched down and stretched his palm out over the sand, I briefly made eye contact with Asten, who wore a half-confounded, half-guilty expression that echoed my own.

As we walked through the field, trying but not succeeding to avoid all contact with the ghosts, I pondered why I was feeling so upset. Asten had done the right thing. I didn't know what had come over me or why being close to Asten inspired thoughts of tearing off his shirt with my claws.

There was no denying now that I was acting horribly disloyal to Amon, and the idea of the pain he would feel over my betrayal made me want to cry. And not just shed a tear or two, but sob in absolute heartbreak like the time Anubis had made me kill him. That was what it felt like. Like I was slowly but inevitably killing Amon. I couldn't stand it.

Tears leaked from the corners of my eyes, and I felt like screaming and ripping out my hair right along with the ghosts who clutched vainly for me when I passed. Through my watery vision, I noticed that the rows of souls near us had access to their hearts. The glowing orbs were almost close enough to touch, but none of them bothered trying. If they helped one another, they might even be able get their hearts back.

Stopping before a sad, broken woman, I stooped to pick up her heart and hand it to her, but Ahmose took hold of my wrist before I touched it.

"Don't," he said. "They're too heavy. The despair will only sink your own feet into the mire." Remembering my inability to pry Asten's heart from the Lake of Fire, I nodded and we went on. It seemed that the only ghosts paying attention to us were those we came into close contact with, and as the hours passed, I began to see a change in the rows. Farther down, the specters were more . . . lively.

Half of them seemed to be affected by their love for me, while the other half clutched hungrily like the Devourer had. With most of them, one or two of their tormenters swirled around their legs, taking little nips now and then. Each soul had its very own brand of persecutor. I saw a variety of bugs, snakes, worms, bats, tiny lizards, and even something that looked like a cross between a miniature garden gnome and a gargoyle torturing them. The number of demons attacking the ghosts increased with each hour.

Aside from the disturbing view, Asten seemed determined not to make eye contact, which was fine by me. The more distance between us, the more in control I was. What was wrong with me?

I tried to ask Tia, but she had locked herself away from my consciousness. She was there. I could feel her, but she was curled up in a ball, and as much as I mentally poked her in the back, she wouldn't turn around to face me. Not that I blamed her. I thought she might be ashamed of me, considering the way I'd been acting.

As we traveled on, the path became narrower. Ahmose apologized and sought a better direction, but there was no better way. We'd have to get up close and personal with the Devourer's victuals. Grasping hands and arms got closer and closer.

Then a specter who appeared to be more solid than those around him, who had at least a dozen fist-sized beelike creatures swarming around his head and repeatedly stinging him, reached toward me and actually caught hold of my sleeve. He plucked at me desperately, crying out to save him. His legs seemed rooted in place, like they'd been planted in the sand. Even though most of his fellows were insubstantial, he had enough matter, for lack of a better word, about his form, that his grip was rather strong.

When I told him I was sorry and that there was nothing I could do, that he had to fight off his own demons, his pleas turned to rage. "You will help me," he spat from his swollen, horribly stung face. "Or you will die alongside me. I've killed plenty of pretty young things like yourself. I wouldn't even bat an eye."

"You're already dead," I said, wondering if I'd have to call forth my claws and if they'd even find purchase in his form.

"I know that, stupid, beautiful girl," he hissed. "I meant the second death. The first for you, the last for me. We'll go down together. It's almost romantic. Maybe if I offered her a pretty girl like you, a live one, she'll take her time digesting you and I'd have enough time to escape." He began hitting himself on the head. "No. No. No. We like her. No. We'll eat her ourselves."

"I don't think so," I said. "Besides, you can't escape the Devourer. I've seen her in action, and she doesn't let anyone go. But cheer up. We're going to try to kill her, so you may make it after all."

"Ha!" he cried. "She can't be defeated. Everyone knows that."

"Well, we're going to try."

"You'll die in the process."

"Better to die fighting than to be gathered up like grain," I said.

The ghost's gray face turned a darker shade and a kind of black spittle oozed from the corner of his mouth. "You'll pay for that."

Other ghosts nearby began to react to the one holding me. Though stuck in mounds of sand, they reached upward, like zombies finally catching the scent of fresh brain, and with expressions nearly as vacant. But none of them were close enough to do much more than paw at my legs and arms, their limbs passing right through my skin, leaving a chill behind on my flesh.

The ghost holding me yanked and struggled, trying to pull me closer, but I was able to dig in my heels enough to stop him from making any headway. Still, he didn't seem to be in any kind of mind-set to let me go. It wasn't until Asten and Ahmose stepped around me and stared the ghost down that his demeanor changed.

"Guardians!" he cried, keening as he rocked back and forth. He released me and went back to beating his own head with his fists. "Stupid. Stupid. Stupid!" he called as he abused himself. "Should have seen them there. Why are they here?" The ghost looked up at us in a hopeful, desperate sort of way. "It's a mistake, right? I shouldn't be here. You're here to take me back?"

"Back!" one ghost echoed.

"It's a mistake," another called.

"Yes! Mistake."

"Mistake."

"Take us back."

Asten took hold of my shoulders and pulled me against his chest while Ahmose approached the corporeal ghost. "I'm sorry," he said. "We're here on our own business."

"Your own business? What business could you possibly have here? This isn't your domain! You don't belong. Get out! Get out!"

The other ghosts began to wail, the intensity ratcheting up and spreading until nearly the entire field was screaming in cacophonous alarm. "Out!" they cried. "Don't belong!"

I buried my head in his chest, inhaling the warm scent of him as he stroked my hair.

"We're only halfway through, and it gets harder after this," Ahmose said. "The ghosts near the front have been here longer. They're less . . . well, less. The ones back here were planted more recently. They'll be stronger. And they'll have the ability to detour our passage."

"We can fly over them, can't we?" I asked, secretly delighted at the prospect of being in Asten's arms again.

Asten shook his head. "We're weighed down here. We feel the effects of their despair. There's no levitating again until we're clear of them."

"Ah, hence the name Mires of Despair."

"Yes."

"Okay, then, we'll just have Ahmose find the best path and—"

My words were cut off when the cries and moans of the dead became screams. A new kind of panic passed from ghost to ghost until it reached the masses where we stood.

Asten and Ahmose each took hold of one of my hands and began to sprint forward. We'd run out of time. The one word we absolutely did not want to hear was being repeated by every single ghost in a field of thousands.

Reapers.

22

Reapers and Jackals

"Lily! Run!" Asten cried, pulling me through the field. As quickly as we tried to move, I was alarmed when our progress had come to a near halt. The path leading out of the field was cluttered with ghosts prostrating themselves and tearing at the ground as they clawed desperately at their fellows and tried to wrest their feet from the mire that held them.

They grabbed our ankles, their sharp nails pricking my skin. When they caught hold, they hollered desperately, "Save me!" or "Take me with you!" Others cried, "Don't let them harvest me!" and "Can't you stop them?" As much as I wished I could do something, I knew there was no way for us to help them. The farther we went, the more violent the ghosts became.

A particularly aggressive specter managed to nearly trip me, causing a snarl to escape from my lips. Ahmose summoned his cudgel and ax, formed from the grains of sand surrounding us, and Asten called forth his bow with a quiver full of diamond-tipped arrows. I pulled my own bow off my back and nocked it with one of the arrows of Isis.

With Ahmose clearing the path ahead and Asten bringing up the rear, there wasn't much for me to do. Once struck with the cudgel, the ghosts withdrew their arms, nursing various hurts, even though some of them appeared to have wounds much worse than anything Ahmose did to them.

Still, they moaned and cried in terrible anguish, and I suspected it was more than just the pain we inflicted on passing. Several of them bit their fists or quaked with fear, then stared off into the distance.

"Keep going," Asten said when I paused to look behind us once again. A crazed ghost took advantage of my unmoving position and grabbed my leg, pulling with such force that I stumbled into its arms. At once I was buried in a cocoon of limbs that yanked at my hair and clothing.

I jerked down the row, far from the path Ahmose had found. My bow tumbled off to the side and was left behind while my knives were wrenched from my grip, tossed with indifference to the ground just out of my reach.

Instinctively, my claws emerged and I raked them across the chests, arms, and necks of those who surrounded me, but they pressed even harder, as undeterred by my assault as zombies would have been. I panicked as the image of a snapping pack of hyenas bent on my destruction filled my mind.

Crying out desperately, I pushed and shoved, so frantic to escape that there was nothing of the sphinx or even a lioness in my demeanor. I'd been reduced to a trembling husk of myself, a weakling that could answer their strikes with nothing but tears.

A shadow fell across the pile of bodies, and one by one the assailants disappeared in a cloud of sand that blew across my face. Asten was using one of his diamond-tipped arrows, filling me with relief and a fervent hope. At first I thought he was jabbing it into the skulls of the dead, but after he'd cleared enough of them away, I could see he was targeting their hearts instead.

Some of the ghosts realized what he was doing and they screamed, attempting to scramble away from him or, when that didn't work, to distract him from the gleaming orbs of their hearts. He let them wrench their bodies as far as their rooted feet allowed them to and then quickly finished off the more aggressive ghosts still in my vicinity. The others nearby were cowering like punished dogs, their arms folded over their stomachs, backs hunched as they drew away from us.

"Are you all right?" Asten asked, crouching down next to me. His eyes flicked over my face and then down my trembling torso. I ached to be held. To be stroked and comforted. *Why isn't he wrapping me in his arms?* Asten touched the underside of my chin and lifted my face until our eyes met. Through my eyes alone, I tried to express just how much I needed him, how much I burned for his touch, but I must not have been successful. Again he asked, "Are you hurt, Lily?"

Something inside me shrank and shied away, much like the ghosts around me.

"Yes," I answered, feeling the confidence and control over my emotions return with each passing moment. "I'll be okay."

Asten cocked his head and peered at me as if not trusting my words, but then he nodded and offered his hand. "Come on, then."

Helping me to my feet, he handed me my spear-knives and my bow with the precious arrows of Isis.

"Asten?"

"Hmm?" he answered, intent on watching the surrounding ghosts.

"Why are they so fixated on me?"

"It must be the heart scarab. As immortals, they can sense things beyond the understanding of a living being. Such a thing as love becomes tangible to us. A physical, heady thing. As the Sons of Egypt, we can manipulate spells to control the unseen but love is unrivaled, uncontrollable, a more powerful spell than anything the gods could fabricate. Perhaps this is why even they fall victim to it."

I was sorting this out when the ghosts around us fell absolutely dead quiet. We froze and looked around. Every ghost in the field was hunched over with their arms wrapped around their legs and heads tucked down almost between their knees.

"What's going on?" I asked.

"I'm not sure," Asten said, placing a hand on my shoulder in a gesture of assurance that a part of me deeply needed to feel.

Whatever was happening, it didn't bode well for us. We'd already been conspicuous in the field of gray forms, but now that we were standing upright in a nearly flattened field, it quickly became obvious that we would make easy targets. It only took a few seconds for our deepest fears to surface.

"They're here," Ahmose declared. The eerie calm was now punctuated with a new sound—a clacking noise that grew in intensity with each passing moment.

There was nowhere to hide.

Ahmose knelt on the ground and murmured a spell, holding his hand out over the sand. After a few seconds he rose. "This way," he announced. "There's a large rock over this hill that we can put our backs to."

As we made our way to the rock, the clacking noise grew, then subsided over and over again. The ghosts around us sank deeper into the mire. I noticed that my own steps became sluggish, my feet sticking, though the soil still looked the same to me.

When I told Asten and Ahmose, they glanced quickly at one another and then Ahmose explained. "It's the despair. You feel it weighing on your heart. Try to focus on the things that lift your soul."

"Is it affecting you, too?" I asked.

"Yes. But hearing that the soil feels sticky to you is alarming. It means you're further along. Are you worried about Amon?" he asked.

"Amon?" The truth was that since descending in Asten's arms, I'd thought of little else besides him. *That's not right,* I thought. I considered my feelings. There did seem to be a kind of dark unhappiness filling my frame that wasn't normal. I wasn't the kind of girl to wallow. I got up and did something to fix whatever was bothering me. I wasn't prone to depression.

If that indeed *was* despair weighing down my heart, it wasn't because of Amon. I was reasonably assured that I was taking the right path to save him. I was concerned about him, of course. Saving him was the thing of utmost importance to me and yet, somehow, it wasn't. There was something else gnawing at the back of my mind. And the more I thought about it, the more foreign the emotion seemed. Like it didn't belong. I bit my lip, trying to figure it out.

We reached the rock and Asten gave me a long look before stepping close to Ahmose to converse with him quietly. Something hungry and fierce took hold of my being, and then that something shattered and the soles of my shoes sank a full inch into the sand. I panicked, remembering the quicksand that had almost killed me. That wasn't going to happen again.

I tried to breathe deeply to calm myself, a focus like Ahmose had said, but my lungs wouldn't expand. Wrapping my hands around my throat, I closed my eyes and concentrated. It felt hard to swallow, and there was a painful burn stinging my eyes.

Suddenly, my eyes fluttered open. I knew the emotion roiling through my frame. It was heartbreak. That didn't make sense. Amon was alive. He loved me. Why was my heart hurting like it had when Anubis returned me to New York? The idea that something horrible, something . . . conclusive had happened to Amon froze the blood in my veins. But I still felt his heart beating steadily where the scarab rested against my skin, so that couldn't be it.

Ahmose left us briefly to scout for a better position.

"What's wrong?" Asten asked, concern etched across his handsome face.

"It . . . it hurts." It was a guttural proclamation ripped from the hidden depths of my soul.

"What hurts?"

"I don't . . . I don't know," I whispered, my lips trembling as tears leaked from the corners of my eyes. I shook my head slightly, trying to clear the waves of sadness that seemed to overwhelm me.

With a pained yet resigned expression, Asten put an arm around my shoulder and awkwardly patted my back. A desperate cry escaped from me and I burrowed into his chest, wrapping my arms around his waist. I felt more than heard his sigh as he put his other arm around me, enfolding me completely in his warmth.

"Tell me what ails you, little lioness," Asten murmured as he rubbed my back in small circles. "What has brought my fierce warrior to this?"

"It's my sister," I heard myself say.

Asten leaned back and looked at me with a note of confusion, which only deepened the gorgeous cleft in his chin. "Your sister?" he echoed. "I didn't know you had one."

I blinked, and a glistening tear that had been clinging to my eyelashes fell on his shirt. Touching my fingertip to the wet spot, I closed my eyes and then splayed my hand on his muscled chest.

"Do you mean Tia?" he pressed.

Sucking in a deep, cleansing breath, I lifted my head. "No. I don't mean Tia." A wave of deep resentment and disappointment filled me. "It's okay, Asten," I said with a slight tremor to my voice. "I'll be fine."

He gave me a look that said he wasn't at all sure about that; then Ahmose ran quickly back to our site, shouting, "Here they come!"

The clacking sound that had surfaced since the ghosts went silent increased until it became impossible to tell where it was coming from. We were enveloped by sound, and I was quite confused by it. I wanted to lash out and protect us, but I fought with myself, waiting for Ahmose's direction. I reached for my bow but halted abruptly with my arm in the air. *No!* Tia shouted in my mind. *Not the bow!*

What? I answered back, upset that I could no longer control my arm. *Why are you doing this? You want to have a fight about weapons now? The reapers are coming!*

I know the reapers are coming, Lily. She almost spat my name. *And we're fighting them on my terms this time. Not yours. Just because I share your body does not mean I share your mind-set all the time.*

What is wrong with you? First you ignore me when I try to talk to you and now you're yelling at me. Do you think you could pick a better time to argue?

I'm not arguing with you. I'm simply telling you how this is going to happen. And we're using our knives, not *the bow.*

I struggled for power but quickly learned that Tia was determined and my mind was immobilized by her rebellion. It was Tia, not me, who reached behind our shoulders and took hold of the knives. Tia who twirled them in her hands and pressed her thumb against the nob that elongated the weapons into deadly spears. Planting them into the sand by our feet, she peered into the field, cocking our ears for the source of the clacking noise.

We didn't need to wait long. Dark shapes circled lazily over the field. They were airborne, and every so often descended at random intervals to harvest a chosen victim. Like grim reapers, the angels of the ghost's second death held a curved blade of some kind, though it wasn't nearly as long as the scythe carried by reapers in horror movies. The reapers acted like large birds darting in the field after a kernel of corn or a worm, but the act came to a deafening end with a slicing noise, followed by a quick, bloodcurdling scream.

A moment later a gray, loose-limbed ghost, after having his gleaming heart unceremoniously shoved down his throat, was stuffed matter-of-factly into a bag slung across the robed reaper's shoulder. That was one thing the legends had gotten right. Reapers did wear black robes, long ones that fluttered in the hellish desert wind. They smelled of desperation and decay.

We remained quiet, ready to fight but hoping to be ignored. I watched the reaping with fascination and wondered what Dr. Hassan would think about this place. Asten and Ahmose stood nearby, weapons clenched in their hands, their breathing ringing in my ears.

Just when we were finally safe to flee, a ghost not too far away, one targeted by a reaper, began waving his hands in our direction and screaming, "Invaders!"

Throwing the seized ghost down as if he were a sack of discarded trash, the reaper turned and looked in our direction. The abandoned ghost, with one remaining leg stuck in the mire, frantically attempted to escape the confines of the field. He wasn't successful. Within the span of a few moments, another reaper appeared, grabbed hold of the struggling specter, and finished harvesting him, along with his heart.

The black-robed form watching us drifted closer and straightened his body out in the air. The horrible clacking began as he twisted his head one way and then another. His hood fell back from the motion, and I saw where the noise was coming from. It was the reaper's jaw.

From Tia I knew the creature was scenting us through the movement of its jawbone. When it opened its mouth, the tongue, a long black muscle, tasted the air. After it drew the organ back into its gaping maw, the jaw clacked a dozen or so times, as if it was chewing up our scent.

The creature looked more buglike than skeletal, but I could see how it might be mistaken for a skeleton. From a distance, the black-and-white patterns of its face slightly resembled a human skull, but the jaw was shaped differently, more like an ant or a wasp.

The clacking mouth wasn't moving up and down like a human jaw would but instead clapped together horizontally from either side. And it was a wide mouth, much bigger than a creature that size should have. The noise it made as it hovered above the ghosts reminded me of a swarm of hornets. Glowing eyes burned as it studied us.

After a tense moment, the buzzing noise ramped up several degrees and we noted several other reapers closing in on our location fast. Asten must've decided that fighting one off now would be better than waiting for a group to attack, so he loosed an arrow. The starlit diamond head found its target and sank into the neck of the reaper. An unholy screech filled the air, and then the creature floated slowly to the ground, roiling in its death throes.

More screeches rose as Asten loosed arrow after arrow. Soon they were close enough to reach by spear, and I threw one and then a second, managing to seriously wound one while killing the other. The creatures swelled in numbers and we were quickly surrounded, fighting hand to hand. I summoned my claws and slashed, continuing to kill. There was something cathartic about being in combat.

All the confusion I'd felt dissipated, and my mind emptied of its worries and errant emotions. Suddenly I found myself in control of my body. While fighting, my limbs moved seamlessly, instinctually. I drew upon the powers of the sphinx and my call was answered. Never before had Tia and I worked together in such a unified manner, and I relished the feeling. With a bare hand, I crushed the windpipe of one reaper while sinking my claws into the heart of another. There was no struggle. No dominance. No uncertainty. We were one, with a connection even stronger than we'd experienced on Cherty's boat.

The second wave of reapers approached, this time their stingers bared. I fought off my two attackers easily, but five flew down to surround Ahmose, who had been struck more than once with a reaper's short scythe. Blood colored the sleeve of his tunic. I smelled its sharp tang in the air, but I could tell his injury wasn't life-threatening.

I headed toward him, but then Asten was stung in the leg and I wavered. Without thinking, I went to Asten instead, using my claws to remove the stinger from the reaper's body. I then grabbed the reaper's robes and smacked his head against a rock until his body went limp. I longed to comfort Asten, but I heard Ahmose's cry and gritted my teeth.

Feeling like I had no other option left, I nocked one of the precious arrows of Isis, raised my bow, and aimed. The arrow sank deep into the shoulder of a reaper, but the creature responded in a very different manner to my arrows than it did to Asten's. Instead of screaming or falling when injured, the reaper immediately stopped fighting and came toward me, its injured arm hanging loosely by its side, the arrow still protruding from its body.

The familiar buzzing noise filled the air, the sound so powerful my skin tingled with the vibrations. The other reapers paused, watching the first, and one by one they followed him as he drifted to the ground by my feet. Gradually the sounds made sense and words took form.

"How may we serve the goddess?" said the injured reaper. Neither Asten nor Ahmose seemed to understand him.

"You can stop attacking us, for one thing," I said, my claws still brandished in a threatening manner.

"We will let you pass," another said.

"What will we tell the mistress?" an alarmed reaper asked his brothers. "Many have died!"

"She will know!" chimed another. "She will devour us!"

The reaper I'd just injured said, "We will distract her with double the number of hearts and attempt to hide our injuries and our dead."

"She will discover us!" one lamented in despair.

"It matters not!" the first shouted. "The tears of the goddess call to us. If it means our death, then so be it."

"Thank you," I said. "My friend has been stung. Can you heal him?"

"Regrettably, we cannot," the reaper said, his words buzzing in my mind. "But the salve from the mother tree in the Turquoise Forest can nullify the poison."

"Yes," another echoed, "if you reach it in time. He has only a few hours."

"Hours?" I questioned, fear for Asten blooming in my chest. So far he showed no signs of poison, other than a slight limp and a sheen of sweat across his forehead.

"Head west," one said. "Find the Fountain of the Jackals. The path underneath will show you the way to the trees."

The reapers turned to go, but one hesitated. "We will hide your presence for as long as we dare from the Devourer, but her mind is sharp. She will discern our duplicity soon enough. It would be best for you to make haste."

"Wait!" I cried before the last reaper rose. He hesitated, floating in the air above us. "After we heal Asten, we plan to attack the Devourer. Will you help us?"

The reaper stared down at me, his mandibles clacking softly as he considered my request. "You are brave fighters, but you are three, and she has the power of thousands at her disposal. We reapers are her votaries, sworn to her service. She will know if we dared to defy her. Once, a very long time ago, we served a goddess of a different sort, but we were tricked into aiding Chaos, and now we are here at the beck and call of the Mistress of the Dead. But we will always remember she who is our creator. She who was lost to us."

He paused. "I will ask my brothers to deliberate upon your proposal. But know that the thing you speak of is very dangerous. We will likely all perish in the attempt, and she will wreak her vengeance upon our whole hive. If she kills our queen and our unborn, our species will perish."

"But if we succeed, then you will no longer need to serve her," I said.

"That is true." The reaper tasted the air as he thought. "When you come to battle, let loose one of the goddess's arrows into the sky and we will see what we can do."

"Thank you," I said, and nodded my farewell.

As the reapers left, I approached Asten. "How are you feeling?" I asked.

"My leg is just a little numb at present. I believe I can walk on it with some help."

I grimaced as I examined the wound. "Can you make some cloth, Ahmose?"

Within a few seconds, Ahmose created a stack of mummy-style bandages that neatly folded themselves into my hands. I raised an eyebrow at him.

"What?" he asked when he noticed my expression.

"Could you be a little bit more foreboding?" I asked, wrapping the bandages around Asten's leg. "These are mummy wrappings."

Ahmose shrugged. "It's the first thing I thought of."

I sighed. "I guess I can't blame you. When we get back to the real world, I'll have to take the two of you on a tour of all things modern, including hospitals with sterile supplies."

"And food," Asten added. "I should like to try more of the pastries Amon introduced me to."

"You got it," I said with a grin.

For a moment, I stood still, remembering how much Amon liked to feast, especially on the round discs filled with fruit. There were so many places I could introduce him to. So many new foods we could try together. Then Asten's next words pierced my tiny bubble of happiness.

"Sadly, we aren't going back with you," he said. "You know that even if we defeat the Devourer, Ahmose, Amon, and I cannot return to your world. We aren't due to rise for another thousand years."

"Maybe they'll let you take a tiny, well-deserved vacation?" I ventured. "Maybe for a hundred years or so?"

"It is doubtful, Lily," Ahmose said. "We have never in our long centuries of existence been granted a reprieve."

"We'll have to do something to change that. But first things first. We need to save Asten and then Amon. Can you find a path to the Fountain of the Jackals, Ahmose?"

"I believe so."

He let go of Asten's arm and I took it, offering my support as he tried to stay upright on his injured leg. Ahmose raised his arms in the air to chant a spell, then clapped his hands together.

The entire valley began to shake.

"What's happening?" I cried.

"I don't know!" shouted Asten, stumbling against me. We clung to each other as the cliffs surrounding us rumbled, ready to crush us beneath them.

A crevice opened in the mountain at the end of the valley, dust and rocks showering down into the dark space inside. Ahmose had cleaved the mountain in two. When the quaking was finished, the three of us stared at the newly made gap that led up and out of the valley.

Within the hour we were at the gap, and it quickly became obvious that Asten was going to struggle to climb the rocky terrain. "You should leave me behind," he said after we came to a stop, the two of us panting with exertion. Ahmose was scouting the best places to climb, finding the spots that were the most stable while we rested. Still, Asten was exhibiting signs of strain and we had a long, long way to go.

"We're not leaving you behind," I said. "It won't happen."

"Time is of the essence. You must save Amon. Surely the world is more important than I am. I'm not even a chosen vessel. I'm just a human who was swept up in this."

"And what do you call me?" I asked. "I didn't exactly set out to become what I am now. We do it to save the ones we love, and I consider you a part of that group."

"Do you?" he asked. His eyes lit on my face, studying me as if seeking the answer to his question.

"Do I what?" I answered softly.

He didn't clarify but lifted his hand to my cheek and brushed away a smudge of dirt. I pressed my hand against his, willing him to feel the touch. He gave me a sweet smile that told me he could indeed feel it. The hurt I'd felt before, though I still didn't fully understand its cause, melted away with his smile. Asten leaned closer and my breath caught, my heart fluttering in my chest as the air around us became thick.

Ahmose called out, "Just a little farther and you can go airborne, Asten!" He slid back down to us and the intimate moment passed. "The pull of the Mires of Despair weakens about fifteen feet up," he said. "Once we get you there, it should go much easier for us."

I felt pleased that we were going to make it. We'd save him. But then, why did the Mires of Despair still tug at my heart? I mused on that until we reached the point where Asten was able to take flight.

A moment later, Ahmose reached for me and pulled me into his arms. The three of us floated up and over the side of the cliff. We remained airborne, passing rocky terrain littered with pulsating mounds of dirt that surely housed monstrous beasts we didn't want to meet. Jagged peaks pierced the sky, casting ominous shadows.

There was no sun and yet there was just enough light to see by. Unlike dawn, there was no promise of brightness and hope, nothing to look forward to. We knew only misery awaited us. All was dusk. Twilight. But it was ugly and devoid of stars. It was as if we stood on the edge of a desperate horror, waiting for the monsters that hid under the bed to feel comfortable enough with our presence to reveal themselves.

The haunted air of expectation that kept me feeling jittery was echoed in the landscape. Even with enhanced vision I could only see so far. Dark caves and pockets, hidden dens and craggy overlooks were everywhere, each one potentially hiding something or someone bent on our destruction. Tingles lifted the hairs on the back of my neck. I was sure we were being watched. Followed.

To distract myself, I asked Ahmose about the reapers. "Why didn't they turn to dust like the ghosts?"

"They're like you," he replied.

"Like me? What do you mean?"

"They are living. When they die, it is their first death. Their bodies are buried here and their souls are judged. The ghosts die a second and final death."

"And that could happen to you? Turning to dust, I mean?"

"It could, but the Devourer will keep Amon alive as long as possible," he said, assuming I was thinking of Amon. "His heart can power her for a long time."

"How long?" I asked, distracted.

"How long, what?"

"How long until she's absorbed enough of his power to break free?"

"I do not know. Amon is the most powerful of the three of us, since he possesses the Eye. But it could be that it won't take long at all."

I thought about Amon, marveling that he'd been able to survive as long as he had in the netherworld. Unlike me, he was by himself.

Eventually, the bleak landscape changed and we came upon a sort of alien oasis. Strange trees rose into the air, and the sound of water drew us closer.

We touched down and Ahmose went to his brother. Feverish heat and sweat had broken out on Asten's face, and despite his attempts to reassure us, he cried out when his foot touched the earth. Even though his leg was bandaged, I could see how swollen it had become.

The trees were too close for Asten to remain airborne, so Ahmose carried his brother on his back while I took the lead, knives at the ready. The moment we found the source of the water—a large bubbling pool in the middle of the oasis—the noise of the birdlike creatures in the trees ceased. The all-too-recent experience with the ghosts and the reapers came to mind, and I knew from Tia that the sound of tiny creatures in the vegetation around us meant everything was fine. The moment the noise ceased was the moment a predator had arrived. I hoped, though I didn't hold out much optimism, that the predators they sensed were us.

I was wrong.

A musky, dark scent, like that of a burrowing animal, tinged with the slight stench of decay, assaulted my nostrils. I spun in a circle, keeping the water at my back and the brothers behind me. Ahmose set Asten down and drew his weapons also, positioning himself alongside me.

Before I could even prepare to throw a knife, dozens of huge, wolflike creatures encircled us. Their hunched backs were bristled with fur, their sharp claws clacking against the pebbles and rocks in their path. They crouched low, baring glistening fangs, their yellow eyes gleaming with deadly intent. Their reverberating growls sent little shivers dancing along my skin. My breathing quickened, and a cold fear licked my veins. *Jackals!* my mind screamed.

Before, when fighting the reapers, I was confident, sure of myself. For some reason this was different. I knew the razor-sharp fangs would rip into my throat, devour me. They had no mercy. They wouldn't hesitate to destroy. To kill.

One of the beasts came closer, his form melted like liquid smoke, and then solidified much too near for me to feel comfortable.

Why are you here? the creature resembling a giant werewolf asked in my mind. *Have you come to feed our hunger?*

"The reapers said you can help us get to the Turquoise Forest."

And why would we do that? the beast asked with a gargling sort of laugh, his jaw opening and then fleetingly disappearing before snapping together again like a trap. The gust of air he blew out from his nostrils tasted peppery and feral on my tongue. He lifted his face and then melted, reappearing a few feet to my right.

Outsiders. The scent of you tantalizes us, the head jackal said. *You stir our blood with the slavering tang of your dread. It drifts over us lazily and invigorates us until we are crazed with what it promises.* He shifted his head excitedly. *We jackals have the strength of great boulders. Our flesh is as iron. Our teeth sharp. Our jaws steel traps. Your teeth are broken, dull. One of you lies weakened. Poison drinks his spirit. And you?* he said right to me. *You reek of fear.*

I think the pack will dine well tonight.

23

Heart Blood

I pulled an arrow of Isis from my quiver. *Eleven left.* The creature's yellow eyes widened, his body turning to smoke. But before he could fully disappear, I jabbed the arrow deeply into the thick muscle of the jackal's neck, hoping it would find purchase.

Fortunately, it did. An unearthly howl filled the air and was soon echoed by every member of the pack. I wondered if my actions had saved us or if I'd just given the hounds of hell the reason they needed to attack.

Drawing back my arm, I summoned my claws, preparing to sink them into the throat of the beast writhing beneath my arrow.

"How do we get to the Turquoise Forest?" I shouted.

We do not bend to your will. No matter who protects you.

"You will tell me, or you will die," I hissed.

The jackal quickly turned his head to snap at my arm, but missed. His entire body shook while attempting to turn to smoke, but the arrow forced him to stay as flesh and blood each time.

We don't serve her. *Not any longer,* he hissed. *We are pledged to a new queen now.*

"The Devourer," I said, and I wondered then if I had made a grave error in thinking these beasts would be as easily pacified as the reapers. "Fine. You choose death, then!" I exclaimed, grabbing the arrow and twisting it deeper.

The beast cried out with a pathetic yelp. *Wait!* he spat.

"Change your mind?" I asked with an innocent-seeming air.

He didn't answer right away, and I shrugged, moving to finish him off. *He deserves it regardless,* my inner voice assured me. *The mongrel, scavenger of death. His kind is a plague on the grasslands. Unfit even for carrion birds. Their entire species needs to be eradicated.*

What is going on with me? I blinked, trying to sort through my thoughts. I had never been vengeful. Especially when it came to animals. Sure, this one wanted to serve us up for dinner and I'd kill him if I had to, but my preference would be to scare them off at worst and wring the information we needed from them at best. These dark thoughts of killing each and every last one of them must be a sphinx thing. *I hope. I have to hold it together.*

"Look," I said. "I'd rather not kill you." The voice inside me screamed in opposition. "All I want is to get my friend to the Turquoise Forest. There's no need for this to turn bloody."

The only thing that prevented me from attacking—a gesture that would surely end in either my first death or Asten's and Ahmose's second, or all three—was reminding myself that Asten was deteriorating rapidly. He needed to get to the cure. That was much more important than any perceived need to kill the pack of monster jackals.

"Tell me what I need to know, right now!" I shouted to the group. "Tell me or your leader dies!"

I stared at the circle of blinking yellow eyes until I noticed a movement on my right. A smaller jackal, a female, crept forward. *We have no choice but to obey you, though my father fights against the coercion valiantly,* she said.

Howling pitifully, she crawled forward and pressed her head against the flanks of her father. He turned and snapped at her, grabbing hold of her leg and biting until she bled, but still she spoke. *You must enter the*

Waters of Forgetfulness. Dive deep. When you emerge, you will find yourself in the Turquoise Forest.

I heard a snap and the small jackal cried out. The father had broken his daughter's leg. She collapsed and licked the blood from her broken limb.

"One last thing," I said as I bent to address the suffering pup. "Why haven't you attacked yet?"

We cannot, the little thing whimpered. *Not while the arrow rests in our leader.*

The head beast snarled viciously and barked at his pack. They echoed his bark, and I knew it was only a matter of time before they came for us. Straightening up, I said, "Then we'd best go. Ahmose, get Asten to the water. I'll join you momentarily."

The jackal's hatred for me was tangible. *I'll rip open your belly and feast on your succulent insides while you watch,* he promised, his jewel-like eyes never leaving mine. *If the Devourer finds you first, she'll stew your bones and toss me your boiled bowels for a treat. Either way, we'll consume you.*

"No *jackal*"—I spat the word at the wounded beast—"will ever take me unawares." With that, I took hold of the arrow and pushed it as deeply into his neck as it would go and then broke off the shaft, leaving the head embedded in his body. He collapsed in a heap, but he was still alive. I hoped he'd stay that way long enough for us to escape.

The pack started barking wildly, a cacophony that I instinctually understood and feared. They would hunt us. Though they bowed to the power of Isis, they now served the Devourer. Unlike the reapers, this group of netherworld creatures would not assist us against the one they served.

Keeping my back to the pool, my eyes trained on the shuffling animals who crept closer, I shifted one foot backward and then another. Within a few steps I was at the water's edge, and without looking down, I moved deeper and deeper until the water lapped my chest. I hoped the water wouldn't ruin my bows, but there was no other option I could think of than to just go through with it.

For a few seconds I thought the jackals had tricked us, getting us into the most vulnerable position they could before attacking. But then I remembered the reapers. They'd said we'd get to the forest by finding the Fountain of the Jackals and following the path underneath. Diving beneath the pool was about as underneath as we could get. I took a deep breath and dove, Asten and Ahmose following close behind.

Down, down, down I swam but still couldn't find the bottom. I felt an arm scrape mine, but when I groped in the dark and looked in that direction, I saw nothing but blackness. Kicking my legs, I continued. Unlike what had happened in the Lake of Fire, my lungs began to tingle. Whatever it was we were looking for, we'd better find it soon. I blinked. *What was it again?*

There was something we were seeking. *We? Who are we? Why am I in water? Is this a dream? A nightmare?* My mind was a blank slate. I screamed but cut it off quickly to save my air. Bubbles trickled from my mouth, heading down the way I was facing, not up. Paddling with my arms, I swam in a circle, searching for something, anything, to tell me where I was and how to get out.

Then, all at once, a light flared near me. It took the shape of a man. He was handsome and strong, but his face indicated pain. He moved awkwardly in the water. I swam closer, yearning to help him, and as I did so, I forgot the twinge in my lungs. He watched me approach with a curious expression, but it was clear he didn't know who I was any more than I knew him.

Hesitantly, I reached for his hand. When our fingers touched, my memories suddenly rushed back to me. *Asten.* Together we searched for Ahmose and found him nearby. When Asten grabbed his shoulder, Ahmose looked our way. His body lit up like Asten's, with one distinction: Asten's body was a white so bright it was almost blue, and Ahmose's was a softer, paler white. Both of them were different from Amon, whose skin had gleamed an almost buttery gold. I wondered if the variance had something to do with their powers or the celestial bodies they represented.

Then I remembered the token Horus had given me. He'd said the stone would not only heal me but would also help me right myself. Upon cupping the stone in my hand, everything shifted. My body moved in the water as if an unseen force were pulling me. The three of us began moving, but not under our own power; it was the water. Just as the three of us united, it rushed around us so forcefully I had to close my eyes.

I could barely see Asten or Ahmose through the cloud of my hair, but their gleaming auras still lit the surrounding water, so I knew they were close. Daylight beckoned us upward, and just when I could no longer hold my breath, we broke the surface.

Tia? I tried to reach out to her, but she'd been silent since our fight. I mentally searched for her but couldn't sense her presence. I realized then that it had become increasingly difficult to find her when she didn't want to be found.

My worries over Tia had to take second place, though. The first thing we needed to do was get the salve from the tree to save Asten. We just had to figure out which tree in the forest was the mother tree. Scrambling to shore, I stood up, vigorously shaking my body to get the excess water off and wringing out my hair, feeling disgusted that I'd kept it so long. I knew should shave it off or, at the very least, cut it. It was a mess, and the long strands were getting in the way.

Tossing it over my shoulder, I immediately checked all the weapons, dumping at least a gallon of water from the quiver of arrows. Crouching down to Asten, I pressed a hand against his brow. His skin was cold; I wasn't sure if that was natural for him in the netherworld or if he was truly close to death. "We'll find the cure," I whispered. "And this misery you feel will float away like the passing water of a deep river." I frowned. When did I become so poetic? I was rewarded for my eloquence, however, as Asten took my hand, gifting me with a soft smile that deepened the cleft in his chin. I returned his smile but then shook my head slightly and withdrew my hand. "Ahmose, we've got to find the mother tree."

"I'll go," he volunteered. "You should stay with Asten."

"No. You'd better let me. This forest is the same one I traveled to in my dreams"—I glanced down at Asten, whose eyes were openly watching me, studying me—"with Amon," I finished. And something about saying his name out loud made me feel guilty.

Asten turned his head. "Let her go," he said quietly to Ahmose. "But if you're not back in a few hours, we're coming to find you."

I nodded in agreement, though I knew Asten wouldn't be moving from his current position anytime soon. He was no longer looking in my direction regardless. "A few hours, then." Rising, I headed off into the forest, memorizing the scents that would guide me back to the place I'd left them.

Skirting the wide pool, I scanned the surrounding trees, wondering what a mother tree looked like. I imagined it to be the oldest tree in the forest, and the trees near our camp were at most ten years old, at least by my way of reckoning the flora at home. Also, the leaves on the younger trees were a brighter blue.

Knowing I needed to find an older section, I headed west, looking for the darkest patches. My footfalls were soft, nearly silent, as I moved across the springy moss that grew in blue-green tufts. Muskier scents of age and death alerted me that I was going in the right direction.

The forest was eerily quiet. The normal buzz of insects or the chirping song of birds was missing. Larger animals hid in the bushes. I could hear them shifting uncomfortably at my presence, but the stench of ammonia clung to them, making them entirely inedible.

Twice I caught the scent of something that made my mouth water, and when I paused for just a moment or two, I got lucky enough to snare one of them. Quickly, I tossed its body into my sack. What I'd caught wouldn't provide much in the way of dinner.

The forest was cold. The coldest place I'd been in the netherworld, in fact. I longed to have the sun heating my back. How lovely it would be to stretch out on the heated grass and bask in the sunshine.

Around and around the forest I wandered, but the trees I saw were young, their turquoise leaves sparkling and dancing in the cold breeze.

"Hello?" I called out to any creature listening. "I'm searching for the mother tree."

There was no answer, and an hour later, I finally found myself in an older part of the forest. This section was dark, especially in the never-ending twilight of the netherworld. Again I called out, but this time more quietly, "Hello?"

Nothing. But I could sense something watching me. I felt the telltale warmth tickling my spine.

I paused at the base of a large tree that looked very much like the one that had given Amon water in my dream. A tiny fluttering of wings caught my eye, but when I turned to look they'd disappeared.

I might have imagined it, but for a moment, I thought the overhead branches had shifted, arching over me. "Such a lovely forest," I said with a yawn, hoping to use compliments to coax out the one watching me. "This is by far the most beautiful and safest spot in all the netherworld. A girl could almost forget all her troubles by staying here. It's a paradise in an otherwise hellish place."

"I don' *care*!" I heard a tiny voice whisper.

I blinked and held my breath, trying to catch the words again. I would have missed it completely if it wasn't for my super-sphinx hearing.

"So *what* if you like 'er? I'm *not* going down there." A pause. "If we're quiet, she'll go away."

Taking a chance, I said, "Is that you, little fairy?" The rustling branches were my only answer. "I'm not going to hurt you," I added. "Won't you please come out and talk to me?"

After a few quiet seconds a limb snapped above and a glowing object shot out from the tree. She floated down in front of me, crossing her arms as she said, "I am not *little*. And *you* don't belong here. I suggest you move along."

I smiled. "You look pretty little to me."

"Oh, I'm pretty," the fairy said while stroking her gleaming red hair and fluttering her nearly translucent wings, "but I'm not little. I'm as big as you are." She pointed her chin in the air proudly and then gave me the once-over. "Or I was once. Well, perhaps not quite as big as you are. Your hands are ginormous!" She gaped openly at my hands.

"What?" I lifted them up to study them and frowned at my fingers. *Are my hands too big? Have the claws done something to them? Do I have gorilla knuckles now?* I'd never felt self-conscious about any part of my body before and I didn't like what I was feeling. I frowned at her. "My hands are perfectly proportionate to the rest of my form."

"*I* disagree," she said, flying around me in circles. She sniffed delicately. "And what's more, ya smell a bit manky ta me, too."

"Look," I said. "I've been through a lot. I didn't come here to fight with you either. I need a favor."

"Ha! Told you she was after somethin'." She shook her finger at the tree in an I-predicted-it manner. "What do ya want?" she asked, placing her hands on her hips. "Not that we'll give it to you. I'm only askin' so we can speed this thing up and get rid of you."

I narrowed my eyes at the fairy. "You're a pesky little thing. To think I almost felt sorry for you, seeing as how you helped Amon when he was dying of thirst."

The sprite gawked at me in shock.

"It's a trick. Don't ya see?" the fairy said to the tree. "Her pretty words are just that. If we heed what she says, it will lead ta harm. I'm sure o' it." She cocked her head to listen, but I couldn't hear anything. "Don't eat the head off of *me*! You're far too trustin'!" she shouted at the tree. "You're cracked in the trunk, you are. Maybe the Devourer sent her. Did ya ever think o' that?" The fairy spun in a circle and threw up her hands. "Fine! I'll ask. Will that make you baggin' happy?"

"I don't mean either of you harm," I said, "and the Devourer didn't send me. I'm here to destroy her, actually. She has my . . . my Amon prisoner and is siphoning the energy from his heart as we speak."

The fairy blinked. "Is Amon your fella, then?"

I nodded.

"And you said the Devourer's got 'im?" she asked, immediately ceasing her rant.

"The two of us, we're . . . connected. That's how I knew you were here."

The little winged girl drifted closer and looked me in the eye. "What is it you need from us?" she asked.

"My . . . friend, Amon's brother, was stung by a reaper. They told us the salve from the mother tree in the Turquoise Forest would save him. I'm assuming this is the mother tree," I said, gesturing to the leafy canopy overhead.

"Of course it's the mother tree," the fairy said huffily, and puffed out a breath. "It doesn't matter, though. She won't give you any o' her sap."

"What? Why not?" I asked. "Don't you want us to save Amon?"

"I do. That is to say, I'm not happy he ended up in the Devourer's clutches but it's his own fault, really. If he had just stayed here, hidden, like I told him to—"

"Well, now his brother is dying. Is that what you want? Don't you have any empathy for others?"

The fairy sucked in a breath as if she'd been slapped. Tears filled her glittering green eyes, though she refused to let them spill over, and her rosy cheeks turned even ruddier.

She took a few deep breaths, then said in a muffled voice, "I . . . I don't wish Amon or his brother harm. And don't think that I'm an ungrateful sort of person. I'm not. I've just learned ta be careful. You have to understand that giving up her sap weakens the tree. Her strength keeps the evil out there from enterin' our forest. If she gives up her energy ta save him, she won't have enough left ta protect all of us or herself. She could die."

Letting out a small sigh, I said, "I'm sorry. But you need to understand that I'll do anything to save Asten. I'm asking because it's the proper way to do things, but I . . . I need him. He's got to live. Anything else is unacceptable."

"Am I ta understand that you're threatening us now? We don't take kindly ta threats. Especially bandied about from fresh-from-the-country girls such as yerself."

I had no idea if she'd just insulted me or complimented me. "It's not a threat," I said. "It's just the way it is."

The sprite eyed me suspiciously.

"Look," I said. "Just give us enough to save him. That's all I ask. We can even stay here and camp, guarding the tree while he heals, but as soon as he does, we'll have to move along."

"I don't like ya vera much," the frowning fairy said, "and furthermore—" She stopped and jerked her head upward. "No!" she shouted. "I won't do it, ya daft bush." She zoomed up five feet and stared at the trunk with an expression of incredulity. The leaves of the tree quivered. "Ya can't! Don't do this!" she screamed, shaking her fist.

The fairy flew around the trunk, shouting and pulling on her red hair. I stood up and tried to follow her erratic flight, but then a moving branch caught my attention. It passed over my head and the thin tip of it touched the trunk. Slowly, it trailed a path downward, and as it did so, light burst forth from the trunk, splitting it open as if the branch had been pulling down a zipper.

I squinted from the brightness while inside the trunk something beat. Sucking in a breath, I realized I was seeing the heart of the tree. The gleaming orb thumped in a slow, steady rhythm. It was beautiful. The tree had gotten her heart back. She'd fought off her demons just like Asten had. I smiled, but then the thin limb pierced the tree's heart.

"No!" I called out, just as the fairy rushed down to see what was going on.

She burst into torrential sobs and grabbed hold of the trunk. "Quickly, catch the fluid that seeps from the heart," said the fairy. "Don't let any of it go to waste!"

I ran up to the tree and cupped my hands next to the heart. The warm and sticky white sap flowed onto my fingers. The fairy came back just as the sap threatened to spill over and brought a huge leaf that was obviously much too heavy for her, but she somehow managed to position it under my hands. Bringing my knee up to support it, I carefully let all the sap trickle into it. The fairy held up a side to prevent it from seeping over the edge.

"Now stop!" the fairy commanded. The light inside the tree had diminished significantly. After daintily dipping her hands into the sap, the fairy pressed her glowing palms against the wound in the trunk, rubbing sap over the edges, and the deep cut sealed itself shut.

"You stupid, selfless, overly generous, chancer tree," the fairy lamented. "Wasn't dying once enough for you? You had ta fight so hard ta get your heart back, and now you give it away ta the first person who asks for help."

The fairy turned to me with a glare that spoke volumes. "I hope you're happy. Now get out of here and save Amon's brother. If you manage to accomplish half of the things you've promised ta do, then I'll be impressed. More likely, though, this precious gift will be squandered. I'd suggest using yer giant hands ta make sure not a drop is spilled. And here." The fairy snapped her fingers and a bag materialized, its weight centered on my hip.

"What's this?" I asked.

The fairy shrugged. "It's not my idea. The tree thinks you'll need it. If it were up ta me, I would have given you nothin'. And I'll warn ya right now. If I find out you're a forger o' lies, I'll hunt ya down and make ya suffer until all the shamrocks in Ireland couldn't save ya."

I nodded soberly. As diminutive as she was, I took her at her word. "Thank you," I said to the tree, then turned to the fairy. "Now, how do I make the salve?" I asked, irritated with her, yet somehow respectful and grateful at the same time.

The fairy shook her head as if my question had been ridiculous. "The sap *is* the salve. It's the heart blood of the tree. Now go. Crack on. And I hope ta never lay eyes upon you again."

I nodded and rose carefully, making sure the sap was stable in the leaf. When I'd walked a few steps away, I turned. "Thank you. Both of you. I promise this gift will be remembered and will be used well. If there's any way to return the favor, I will."

It took me two hours to return to our camp, and when I entered the clearing, I smelled two things. The first was fire, and I was grateful to Ahmose for getting one made. If he hadn't hunted yet, I figured we could eat what I'd brought, and then we could hunt again in the morning. Honestly, sleep was now more important to me than food. The second thing I smelled was decay. Rot. And I stopped in my tracks, a feeling of horror spreading through me.

"Ahmose, is he . . . ?"

"Dead?" He shook his head. "Not yet."

"Then we'll have to hurry. I hope we can save the limb," I said. "This salve should heal him. I just hope it's enough." I brought the sap-filled leaf next to his leg and overturned it onto the wound. Gleaming liquid pooled slowly beneath the leaf and trickled sluggishly down his thigh. I rubbed the leaf in tiny circles, making sure to get the bulk of the sap into the wound. Asten moaned and thrashed. "Hold him down!" I shouted.

I didn't know what I would do if I lost him.

"I'm going to wash my hands. Can you make new bandages?" Ahmose nodded and I headed to the pool and thrust my hands under the water, scrubbing hard.

The gleaming liquid fizzed and bubbled, creating a cloud of light beneath that slowly dissipated. Where the sparkling water lapped the shore, tiny green things began to glow, and as they did, they grew. Little plants stretched out their vibrant leaves and the moss thickened and spread. I watched in fascination and then raced back to Asten.

Ahmose was wrapping his leg. "His fever has broken already," he said. "Your salve appears to be working."

"Let's just hope it's not too late."

Finishing up, Ahmose stood and stretched. "What's that?" he asked.

"What?"

"What's in the bag? You didn't have it when you left."

"Oh. It's something the fairy gave me. That and some kind of forest creature I caught."

"Fairy?"

"Yeah. It's a long story." I pulled the tie, freeing the bag, and opened it. "Food!" I said. Inside was an assortment of nuts and dried fruit. "The tree made sure I took it, along with the sap."

"We'll have to thank her," he said as he reached into the bag for a handful. He handed me a skin of water as well, and I could tell from the thick fabric folds of cloth that he had made it and likely filled it from the pool of water. Several others sat at the base of a fallen log, plump and bursting with precious liquid.

Ahmose suggested we take turns keeping watch, and offered to keep an eye on Asten while I slept. I was so very grateful, and had just allowed sleep to creep up when a thought occurred to me. I remembered that there was no way I could sleep until Asten was able to watch over my dreams. The likelihood of the Devourer finding us by following my sleep self was too great to risk.

Ahmose had already wandered off, circling our little camp. Not wanting to disturb Asten or interrupt his healing process, I peeked at his wound, noting that a medicinal smell had replaced the scent of decay. It seemed to be healing at a very fast rate. He stirred.

Scooting over next to him, I pressed my fingertips over his brow to check for a fever. "How are you feeling?" I asked.

Asten cracked open his eyes. "Not as good as you're looking." He gave me a weak version of his cheeky smile. But it was as welcome as a monsoon after a drought. I didn't realize how much I'd ached at the thought that I'd never see it again. "Hello there, little lioness," he said quietly. "Glad to see you made it back. If I'd had to go after you, I'd have made you regret it."

I answered his smile with one of my own. "Why don't you save that threat for a time you can act on it," I suggested.

"I just might," he said, and sighed, closing his eyes once more.

When I thought he had drifted off again, I tried to draw away, thinking to find Ahmose and tell him there was no point in both of us staying awake, but Asten caught my hand and pressed it to his chest. "Don't leave me," he murmured sleepily.

Slowly, I lifted my other hand to smooth the hair away from his forehead. "I won't, *Tene*." I frowned, wondering where I'd heard that word before. Was it Egyptian? Asten inhaled deeply and I felt the thump of his heart against my hand. "Shush now. You need your rest," I said.

"You need to sleep, too," his voice rumbled faintly beneath his chest.

"I . . . I can't. You need to be well first."

"I'm healing. I can feel the effects of the poison ebbing away. So relax," he urged. "I'll live."

"It's not that," I said. My cheeks colored. "You need to be well enough to . . . watch my dreams."

Asten opened his eyes then, cocking his head to look at me. "I can do that," he said softly.

"But I thought—"

"Come." Asten held out his arms. When he saw me hesitate, he explained, "It will be easier for me if we are touching while we sleep."

I nodded and shifted awkwardly to his side as he wrapped an arm around me. Pulling me closer, my head cushioned on his shoulder, he captured my hand and brought it to his chest.

"There," he said. "Much better. Now try to still your body. I promise I will be waiting for you in your dreams."

There was something both frightening and thrilling about the idea, but I attempted to follow his instructions and still my racing heart. Fortunately, my body was so achingly tired that it didn't put up much of a protest, and I closed my eyes, letting my mind drift far, far away.

24

Where There's Smoke

The dream came upon me softly, slowly, like layers of twilight that deepened and darkened, as silky sheets of light were peeled away with a caress and a whisper. I lay on my back, my hands tucked behind my head. A night breeze ruffled the leaves of a nearby tree, but the canopy did nothing to block my view of the evening sky.

Opalescent stars glittered above me, so close they seemed to ache for my touch. The crushed grass beneath my body smelled sweet and I wiggled slightly in the indentation I'd made, feeling wild and wanton. I closed my eyes, basking in my surroundings and the peace I felt.

"Hello, little lioness," said a voice behind me.

I turned over on my belly, twisting up to see who spoke. Asten stood with his back resting against the trunk of an old tree. He was long and lean and, strangely, seemed to be just as at home in this landscape as he was in the waking world.

There appeared to be no trace of the fever or the gash in his thigh. One of his legs was crossed over the other in a casual pose. His brown eyes sparkled in the shadows of the tree as he watched me, his demeanor reminding me of a lazy cat who'd just finished a satisfactory meal and was looking for something to play with.

"So this is the place you dream of," he said. His gaze took in the scenery, the starry sky overhead, and then settled back on me. "I like the view," he murmured softly, his eyes tracing my form, lighting little fires everywhere they touched.

A burgeoning storm built inside me, though I didn't fully understand why. I licked my lips, imagining his touch, and the tempestuous feeling coated the tip of my tongue. I liked the dreamy, honeyed taste. "Why do you remain so far away?" I asked. "The view is better from here."

Asten laughed softly, the sound an electric thing that left my limbs feeling quivery. "That it is."

He came closer and I turned onto my back once more, stretching luxuriously in a slow purposeful way, limb by limb. When I settled back, I kept my hands by my sides. Putting them under my head again made me feel vulnerable. Asten's shadow fell over me and I gazed up into his face, now haloed by the stars. I sucked in a breath. "You're beautiful," I said.

Asten froze briefly, and a guilty expression stole across his face. "Don't say that, Lily. You don't mean what you're saying."

I frowned for more than one reason. "But I do. I've never seen a form as pleasing to my eyes as yours."

He gave me a curious glance and then said, "You should be careful of the things you say in a dreamscape."

"Why?"

The corner of his mouth lifted. "Sometimes I forget just how young you are." When I narrowed my eyes, he clarified. "What I meant to say is that your innocence is charming. Sometimes, it causes me to forget myself. It's not always a bad thing, mind you. In truth, I particularly appreciate your straightforwardness, but in this case, it can cause . . . problems."

I mulled over his comments and then asked, "Do you not speak your mind as I do?"

"Not as often as I'd prefer. Hearing you . . . well, it makes me feel . . . free." He said the last part with an embarrassed glance.

"Do you feel trapped, then? Is it your past that haunts you?"

Cocking his head, Asten knelt next to me. I took his hand and drew him down. Almost reluctantly, he lay down alongside me, his head propped up by one hand so he could look at me.

"There are a number of things that haunt me, little one."

"Is that why you didn't wish to share my dreams? Ahmose said you're afraid of me learning too much."

"Ahmose is right, in a way, though you already know the bulk of my secrets since you witnessed my judgment."

"You did not deserve banishment. Even Ahmose agrees with me."

Asten sighed, lying back and placing his hands behind his head like I had done earlier. "Ahmose is tenderhearted and quick to forgive."

"Don't you feel you're worthy of forgiveness?"

"Perhaps, for some things."

A winged creature of the night cried out as he took flight, and we followed its path until it disappeared.

"Which of your former actions continues to plague you?" I asked bluntly.

He gave me a wary look. "It's not my past that plagues me. I've come to terms with my demons. It's my future."

"The future? You know what is to come?"

"Being the Guardian of Dreams is a very weighty responsibility, especially when those dreams involve myself."

"You said you'd dreamed of me. Tell me, what was your dream of?"

"I . . . ," he began, but then shifted uncomfortably. "It would be better if I kept those things to myself."

"Do you think that I will judge you?"

"No. I think that you might encourage me and encouragement is the last thing I need. I'm barely able to control myself as it is."

We remained quiet for a few moments, and then I leaned up on my elbow and said, "You do not need to play the part of a prince or a godling or even a brother while you're with me if you don't wish to. When I look at you, all I see is a man, a man that pleases me in countenance and in temperament. A man I admire and am proud to fight alongside of. There is no secret you could share that would alter my perception of or my feelings for you."

Asten gazed up at me with an expression full of something hopeful and euphoric. Gently, he reached up to tuck a strand of hair behind my ear, and when he did, his fingertips glowed. The section of my hair was now sparkling, the strands turning as white as the stars. I leaned into his touch so that his hand caressed my cheek.

"I can feel you here, you know," he said, "without you using your power, I mean. In the dreamworld a touch happens on a different plane. It doesn't matter that you are living and I am not."

I closed my eyes and said, "When you touch me, my heart races faster than I've ever experienced before. I feel as if I am running but I am utterly and absolutely still. To move right now would be torturous."

His fingertips traced my lips in a deliciously slow way. The feeling was glorious, tantalizing, transfixing. I opened my eyes and remembered what it was like to bask in the warmth of the afternoon sun. Asten was a burning star, and the warmth with which he looked at me heated my blood to a point that I wanted to give myself over to it, to him, forever.

Moving my lips against his hand was heady, intoxicating, and it soon became evident that the passion inflaming me was echoed in him. I made a tiny involuntary sound and then his hand dropped. The tenderness I'd seen in his face was now gone, replaced by an expression of doubt and concern.

He sat up and wrapped his arms around his knees, seemingly wishing to forget the passionate experience we'd just shared. "Have you seen Amon at all?"

"Amon?" I echoed, confusion filling me. I sat up beside him. "No. Should I have?"

"No. Not tonight, anyway. That's good. It means I've been with you since your dream began." A red flush crept up his neck.

"You're embarrassed," I said.

"No. It's not that." He got up and walked a few steps away, staring up into the night sky.

I watched him, feeling swirls of uncertainty eating away at the pleasant experience I'd just had. That he regretted touching me just now was obvious.

I longed to join him but I couldn't bear the thought that he didn't want me. Didn't crave my closeness as much as I did his.

"I miss them," he said, interrupting my thoughts.

"Miss what?" I asked.

"The stars. It feels wrong not to glance up and see them. They are what I miss the most on my long sojourns."

"Are they?" I asked, finally mustering up the nerve to approach him.

He shot me a quick glance. "Yes. Though now I'll have something else to miss."

I was going to ask him what that was, when over his shoulder I saw something.

Pointing up to the heavens, I said, "Oh, Asten. Look!" A shooting star blazed across the sky. I was delighted to see it, and a bit envious of the speed and freedom it had to race across the expanse of space.

When it was gone, I turned to find him watching me, an air of sadness and longing on his face. "I'm surprised," Asten said.

"What about?"

"That this is what you dream of." He held out his hands, spinning in a circle. "It's . . . it's peaceful," he said, turning back to face me.

"Aren't most dreams?" I asked.

"No."

"What do most people dream of, then?"

"In dreams people process the day-to-day things. Their worries and concerns are puzzled over, and they find solutions. Some dream of terrible things they'd dare not speak of or do in the real world. But in a connected dream such as this one, I can see what it is a person wants most in the world."

"And what is it that I want?" I asked, taking a step closer.

Asten regarded me with a mixture of fascination and fear. His reaction made me feel powerful. I got up and stepped past him to brush my hand along the thick limb of a nearby tree. Arching my back, I stretched like a cat and then turned to him, an arm still draped across the limb. He swallowed. Then, eyes glittering, he closed the distance between us. "You want to bask in the starlight on an evening still warm enough to heat your skin," he said. He lifted his hand, tracing a path from my elbow to my wrist. The surreptitious touch was tantalizing, and I desperately wanted more.

"What else?" I pressed with a mysterious smile.

He leaned against the branch and looked up at the sky. "You gaze at the stars as if they hold secrets you wish to find answers to. Why do they intrigue you so?" he asked.

"The stars are . . . beyond," I said.

"Tell me what you mean."

"They beckon me. When I was first joined and became a sphinx, there was a part of me that belonged to the earth, to my former home, but there's also a part of me that belongs elsewhere. I want to race through the stars and discover all the worlds and all the beings found there. The idea of getting lost and leaving my old life behind entices me."

"Surely there's something of your old life you'd like to keep," he murmured.

Unbidden tears filled my eyes. "No." I shook my head sadly. "There's nothing left for me there."

"Nothing?" he asked as he brought his hand to my face, brushing away the fat teardrops with his thumb.

I blinked and his hand slid down from my cheek, gliding over to the corner of my mouth. His touch stirred my despair, coaxing my emotions from drowsy flames into a blaze so powerful I was overwhelmed by it. His gaze, before full of sympathy, was now fired by something else, something smoldering.

"There's something else I want," I said. "Do you know what it is?"

"I do," he said, his eyes roving over my face and fixing on my mouth.

A subtle cry escaped my lips—part inhale, part whimper. Before, it had caused him to take a step back but this time he came closer, so close that our bodies touched. Had I thought he was cold before? It must not have been his natural predisposition because he was hot now. Being near him felt like I was baking beneath the light of a thousand, thousand suns.

The anticipation of something I couldn't describe burned, inflaming every inch of my skin. I trembled, yearning, not knowing how to make the thick pounding in my veins stabilize. Slowly, almost hesitantly, he lowered his head until his lips made contact with the delicate skin where my pulse beat erratically.

I flinched momentarily, but he didn't bite. His caress was gentle, soft, like the barest of touches. He trailed soft, deliberate kisses down my jaw to the cor-

ner of my mouth. I was lost in the sensation, and savored each press of his lips against my skin, yielding to his embrace.

As his mouth grazed my ear, he paused and slid his hands to my shoulders. I panicked, thinking he was going to cease touching me in the lovely and delicious way he had been. "Asten? Don't stop," I begged.

He shifted his head away, his breathing deep. As if unable to keep his hands off my skin, he slid them up to cup my neck. Asten lifted his gaze to look directly in my eyes, his expression haunted. "I'm sorry," he said.

"Why?"

"Because my desire for you isn't something I can control in the dreamworld."

"Is this what you were afraid of?"

Reluctantly, he nodded.

"And you've seen us together like this in the future?"

He paused a moment, as if deciding what to tell me, but then he sighed and said quietly, "Yes."

"Then I don't understand your hesitation."

"My"—he swallowed and sucked in his lower lip, a gesture I found transfixing—"my hesitation came with knowing how you feel about Amon."

"Amon?" I blinked, and a cold irritation piqued, settling in my stomach and threatening to squash the escalating ardor I felt. Resentment washed away every happy sensation from moments ago.

"Am I not allowed the freedom to love whom I wish? To explore my feelings? To follow the urgings of my heart? Of my soul?"

"Of course you're allowed those things."

"Then you need to understand that there's a fervor running through my blood that calls to you. I will work to save Amon. I will fight the Devourer. I may even die. But before I do all these things, I want to understand these feelings. Discover the tiny pleasures that I've only just begun to learn." I stroked his cheek and found the roughness of the stubble on his face a soothing distraction.

He stilled my hand, placing his on top of mine. "Are you sure this is something you want, little lioness?" he asked.

I smiled. "This is something I very much want, Tene." Love. *The word felt right. He felt right. And yet, a nagging thought plagued me. "But . . ."*

"But?" Asten frowned.

"There is something I need to know." He nodded, encouraging me to speak, and squeezed my hand. Hesitantly, I asked, "Is the desire you claim to feel for me the result of the scarab's pull?"

"You're asking if I can love you for yourself?"

I nodded, relief and gratitude filling me. He understood me in a way no one else could. He could see into my heart.

Asten studied me for a moment and then slowly, purposely, his eyes never leaving mine, brought my palm to his lips. His kiss so sweet, my entire body hummed. Then, wrapping his arms around my waist, he drew me closer. "The scarab has no sway in the dreamworld," he murmured, nuzzling my ear. "What I feel for you here is genuine and comes from my own heart. Does that answer satisfy you?"

I nodded.

He pressed a kiss against my temple and continued. "I was a man who usurped another man's place. Who hid who he was and what he wanted. If all I ever get is to love you in my dreams, I'll take it and praise my good fortune."

I was about to protest, but he raised his head and pressed a finger against my lips. "And if, when you wake and decide that the things we've said and done were a mistake, I'll understand. A long time ago, I made a vow never to take what belongs to another man again, especially my brother. But where you're concerned"—he paused, trailing his fingertips across my skin and down my jaw, leaving little tingles in their wake—"I find oath breaking an all-too-pleasing prospect."

I leaned into him, a tiny groan escaping from my lips, but he took hold of my shoulders. Pressing them lightly, and letting the cold, unfeeling wind flow between us, he waited for my eyes to open and meet his. "I need you to understand," he said. "If, after this trial is said and done, you decide that you want to pursue this . . . this feeling between us, I will. I'll move the stars in the heavens to find a way to be with you. This I vow."

I smiled, teasing him lightly, "Do you ask me to trust you, then? A self-professed oath breaker?"

His eyes pierced me. "I would break every oath I've ever made or will make just for the chance to capture even a moment of what I've seen in my dreams. But the time is not yet, little one."

Asten paused, watching my expression as if to make sure I understood what he was saying. I understood, unfortunately, all too well. He was saying we should wait. Push the ardent feelings aside and pretend we were simply accomplices until we defeated the Devourer. I didn't know if I could do that.

I cocked my head in an impish manner, which was very unlike me. "If I agree, would you grant me one little boon?"

"What do you want?" he asked uncertainly.

"I want to experience just one tiny pleasure, even if it only happens in this dreamworld."

"And what is that?" he asked.

"The feel of your hands in my hair and your lips on the corner of my mouth again. Right here." I pointed to the place he'd kissed me so tenderly before.

"Ah." He smiled and I knew I'd won.

"Would you mind doing it again? Just once?" If he rejected the notion, I wasn't sure what I would do. It felt like my entire being was centered on obtaining this one touch, being held by this one man. At that moment nothing in the world was more important to me.

"Hmm." He must've sensed my desperation because after warring briefly with himself, he gave in and said, "Perhaps I can do one better."

Breathless anticipation swept over me as his lips came closer. He smiled and stopped, teasing me with the distance but then just as I was ready to cry out in frustration, he cupped my neck, running his thumbs slowly and tenderly over my jaw before he slid his hands into my hair.

Why had I ever thought hair had no purpose? Obviously the purpose of leaving hair loose and long was for this—to have a man run his hands through it and cradle your head as he kissed you. Asten did just that. Tilting my head, he finally, finally touched his lips fully to my own in a perfectly slow, perfectly deliberate way.

His hands were in my hair and then cupping my face, stroking my neck while his lips moved over mine, melting me into a hot pool of sensation. The kiss was heady, exhilarating, and so, so much better than anything I'd anticipated.

I gradually drifted awake and checked Asten. He slept peacefully, a half smile on his face. I no longer felt restless. There was something soothing about being close to him, our limbs intertwined. The lids of my eyes lowered sleepily, but I remained in a half-dozed, half-wakeful state, which is why I was able to react so quickly when incipient, dark plumes of smoke rose from the west.

Quickly, I disentangled myself from Asten and shook him. He groaned, reaching for me and trying to pull me back. "No!" I hissed, patting the nearby ground for my leather harness. "Wake up, Asten! Ahmose?" I called out.

"What is it?" Ahmose was at my side almost instantly.

"There's smoke," I said.

He peered into the murky twilight. "Could it be another campfire?" he asked.

I shook my head. "Too big. Do you want to stay with Asten or come with me to check it out?"

At hearing his name, Asten finally roused himself enough to open his eyes. "What's going on?" he asked.

"Smoke on the horizon," I answered matter-of-factly. "We're debating on who's going to stay and watch over you."

Asten gave me a long look, one that I couldn't decipher. "I'm well enough I think to go with you," he finally answered.

"Are you sure?" I asked. "You slept like the dead."

Again Asten paused, a slight frown wrinkling his brow. He had an air of expectation, as if he was waiting for me to say something else, but then, dutifully, he began unwrapping his bandage. His thigh was perfectly healed.

"Can you stand?" Ahmose asked.

With the help of his brother, Asten took a few cautious steps and then bent to stretch out, testing his muscles. "I don't understand how this happened," he said, remarking on his returned strength.

"There's no time. We'll explain on the way. Hurry!" I added when I felt like they were moving too slow. "The smoke is coming from the area where I found the mother tree, and I've made a vow to protect her."

Asten helped me shrug into my leather harness, his fingers sweeping along the hemline of my shirt at the back of my neck. I started and stared at him in puzzlement as he murmured, "We wouldn't want you to be an oath breaker, then, would we, Little Lioness?"

"Uh, no," I answered blankly, feeling like I must've heard him wrong or missed something. "Let's go already!"

They followed, trusting me to find the right path, which I was able to do easily. Even with the smell of smoke filling my nostrils, I knew the direction I'd walked before and recognized the trees. The smoke overhead billowed, becoming blacker with each step.

The closer we got to the mother tree, the more certain I was that the fire would harm her soon if it hadn't already. Tension bubbled up inside me, filling my frame, and I pushed the two men harder, running and darting through the underbrush faster than they could, even as immortal guardians of the afterlife. My claws came out, and I tore at the vines and branches that got in my way.

We hit the fire line all too quickly. Ahmose stepped forward and used his power to find the safest path. Despite his ability, we were often burned and our progress slowed but we were able to move along despite the char in the air and the fog of black smoke. When it became too difficult to see, I learned of another gift Ahmose possessed.

Taking hold of my arm, he stopped me. "Stand still for a moment."

Raising his hands in the air, he chanted a spell, and a gentle wind lifted my hair and the hem of my shirt. A stiff gale moved all around us, and I had to squint and brace myself against a tree in the maelstrom. Within the span of a few moments the smoke had cleared away enough for us to continue, but the wind he'd created had stirred up the fire even more.

The mother tree was just ahead. The trees around her were black and burned like charred skeletons reaching toward heaven for divine assistance. Around the mother tree, white, sparkling smoke lifted into the air, and though her leaves shook and her branches trembled, she was still alive. Hope blossomed.

"Hurry!" I cried. "She's still there!" We closed the distance and ran to the tree, stamping out flames in the grass at her roots. I turned to Asten. "We have to stop the fire!" I shouted. "Can you make blankets so we can smother it?"

Asten shook his head. "A few blankets aren't going to matter! The fire has spread too far."

"I've got to do something! I promised her!" The roar of the fire overpowered my voice, but I cried out as loud as I could. "Fairy!" I shouted. "Fairy, are you here?"

There was no answer. I ran up to Asten, wrapping my hands in his shirt and shaking him slightly. "Asten, we've got to do something! Please!"

Gently, he placed his hands on my shoulders and squeezed. "Ahmose?" he said. "If I lend you my strength, do you think you can manage?"

"I can try," he answered.

Asten quickly explained, "Ahmose is the Bringer of Storms. It's how he was able to clear away the smoke a while ago, but to call forth rain in the netherworld is very tricky. There isn't much water here. Attempting it will leave us both weak."

Asten gripped his brother's hand as their arms rose in the air. They chanted a spell and the wind expanded, whipping the flames around us to increasing heights. Clouds formed overhead, bumping and piling against each other until the sky became gray and even darker than it normally was.

Fat drops fell, one at a time at first, and then faster and faster until a torrent soaked us. It lasted only a short time, not long enough to put out the fires, but it diminished them at least. When the last drop fell, both brothers slumped to the ground, utterly spent and panting. "That's . . ." Asten swallowed and sucked in another breath. "That's all we could manage," he said.

I nodded and took up the search again. I'd just rounded the tree when I sensed something. Quickly, I leapt to the side just as a sharp, pointed weapon slammed into the trunk not inches from where my head had been. I gasped when I saw the black weapon violently wrenched from the trunk, taking whole chunks of wood with it. Turning around to face my enemy, I drew my spear knives and came face to face with a giant scorpion.

Its razor-sharp claws snapped quickly, threatening to behead me while the thick tail towered overhead waiting to strike. When I struck them with my spear-knife, sparks flew, but I didn't even make a dent in the armor-like carapace. I shifted around the tree, the scorpion tracking my every move, following me.

The tail struck again, and before it could withdraw, I seized my opportunity. I catapulted into the air, leaping on its back and plunging my spear-knife between the plates around its neck, pressing the button as I did so. When the knife lengthened into a spear, the demon scorpion trembled, letting out a terrible screech before slumping to the ground, dead.

I heard a shout. Asten pointed overhead. Two more scorpions that had been camouflaged by the massive blackened trees surrounding the mother tree descended, pinchers cutting the air with sharp shearing sounds.

As I faced off with one, the other circled behind and engaged both of the brothers. Asten managed to cut off one of the monster's legs, while Ahmose used his ax to slice off the stinger. Then the black exoskeleton lit up from the inside, turning the creature as red as a boiled lobster. Waves of heat emanated from the monster and then the red color deepened by degrees through the segments of the damaged tail.

When it reached the zenith, fire shot out of the appendage. Like liquid lava, a viscous red gel plastered the ground where Asten had just been. It smoked and fumed, and anything living in the area caught fire.

Some of the liquid hit the already weakened mother tree. She fought against the onslaught valiantly, even managing to absorb some of the fiery liquid, but flames now licked the side of her trunk.

By the time I slew the second scorpion and helped Ahmose and Asten finish off the third, I knew it was too late. Flames engulfed most of the top, the ashes from her burned leaves raining down on my head. Tears of exhaustion and sorrow dripped down my cheeks, and despite the burning debris, I wrapped my arms around her trunk and cried, "I'm so sorry. I wasn't here to protect you. I know I promised."

A tiny half-charred limb stretched down toward me and tugged on my shirt. I wiped my eyes, black streaks of soot coloring my fingers. "What is it?" I asked the tree. "Is there something I can do?"

The trunk parted and the thin branch disappeared inside, then pulled out the tiny broken form of the fairy. Half of her small body was burned. What was left of her glorious red hair hung around her face in clumps, and she wheezed as if she could barely breathe.

I took the fairy, cupping her in my hands as the limb unwrapped itself from her waist. "What can I do?" I beseeched the tree. "How can I save her?"

The tree shuddered, and a large towering limb snapped completely off, splitting away from the trunk. I sensed it wouldn't be long until she died as well. Leaves trembling on the barely mobile limb, the tree stretched toward it me and touched its tip to my temple.

A matronly voice said, "Take care of her. Please protect my precious Ashleigh."

"I will," I promised. No matter how long the little fairy lived, I would try to offer as much comfort as I was able.

With that, the mother tree quaked, and with a mighty crack, the trunk split into two, sparkling white smoke dissipating into the air before disappearing. The once magical fairy tree, the great mother tree and guardian of the Turquoise Forest in the netherworld died a second and very final death.

My shoulders trembled as I cried. Asten put his arm around me, trying to offer his support, but I was comfortless. Carefully cupping the horribly injured fairy, I managed to scrub my face against my shoulders, dashing away the tears that blurred my vision.

I looked down at my hands and gasped in alarm.

The little fairy was gone.

25

Shadow of a Man

The disappearance of the fairy was soon to be the least of my concerns. My vision was spinning, the sounds of waves filling my mind. The weight of our situation was finally settling in, and all I could do was release a bloodcurdling scream.

Arms caught me and I heard a voice like rushing wind calling my name. "Lily? Lily!" it cried, but there was no way for me to answer. My mind disconnected with my body, and I felt like I was falling down, down, down. And then nothing.

I faintly became aware of the voices. A crackling fire burned nearby, and shadows encompassed it. All at once, panic filled me. I tried to scramble away from the flames, only stopping when I hit something . . . no, someone, and that someone wrapped their arms around me and steadied me.

"Calm down, little lioness," the man holding me said.

"Where? Where are we? What happened?" I asked.

"You fainted at the base of the tree. We don't know why."

Ahmose knelt in front of me. Awkwardly, I sat up and wrapped my arms around my knees. I shivered despite the heat of the fire and rocked back and forth, tears filling my eyes. A small, almost indecipherable keening hummed in the back of my throat.

"I'm sorry we lost the mother tree," Ahmose said quietly. "There was nothing we could do. We were too late. The Turquoise Forest is gone."

The keening grew louder. "And the . . . the fairy?" I asked. I felt like I was leaking from every possible part of my face.

Shaking his head sadly, Ahmose said, "We weren't able to locate her body. We carried you here and, seeing it was a safe place, thought you might need the rest."

"How long?" I asked numbly.

Ahmose frowned. "How long what?"

"How long was I unconscious?"

"Nearly twelve hours," Asten answered soberly. "You didn't dream either." He added quickly, "I was . . . was monitoring you, but you never appeared in your dreamscape. That means you were knocked completely out."

I blinked and cocked my head quizzically. "But weren't you too weak to carry me?"

"We levitated and took turns," he explained. Asten reached out a hand like he wanted to touch my shoulder but then stopped before he made contact.

Turning away, too wrapped up in my own despair, I took in our surroundings. The landscape looked hilly and rocky again, like the Painted Desert. The only trees visible were stubby and filled with blinking eyes that watched our every move. "We're in the Devourer's territory," I said.

"Are we?" Ahmose asked as he looked around. "We got lucky, then. Without you sensing Amon's heart, there was no way to tell if we were going in the right direction. I just sought the easiest path away from the fire."

I looked up at the grayish, muted version of the sky and wished there were stars. It felt wrong that they weren't there, but I shook off that notion quickly. We wouldn't see the stars again until we saved Amon. I shifted, uncomfortable on the sand, and Ahmose handed me a skewer of cooked meat from his hunt. As I nibbled on it, I said, "Surprised you found something edible out here."

"Hunting would've been better in the forest," Ahmose said. "There's only a bit left of the supplies the tree gave us, and we ate the meat before it went bad. We saved what we could for you, but we needed the energy to carry you. Sorry there isn't more."

I nodded, and suddenly overwhelming grief flooded through me again. Errant tears trickled anew down my face. "Trees are scarce as hens' teeth in the netherworld," I said with a sniffle. "The heat out here is fierce enough to cook a grazin' sheep in its own hide. She protected the forest from the worst of it. It's all your fault that she was too weak to defend herself," I accused. "You shoulda let him die," I finished, jerking a thumb at Asten.

Ahmose narrowed his gaze, but Asten gasped in shock. I glared at him, my body shaking with defiance as I waited for him to tell me I was wrong so I could lash out at him. "She was more important than anything," I spat.

Asten stared at me, a cold void filling the space between us. A part of me knew I'd said something extremely offensive, hurt him much more than he deserved, but my mouth seemed disconnected from my brain and my heart broke because of it. I would have expected Asten to try to bridge the distance and offer solace, but it was Ahmose who reached out.

He put a hand on my shoulder and said, "Come now, you don't mean that. You're not in your right mind. You've suffered a great loss, and we weren't much help. I'm sorry about your . . . your friend. She was noble and worthy and didn't deserve such an ignominious death. Her sacrifice should be honored."

Sniffling, I nodded in agreement. Ahmose created a piece of cloth for me to wipe my nose. My head felt weighty and my heart fragmented. "No matter how long the day, the evening comes," I murmured.

"What does that mean?" Ahmose asked.

"My mother used to say it when bad things happened. It means that sorrows will end. We might not know when, but a new day will dawn sometime."

He smiled. "I like that," he said.

"The fairy tree died well. I guess I couldn't expect any different from her. She did it once before, so I should'na be surprised that she'd do it again."

"Did the fairy tell you that?" Ahmose asked.

I shook my head slightly as if to clear away the fog. "The fairy? Oh. Yes. Her name was Ashleigh," I added morosely.

"Ashleigh. That's a pretty name," he said.

"It was." I nodded. "I'm not sure what to call myself now."

"Call yourself? What do you mean?" Ahmose asked.

"What?" I blinked in confusion and a fog seemed to lift within me.

"You said you didn't know what to call yourself."

"Did I? That's strange." I tossed the skewer into the fire and pressed my palms against my head, trying to alleviate the headache I felt coming on. Ahmose offered me a sip from the water bag he carried. "Thank you," I said as I nearly downed the entire bag, then froze. "Tell me there's more."

"We have only what Ahmose was able to collect before the fire. Two bags burst in the flames," Asten said. He pointed to the ground, indicating we had three left. "Ahmose can summon some, but it won't last for long."

"Then we don't have much time. The forest and the pools are the only pure sources of drinking water in the netherworld," I said.

"How do you know that?" Asten asked.

"I'm not sure. I just do. Have the two of you slept?"

"We don't need much," Ahmose said. "If you're ready, we can move on."

"Good." I nodded, moving to stand on shaky legs, determination pushing my grief to the back of my mind. "It's time to find Amon."

We'd only traveled for a few hours when we discovered we were being followed. Reaching the summit of a jagged peak, we paused to take in the view of the wide valley below, and I spotted a dark herd of something on the horizon. "What's that?" I asked. "Some kind of netherworld buffalo?"

Even though I'd asked the question, a part of me suspected—no, knew—it was wishful thinking. Still, I hoped I was wrong.

"No, they aren't buffalo," Asten said, finally ending the stony silence he'd maintained since we broke camp. He peered down, watching the moving animals for a time. "Is it what I think it is?" Asten asked his brother.

"I'm afraid so," Ahmose replied.

"What do *you* think is it, then?" I asked, not really wanting them to confirm what my mind screamed was true.

"It's the pack."

No! We mustn't let them overtake us! I felt Tia's panic and tried to soothe her, but she wouldn't listen.

"Are you sure?" I asked quietly.

He nodded. "They must've gotten themselves freed somehow."

"And now they're coming for us." The three of us watched the pack of hellhound jackals, which I estimated were still a few miles off but they were closing in fast. If we'd been downwind, I would have already been able to smell them.

"The mountain will slow them down," Asten said.

Ahmose rubbed his jaw. "Yes. But they'll overtake us eventually."

"Can we fight them?" I asked.

Asten shook his head. "No. There are too many. We could fight off a pack half that size, but all the hellhounds in the netherworld? It's not possible." He glanced up at his brother. "I say we make a run for it. Worst-case scenario, we take to the sky."

Ahmose considered this and then nodded. "Agreed. It's time to go, Lily. Let's test your speed. See if you can outdistance us."

I was eager, afraid, and hesitant all at the same time, but thinking of Amon drove me forward. Realizing that he and his suffering had not always been at the forefront of my mind racked me with guilt. When the descent from the mountain became treacherous, Asten picked me up, and the three of us floated down. I wrapped my arms tightly around his neck.

Flying felt more natural now than it had the other times. It was almost . . . instinctive. I wasn't affected by dizziness or vertigo. I didn't realize until we touched down that I'd been absentmindedly playing with Asten's hair. All my concerns of before had lessened significantly just by being near him. He hadn't said anything about my mood shift, and I flushed with embarrassment at my actions. What was going on with me?

I'd say acting like a bit of a hoyden, a voice whispered in my mind.

That sounds about right, I thought. *To be fair, though, I wasn't doing it on purpose.*

A part of you was, the voice argued. *A part of you wanted to.*

Tia? I asked.

What? I heard her sullen, dull voice respond.

Tia, you know how I feel, I said.

It's the same as before, she finally said after a tense silence. *If you weren't open to the idea, these feelings wouldn't be there.*

I sighed. How was I ever going to straighten this mess out? *Still,* I rationalized as I ran, *the most important thing isn't my love life; it is saving Amon.* Everything else I could figure out later.

Are ya sure ya want to fight? my inner voice countered. *A good run is better than a bad stand, ya know.*

What was I saying?

Did a part of me fear standing up to the Devourer? We could win. I believed it. The gods must believe it, too; otherwise why would they have sent us here? When I first began to run, I staggered. My skin burned and sweat poured down my face. Something was wrong. I felt like I was in a three-legged race and my stride was strained and disjointed. The power and grace of the sphinx eluded me. Bending over, I panted and begged Tia for her help. *We've got to regulate our temperature or we'll burn up before we get there,* I said.

I tried again, and it took a few minutes, but then something clicked into place once, twice, and I found my rhythm. My body cooled, and I ran faster than I ever had before. The speed I was capable of astounded both brothers, and I could have easily outdistanced them if it hadn't been necessary to stick to Ahmose's path.

We'd run for a couple of hours when Ahmose called for a halt. They were drained, and I knew it was because they were feeling the effects of Amon's torture again. The three of us rested as we felt the energy leak out of us. When we came to our senses, I was famished and quickly scarfed down the meager remnants of the food the tree had given us after the brothers insisted that my living body needed the fuel more. Seeing Asten and Ahmose only drinking water didn't sit right with me.

I offered to hunt for them, but they determined that hunting would take too much time, and I knew they were right. When I lifted my nose to scent the air, the wind now carried the stench of jackals. I shivered, and the part of me that wanted to kill every last one of them and rip them apart with my claws rose to the surface. I sneered. "Mangy beasts," I hissed. "They don't deserve a calm, simple second death. They should be killed over and over until there's nothing left of them but a smear in the dust where they died." Pausing, I tilted my head to the left and murmured, "Many a time a man's mouth broke his nose."

"What's that?" Ahmose asked.

"Uh, nothing," I replied. "I'm finished. Let's get going."

We ran and ran until I was certain that even the power of the sphinx couldn't carry me forward another step. "We've got to rest," I cried. "I'm shattered."

"Shattered, are you?" Ahmose chuckled, then bent over, his hands on his knees as he tried to catch his breath. "I've never heard that term before," he added.

I smiled. "Ya have a nice laugh. Me mother says, 'A good laugh and a long sleep are the two best cures.'"

"And what do they cure?" he asked.

"Ach, everything. All the pains of the world disappear if you can find something to laugh about and, if not, things often look different in the mornin'."

Ahmose was about to say something when a hand grabbed my arm. "What are you saying, Lily?" Asten demanded.

"What?" I replied, irritated that he would manhandle me so. "I'll thank ya ta let me go now."

He sucked in a breath and glanced briefly at Ahmose. "I think we need to talk. Alone," he added with emphasis.

Now I was thoroughly upset. "No. Anythin' ya need ta say, ya can say in front o' him. I've got nothin' to hide."

"Nothing to hide?" Asten barked, running a hand through his hair. The cleft in his chin deepened and his eyes flashed dangerously. "You're—" He gritted his teeth. "You're not yourself, *Lily*."

"Do ya mean ta traduce me, then? And in front of this lovely gentleman, too?" I said, jerking a thumb over my shoulder to indicate Ahmose. *"Lily,"* I spat, scoffing at his use of the name. "Who are you to judge what I am?" I asked, jabbing a finger into Asten's chest. "*Lily* is a fragment of what we are. I am much more than *Lily*. When ya call me that, it diminishes the other parts o' me. I do not appreciate it. Perhaps, mah friend"—I twitched my fingers, running them up his chest, over the cleft of his chin, and then tapped his nose—"ya should consider that it's often better ta be found with good manners than good looks."

Asten raised my wrist as if I were a fish at the market he was showing off and looked at Ahmose. "Do you see?" he asked as I struggled against him to free myself. "She's different. Even more so than when she appeared as the sphinx."

"Let. Me. Go!" I insisted, and Asten finally released me. I rubbed my wrist and glared at him all the while a part of me yearned to feel his arms around me.

Ahmose cautiously approached me, exuding tenderness and compassion from his gray gleaming eyes.

I sniffled and scrubbed my palms against my eyes. They itched. My brain did, too. I pressed my hand against the stela but didn't feel any surge of energy.

Gently, Ahmose took hold of my shoulders.

"You don't wish to be called Lily any longer?" he asked.

I shook my head no but felt confused as to why I did so.

"Then what should we call you? Sphinx?" he asked.

"Yes. I mean, no." I let out a breath and pressed my palms against my temples, squeezing to stop the pain. "I guess it's the best thing to do for now."

I could feel Ahmose's eyes on me. "Does your head hurt?"

Wincing, I nodded.

"Will the stela heal you?"

"We've been tryin'," I said. "It doesn't seem ta work."

"We can try to help you, if you'll let us. I'm a healer. Remember?"

"Yes," I murmured quietly. "I remember."

"Then close your eyes and try to relax. Breathe deeply."

Obediently, I did what he asked and took in a cleansing breath. Ahmose gently took my hands from my head and began massaging my temples. "Ach, that's lovely," I said, feeling the tension in my body ease for the first time in what felt like forever.

A lilting hum intertwined with a purr filled my mind.

Asten came close and spoke softly in my ear. "Do you recognize me?"

"Yes," I answered, feeling as if someone else was communicating for me. "You are Asten." My cheeks tensed briefly as I felt myself smile. "A handsome and brave warrior. One who sends my heart to the stars."

There was a pause. "Ah, yes. When I speak, you will answer me truthfully. To do otherwise would bring you great sorrow. Do you understand?"

"Are you sure this is necessary?" I heard Ahmose ask. His voice sounded distorted like I was eavesdropping from underwater.

I never heard Asten's reply.

"Tell me," Asten demanded. "Who are you?"

I worked my jaw back and forth, my mouth forming words that seemed to be lifted directly from my mind. In a trancelike voice, almost unrecognizable to me, I said, "I am Lily." A rumble echoed deep from my chest and I turned my head to the right with my eyes still closed and heard a silky, yet powerful voice announce, "I am Tia." I sensed Asten preparing to ask another question but I wasn't finished. I cocked my head to the left side and a third voice, one with a halting Irish lilt, said, "And I . . . am Ashleigh." After the third voice spoke, something ruptured inside my brain, and if Asten hadn't caught me, I would have hit the ground, hard.

When I woke, it was to the sight of Asten and Ahmose staring at me with concern but there was something else in their eyes, too. Something I didn't think I'd ever seen before, not even when they'd faced a giant zombie army. It was pure fear. "What is it?" I gasped. "Have the jackals found us?"

"No. We are safe enough for now," Ahmose answered softly.

I glanced around and saw we were atop a steep and narrow butte. The area we sat on was flat and just big enough for the three of us if only one of us slept at a time. Just behind me the vertical drop-off plummeted straight to the ground below and it appeared that this was true all the way around the formation. In fact, the only possible way we could have gotten to the top would have been to fly there. Dark forms circled our tiny perch far below.

"They've overtaken us," I said.

"Yes," Asten answered, "but that is the least of our concerns at the moment."

"The *least* of your concerns? I'd say it's a pretty big concern, especially since the Devourer likely knows where we are. What else could possibly be concerning you at present?"

Asten frowned and opened his mouth but seemed hesitant to speak. Instead, he looked to Ahmose, who furrowed his brow before finally saying what was on his mind. "How are you feeling, Lily?" he asked watchfully.

I folded my arms across my chest. "Fine. Considering everything. Why?"

"Where are you from?"

"New York."

"What's Dr. Hassan's first name?"

"Oscar."

"Why are we here?"

"To save Amon." I threw my arms up. "What's with the twenty questions?"

"We just wanted to make sure you're you," Asten said.

"Who else would I be?" I asked testily.

Ahmose sighed. "We did a spell on you and"—he seemed uncomfortable—"we discovered that you're not alone in your mind."

"What are you two talking about? You know I have Tia, too. Though she has been extremely quiet as of late. It's like pulling teeth to get her to talk."

"That's just it, Lily. She has been quiet but now another voice is taking over."

"Another?"

Ahmose nodded. "You're still there, which is a relief, but there's Tia and now . . . Ashleigh."

"Hold on. Are you saying the fairy is in my mind, too?"

"The spell confirmed it," Asten said. "We aren't sure how it happened. Perhaps it had something to do with the tree?"

"Or fairy magic?" Ahmose suggested.

A humming sound started to fill my brain again. "No. No. This isn't possible. How is this possible?" I started rocking back and forth, my arms clasped around my knees. "I'm going crazy, aren't I? This happened to the other sphinx. She went crazy. Asked to be killed. What am I going to do?" Reaching out, I grabbed Asten's arm and took hold of Ahmose's hand with my other one, shaking them both. "You've got to help me. Isn't there something you can do?"

Ahmose shook his head sadly. "We've never encountered anything like this before. What's . . . disturbing is that there are times when you don't seem to be aware that you're not in control."

"What?" I gasped. "Are you sure?"

"There's only one way to find out," Asten said. "Do you remember . . . dreaming with me?"

"Dreaming? What specifically are you talking about?"

"There was a shooting star, a grassy hillside?"

"No." I shook my head. "The last dream I remember was seeing Amon being tortured."

Asten nodded curtly. "That proves it, then. It wasn't you."

"Wasn't me? You saw me, but I wasn't me?"

"It was you, in body, but not in mind. Did Hassan say anything about the merging of your consciousness or about one of you disappearing?"

I thought for a moment. "Hassan said that because I didn't kill Tia, our minds would fight for control over my body. And Horus said something about the power of the sphinx working when the two of us agreed on what we were doing and that the only time we could be fully ourselves was when the other—or, I guess, others now—acquiesces or sleeps."

"So it was Tia who dreamed with me," Asten mused thoughtfully.

I pressed my hands against my face. "This is really confusing." Taking a deep breath, I looked up at the netherworld sky and wondered what was going to become of me. Then I realized it didn't matter. What did matter was finishing what I set out to do. Crazy or not, possessed by a lioness and a fairy or not, I was going to save Amon.

Standing up, I dusted my hands on my leggings and assumed control, silencing every other voice in my mind. "Let's put these multiple personalities-slash-psychosomatic issues of mine in the parking lot and decide what to do about that at another time. For the moment, we've got bigger fish to fry. Let's hope we'll find a solution later on down the road. If either of the other girls comes out to play, I trust the two of you will keep them aimed in the right direction."

Asten and Ahmose looked at each other and then nodded.

"Good. Shall we go, then?"

Asten handed me my weapons and I noticed that his fingers lingered over my hand for just a moment longer than necessary, but I ignored the gesture. When he offered to carry me, I purposely went to Ahmose instead, attempting to pay no attention to Asten's clenched jaw and how it made the cleft in his chin deepen. I itched to question Tia about what she'd been doing while in control of my body, but I tamped down those thoughts, which smacked of betrayal. The truth was, I needed her and I knew it.

Ahmose seemed willing and happy to help and didn't appear to notice how quiet his brother was. Pressing my hand against Amon's heart scarab, I felt the thump of it against my palm and turned in a slow circle until I knew the direction we should take. The feel of it steadied me. "That way." I pointed, and as we rose into the air, I heard the cries of jackals far below. Though I knew they followed us, we soon outdistanced the pack.

A few hours later, I spied something that looked very familiar. It was the iron wall my dream self had climbed when I first saw the Devourer. I wasn't sure if she was there, but I knew Amon was. His heart called to me. It was so much weaker now than it had been before, but at least I knew he was alive.

We touched down on a lip where we could crouch and peer into the stone theater beneath us. There was no sign of the woman I'd seen before, but I knew that didn't mean much. I scanned the area, and though the pole Amon had been chained to previously was still there, he wasn't. The iron chains that had held him hung limply, clinking softly against each other as they stirred in the breeze.

"Where is he?" I whispered.

"Does your heart tell you he's here?" Asten asked.

"Yes."

"Perhaps it is a trick," Ahmose suggested.

"I suppose it's possible," I agreed. "Let's try to get down there."

I was about to reach for my weapons when I paused. "She'll suck us dry sure as I'm talkin' to ya right now. Fightin' this many is like tryin' ta empty a pond with a pail. I think it's best we leave. If we're real quiet-like, she may not even notice us at all."

"What did you say?" Asten asked, a look of surprise crossing his face.

I glared at him, not liking his wary expression at all.

"Ashleigh?" Ahmose patiently turned toward me.

"Yes?" I smiled at him, enjoying the look of those gray eyes twinkling in my direction.

"We really need Lily to be here right now."

My smile disappeared. "Don't I have a right ta go where I please?"

"You do." He cupped my hands in his warm ones and something in me quivered. "But right now we need to fight a battle. You might be safer staying back as far as you can. But lend her your strength if possible."

I peered at him, looking for insincerity, but found none. "All right, then. I'll hide. You just keep us alive. Do ya understand?"

"I do. And I will."

"I'll hold ya ta that."

Blinking, I found I was staring too deeply into Ahmose's eyes. His brows were lifted. I gave a curt nod, my cheeks burning over the things I'd been thinking—that *she'd* been thinking, I corrected myself, and sighed. This was all so confusing. A part of me knew the thoughts weren't mine, and yet they felt as real to me in the moment as the touch of his hand had. Squaring my shoulders, I signaled the brothers.

We'd just stood when there was movement below. Quickly we ducked down as the grating of stone echoed up to our ears. Sand shifted on the arena floor and disappeared down a crack that grew wider. From beneath the sandstone surface a dais rose, and on top was a large black cauldron. A door opened in the forum and creatures of all descriptions entered, filling the space around the giant kettle.

When all were in place, a drum sounded, and as one, the creatures looked to the sky. Thousands of winged beings filled the air, screeching as they called out below. I ducked, knowing they were minions of the Devourer and hoping in vain that they wouldn't notice us.

While they flew overhead, the Minotaur henchman entered.

"Ach! Look at 'im!" I remarked too loudly. "Ya wouldn' wanna ride that into battle, now, wouldja? I mean, he's got the kind o' face that looks like a bulldog chewing a wasp!"

Ahmose elbowed me. "Ashleigh, you must try to keep your voice down."

"It's okay," I said, shaking my head. "I'm still here. She's just got very loud thoughts, is all. It's hard to block out."

The Minotaur was followed by a shrouded figure in the form of a man. I felt my heart lurch, thinking it might be Amon, but then I saw that the person wasn't chained. He walked of his own free will. The man I knew would have fought to his dying breath. No. Amon was here somewhere, but it wasn't the man in the hood.

The winged batlike creatures fluttered madly, dipping lower and lower until a form materialized in their midst. Quickly, the leathery wings stilled, becoming a cloak. The Minotaur smiled—a chilling, slightly nauseating sight. "All hail the Devourer!" he cried out. The sentiment was echoed among the rowdy crowd of monsters so terrifying I knew I'd have nightmares about them for years, assuming, of course, I survived long enough to dream again.

The personification of all I loathed took a step forward. She raised her arms to the crowd, her back to us, and laughed.

"Thank you all for attending this most auspicious occasion!" the Devourer said in her lovely, monstrous voice. She turned in a circle, swinging her curvy hips as she did so, and I saw that this time she was dressed in a gown of sparkling silver, a very *clingy* one. The living cloak trailing behind her was spiked from the horns of the winged minions that clung to one another, and the skulls of some little beasts adorned each shoulder.

Her long, dark hair hung down her back in lustrous undulating waves, and even from a distance, I noticed that the small silver beads adorning the locks of her hair were also living, clutching sections with their claws and affixing a gleaming, jeweled crown upon her head. The gems were as red as blood. *How appropriate,* I thought.

She looked even lovelier than she had the last time I'd seen her. The greenish-gray veins that surfaced during our last encounter had disappeared. Now she was all creams and pinks except for the same bloodred lips. It was as if she'd blossomed while feasting on Amon's power. Technically, she'd been siphoning off energies from all of us. The idea that the bloom in her cheek might have come from me sickened me. I shivered, knowing it was highly likely that was what had happened. She thrived on our shared power.

"She's not at all what I expected," Ahmose whispered.

"In all the stories I've heard about her, she was always referred to as the ugliest of immortals," Asten added.

"You might think she's beautiful now," I said. "But wait until she opens her mouth like she's about to stuff an entire Thanksgiving turkey down her throat. Turns your stomach." Ahmose and Asten stared down at the woman like they were in love or, at the very least, entranced. I elbowed them. "Do I have to leave the two of you here? Are you going to be able to fight a pretty girl?"

Ahmose had the decency to look chagrined. "Sorry, Lily. We will fight when the time comes."

"I expect so. It's going to be hard enough to defeat her even with the both of you backing me up. If it gets too difficult, then focus on the Minotaur and the rest of the demons and I'll take her out. Got it?"

"Yes, little lioness," Asten said with his cheeky smile.

I gave him a suspicious look. "Okay, then."

The Devourer motioned to her manservant and the Minotaur stepped up onto the dais, followed by the man in the hood. With a wave of her hands, the cape she wore lifted, baring her creamy shoulders, and the screeching, leather-winged beings disappeared in a puff of smoke. The black mist created by their bodies zoomed downward, entering the cauldron and filling it with roiling dark liquid that sizzled and popped. A sickly sweet stench filled the air.

"There," the Devourer said. "Now it's time to add the final ingredient." She crooked her finger and the cloaked man stepped forward. With a snap, the hood fell back, and standing there on the dais was Amon.

I let out a sharp gasp.

Amon stood bare-chested with a slack expression as the Devourer ran her hands over his shoulders. More disturbing than his lack of emotion was the state of his body. He was pale. So pale I swore I could almost see through him. He looked a lot like the ghosts trapped in the Mires of Despair, and I felt my heart break, thinking it might be too late for us to save him.

"Amon!" I whispered desperately, and felt Asten's arm wrap around my back. His touched calmed and steadied me.

The Devourer's voice carried through the arena. Though she spoke quietly, each word pierced me as if she were screaming. "Before we roast your bones so that I might suck every last living bit of your remaining energy"—she paused and tilted her head, pursing her lips in a girlish pout—"how about a final kiss?"

Amon didn't answer. Or blink. He simply obeyed. He stepped closer and the Devourer wrapped her arms around him, pressing her curvaceous form against his once muscled but now emaciated body. She pulled his head down, capturing his lips to hers, and I cried out, my energy bleeding right out of me.

When she pulled back from the kiss, sparkling white tendrils of fog framed by a green light trailed from Amon's mouth to hers. Delicately, she brushed his lips with her fingers, capturing the thick stuff, and swallowed Amon's life energy like she was eating a bowl of buttery noodles. She shuddered. "Absolutely delectable. I'm so going to miss you."

She gave a nod and the Minotaur commanded Amon to climb into the boiling cauldron.

He'd only taken one step when I clambered to my feet. Asten and Ahmose weren't recovering as quickly, and I whispered a quick thanks to the other two occupants of my mind. It was likely their presence had helped me regroup. In an instant, I locked minds with them. We all agreed that it was time to rise to our potential.

Something primal and fixed centered my core. Confusion, indecision, and hesitancy no longer existed in my mind. I was sphinx—decisive, deadly, and determined. I drew my bow and shot an arrow of Isis into the sky. *Ten left*. As Amon took another step, I leapt atop the iron wall, running toward him, and jumped. Tumbling through the air, I drew my spear-knives from my shoulder harness. I landed, touching down as gently as if I'd been defying gravity, between Amon and the bubbling cauldron.

Pressing my shoulder against Amon, I stopped him from progressing. "Don't," I begged. "Please stop." But he kept pushing against me, trying to get to the cauldron.

The Devourer laughed in delight. "Amon, dear. Come back over here by me. We have a guest."

Immediately, Amon turned and took up position right next to the Devourer. "We were so hoping you'd make an appearance," she said, as if she and Amon were hosting a social gathering.

"Yeah?" I replied acerbically. "I guess your invitation got lost in the netherworld mail. Sorry to crash the party."

26

The Crown of the Mistress of Dread

The Devourer's frown did nothing to diminish her beauty. "Perhaps destroying the Turquoise Forest was too subtle. Ah, well. Lesson learned. Next time I'll be more direct."

My fists clenched, and before I could stop myself, I shouted, "You pompous, evil, she-beast! You killed her! The forest was the only good thing left in this blinkin' hellhole you call a home."

A part of me recognized that I wasn't the one speaking, and yet every utterance and twist of my tongue felt natural. The things I said, I owned. The passengers riding in my mind were just invisible layers of my psyche. They had integrated themselves into my being to the point that their thoughts were mine and mine were theirs. Our connection made me feel more well-rounded. More . . . whole.

So it was I, just as much as it was anyone else, who raised the spear-knife toward the Devourer menacingly, puncturing the air with it as my words continued to pour forth. "'Ur maggot-filled breath been ablowin' down our necks long enough. It's time you pay for what you done! When we're finished with ya, the wolves'll tear ya asunder an' feast on 'ur bones till there's not enough left for even the tide ta take ya out!"

She pursed her lips. "My, my," she said. "Such a temper on you. Your manners are atrocious." A feral smile lit up her face. "But speaking of wolves." The Devourer dramatically waved her hand and smoke poured into the arena from every side. Dark clouds split into pulsating masses, gleaming yellow eyes shining from their depths before the pack took physical form.

The leader, snarling mouth glistening with saliva, took his place next to the Devourer. Licking his lips, gaze lethal, his voice filled my mind. *Let me have her, my queen. I long to taste her death.*

"Now, now. Patience, my pet. This one's powerful, and I won't have her drained." The jackal whined and she soothed him by ruffling his ears. With her eyes locked on mine, she slowly leaned down and whispered to him, "Yet."

At his low snarl, she laughed.

I glanced around the arena. There were too many. How could one girl—or rather, three girls in one body—take on so many, power of the sphinx or no? Even with Asten and Ahmose helping, we were heavily outnumbered. The best-case scenario would be for me to distract the Devourer while Asten and Ahmose flew down, nabbed Amon, and made an escape. Defeating her wasn't very likely. *Why haven't we gone over a plan?* I thought.

"I must confess," the Devourer said, interrupting my thoughts. "I didn't expect you to have so much fight left. Not after a sojourn of such length in the netherworld." She tilted her head. "I wonder how it was you lasted this long," she mused.

I didn't miss the gravitas she lent to her words, and it caused a prickly nervousness to shoot up my spine, one that left an uncomfortable tingle at the base of my neck. So far Asten and Ahmose had remained hidden, which was good. I didn't want her to know they were with me—at least, not yet. It wouldn't do to play my trump cards too early. In a game like this, anything could be wild.

"Don't get me wrong," she continued. "I'm quite happy about your . . . vitality. After all, the more strength you have, the longer I can feed off you." The Devourer inhaled deeply and smiled. The pupils of her reptilian eyes elongated, coloring the entire orb black as if she'd been overtaken by bloodlust. "Such a delectable aroma," she said. "Imagine! A living heart. It's been eons since I've had something so fresh. Knowing such a feast is imminent puts me in the best of moods." The jackals barked in happy agreement, as if their master was preparing to share the choicest tidbits from her plate.

I twirled my spear-knives and snickered. "Do you really want to be eating more right now? You're looking a bit pudgy, if you ask me. Might want to lower your caloric intake, if you know what I mean."

Her eyes narrowed and tiny plumes fanned out around them, sharpening into dangerous spikes. The hair that hung down her back rose around her body in a halo, like serpents I'd just foolishly startled awake. "I assure you, your silly games will accomplish nothing. You can't possibly think to win."

Tilting my head in consideration, I snapped my teeth and eyed the swaying barbs of hair, careful to stay far away from their striking range. "What a shame. Didn't anyone ever tell you how much cholesterol is contained in a heart? It can't be good for you." I leaned forward with raised eyebrows. "Just between us girls, you're not looking your best. Why, you're bloated as a mattress left out in the rain."

Wrinkling my nose, I added, "There's a particular odor about you, too. It's a bit like mildew. Maybe mold. Whatever it is makes the eyes water." I pointed my spear-knife, angling it from her head to her toes, part insult, part threat. "Probably comes from consuming more than your fair share of rotten hearts. But I imagine that comes with the territory. You know what they say—garbage in, garbage out. All things considered, I think my chances are good."

The Devourer's red-tinged mouth fell open and I grinned like the Cheshire Cat—that is, until she turned to Amon and ran her now-green-painted fingertip down his bare chest. "Amon?" she asked sweetly.

"Yes, my queen?" he answered in a monotone voice.

"Would you mind teaching this slip of a girl a lesson in respect?"

Amon blinked once, twice, and then sucked in a breath and headed toward me, arms raised, ready to destroy.

"Amon?" I called out. "Amon, stop!" He grabbed for me, arms flailing, but I easily spun out of his reach and darted away. He fell against the bubbling cauldron like a broken toy and I heard the hiss of burning flesh. He didn't cry out, despite the injury, and when he turned back to me, I saw a huge red welt along his side, pocked with angry blisters. "What have you done to him?" I cried. I stowed my spear-knives and raised my bare hands, afraid I'd injure him further.

"It's a simple thing, really," she said as she watched Amon cornering me, a jubilant expression on her face. "His mind is broken, which means he's easily controlled. You see, when I take his energy, I replace it with the bile of the damned—a scourge that poisons what little remains of him. It makes him easier to digest," she added as an afterthought, then frowned. "It's been terribly difficult to siphon off what's left of his energy. Boiling him is a last resort and carries with it the risk that what remains of him will be lost. Ah, well. Now that you're here it doesn't matter much anymore."

That she'd been unable to finish him off was likely due to Amon's having the Eye of Horus. Long ago Amon had told me that the symbol of the Eye was a sign of protection. Having possession of the real thing must have kept him alive. I glared at her with all the hatred I could muster. It should have been enough to light the woman on fire, but she wasn't even looking at me. The Devourer was biting her thumbnail and studying Amon as he lunged toward me again like a drunken man.

"Perhaps I'll keep him around a bit longer," she said. "His presence should motivate you to cooperate. And Amon is under my thrall, after all, mind lost in the Caverns of the Dead, until such time as I release him to a second death, anyway. Which is what I was about to do until you showed up. Lucky for you, I decided to wait. To think, you might've been too late to save the one you love. Even now I can hear how your heart beats for him. The sound of it . . . diverts me. Such deep emotions. They taste like the richest dessert."

Amon lunged and I leapt to the side, throwing a leg out to trip him. He tumbled to the ground, loose-limbed and sprawling. I was grateful that he wasn't at full strength. Otherwise he would have been a formidable opponent and I'd have no other recourse but to defend myself. Already I sensed the Devourer tiring of the display. The jackals stood nearby, watchful, stretching out their necks surreptitiously to snap when they thought the Devourer wasn't paying attention.

I roughly kicked one of them and the jackal tumbled into his brothers, knocking several others over. They rolled to their feet and snarled. I took the opportunity then to move back into the more open area in the center. Even though it was too close to the hot cauldron, I deemed it safer than being in the midst of the pack.

Amon summoned his weapons from the sand, but his weakness made them unstable. He struck me with a sword that gleamed one moment and then turned to sand when it hit me. Ducking his next swing, I grabbed him from behind, trapping his arms.

Part of me reveled at being able to physically touch him again, even in this dire circumstance. His hair brushed my face, and the weight of his body against mine felt like home. How I longed to be held by him. To feel his warm kisses on my eyelids and cheeks. He smelled of blood and sweat and pain but beneath it all I could still catch the faint scent of his that drove me crazy—liquid amber with a kiss of cashmere and a hint of myrrh that's been warmed in the sun.

The absolute certainty that I was in love with him rocked through me, and I smiled. We belonged together, though the cosmos seemed determined to keep us apart. As the sphinx, I could discern the truth of things, even about myself, and I knew in my heart that my love for Amon was true; no matter what else had happened, no matter what other feelings I entertained, I loved him.

While Amon struggled, I attempted to distract the Devourer, hoping her hold on Amon would lessen.

"Obsessed with love?" I called out. "I guess a heart-eater would be. I'm surprised you'd even recognize it. Speaking of which, it's a wonder you don't have a boyfriend, what with your poisoned kisses and all. Does the netherworld have a dating service for people like you? Maybe you should set up a website. You could call it mybreathreeks.com." The Minotaur eyed me with interest and I winked at him, going out on a limb to see if I could bring him over to my side using the power of the heart scarab.

The tinkling of laughter filled my mind. It buoyed me, and I glanced up at the wall, hoping to catch a glimpse of Asten or Ahmose. I didn't see them. I prayed that meant no one else had either. *What are they waiting for?*

Amon slammed his head back, hitting my nose. Stars danced before my eyes. Taking my arm, he yanked me forward, pushing me not into the jackal pack, but into the crowd of Devourer devotees. Claws raked down my back and arms, attempting to steal my weapons.

I was dimly aware of the little rivulets of blood that trickled down my arm, dripping off my elbow, but my nose was throbbing and I couldn't see straight. A frenzy of screeching and grabbing ensued, and Amon became the least of my problems. I was caught in a whirlwind of demonic limbs. Bodies tumbled on top of me as if I were the ball tossed into a scrum circle.

A roar blasted through the arena. It had come from me. A dam had broken inside me, pouring out all the pain and frustration and sadness that had built up since the start of my journey. Since I'd stowed my spear-knives in an effort to keep from wounding Amon, I attacked with claws. I fought like a cornered animal, slashing and ripping. Bile filled my mouth and I blinked, realizing I'd actually bitten someone, and that someone tasted vile.

"Do not destroy her!" I heard the Devourer cry out. "Bring her to me. Now!"

The creatures ceased thrashing, though one of them gave me a final punch in the jaw, knobby stubs on the ends of its knuckles scraping my skin as it did so. My arms were held by no less than six of her goons, who had no problem kicking me in the kidneys when I tried to thrash against them. They dragged me forward, presenting me to their queen. I used the stela to heal my little hurts while I stood there. Amon, who'd trailed along beside the demons holding me, lingered nearby, his eyes fixed on nothing.

"Foolish girl," the Devourer said as she moved closer. "As strong as you may be, you must know that my power here is irrefutable." She waved her arm at the crowd. "Look around you. You stand alone. One weak, pathetic child pitted against every evil creature in the netherworld."

She reached me and ran her ice-cold fingertip from my temple down to my jaw. Her breath smelled of death, decay, and despair. She was the absence of all things bright, good, and strong. I wanted to flinch, but something inside me demanded that I hold my ground, knowing that looking away would be a mistake.

The Devourer whispered, "You see, we are the things that go bump in the night." Her voice was as frigid as the blackest abyss in the deepest ocean. Goose bumps peppered my neck. "We are the tingles you feel creeping up your spine. We are the secret fears of your heart. Always disquieting, always disturbing, and always seeking your demise."

When she trailed her finger down to my heart, I felt it flutter. She paused, a triumphant smile on her face. "Even you can feel it," she stated. "Your heart knows the power I hold over it."

Her smile faltered. "But wait," she said, her brow lowering in reflection. "I nearly forgot. There's more than one heart here, isn't there."

I froze, panicked that she knew about Tia and Ashleigh, but then she shifted my leather harness and found the heart scarab. "It's weak now," she said. "I nearly missed it."

The Devourer stroked the jeweled carapace of the scarab. If I'd had control of my arms, I would have shoved her away. Her touch felt like defilement. "Perhaps *this* is why I was never able to fully drain him. Hmm . . . I wonder if the spell of the cauldron would have even worked, then. What a challenge," she said brightly, and then patted my cheek patronizingly. "I so look forward to breaking you, my dear."

She turned and began whispering instructions to her Minotaur slave. As she did so, I relaxed enough that a single tear escaped my eye. *This is it. Something must've happened to Ahmose and Asten.* I was feeling so sorry for myself that I nearly missed the sparkling dark mist that hovered on the outskirts of the demons. My eyes glued to the shape. It enveloped a demon completely, and when it passed over the place where the beast had once stood, there was nothing. Not even its brother demons close by had noticed that he'd gone missing.

How long had Ahmose and Asten been quietly working? Doing some quick calculations, I could see there were significantly fewer demons than there had once been. It wouldn't be long before the Devourer would spot the difference. I needed to buy them more time. Unfortunately, I didn't have time to think of anything.

The stench of godlings fills my nostrils! the jackal leader cried. *I cannot see them, but they are here.*

"What?" the queen demanded. "Who is here?"

The ones she traveled with.

In a fit of rage, the Devourer grabbed hold of the jackal's muzzle and inhaled. Green light glowed from the creature's face as tendrils of gray smoke trickled out of his nostrils. The jackal whined miserably, vainly attempting to wriggle his way out of her grip.

She took a deep breath, drawing in the smoke, and then closed her mouth. "Mindless dog!" she spat as she tossed him aside. "Why didn't you think to tell me of this?"

The defeated creature cowered, tail between his legs, and lowered his head until his nose touched the earth. *We did not think them important,* he said. *You only mentioned keeping watch for the girl.*

"You thickheaded mongrel. Am I the only one in the netherworld with a brain? They are the Sons of Egypt!" she screamed. "Go! Find them! Bring them to me!"

The pack began barking wildly and headed toward the scent that assailed their nostrils. Though Asten and Ahmose were hidden in Asten's magic, the pack soon found the source. They barked and yipped triumphantly as they danced around the mist. Those that entered were quickly tossed out, their bodies broken.

The smoke dissipated and two golden gods emerged. Asten, adorned with bronze armor that mirrored the shade of his glow-in-the-dark eyes, raised his bow, firing his diamond-tipped arrows into the pack and taking down six jackals in quick succession.

Ahmose, his armor as pale as silvery moonlight, lifted his gleaming ax and cudgel and raised his voice in a battle cry. Between the two of them, the pack couldn't get so much as a bite in. The queen watched the fight, incredulous that the two brothers could keep the jackals at bay for so long. Then I caught her assessing gaze. Her nostrils flared and I knew she was scenting their hearts. Their very immortal, very powerful hearts.

A smile spread across her red lips. "Tear her limbs from her body!" she shouted to her minions loudly enough to make Asten and Ahmose pause. Both brothers stopped and, as one, took to the sky. The Devourer watched their progress with fixed attention.

One of Asten's arrows zoomed forward, headed for the queen's head, but she stood her ground, calmly, placidly, and barely took note as her Minotaur henchman caught it in his bare hand and broke the shaft in half. Meanwhile, the demons holding me began to pull.

The strength of the sphinx was the only reason I wasn't immediately ripped apart, but the action swiftly brought tears to my eyes. I knew I didn't have enough strength to stop them for long. She'd tear me in two, then suck the energy from my heart and the marrow from my bones, and Egyptian heaven help me, there wasn't a blessed thing I could do to stop her.

Amon stumbled toward me, stretching out his hands once again, like he wanted in on the action. His face held no emotion. No sign that he was aware of what he was doing. He moved like a zombie obsessed with a juicy brain. Lifting his hand to my arm, he ran it up and over the hands of the demons holding me.

They paused, confused.

The Devourer laughed. "How appropriate that you should be broken asunder by the one you love. What a terribly delicious emotion to swallow. I'll save that luscious treat for last."

Amon turned to her as if asking permission. The demons, breathing heavily around me, waited to see what she wanted to do.

She waved her hand at Amon as if encouraging her little boy to go play in a sandbox. "Go on," she urged. "Pull her arm off."

Amon faced me again. Tears coursed down my cheeks as I watched him, wishing I could say goodbye properly, could see his loving gaze just one more time.

Something changed.

I got my wish.

Beads of sweat stood out on his forehead, a sign of monumental effort, though he'd barely moved in the last ten minutes. He raised his head and I saw not only recognition, but also something more. He licked his lips, his weak voice cracking as he tried to speak. It was just one word, but in it I found hope.

"Lily," he said. His piercing green eyes locked on to mine, his hand sliding over my arm to my shoulder where he cupped the heart scarab. If my arms hadn't been held, I would have placed my hands against his cheeks and kissed him. Heat burned where his palm lay, and when he backed away, a smile crossed his face before he collapsed to the ground.

"Amon!" I cried, but immediately, heat from my shoulder spread across my chest and down my body. I flicked my arms and the demons holding me flew away, like water shaken off a tiger's back. In my hand a gleaming green shield formed and armor encased my body, each segment snapping into place. The heart scarab had shifted and now sat at my waist like a belt. Renewed power surged through my limbs, and I knew it had come from Amon. He'd given me what little remained of his energy.

I panicked, thinking he'd died, but as soon as I saw Asten's flying arrows and heard the smack of Ahmose's cudgel impacting a demon, I knew he was still with us, if barely. I made a vow right then to use Amon's gift to save him. What it had cost him to break free of the hold of the Devourer was not something I wanted to think about. The queen, obscured by the rising cloud of her living cloak, shouted to her minions to seize us.

When the demons returned, I kicked the giant cauldron, knocking it over and spilling its abominable contents all over the ground. The creatures stepped into the viscous substance, screaming an unholy, piercing sound that was soon cut off as the black tar closed over their forms, melting their flesh and leaving nothing but misshapen bone behind.

I summoned the wind. It poured over the iron wall and stormed around the demons with such ferocity that they staggered back, shielding their eyes from the grit and dust. The few that fought their way through to face me I strangled. My power was so strong that I could incapacitate three at a time, but killing them that way still took too long. While my attention was fixed on three, a jackal attacked. I crushed his skull between my gloved hands as if his head were a melon. Maintaining the wind kept all my attackers away from the place where I stood. Only the queen, her bodyguards, and Amon were within the circle of calm.

All around us was chaos.

With the deadly pool at my back, and Asten and Ahmose safely flying above the maelstrom picking off the other fighting demons, I felt confident enough to turn my full attention back to the queen.

Amon lay at my feet, unconscious but breathing. I looked up at the Devourer with narrowed eyes, making her out clearly despite the creatures shielding her, and drew my spears, which had been safely locked by the magic in the leather harness. Dashing toward her, I slashed, aiming for her neck, but she spun away at the last moment, nearly tripping on her tight silver gown.

Her gleaming crown tumbled from her head and rolled in my direction. Reaching my foot out, I stepped on its rim, halting it mid-roll. A bloodthirsty desire for her head to be the object beneath my foot flashed through my mind. "I guess this belongs to me now," I bragged, jabbing the knife through the crown before I tossed it aside. Elongating one of my spear-knives, I drew my arm back and aimed for her heart.

"So much for your rule. Have a nice trip to wherever it is bad little queens like you go."

27

Secret Names

The Devourer's body disappeared in a burst of winged creatures just as my spear tore clear through them. The bats were replaced by dozens of demons that had surged up from cracks in the ground. They rushed me. Just as I raised my remaining knife to defend myself, two bodies descended from the sky and met the group with a clang of weapons.

Asten had stowed his bow and now fought with his fallen brother's golden scimitars. We positioned ourselves so that Amon was protected in the center of our formed triangle. Facing outward, we protected each other's backs as we fought.

"Just take him and go!" I yelled as I speared an opponent through the throat. "I'll hold them off!"

"Can't do that, little lioness," Asten said over his shoulder as he swung both scimitars in opposite directions, decapitating a demon. It disappeared in a cloud of dust. "We've got to kill her. If we do, Amon will gain his power back. If not, he might never recover."

"Fine."

The demons and what remained of the jackals, which the queen managed to funnel into our circle in the center of the storm, were still far too many in number and continued to rush us in a never-ending stream. The queen was nowhere in sight.

I instinctively raised my shield, and when I did, the heart scarab burned at my waist. A powerful burst of green light shot forward and felled dozens of creatures, their shrieks of agony echoing off the iron walls before they turned into clouds of dust. "That's handy," I said, and attempted to use the power again as the next wave warily gathered around us.

Unfortunately, I couldn't figure out how to duplicate the process. Frustrated, I jabbed my emerald shield down into the sand and tossed aside my helmet. Asten had been able to recover my lost spear when a demon decided to use it as a weapon against him. He tossed it to me and I immediately felt better having both spear-knives.

There was definitely a side of me that thirsted to test myself in battle. I wanted to see the fear in my opponents' faces as I gutted them. It was much more satisfying up close rather than from the distance of a spear length, especially when killing the jackals.

"I liked you better with your bow," Asten said with a backward glance as we waited for the next onslaught of demons.

The three of us breathed heavily. Even with the strength of a sphinx, I was tiring. The wind died down, and the demons that'd been pressed against the wall began making their way toward us. My chest rumbled in anticipation. "I prefer claws, actually, if given a choice." It was Tia who'd risen to the surface to speak. The three of us had been acting harmoniously for the most part, but standing back to back with Asten had brought her out.

"I'll bet you do," Asten said with a triumphant grin that was totally out of place but somehow made me smile. "Let's swing things a bit more in our favor, shall we?" He began murmuring a spell, and I thought the result would be his familiar cloud of obscurity. Instead, the entire arena was quickly bathed in starlight.

Stretching forth his hands, Ahmose joined his own power to the spell and the light increased tenfold. "Let's see if those who conspire in darkness scramble like roaches in the light of day," he cried.

Their instincts were spot-on. The demons blinked and began groping around blindly, bumping into one another as they searched for us, leaving them much more vulnerable to attack. It evened the odds a bit. But the jackals still found us easily, snapping at our ankles and trying to separate the three of us.

We held our ground—that is, until the queen who didn't have the same problem with the light as her demons did performed some magic of her own. I caught sight of her standing just behind her Minotaur slave. His arms were folded and he wore a smug expression on his face, like he was enjoying the spectacle before him.

From the corner of my eye, I saw the queen's arms raised in the air. I got a very bad feeling and shuffled back a few steps.

"She's up to something! Watch out!" I warned.

The demons we'd killed had disappeared in a cloud of dust, but the jackals, being natural-born creatures of the netherworld and only dying their first death, lay piled up on the ground around our feet. Her spell was bringing them back to life.

Like zombie dogs, the jackal's limbs quivered and they slowly rose to their feet. Soon we were surrounded, fighting legions of undead jackals, and it wasn't until several agonizing moments later that we remembered the only way to bring them to a second death was to stab them in the heart.

Unfortunately, their hearts were not in the place one would expect. Through Ahmose's lucky strike, we quickly found out that the heart of a hellhound lay just beneath the thick ruff of their necks, a bony plate the only thing protecting it. He quickly shouted what we were to do after his undead jackal disappeared in a cloud of dust. The weapon had to be driven in at just the right place.

Ahmose was bitten savagely on his dominant arm, making it useless. I lost one of my spear-knives in the body of a jackal that went off to die his first death too far from my reach. Then, just as we thought things couldn't get worse, my wind power failed altogether, and newly arrived ghosts began to attack as well.

They rushed us in a crazed fury. Evidently our doggedness in battle warranted pulling in the second-stringers. They weren't as strong as their compatriots, but they still managed to yank my hair, scratch at my ankles, and bite my ears. Desperate to live, they did anything and everything they could to distract us. My determination was faltering. There was no possible way we could overcome them.

Then a glorious, ominous hum filled the air.

The reapers had arrived.

We still stood a chance.

As they descended by the dozens, their mandibles clacking, short scythes gleamed as they carved ghosts and jackals in two. But the jackals were quicker. They leapt into the air, taking down the reapers before they could swing.

When the reapers died their first deaths, they disappeared in a burst of light. I hoped that meant they'd be taken back to Isis, the goddess they still served. They deserved peace after all the suffering they'd endured in the netherworld. When the queen saw we were at a stalemate, she changed tactics and commanded all who remained in her army to target Amon. Though we'd tried to keep him at the center, in the course of battle we'd moved away from him. I cried out and made my way back in a desperate attempt to save his life. A demon with a face full of piercings lifted a wicked-looking cleaver, attempting to remove Amon's head from his body.

I knew there was no way for me to get to Amon in time. Asten was fighting off three jackals at once, and Ahmose was engaged in hand-to-hand combat with a thick-fisted demon three times his size.

I ran, leaping over jackals and ducking under swinging weapons. A fire blazed in my core. And then time slowed. The cleaver continued its downward arc, but it only moved a fraction of an inch at a time.

One moment I was running, and the next I'd come to a complete stop.

A cacophony of voices filled my mind. They screamed. Roared. Begged. Then, like gears fitting into place, I felt a snap.

One . . . two . . . three.

My body lifted into the air as if I weighed less than a cloud. Light shot across my vision and overhead I saw three shooting stars rocketing toward each other, their tails arcing across the sky in a symbol I'd seen before—the impossible triangle.

When the stars reached their destinations, the light burst in a showering display, raining down upon the entire theater. No one below appeared to notice the phenomena and as I regarded them, they looked so tiny and powerless. The bright fragments touched my skin and I absorbed them. I closed my eyes, taking in a deep, cleansing breath and allowing the weight of my corporeal form to float me back to the ground.

My feet touched lightly upon the battlefield and I moved among the demons and warriors like a ghost, unseen and untouchable. When I exhaled, the scene around me jerked haltingly, awkwardly, as if the players on the field were more like puppets, ones I could manipulate if I could just find the strings.

The stars had given me a gift.

I knew what to do.

I knew how to control them.

Smiling, I tilted my head as I considered the demon ready to strike Amon. A name bubbled up in my mind, filling me with a sense of power. Calmly, fluidly, I spoke, and the sound resonated like a cannon on a battlefield.

"He Who Wields a Sharp Knife," I cried. The demon froze in place, his cleaver suspended as he turned to me.

"Set down your weapon," I said gently. Immediately, he obeyed. "Sit down and do not move."

To my surprise, he did. Turning, I peered at the monster fighting Ahmose. Another name floated up into my consciousness. "Raging Hippo," I said calmly. "Stop. You will fight no longer." One by one, I repeated the process, shouting name after name. "Serpent of Mud," I cried. "He Who Dances in Blood, Teeth of the Wax Crocodile, He Who Burns with Fire, Worms Devour Him, Inert Rebel, He Who Eats Snakes, you will cease fighting immediately."

Once I'd named all the demons, I turned to the jackals. "Carrion Eater, Crushed Paw, Stump Tail, Eye That Sees Nothing, Biting Flea, Offal Eater, Tufted Ear . . ." I went on and on, naming each creature that struggled against us. When I reached the leader of the jackals, I closed my eyes and then opened them with a smile. "He Who Voids His Bladder in the Wind." The head jackal whined, lowering his head. His pack snarled at him softly. "Sit!" I commanded in an authoritative voice. Each obeyed.

The queen screamed in rage, her pretty face souring as she stormed at me. Ahmose and Asten flanked my sides, their weapons raised. Above us the remaining reapers hovered, black cloaks rippling in the hot wind.

The smell of death overwhelmed me as I watched the Devourer approach. I felt no fear. No emotion except curiosity. Some other force pulled this one's strings. Cocking my head, names rose in my mind.

I pointed to her and said, "The Eater of Hearts. The Queen of Gluttony."

She staggered but recovered quickly. Those names belonged to her. I knew it. Yet there was an element missing. Some part of her I'd overlooked.

She spat furiously, "How do you, a mere human girl, know of the names in the Book of the Amduat?" she demanded. "No mortal has ever had access to it. Only my master and I know the secret names of those recorded there."

The queen of the netherworld took a step closer and I licked my lips, attempting to compel her as I had the others. "Stop," I said.

Her eyes widened but she then smiled, realizing she could still move. "Did you think to best me in my own realm?" she laughed, confidence growing with each step. "You might have control over these mindless underlings but not over me and not over the one I serve."

"Seth," I murmured.

"Yes. The barrier is thin now. He's nearly able to break through, and there's nothing you or your pathetic Sons of Egypt can do to stop it." She took in our surroundings and clucked her tongue. "And just look at what you've done to my immaculate home."

"You destroyed my home," I hissed, thinking of Amon and the Turquoise Forest at the same time. "We destroyed yours." I waved my arm, indicating the death surrounding us. "I'd say we're even. Or we will be, once we finish you off."

The Devourer laughed. "You can do no such thing. I'm the Queen of Hearts, remember?" She took a step forward. "And last time I checked"—she bared white teeth, a feral gleam twinkling in her eyes—"you all had one."

She snapped her fingers and the white Minotaur, her only remaining loyal servant, stepped forward. "Yes, my queen?" he said.

"Bring me her heart."

A fiendish look of delight lit the frightening contours of his face. Asten and Ahmose raised their weapons and charged, but he batted them aside like flies. They looked beyond exhausted. When the reapers tried to intervene, he unfurled the qilinbian and cracked the whip.

An electrical charge shot through the air, and one by one, the reapers dropped to the ground, stunned unconscious.

Ahmose's and Asten's weapons appeared to have grown heavy in their arms as they struggled against the fresh and very powerful demon. Closing my eyes, I focused, trying to summon to mind his name. Bits and pieces of what he was made of linked together, but no name I could think of was exactly right.

It was as if she'd created him like Frankenstein, sewing together various parts of other demons until she fashioned the perfect servant. Each piece retained a bit of what he once was, but none of them comprised what he was now. I struggled as I drew my spear-knives, giving up on naming him as I had the others.

I'd pulled back my spear, ready to throw it, when I saw Asten and Ahmose lower their weapons and walk trancelike over to the Devourer.

"There," she said to her servant. "Now take her."

The Minotaur closed in, but I ignored him and called out to them. They didn't respond. The pale creature filled my view just as I heard the evil queen say, "Hello there, handsome. How about a kiss?"

I ducked as the whip cracked above me and caught a glimpse of Asten lowering his head. A piece inside me snapped and I struggled to maintain the serenity that had come so easily before. Desperately, I clung to my newfound power, but then his lips touched the queen's and a snarl escaped from me. "Asten!" I cried.

Spinning, I went into reflex mode and kicked the knee of my opponent. It didn't even cause him to stumble. The next second, he knocked the knives from my hands. The whip sounded again and made contact. Even though it hit my green-armored back, the pain was unlike anything I'd ever felt before. It was raw and jagged, and my breath left my body. I didn't know how poor Amon had been able to suffer through it. My claws emerged and I sank them deep into his chest, but it did nothing to deter him. *He must've already died a first death,* I thought. *I have to find his heart!*

Over and over I sank my claws into him, but I might as well have been sticking pins into a pincushion for all the attention he gave the wounds I inflicted.

Hurry! a voice screamed in my mind.

"I can't find it!" I cried, tears streaming down my face. "Where's his heart?"

I heard Asten's body fall and another piece of my heart broke.

"Scrumptious," she said. "That one was a bit spicy." The evil woman crooked her finger, gesturing to Ahmose, who stepped toward her like a robot. "I saved room for dessert," she declared throatily. "I'll bet you're sweet. Let's have a taste."

"I'll thank ya ta be leavin' that bonny lad alone!" I shouted. The other link in my mind spun out of perfect harmony. I ducked as a beefy arm swung, just missing my temple. *Come on, girls! Think! We can do this!*

My mind swirled with the possibilities of my opponent's name as I tried to draw upon my waning ability. Time was running out. We'd lost Asten and Amon, and we were going to lose Ahmose, too. It was hopeless. Then, suddenly, I had it.

"Browbeater," I whispered. "He's called Browbeater. Where's your heart, Browbeater?" I demanded. He pointed to his forehead, the last place I would have ever thought it would be. Aiming for the creature's thick brow, I was just about to sink my claws into it when the Devourer realized her minion was in jeopardy.

"Stop!" she cried out, and I froze in place, immobilized, my claws inches from his forehead. It felt like an icy hand had taken hold of my heart.

The Devourer lifted her head, tendrils of sparkling smoke trailing from her lips to Ahmose and dissipating as she closed in on me.

"How did you know his name?" she asked, narrowed eyes peering into mine. "I never recorded it." When I didn't answer, she frowned. "I've had just about enough of you," she spat. "I've got sufficient energy now to release my master, but before I do, I'll have the satisfaction of killing you."

The Devourer opened her mouth and stepped closer. Her green light bathed my face in an icy fog, but when it touched my skin, there was a blast. The queen's connection broke, her body thrown from me. I could feel the control she had over my limbs ebbing as she landed in a tumble at her Minotaur's feet.

"What is the meaning of this?" she demanded, rising in fury.

I didn't answer, and this time when she approached, it was with hesitation. She pressed her frigid fingertips against my throat and slid them down until they rested against my heart. Surprise registered on her face, and then her expression quickly turned to one of horror. "Three?" she whispered. "Three hearts? How is it possible? I didn't sense this in the dream before." She twisted away from me and tripped, sprawling on the ground, her body trembling.

"The Triangle of Impossibility," she cried. "The prophecy is true. You've come to kill me."

"Uh, duh," I said. "I've been saying that the whole time."

"No. No. No." The queen scrambled to her feet. Wringing her hands, she strode back and forth. "What will I do?" Her hair fluttered, the strands rising in defense, while some of the snakelike barbs wrapped around her shoulders as if seeking to offer comfort.

"Master!" she cried, looking up to the sky. "Master, what do I do?"

I didn't hear a reply and wondered if she'd finally gone crazy. I tried a new name. "The Demoness of Punishment," I said, wrapping my lips around it, though I knew it still wasn't exactly correct. Why was my new ability eluding me just when I needed it most? "Give up your power."

She screamed and clawed at her hair, dislodging the little creatures that held on. Concentrating, I tried again, my mind spinning as I strained. "The Great and Final Death, relinquish your life to me." It wasn't quite right. Still, the effect the names had on her was tremendous. I was getting close. Her hair fell out in clumps, thick strands writhing as if each one was dying little deaths. Her true name was on the tip of my tongue. I could taste it. If I pushed just a bit more . . . "Gall of Asps!" I cried. It was still not her true name, but I was close. Very close.

"Browbeater!" she cried. "I need you!"

Jerked from his immobile state, he knelt at the feet of his queen. The Devourer reached out a hand shaking with tremors and stroked his brawny arm. "My first and best slave. You'd do anything for me, wouldn't you?" she asked.

"Yes, my most beautiful and beloved Devourer."

"Very good." She smiled. "I have need of your heart."

"Of course."

I shouted, "No! Browbeater, stop!" But my words had no effect. She had created him, and therefore she held ultimate control. Suddenly I realized that it wasn't just another heart she wanted. In unmaking one of her own creations, she would gain tremendous power. It was what Seth had tried to do with Asten, Ahmose, and Amon. I tried to stop Browbeater again, but he only had ears for his mistress.

In a horrific kind of slow motion, I saw him press thick fingers into his own brow, tearing aside skin and jabbing the whip into his skull. The bone broke easily, and before I could blink, his glistening white heart was there in his palm. He held it out to her like a priceless gift, a triumphant look of jubilation on what remained of his face.

"Thank you, my precious one," she said, cupping her hands around the shiny organ. "With the breath of my nostrils he is consumed." I scrambled forward in a desperate attempt to stop her, but she quickly crushed the heart in her hands. It turned to smoke that swirled around her while the Minotaur disappeared in a cloud of dust.

The ground beneath us began to shake. I fell to my feet next to her, feeling as if I'd won the battle but lost the war.

Everything I loved had been destroyed. Asten and Amon lay on the ground and Ahmose stood frozen in place. The Devourer turned her head and smiled. "Until we meet again, *Wasret*."

The netherworld quaked, the arena walls tumbling down, and the woman who'd taken everything from me disappeared.

28

The Waters of Osiris

The dust settled and I knelt in place as if frozen. Minutes passed, or perhaps it was mere seconds. Either way, I wasn't aware of anything until I felt a hand touch my shoulder.

"Lily?"

I didn't respond. Then Ahmose was in front of me, crouched down. I saw him snapping his fingers but couldn't even feel it when he slapped my face.

He tried a different tack. "Tia?"

I wanted to answer him but I couldn't. I was trapped inside my own skin.

"Ashleigh?" he said.

"Yes? I'm here," I answered, my voice as if from a great distance. It was mine, and yet it wasn't.

"You'll have to help me," he said. "There's something wrong with Lily."

My head nodded. "Tia, too. They've gone to a very dark place. Will they come back?"

"I hope so. We've got to leave this place. Asten and Amon are still alive. Barely. Our energies seem to be maintaining them. I'm hoping that the gods will be able to help them recover."

"What should I do?" Ashleigh asked.

"Can you heal them using the stela? The Devourer drained me. I'm too weak to fix what she's done to them."

"Sorry, darlin'," my voice said mournfully. "I can' work the healin' without Lily."

Ahmose turned in a circle, scanning the arena. "All right. Then you'll have to invoke the power of the tether to draw us back." Ahmose picked up Amon and placed him next to his brother, then knelt down and held out his hand, indicating that Ashleigh should take a position between them. When she knelt in front of Ahmose, she placed a palm upon his cheek. His gray eyes lifted, and in them I could see the pain, the loneliness, and the all-encompassing fear that he would lose those he loved.

"Don't worry over them so," Ashleigh said. "Your brothers will live."

"How do you know?" he asked.

"Fairies have a gift of knowing things. Besides, ya have good arms," she said, patting his strong shoulder.

Ahmose gave a sad, halfhearted laugh. "What does that have to do with anything?"

"The fairy tree always said, 'The higher and stronger your reach, the more people ya can shelter beneath 'ur branches.' I've got a feelin' you've got enough strength ta carry the load."

"I hope you're right, Ashleigh."

"Fairies usually are, though they don't always share what they know. Now, what do you say we leave this foul and fiendish pit?"

Letting out a breath, Ahmose nodded.

Ashleigh placed one hand on Asten's arm and one on Amon's. "Now what?" she asked.

"Close your eyes and reach out for the tether."

Ashleigh obeyed, and I felt my body shiver slightly when Ahmose's hands gripped our shoulders. We felt a light tug, but it was nowhere near strong enough. "I can't do it," she gasped. "Not without Lily and Tia."

Guilt assailed me. I knew I should be more in control. The fact that I couldn't feel my connection to Amon at all anymore made me cower in the back of my mind. Forcing Ashleigh to take the lead was wrong, but I just couldn't be an active participant in what was happening. The Devourer had escaped. It was all my fault. Amon had gifted me with whatever energy he'd had left, and I'd wasted it. I hadn't killed her. She'd fled, and now the world was at risk. If only I'd been able to discern her true name!

"Tia! Lily!" Ahmose cried. "We need you! Help us!"

Tia roused herself and attempted to nudge me forward, but I turned my consciousness away from her. Without Amon, my mind was a black hole so complete, I felt like it could swallow me.

"Hassan," Tia whispered. "Think of Hassan."

Tia joined her mind with Ashleigh, and she fed the fairy images of her brief encounter with the Egyptologist. Wind swirled around us, kicking up dust. It churned in a cyclone, circling our bodies, and a thin pillar of light fell upon us.

"I see the tether!" Ashleigh cried. "But it's still not enough!"

"Forgive me, Lily," Tia whispered in my mind, and then my consciousness moved.

Awareness impaled me, stabbing me like needles. "No!" I screamed. "I can't! Not without Amon!"

Tia and Ashleigh burrowed into my thoughts, digging through my brain with sharp claws seeking the bits and pieces they needed. An image of Hassan was dragged to the surface. Then another and another. I heard his voice, saw his eyes, smelled the dust that wafted from his cargo vest as I hugged him. The light brightened, encompassing us completely, and we were drawn into it.

Then everything went dark.

Tiny lights pierced the shadows surrounding us. I heard voices.

"They're passing through the Waters of Osiris, headed for the Cosmic River."

"The three are now one," another voice murmured indistinctly. "They are more important than you can possibly imagine."

"They are not quite one. Not yet."

Stars came into view. They roiled beneath me, moving and shifting without pattern, but then I recognized a fixed constellation. It had formed a kind of symbol. One I recognized.

It was the rising sun. The symbol Dr. Hassan had taught me. The setting sun had guided me to the afterlife, to death, and if this was indeed the rising sun, then that meant it was truly the way out.

It would bring life.

Vertigo assailed me and I closed my eyes, breathing through my nostrils to try and still the nausea.

"She will be of no use if this melancholy continues," Ma'at said.

A voice sounding like the goddess Nephthys suggested, "Perhaps if she said goodbye . . ."

"She's not the only one suffering," Anubis reminded them.

"Then we must give them what they need. Utilize the dreamer," Osiris instructed.

A humming sound filled my mind and I was caught up in a dream.

Asten stood on the edge of a cliff looking up at the stars. I put my hand on his shoulder. The glimmer of life in his body was so faint, I could barely sense it. "The stars beckon," he said softly. "It is as we imagined in our dream."

Turning to me, he smiled and touched his forehead to mine. "It is my most fervent wish to see you again. That is what I will dream of now." Sighing deeply, he added, "As much as I wish you were here only for me, I know there is another you seek."

Before he could turn away, I touched the tip of my finger to the little cleft in his chin and then pressed my lips against his. The taste and scent of him were familiar to me now. Asten felt like the wild, the savanna, and the stars all wrapped up in one. He was past, present, and future, and in him I found something that I thought had been lost to me forever and never knew I'd been missing.

With a little mewling sound, I let him go, tears coursing down my face. He swiped the tears away with his thumb and closed his eyes, and his body shimmered before he disappeared. Instead of Asten's hand, I clutched someone else's.

"Amon?" I asked, incredulous.

"I am here, Young Lily."

"Are you really?" I asked, pressing a hand against his cheek.

"I am always here. I've never left you and I never will," he declared, gathering me in his arms. "Do you believe this?"

Taking a deep breath, I nodded slightly, but asked, "Why must we be separated?"

Amon took my hand. "Our hearts are knit together, Lily. Do not forget. Palm to palm . . ." He threaded our fingers, clasping my hand to his and pressing it against his heart. "We risk together, we live together, or we die together."

"I won't forget," I said as I wrapped my arms around his neck.

"Good," he whispered against my lips. "Lily?"

My frame trembled. "Yes?"

"Promise you'll come and find me in your dreams."

Sucking in a shaky breath, I answered, "Always. I promise."

Then he kissed me. The sting of a sharp breeze danced over the trails of tears on my cheeks, but I ignored it, pouring all my emotion, all my longing, and all my love into the embrace.

Amon's lips passionately moved over mine. His arms locked around me so tightly, I couldn't breathe, couldn't move, but I didn't want to. I relished his warmth, the sunshine touch. The radiance of his love settled so deeply in my heart, it felt as if it was forever rooted.

We spun in dizzying circles, linked together in an embrace so powerful, even the rushing squall that erupted around us couldn't pull us apart.

Then, suddenly, Amon was ripped from my arms.

I was alone.

I plummeted, crying out for him. The constellations swirled around me, horror flooding my body when I looked ahead to find a churning nebula. It waited for me with a gaping maw ready to swallow me whole.

The cosmos spun, stars gleaming brightly as they watched my descent with icy, detached gazes. Faster and faster I turned; the lights blurred into long lines until I could no longer tell which way was up and which way was down.

Time slowed. Froze like the winking stars.

Then, gently, like a feather falling, my body was rocked and I slept as one dead.

EPILOGUE
Beacon

Feeling drowsy, my mind sluggish, I stirred. The comforting weight of a quilt drawn up to my chin felt both right and wrong. The thought occurred to me that maybe everything I'd experienced had been a dream. That there was no Tia. No Ashleigh. That I was in my bed back at my nana's house. That the hum I heard in my mind was the sound of crickets chirping outside. And that the slight breeze that wafted over my skin was because I'd left the window open.

It was still dark. The scent of bacon tickled my nose. My stomach growled.

Then I heard the voices. "You are her guardian and remain her tether. As such, you are charged with guiding her on the right path. You know the stakes should you fail."

"Yes, Anubis," I heard a familiar voice say. "I understand my duty."

"Good. Find what's engraved on her heart. Until you do, her powers will be weak."

"Yes. But may I ask, what about the Sons of Egypt?"

"They are safe enough for now. The three of them again reside in the afterlife and have resumed their positions as guardians." There was a pause. "He is resigned to his fate. The protector of the Eye of Horus knows what he must do and is content to wait." The person speaking sighed. "Only she has the power to return them to the Earth now."

I heard the whine of a dog. "And how long will she be like this?"

"It is hidden from us. Her mind is like an adder stone. Not even Amun-Ra himself could discover her now should she wish to conceal her whereabouts." There was a pause. "This is a good thing, I promise you."

"Yes."

"Prepare her, Vizier. A cloud of darkness overshadows us. The fiery darts of the adversary have already begun to fly, but rest assured, light is always more powerful than darkness. We are mere candles casting our weak light upon the universe, but she can be so much more. If she will stand as our beacon, there is still hope."

ACKNOWLEDGMENTS

There are a few people I'd like to thank for helping me with *Recreated*. First, I want to recognize all the amazing teachers I've had over the years, especially my English teachers for nurturing my love of literature. There is one teacher in particular who stands out in my mind. It's likely she departed this world some time ago, since no one at my old middle school even remembers her.

She had large posters all around her classroom depicting the Greek gods and goddesses, and I spent my entire seventh-grade year staring at them and wondering what their stories were. That teacher gave me a powerful love of mythology that I still feel today. On the back of her classroom door, where the administrators couldn't see it, she had another poster—Tom Selleck in a Speedo. It is possible that that poster might have influenced me a bit, too.

As always, I am grateful for my husband, who reads every chapter as I write it, and for my mom and sisters, including my sister-in-law, Suki, who all function as my assistants in pretty much every aspect of my life.

I can never show enough appreciation for my early reading group and fact-checkers, Linda, Neal, Fred, Liz, and Cindy.

My agent, Robert Gottleib, is so enthusiastic and supportive that I wish you all had such a person in your corner. *Recreated* wouldn't be what it is without the encouragement, guidance, and insight of my editor, Krista Vitola.

Thanks to everyone at Delacorte Press, including Beverly Horowitz and Angela Carlino, to copy editor Carrie Andrews, and to Chris Saunders for the outstanding cover art.

And to my fans, you have made it possible for me to walk with lions and tigers and unicorns every day, both in my dreams and during my waking hours. It's such a delight to be able to craft these stories for you and to know that they are as near and dear to your hearts as they are to mine.

Continue reading for an exclusive mythological story from

RECREATED

The Unicorn and the Lion

"Why don't you tell me the story of the Unicorn and the Lion?" I asked.

He won't tell you the truth, Tia grumbled in my mind.

"I'm sure you'll correct anything he gets wrong," I said, trying to console her with good thoughts and play the diplomat.

Since I am a gracious sort, Nebu said, *I'll oblige and tell you the story you wish to hear, as long as you keep stroking my neck. I'm rather fond of that,* he added.

"It's a deal."

First of all, you need to know it isn't the story of a Unicorn and a Lioness. It's the tale of the Unicorn and the Lion.

The Lion and the Unicorn, Tia corrected.

"Shh," I said. "Let's listen."

The golden stallion began. *There was once a lovely young maiden, a princess, in fact, who was blessed by the gods with transcendent beauty, unmatched charm, heartwarming kindness, and heartbreaking purity.*

"Why was her purity heartbreaking?"

I'll get to that. She was as fresh as the dew on the meadow and as happy as the sunshine in springtime. Every man who saw her fell instantly and hopelessly in love with her. She filled their dreams with warmth and gladness as each imagined what life would be like if the lovely girl could be theirs.

So virtuous was she that those who came near her formed a feverish desire to become her equal, for it was widely known that only a companion as beautiful and as unique as she would make a good match. This was the cause of many a man's heartbreak. You see, their hope was ephemeral. Most of those who sought her hand in marriage couldn't even dream of coming close to that level of perfection.

They imagined that if she was a little less than flawless, a little more swayed by a handsome form and face, or, perhaps, a little more willing to compromise her virtue, they might persuade her to select a husband based on a moment of passion. Alas, she was not won so easily. When it was determined that the time had come for her to marry, her father, the king, sought the bravest, most stalwart, and worthiest companion to be her mate.

Tia had said nothing during this time, though I could tell she was listening, too, scrutinizing every word Nebu said. "Please, go on," I encouraged.

Men came forward from great distances. They were princes and peasants. Knights and knaves. Servants and slaves. Their various stations, riches, and fine figures didn't matter, for the girl concerned herself only with what they carried on the inside. Every suitor was brought before the princess, and she took the hand of each man, staring into his eyes and through his soul. She never encouraged or denied any of them, but still, one by one, they left, unhappily accepting the fact that she would never belong to them.

"How did they know they weren't the one?"

When she looked into their hearts, they flinched, he said. *They could not endure her gaze. It was like staring into the face of a goddess and having every sin and secret revealed. They were unworthy and there was no denying it.*

"Then what happened?"

When all the would-be suitors had come forward and there was no one left to try, the princess despaired of loneliness. She feared there would never be one like her and she was destined to continue her mortal sojourn alone. One day she was in the forest, dipping her feet in a cool pond, when a lion happened upon her.

He, too, fell hopelessly in love with the girl. The lion came forward and begged her to let him stay by her side. Though she was frightened, she looked into the lion's heart and found no malice there.

You see, a lion is not greedy, envious, drunk on his own power, or selfish. He is an animal, and his actions are based on instinct and survival. As she looked into his heart, she realized that here, finally, was a match who would prove to be her equal.

"So she, what? Took him home to meet Dad?" Both Tia and Nebu bristled at my blasé observation regarding the fairy tale that the two of them obviously took very seriously. "Forgive me," I apologized. "I didn't mean to interrupt."

When the king met his daughter at the postern and found her accompanied by a lion, he was surprised, to say the least. He'd never expected a lion to become the heir to the throne.

"Wait a minute. So the lion was actually going to marry the girl?"

Yes. The king had promised his daughter to the one who proved worthy of her.

In my head, I asked Tia, *Is that how the lion became known as the King of Beasts?*

She snorted derisively. *Lions do not need the help of human royalty to be branded with that title. We are majestic predators with no equal. However, there may be some evidence that this story is how humans came to recognize lions in such a way.*

Nebu continued. *Since the girl was suffering from loneliness, her father, the king, agreed to the idea of a spring wedding. The princess and the lion spent all their time together through the summer, fall, and winter, but there was a downside to being betrothed to a lion.*

"Only one?" I smiled.

Tia didn't appreciate my comment.

The young maiden was used to being surrounded by people clamoring for her attention. With a lion nearby, the citizens of her kingdom, even those who professed a deep and abiding love for the princess, wouldn't risk the lion's wrath to approach her. The lion didn't see anything wrong with this. In fact, he preferred to keep her all to himself, though he was troubled at seeing her so unhappy.

"So where does the unicorn come in?" I asked.

He comes into the story now, actually, Nebu replied.

Here's where it gets interesting, Tia added.

The lion was the equal of the princess in many ways. All ways but one, in fact: the princess didn't eat meat.

"Oh." I blinked. "Why should that matter?"

It wouldn't normally, and she knew the lion only ate meat to satisfy his hunger. He didn't kill arbitrarily. Still, it bothered the girl. She who loved all beings couldn't stand knowing that her fiancé caused the death of innocent creatures.

"So what did she do?"

She cried over each kill until the lion stopped eating altogether. A few months passed, and though the lion tried to eat fruits and vegetables as she did, he became weak. Never in his existence had he experienced such lassitude. But so great was his love for the girl that to make her happy, he went on ignoring his instincts.

One afternoon, they headed to the forest and unpacked a picnic of apples, carrots, and strawberries. The still hungry and unsatisfied lion lay down beside the girl he loved, and with her hand on his back, he fell asleep.

While he slept, the girl walked through the trees, seeking flowers, and came upon a secret grove, opulent and lush, that only one with an innocent and pure heart could find. It was the home of a unicorn—a great, noble beast, who had also been blessed by the gods.

Tia gave me the mental equivalent of rolling her eyes.

Interested in meeting the person who'd found his home, the unicorn stepped into the clearing and saw the beautiful girl picking his flowers. He approached, and when she looked up they both knew that they were meant to be together. His great heart melted.

All at once he loved everything about her, from her demure expression to the warmth of her presence. The unicorn found her effervescent laughter delightful, but most of all, the purity of her heart, the richness of her soul, drew him. Like the girl, the unicorn was beautiful both inside and out. He, too, could read the hearts of others.

He possessed the same kind of magic that drew others to him and made them want to better themselves. His heart was pure. He was worthy. He was her perfect match. She was as drawn to him as he was to her. It was a feeling, a conviction unlike she'd had with any other, and yet the knowledge broke her heart.

The princess stayed with the unicorn all afternoon and told him that being together would be impossible. She was betrothed to a lion, and the goodness inside her would not allow her to break her vow to wed. The unicorn wept with despair, for he knew her heart better than anyone else's and he would never ask her to be less than she was. He laid his head in her lap, determined to make the most of the stolen time they had together.

She left as the sun set, and told him she'd never seek him out again. He accepted this, though his heart broke at the knowledge. He brooded as the days passed, but the princess was true to her word and did not return to the unicorn's hidden grove. He tried to tell himself it was over. That their love was a mere dalliance, hotly burning but quickly extinguishable. In his truest heart, though, he knew that he told himself lies.

He was wild with love for the girl, and the separation from her caused him unbelievable pain, ineffable torment. So he stole into the human world just to catch a glimpse of her once more. When he did, the unicorn could see that she was as despondent as he was. That their being together was essential.

That's your opinion! Tia hissed, though the unicorn was not privy to her thoughts.

Neby went on to say, *Now, a unicorn possesses a certain amount of magic, and it's centered in the alicorn, the horn that protrudes from the top of its head.*

"But you don't have one."

That is correct. And now you'll understand why. The unicorn was desperate, so he did something no other unicorn had done before.

He tricked the lion! Tia shouted in my mind.

He sacrificed the power he had to offer a gift to the lion.

It's a lie! It was no gift. The lion was deceived! Tia exclaimed.

"Tia, shh," I said.

This is the part where the lion and the unicorn disagree, Nebu explained. *It's likely she will give you her own version of the story. The gift,* he went on, *which the lion attributed to furtive behavior on the part of the unicorn, was the seat of his power, his alicorn.*

"Why would he offer that to the lion?"

He met the lion and confessed the truth: that he was as in love with the girl, as the lion was, and that he hated seeing her unhappy. He told the lion that there was great power in his alicorn, and that if the lion would take it from him, he could use it to change his body so that he could thrive on the grains, fruits, and vegetables that the princess ate and still retain his energy. In short, he would be imbued with strength once again.

"Then why would Tia say it was a trick?"

It is because of what happened next. The unicorn, not having the wherewithal to remove the horn himself, knelt down, and the lion, desperate to remain with the girl he loved, leapt upon the unicorn and used his sharp claws to sever the horn. Once it was severed, the horn lost its power, making the unicorn nearly as weak as a mortal horse.

"So it didn't work? The lion wasn't made strong?"

Oh, the lion was made strong again, but it didn't matter, for he purposely caused harm to another creature for his personal gain. When the lion took the severed horn to the princess and laid it at her feet, she wept bitterly, for her fiancé was now lost to her. His heart was no longer pure. In despair, the lion cried out that he'd been deceived and insisted he had only done it so he could be with her.

The maimed unicorn went to the girl, asking her if they could now be together since they wanted each other so urgently. Though she loved the unicorn and sensed no malice in his heart—

Bah! Tia said.

—the girl hesitated. The lion insisted the unicorn had tricked him, and he petitioned the gods for help. A tribunal heard the case and determined that both creatures had acted selfishly and would therefore be rebuked. The lovely girl

cried out, for her tender heart could not bear to see either beast she loved punished. She picked up the broken alicorn and plunged it into her heart. When she died, neither the lion nor the unicorn cared any longer about what happened to them. Their only wish was to reunite with the girl they loved in the Afterlife.

The tribunal, angry that love had wrought so horrible an end, did not grant their wish. It was decided then that all lions henceforth be banished to the human world. And to teach them a lesson, they would be forever at odds with mortals. Animals that die a mortal death do not ascend to the afterlife, so the lion would never see his betrothed again.

As for the unicorn, all unicorns would be forbidden to show themselves to mortals. Some have broken this law, but they are swiftly dealt with. Unicorns were given the gift, or curse, depending on your perspective, of immortality. We can never enter the Afterlife, and that particular unicorn would never see his princess again, though his love was truer than any love that has ever been or ever will be on Earth. For it was a love born of a pure heart.

Oh, please, Tia murmured.

I ignored her as Nebu went on. *You see, the great love the unicorn had for his beautiful princess did not die and constantly seeks to be reborn. This is why unicorns have a difficult time resisting those with innocent hearts: they remind them of the girl who was lost. To make sure the unicorn remembered the lesson of the tribunal, all alicorns were taken. The power was completely stripped so that none remained, even in vestigial amounts. It is said if a unicorn accomplishes a completely selfless deed, he can earn back his alicorn, but so far, none ever has.*

Now I understood why unicorns and lions didn't trust each other. It was tragic . A terrible fate for all. Having found the one that my heart spoke to, I could understand the pain of separation. Obviously, I, too, was pretty much willing to do whatever it took to just be near Amon once again.

Finally, I said, "I'm sorry. I'm sad for both of you. You've both lost so much."

The pain of it dulls over time, but I fear my heart will never be fully recovered, Nebu said.

"Wait. Are you saying . . . that was you? That was your story? You were the one in love with the princess?"

What does it matter if I was?

"But . . . you're a father. You have children."

Not in the sense that you believe. Unicorns are not born. We are created. I am simply the eldest of my kind. The younglings call me Father.

Tia? I thought. *Do you think he's the one? The one who really loved her, I mean?*

If he is, she said softly, *then his is a soul damned for eternity. I would not wish that on my worst enemy.*

ABOUT THE AUTHOR

Colleen Houck is the five-time *New York Times* bestselling author of the Tiger's Curse series and *Reawakened*. She lives in Salem, Oregon, with her husband.

Follow Colleen